I0583470

A STRAWBERRY SPRINGS NOVEL

AS IT WAS

ELLE RIVERS

This book is a work of fiction. Any similarities to real individuals are purely coincidental. All events are from the author's imagination and are not to be taken as realistic.

Copyright © 2025 by Elizabeth Irwin. All Rights Reserved. No portion of this book may be reproduced without the consent of the author. Any unauthorized use of this publication to train generative artificial intelligence (AI) is expressly prohibited. For information, please email elle@ellerivers.com.

Cover Design by Summer Grove

Developmental editing by Mae Peredo, Wildwood Author Services

Copyediting by Kasey Kubica, Basic Behemoth Edits

Proofreading by Mae Peredo, Wildwood Author Services

 Formatted with Vellum

PLAYLIST

marjorie—Taylor Swift
labour—Paris Paloma
The Outsider—MARINA
I Hate It Here—Taylor Swift
love is embarrassing—Olivia Rodrigo
We Are Never Getting Back Together (Taylor's Version)—
Taylor Swift
You're On Your Own, Kid—Taylor Swift
enemy—Charli xcx
Jealous—Nick Jonas
Sparks Fly—Taylor Swift
Watermelon Sugar —Harry Styles
Mess It Up—Gracie Abrams
Juno—Sabrina Carpenter
golden hour—JVKE
As It Was—Harry Styles

STRAWBERRY SPRINGS COMMUNITY GUIDE

Jackie Anne Tyler—Owner of Hair Haven salon
Kerry Winsor—Stay at home mom, resident gossip
Nicole Rudder—Teacher at Strawberry Springs Elementary
School
Cain Smith—Farm Manager at Bennie Grove Farm
Tammy Jane and Ron*—Married owners of Center Point
Diner
Hugh Jeffries—Retiree, resident grump
Marjorie and Henrietta Brown—Married retirees
Dr. Atticus Thompson, DVM—Veterinarian
Jade Clark—Owner of Jade's Goodies gift shop
Grace Day—Owner of Treasure Trove clothing store
Dale Garrett—Owner of Food N' Things grocery store
Mike Finch—Sherriff of Strawberry Springs
Dr. Henry Connor, MD—Clinic Doctor
Mark Bell—Owner of Bell's Brews bar
Theo Murf—Town handyman
Brooke Day—Aspiring singer

*Tammy and Ron have not consented to the inclusion of their last name in this guide at this time.

A NOTE FROM ELLE

As It Was contains mature and potentially triggering content that some people might find upsetting. Please be advised that the following content can be found on-page unless otherwise noted.

- Bullying
- Emotional/verbal abuse
- Explicit, open-door sexual content
- References to past physical abuse (not descriptive)
- References to past death of a loved one (not descriptive)
- Child endangerment (off-page, child is not harmed)

None of the dangerous/harmful behavior is committed by main characters. While the story is set on a farm, no animals are harmed in this story.

If you come across a potential trigger not mentioned here, please email me at elle@ellerivers.com.

To anyone who feels stuck where they are:
Beautiful things are just beyond the horizon.
Welcome to Strawberry Springs.

CAIN

Fourteen Years Ago

LIFE WAS A SERIES OF DISAPPOINTMENTS, one after another.
If there was one lesson I'd learned, it was that.

And the biggest one?

The man sitting across the breakfast table glaring at me.

His wife, Jackie, was talking about her plans for the day. She
had a lot of clients in her hair salon in the center of town, and
she had to leave early to get to them. The salon was new and
was a passion project of hers. Donny despised the fact that she
worked at all.

I wasn't sure why he hated her being out of the house so
much, but I had a feeling it was because it meant he was forced
to watch me.

To be fair, I also hated being watched by him. My other
foster parents had left me by myself since I was ten. But he
insisted on it, saying I would steal something if left alone.

I was already dreading the day, and it hadn't even begun.

He didn't like me, that much was obvious. The feeling was
mutual. Since I'd come here three months ago, I'd been the

victim of his yelling fits more times than I could count. And I'd thrown it right back.

He'd threatened to kick me out once a day, but whenever my social worker would come to check on me, he stayed silent while Jackie told them how good of a kid I was.

I tried to be. For her. She was the nicest foster mother I'd met.

Donny, on the other hand?

Worst foster father ever. And that was saying a lot.

I was a difficult kid. No one would say it to my face, but I didn't do well in any of the homes I had been put in. Some were fine, but I was packed in with too many others to focus on my schoolwork. Others were only in it for the money, and it was obvious. With one mess up after another, my options dwindled.

My social worker thought that getting into nature would be the key to me finally assimilating somewhere. When I first saw the tiny trailer amidst a sea of green grass, I thought I would hate it. But there weren't many sounds outside. Only birds and wind.

I kind of liked it.

Which meant it would all end soon.

"I need to get on the road into town," Jackie said. "It's such a long drive."

"Can I go with you?" I asked it all the time. "I can be helpful."

Her gaze flicked to her husband and then to me. "I have a job for you."

"A job he can do?" Donny mumbled. "I doubt it."

I opened my mouth to snap that I could do a lot of things, but Jackie's hand landed on my shoulder, and I focused only on her.

"Bennie is our neighbor up the hill. He owns a lot of farm-land. He's getting old and needs some help around the farm."

"Can't believe he even said yes. I told him this little punk was a thief."

"I don't steal! You're the one who smoked through your last pack."

"No, I didn't. You took 'em. I know you did!"

Jackie glared at Donny, but her eyes softened when she looked at me. "Do you wanna go there today?"

"I'll do it," I said. I would do anything if it meant getting away from Donny. She smiled and grabbed my arm.

"I'll walk you there and introduce you. Then I really need to get going."

I followed her up the hill to a wooden fence. The spring air smelled like tulips and strawberries. Next to a white farmhouse with a blue roof sat a field of pink and white tulips. On the other side, there were multiple strawberry fields. There was a tree line far away with a singular path through it. I'd never seen so much space before.

"Bennie!" Jackie called as she hopped the fence. "I brought him!"

An older man was bent down in the field. He slowly stood and stretched before walking over to us. He had weathered skin that pulled into a smile. "Well, well. Cain Smith. I've heard a lot about you."

That wasn't a very good sign.

"It's nice to meet you, sir."

"You're, what, sixteen? That's only a little older than my granddaughter."

"Yes, sir."

"He'll do well. He listens to me. Most of the time." Jackie laughed. "And I think he'll listen to you too."

"Do you like animals?" Bennie asked.

Who didn't? "Yes."

"Good. Come on. I'll show you what you need to do."

Jackie gave me a wave before I walked off with Bennie. I watched him warily, but followed. We walked along the path through the tree line. The sun gave way to shade for a few moments until we came to a clearing. There was a massive fenced-in area with multiple chicken coops. The large birds walked around, digging in the dirt as they looked for food.

There were white, black, and even red chickens. I had no idea so many different kinds existed.

"So, you have chickens?"

"Not just that."

He pointed in the other direction where a wooden fence marked an expansive plot of land with a barn in the center. Cows were everywhere, eating the grass beneath them. Some lounged in a shallow pond not too far away.

"I need you to be able to hop these fences and feed all of the animals."

"Is there a gate?"

"There was, but it got blocked up a long time ago. I thought hopping the fence would keep me young. Boy, was I wrong."

I looked at both fences. The one for the cows was higher, but not too bad.

"I can do that easily."

"Here," Bennie said, throwing something into my hand.

"What are these?"

"Mealworms." I was sure my face had turned a sickly shade of green because he laughed and added, "The chickens love them. They'll run at you for them."

I resisted the urge to throw them on the ground. I liked animals, but I *hated* bugs—worms included. We walked into the coop, and soon I was trying not to trip over the chickens rushing at my ankles for what I had in my hand.

"Ah! Okay, here!" I dropped the mealworms on the ground. "Please don't trip me."

"Oh, they will," Bennie said. "Come on, let's go check their regular food and water."

I followed him to the back of the coops where we piled up more eggs into a basket than I'd seen in my life. By the time we were done filling their food bins with grain, they were already trying to trip me again, but I managed to get around them.

We walked outside, and I was still thinking about all of their little faces and how they ran. Chickens didn't seem very bright, but they did seem kind of . . . cute.

"The animals are hard to keep up on," Bennie explained. "My passion is with the strawberries, but that's not year-round, and these eggs sell very well around here. As does the cow milk."

We walked up to a field filled with black cows. "There are so many of them."

"I need an employee to work on rounding them up for milking. And someone to collect eggs." He patted my shoulder. "Now I have one."

"I don't know if I'll be good at it."

"Why not?"

"I'm not good at much."

"You're sixteen. Just starting out. You just need time."

"But—"

"No talking down about yourself. Let's just try it and see how it goes, yeah?"

"Y-yeah, okay."

"Now, let's go see some cows."

We entered the fenced part of the yard. The cows were friendlier than I'd expected, some even brushing up against me as I walked through. I didn't smile much, but when an animal liked me for no reason, I couldn't resist.

While Bennie showed me how to milk them, I committed

each part to memory. I was used to letting people down, but I wanted this to be the one time that I didn't.

The next day, he only monitored from a distance as I tried not to mess anything up.

But I didn't expect one of the cows to waltz up to me with a newborn calf. She was only a cow, but I swore she looked at me expectantly.

"I don't have any food. It's all in the barn."

She looked at her baby and then at me.

"What? What do you need?"

"She's showing off her baby!" Bennie called.

I looked at it all with new eyes and smiled at both the massive cow and the tiny one.

"She's cute. You have good genes."

I didn't know if that made me the biggest loser in the world, but there was no one around to hear, except maybe Bennie.

"You're gonna do great," he said when I walked up to him. "You're just like my granddaughter."

"Where is she?"

"Her mama keeps her in the Nashville, but I don't think that's where she belongs."

"Why not?"

"Sometimes you just know. And when I see her on the holidays, all she can talk about is wanting to be here. Hopefully, she'll get what she wants."

"She sounds cool."

"Right now, she's busy finishing up school and doing all the things her mama wants." He smiled, but it seemed a little sad. "But she'll find her way here. I just know it."

"And then I'll get to meet her?" I didn't make plans for the future, but for some reason, I wanted this to work.

"Somethin' tells me you'll *definitely* get to meet her, kid." He ruffled my hair and walked off.

"Wait! What else should I do?"

"Come with me to sell all of this! And then dinner."

"You're feeding me?"

"You're a part of my team, aren't you? You'll get treated like it."

I hadn't ever been a part of anything, but I liked the sound of it. I ran to catch up with him, feeling like just this once, things were going right for me.

I hoped it stayed that way.

1

MOLLIE

I was riding off into the sunset with a hot cowboy when my alarm went off and broke my perfect little dreamland.

"Fuck you," I said to the blaringly loud noise, and laid back down.

My emergency alarm went off five minutes later, just as I was seeing a buff form against an orange and pink sky.

I let out a groan so loud the bed rumbled, and finally forced myself upright. I rubbed my eyes and grabbed the beige comforter, laying it across the bed neatly. Personally, I didn't care if my bed was made or not. But my fiancé, Trevor, did. And if he wanted something, it meant I needed to get it done.

He said he was terrible at cleaning, which I certainly noticed every morning when I tripped on his clothes that he'd left on the floor. Trevor wanted our apartment a certain way, yet he left a trail of things to clean wherever he went.

If I confronted him about it, he'd always tell me that he was too busy thinking about work. Or, if he was in a good mood, our future together. He excused it by saying it was easy for me to grab them off the ground when I saw them.

He said the logic was sound.

I wanted to believe him, but I couldn't help but feel frustrated every time I had to pick up something of his.

After that, I threw on one of my pairs of beige slacks, the one pair Trevor complimented me in, and a white dress shirt for work. I brewed a K-cup, mixed it with the chalky protein shakes he insisted were good for me, and ran out the door to head to work.

Some people found peace in their routine. I only found boredom that grew every single day.

No one paid me any mind as I walked through the lobby of our apartment and out to the streets of Nashville. Everyone was too busy either on their phones or rushing about their day. There was a jogger I encountered every single morning in a pink or purple outfit. She would always run right past me, or *over* me, never giving me a second glance.

Everyone was like that here. Sure, some were friendly. But they were so *busy*.

Nashville was good at being busy.

The streets always were, even when it wasn't rush hour. I lived downtown, and the road noise was ever present, even in my apartment. Cars honked, tires squealed, and loud trucks idled any time of the day.

It was worse whenever I walked to my car.

The only break in my usual routine was a biker nearly hitting me as I crossed the street. I jumped back, momentarily jostled by it, but he only waved an apology and kept going.

No words were exchanged.

I got in my car only to sit in traffic, listening to a podcast drone on about the morning news while I tried not to fall asleep at the wheel.

I wasn't a morning person, but life seemed to only reward morning people. I tried to get to the office at eight, but it took me thirty minutes every morning to go five miles from the apartment to work, meaning I had to be up by seven every weekday.

Trevor was already there. Unlike me, he thrived in the mornings and liked to come in as early as possible to get work done. We used to ride together until I couldn't get up early enough for him. Now, it was only me coming in at eight.

At first, I'd been hurt that he'd left me behind. But then I saw it as a blessing in disguise. At least when I was alone, I could groan and curse about my life as much as I wanted to.

I shouldn't have been in a bad mood, though. Trevor and I had plans today. Sure, they weren't romantic. Or even anything fun. But he was clocking out early for me—something he'd told me to be grateful for.

The feeling of nothingness only got worse when I arrived at work.

There was something about an office that was soul-sucking. It didn't matter what little perks they tried to offer; even if there was a white-marble lobby that was far too expensive, being within four gray walls illuminated by fluorescent lights made me feel like I was in a prison.

I had no reason to feel this way. I had a good job in real estate. I made good money. I worked with my family and fiancé. I did my job well—marketing to people and getting return clients—but lately, it had all begun to feel like a . . . slog.

A few years ago, when I'd graduated college, I was better at going all the time. I liked working. I liked proving myself. But I was now tired in a way I didn't know how to fix.

We were trying to get more clients due to the recession, and I couldn't care less. I tried to tell both Dad and Trevor that the homes in Nashville were simply too expensive for what people could afford, but they didn't believe me. We still had more than enough money, but Dad was sure there was something we could do to fix this, so we were in planning mode.

The first thing on my list was a meeting, which sent me to the break room for more coffee. As I sat and tried to listen, I found it impossible.

I could see outside from our meeting room, and it was the only thing keeping me awake.

In the late summer air, lilies bloomed from their tall sprouts in the ground. The city had curated spots planted around signs and premade gardens.

I had dimly noticed them, but I hadn't had time to stop and truly appreciate one of my favorite seasons.

I missed how these warm months had felt when I was a kid. How, even though the air was oppressive, nature experienced a crescendo every single year. Crops grew. Animals reproduced. Flowers bloomed until the air smelled sweet.

The city always had a certain scent to it. It was either cars or some other pollutant. Whenever I thought of happiness, it wasn't here. It was the farm I'd used to visit when I was younger.

Papa Bennie's berry farm had always been beautiful. Mom and Dad only let me stay with him when they had no other childcare, but when Mom quit her job to stay at home, I no longer needed to go there. I saw him on holidays and spent the whole time catching up with him, but my days of visiting were over.

When he passed ten years ago, I was too lost in my grief to ask about his farmland. I knew Mom wouldn't keep it. Someone must have bought it, but I didn't know if they'd kept the strawberry farm open.

I missed it, though.

He was Mom's dad, but she didn't talk about him. Dad was cordial with him, but they had never been close. Over the years, he'd faded into a warm memory, one that I wished I could go back to. And now that everything had blended together, I wanted it even more. There was a rose-tinted filter over everything, and I wished things could go back to how they used to be.

People always talked about nostalgia, but they forgot to mention one thing.

Nostalgia *hurt*.

"Mollie?" A voice broke me out of my dark thoughts. "What do you think?"

"About what?" I asked, pulling my gaze away from the window and back into the meeting room. Trevor had been speaking, and at my response, he sighed and ran a hand through his pale blonde hair.

"The marketing campaign," another man, Todd, added. "We wanna buy out more emails so we can broaden our reach."

"Yeah, sure." I said it without thinking.

"What?" Trevor asked, shaking his head. "Mollie, I thought you were against buying email lists."

Ah, shit. I shouldn't have said yes. That was going to make work harder for myself.

But I just wanted to be in nature, not in this meeting room.

"She said yes," Todd said. "So I'm doing it."

"Mollie," Trevor urged. "Do you want to clarify?"

I tried to find the same urgency he had. But these were *emails*. Sure, I was morally against this choice, but God, I didn't care anymore. Todd had been pushing this for weeks.

Maybe it was time he learned.

"Test it out. Let me know the results."

Trevor's brow rose, but Todd jumped at the chance and announced his plans. I might regret giving him that concession later, but I was too out of my own head to think about it. Future Mollie could deal with it.

Thankfully, I was pulled out of the line of attention when Dad brought up something else, and I released a sigh of relief. I could feel Trevor looking at me, though, as if he were trying to figure out exactly why I was so distracted at work.

He wouldn't be caught dead not thinking about work. He was perfect in the office and always focused. When I'd met him, I'd wanted to be like him. Now, I wasn't so sure.

When the meeting was over, I made a beeline for my cubicle to get my head on straight.

But a hand on my arm stopped me.

"Mollie," Trevor started. "What was that? You've never agreed to let Todd do anything of that nature before."

"I'm sorry, I just . . . Something else is on my mind."

"What could possibly be on your mind?"

I screwed my eyes shut. He wasn't going to understand what I was about to say.

But he was my fiancé, and I knew he wanted me to say something.

"It's late summer, and I feel like I haven't been outside at all."

His eyebrows creased. "We have a balcony."

"It faces another apartment. I wanna see *nature*."

"Why?"

"It's pretty? It's nice? I'm feeling so burnt out lately that I think it might help."

"Okay, then. Find a park."

"I want real nature. Like Papa Bennie's farm. I wanna go there."

Trevor scoffed. "Why would you want to go there?"

"I miss it."

"You miss *him*. And he's dead."

"Thank you for reminding me," I said flatly, "but it's not that I wanna see him. I wanna see what he left behind. The farm is still around. Or it should be. Someone bought it."

"Or it ended up like a lot of farmland. Abandoned."

"You do realize that farmland is responsible for all of the things you put in your smoothies every morning, right?"

"Of course. And I have nothing but respect for the profession. But it's . . . not for people like you and me."

My shoulders sagged. "You don't get it. I just need to visit. Nothing else. I don't know what happened to the farm, but someone has to."

"I don't understand why you're even thinking about this."

"I just want a reset."

He rubbed his forehead, his typical response whenever I talked about anything he didn't have an interest in. "You need to focus so we can deal with the can of worms you just opened."

"Can of worms?"

"The meeting, Mollie. In case you've forgotten, you're at work and just let Todd get away with something you probably shouldn't have."

I let out a long sigh, still unable to care about anything within the bland four walls.

"This isn't you," he said. "Or at least, not the woman you were when you got out of college. Maybe we should revisit the idea of you not working. You wanted to wait until we got married, but if you're *this* distracted . . ."

I resisted the urge to grimace. I didn't know why the idea of depending solely on him chafed me, but it did. Every single time he brought it up. But that was how he justified his long nights. He spoke about me financially depending on him as an inevitability, not an option.

And I couldn't explain why it made me so nauseous. This was what I wanted, right?

"I think . . . I think I'm just stressed with the house hunting and the recession."

"Oh." His hands came to rest on my shoulders, and I tried to find comfort in it. "Don't worry about that."

I wish I found it as reassuring as he meant it to be.

"I think I might need a little more support."

"Just wait until we get off work. I have the *perfect* thing."

Oh, *God*. I didn't think I had it in me to fake an orgasm tonight.

"I think I need something truly relaxing. You know, like a bath or something on my own."

"You can do that after we finish the house viewing."

"House hunting? That's what we're doing?"

"Yes. What else did you think it would be?"

I tried not to let relief show on my face. "N-nothing! But still . . . Is house hunting ever stress relieving?"

"It is when I've found the perfect one. You're gonna love it."

We'd been doing this for the last six months. I was tired of apartment life, and Trevor had given in to my desire for a home. It had been a long journey, especially since we had very different tastes. But this was promising. Had he finally given in to the idea of an older home with character? Had he finally moved on from only wanting a brand-new place in the middle of a subdivision?

Hopefully, whatever plan he had would get me out of the rut I'd been in.

I needed it.

"I can't wait to see it," I said.

A pleased smile crossed his face, and he patted my shoulder before going to his office.

And the numbness came back.

"A kiss would have been nice," I muttered before returning to my desk.

I ran right into Dad.

"Everything okay, Mollie-bear?"

I wish I could have felt something at his nickname for me.

"I'm fine. Or trying to be."

"Are you sure?" he asked again. "You were off in the meeting."

"I don't think I've spent enough time outside."

He slowly nodded. I knew Dad didn't get it, but at least he wasn't as direct as Trevor.

"Have Trevor take you on a hike. Or go with your friend, Wren."

"She's busy with her huge new project." One that I barely knew anything about. "And Trevor was . . . Well, he told me to go to a park. I don't think he wants to help me with this."

"Are you sure?" Dad's brow pinched. "He's always more than willing to help around here."

Sure. *With work.* Not with me. It was like his work sucked up all of his energy, leaving nothing for anything else.

"Maybe I misheard," I said, shrugging. "I do that sometimes. I should get back to my desk."

"You could go on a speed walk with your mom if you wanted to."

I cringed. Walking through her HOA-curated neighborhood was *not* what I needed.

"It's just a phase," I said, shaking my head. "It'll pass."

I brewed another cup of coffee before I went back to my desk. I clicked around in spreadsheets for hours before Trevor came to get me.

"Ready to go?"

I nearly jumped up. "I'm ready!"

"Someone's excited," Trevor said. "Are you finally over your mood?"

"Yep!" I tried to channel brightness. He looked at my desk before his forehead creased.

"Are you sure? Your desk is a mess."

I looked over, seeing papers scattered. It was slightly worse than usual, but nothing like his had been when he'd asked me to reorganize it last month.

"I'll get to it tomorrow."

"You also need to mop the apartment too. The floors are sticky."

"Could you do it this time?" I asked. "It'll help my mood."

I had hope for all of half a second that he would agree. It would have made me feel better.

But he scoffed. "Come on, Mollie. You know I'm too busy earning my salary for that."

"I work here too."

"But I make way more than you."

I struggled to keep the disappointment off my face. Trevor hardly ever did anything around the house, claiming that working his job was more than enough. He expected our apartment to stay the way he liked it—orderly and clean.

Which was odd, considering he was neither of those things.

"You coming?" he asked. He was already several feet away.

My feet refused to move as I tried to sort through my emotions.

He was nice to everyone else. This was just normal man stuff. There were entire forums filled with wives who dealt with this. It wasn't out of the normal.

So why was I so angry with him?

No, I was angry with his *actions*. Not him.

I tried to remember that as I forced myself to follow. I was sure once we went to this perfect house of his, I'd feel better.

Trevor even drove me in his car, promising to bring me back once we were done. I watched where we were driving, trying to figure out which part of Nashville we were heading to, but then I started to recognize the streets.

"Are we going to my parents' house?"

"No," he said. "Not at all."

I frowned as we passed the welcome sign to their neighbor-hood. As we went by manicured lawns I knew my mom was responsible for as the head of the HOA, even my fake good mood vanished.

Their tan and white home came up, and I crossed my arms.

Then we pulled into the driveway of the house next door.

"What?" I asked.

"Surprise. This is the house we're seeing."

I slowly turned toward it. This was a tan brick home with two stories. It wasn't a new build, but it was also ten different shades of beige, just like my parents'.

Mom and Dad's neighborhood was nice, but it was so regu-lated that there was no freedom to do anything different. She lurked as if catching prey when hunting down anyone out of compliance.

"R-really?" I asked. "But homes here are way too expensive."

"Don't worry about that. Let's just see the inside."

"But it's—"

"You'll love it. It's just like the house you grew up in."

I opened my mouth, but closed it again. When I thought of my childhood home, I saw Mom and Dad's house, but I also saw Papa Bennie's old farmhouse. It had blue and white wallpaper, an old woodburning stove that kept everything warm in the winter, and massive windows that let all the light in.

But there was no way to use the word *farm* with Trevor.

Slowly, I got out of the car, hoping I would like it more on the inside.

But all I could see was gray. The owners had tried to remodel it, but they had done the same thing the modern-day builders did: They'd painted everything one tone to make it appeal to the masses.

It was the same layout as Mom and Dad's house. An office, a dining room, and a cookie-cutter kitchen.

Papa Bennie's kitchen had tiled countertops with leaves painted on them. It was gorgeous.

I wished I could see it again.

"There you two are!" Mom said as she walked through the door. "This is so *perfect*, isn't it?"

"Hi, Maribelle." Trevor turned with a smile. "She's taking it all in."

"I can't wait for us to be neighbors. We can see each other every *day*!" She clapped her hands together, but then leaned toward Trevor and said in a lower voice, "And I can make sure you mow your lawn correctly."

"I-it's nice, but it's way out of the budget," I said, shaking my head. "We'll have to find something in a different part of town."

Mom smiled conspiratorially with Trevor. "Should we tell her?"

"We should."

"Come on." She waved for us to follow her. "We have something to show you."

We walked from the empty house for sale and into theirs. Dimly, I realized I would never have any privacy. Mom would be in *everything*.

My nerves only grew as we walked into Dad's office at the back of the house.

"You have a lot more than you know," Mom said. "And with this"—she pulled out an envelope— "you can afford the house next door."

She handed it over and I slowly opened it. Were they giving me the money for it? Was this a way-too-large check I wouldn't feel comfortable cashing?

Instead, it was a piece of green paper and a letter.

. . .

*And to my granddaughter, Mollie Mae Wilson, I leave the farm
and farmhouse, as well as all employees and income.*

"What? Papa Bennie's farm?"

"He passed when you weren't eighteen yet. It was in a trust
that we never took it out of. I've kept it for when you needed it."

"I'm nearly thirty. Why didn't I know about this when I was
of age?"

"You were doing so well, Mollie-bear," Dad said. "A farm
like that is a lot of responsibility, and in the time since you've
seen it, things have changed."

"We wanted you to have a life outside of what was given to
you," Mom added.

I looked back down. I'd thought Papa Bennie's house was a
place I'd never see again, and now it was *mine*? It had been
mine the whole time?

"She's in so much shock she can't even speak!" Trevor said
with a laugh.

I slowly turned to him. "You knew?"

"Of course he knew," Mom said. "We told him when you
were struggling to find the perfect house."

My grip on the paper tightened. He *knew* how much I
wanted to go back. I didn't understand. Why had he lied to me
about it? Why had he let me think it was gone?

"Here's the best part, Mollie-bear," Dad started. "These
investors would buy it from you at a higher rate. Trevor found
them."

I looked back up at him, trying to keep the betrayal from
showing on my face. Did he even care about what I wanted?
"It's my family's company. They've been looking for a place to
develop for years."

"That area is up-and-coming," Dad added. "It could be the first neighborhood in the area."

Strawberry Springs was a small town, one where everyone bought a large plot of land and lived on it, unless they lived near the town square. I didn't remember a single subdivision in that area. And unless things had changed over the last ten years, I doubted it really was up-and-coming.

"Thank you for showing me this," I said slowly, trying to figure out what to do.

"You should get to work on selling that old place," Trevor said. "Then we can put an offer in on the house next door."

I stared down at the letter, wondering if I could even go through with that before going back to my happy place.

I didn't know if I could let go of it.

"Let me get it into my name fully," I said. "Then we'll go from there."

"I can't wait until you guys can come over every morning for coffee." Mom bounced on the balls of her feet. "Can't you, Mollie?"

"U-um, yeah."

"Is everything okay?" she asked.

"Oh, I'm just . . . thinking. About all of my plans."

And how I might just hate every single one of them.

"Are you sure you're okay?" she asked. "I thought you'd be more excited."

"I'm . . . I miss the farm. I didn't know I had it."

"You have such a rose-tinted view of everything," she said. "But I know it isn't how you remember it. Not at all."

"Still, it's something."

"I have something far better to help," she said. "Come on. This will make you feel better."

Mom pulled a DVD out of the closet and took us to the living room.

"Here you go." She pressed play.

The opening shot was a close-up of a flannel shirt, and then Papa Bennie came into the frame as he set the camera down. His tanned skin was familiar, and my heart gave a lurch at the sight of him.

"All right, I *think* this is right," Bennie muttered. "Maribelle will have my head if it isn't."

"Papa Bennie! Look what I found!"

A young version of me came into the frame, holding up a gigantic worm.

"Oh, that's disgusting," Trevor muttered.

Nostalgia hit me stronger than I'd ever felt. It had been years since I'd laid my eyes on those strawberry patches and rolling hills.

They were beautiful in a way I needed. The screen wasn't enough. I needed to *be* there.

"Your mama said to change into overalls, Miss Mae!"

I blew a raspberry and ran for the tree line where the animals used to be. Papa Bennie laughed.

And the camera cut.

"You were such a menace back then," Mom said, laughing. "Those fields didn't know what was coming whenever we let you stay the night. Though with how messy you were when you came back, I was glad not to have to deal with that anymore. You can have this DVD. That way, you can see it whenever you want to. Problem solved."

But it wasn't solved. Not even close. Now I wanted to go there *more*. I needed to see what had become of the place I'd loved so much.

"Mollie," Trevor said. "Come on, it's just a farm. Your life is here."

"Yes, honey." Mom's voice was gentle. "It's with us."

I bit my lip and nodded, even though every cell in my body

told me not to. I put the papers in my purse and tried to make peace with my decision.

I didn't find it.

Mom handed me the DVD and then talked more about our plans. I nodded along and tried to sound happy, but when Trevor and I were getting into the car, the mask fell.

"I can't believe you knew," I said as we pulled away. "And you're wanting to sell it to your family's company."

"That sale will ensure we can buy that house and have a wedding. Selling the old land will benefit us both. Trust me."

"I'm trying to. But you kept my own farmhouse from me."

He rolled his eyes. "Of course you'd be upset over this. Don't be so sensitive, Mollie. I just wanted you to see our next house before I told you."

"Still. You saw the DVD. You saw how happy that place made me."

"Do you really wanna be that girl with the worm?"

"Maybe I do."

"Absolutely not. I'm not letting you."

I took a deep breath and tried to push down my rising emotions.

"I want to see it before I sell it."

"And that's another thing I'm not letting you do."

"What? *Why?*"

"Because I know you. You'll want to stay. You'll see some shabby little town and think it's right for you."

Dammit. He may not always understand me, but he was right about this one.

Strawberry Springs was the kind of place where everyone knew each other. And to a girl who didn't even know her neighbors, that sounded nice.

"Just get the deed and sell it. Trust me, you won't regret it."

He seemed so sure about it.

"Have you ever felt this way?" I asked. "Like you're in the wrong place, and you want things to go back to how they were?"

"No, of course not." He shook his head. "I know exactly how I want my life to be."

A million thoughts fought for dominance, but none of them were kind. I swallowed all of it and crossed my arms, looking out at the city.

I wanted this feeling to go away. I wanted to like Nashville, the city everyone told me I should love.

But I didn't.

2

CAIN

Strawberry Springs Neighborhood Watch
Kerry Winsor
Look at my little man, ready for school! He's got **@Nicole Rudder** as his teacher! Gosh, I remember when she was a kid.

Comments:
Nicole Rudder: Did you have to tag me?
Kerry Winsor: Um, YES. I'm proud of you both!
Jackie Anne: Oh, you have Nicole! Congrats.
Kerry Winsor: Does anyone else have Nicole?? Who are his classmates gonna be? I need to know who I can chat with about all of these things. Other than Nicole, of course.
Nicole Rudder: Please remember that I have to be professional.
Kerry Winsor: I helped you fix your hair after you turned it orange in high school. Considering I never told your dad, I get a special pass.
Nicole Rudder: You're lucky he doesn't have Facebook!

THE CHICKENS SWARMED me when I walked into their run. I had a ton of them, so it felt a little like being drowned by fowl, but the second I threw the food down, they went for that.

Except for one.

My favorite chicken, Hennifer, flew to my shoulder. She did this every morning since she knew I'd give her something special whenever she landed without scratching me.

"Good job," I said, holding out my hand, which held her daily treat. "There you go."

She grabbed every last mealworm out of my palm before joining the rest of the flock. I watched them for a moment to ease the churning in my gut before going to collect eggs.

Usually, I grabbed the eggs and then focused on packaging them to sell. That, in addition to getting the milk from the cows ready to be sold to a pasteurization plant, took up most of my days, especially when the weather was warm and egg-laying season was in full swing.

And it was all on me since I was the sole employee of Bennie's farm. For a long time, I'd been angry that all of that work had been given only to me. I managed the farm and did the daily tasks, and for a while, it was almost too much. I'd written to his family to ask for more help, but there had been no response.

These days, I was grateful for it. Sure, I'd had to make cuts and focus mostly on the animals rather than the crops Bennie had managed, but I got to make a living while barely talking to anyone. The diner and the local store bought most of the eggs, and the milk I sold to the plants earned a decent income to keep the farm running.

I had enough free time to move my schedule around to spend time with Eric, my nephew I had custody of. But not enough to think too hard about life.

I checked my watch, knowing we needed to leave soon. This

was a day both Eric and I had been dreading. His first day of school.

Weeks before, I'd figured out a new schedule of running the farm and picking him up. It did nothing to quell the nervous feeling in my gut.

He'd already had a hard life since his mom—my sister—had died in a car crash. She was a single parent, and I was the only blood relative the state could find. She and I had been separated when we were kids after being thrown into the foster system. I hadn't known anything about her until she'd died.

And then I had sole custody of a two-year-old.

I could remember the days when I would move from home to home and wonder why no relative had stepped up for me. When I'd had the chance to do things differently, I'd taken it, even when my only knowledge about being a parent had been from calving season in the spring.

Since then, I'd tried to make sure Eric didn't have much stress in his life. He helped with the animals when he wanted to, but most of the time, he could play in the fields and enjoy life without worrying about whether or not he would be cared for.

And him being nervous for his first day of kindergarten? Yeah, that wrecked me.

I was tempted to homeschool him and keep him from every fear there could be, but being the lone person working on a farm meant I was busy. Besides, I was many things, but a teacher was not one of them.

The Strawberry Springs Elementary School was good. Too good. The close-knit town never hesitated to help out the school, and many of the teachers who had taught *me* were still there.

Of course, Eric had gotten the youngest one. Nicole Rudder, one of the popular girls in high school who had always turned her nose up at me. To be fair, those were my worst years, and I'd made a lot of bad impressions at the time. To this day, she hesitated to speak to me, like most of the people around here did.

I only hoped she wouldn't do the same to Eric.

All the eggs were in my basket, and the sun crept over the horizon. I knew I couldn't avoid this for much longer. Eric had asked to go into town for breakfast before school since our diner, Center Point, was open this early.

I couldn't say no.

I went inside and loaded the eggs into the egg-washing machine before I got myself ready for the day. Eric was up and sitting next to his backpack, waiting for me.

"Ready?" I asked as I ruffled his dark hair, eyeing the way he swung his legs. He always moved when he was nervous. Now that the calendar had counted down to zero on his first day of school, he never seemed to be still.

"Yeah," he said. "Can we get pancakes now?"

I was not ready. Not remotely. But I grabbed the keys to the truck anyway.

It was a thirty-minute drive into town. Technically, the town square was out of our way, but I didn't care. If my nephew wanted pancakes on the day his life changed, then he was getting pancakes.

It still didn't stop the way my body tensed when we parked. I hated coming into town. There were reminders of all my mistakes everywhere. Like the corner of the square where I'd let Donny have it. Or the center of it where Bennie had dragged me to sell eggs, and I'd wound up standing awkwardly as people passed.

I'd never been able to integrate into the town dynamics, and it was obvious when Tammy did a double take at seeing me.

Tammy owned the diner, and other than her husband who worked in the back, she ran it by herself. Her daughter some-times helped, but she'd left town to go to college. Since then, she'd hired some of the high school kids, but this morning she was alone and gestured for us to sit anywhere.

Old Man Hugh was here, and he'd called Tammy over to lock her into a long conversation about how taxes were too high. Marjorie and Henrietta, a retired married couple I barely spoke to, took up one of the other tables in the corner. I looked down at the menu, though there was no need. Both of us knew exactly what we were getting.

Tammy came to our table a few minutes later, dropping orange juice for Eric and a water for me.

"So," she said as she turned to him, "first day of school! How are you feeling?"

"Good," he said at first. Then he sank into his seat. "Nervous."

"You'll do great. I bet you'll have a bunch of friends on your first day."

Unlike Cain, I could hear her saying. I wasn't much for friends. Or people.

"Is the food at school good?" he asked. That was always the first thing on his mind.

"It's . . . okay. You might have better luck asking this one"— she jerked a thumb at me— "to make you lunch."

Eric's eyes slid over to me.

"The letter from the school said they wanted you to try school lunch once. But we'll talk about it after."

"Fine," he said before turning back to Tammy. "Can I have pancakes?"

"Of course. Your usual, Cain?"

"Yes," I said. "Thanks."

She nodded slowly before going to put the order in. I let out a breath. I tried to put on a brave face for Eric, but this was like pulling teeth for me. All the people here saw me as the kid I used to be, not the man I was.

Tammy didn't waste time. We got our food the second it was done, and we ate quickly before leaving to go to the school.

Other parents were waiting in the courtyard. I parked the truck and walked hand in hand with Eric up to the front, trying to ignore the pounding of my heart. My teeth clenched, and I knew if I saw any tears gathering in Eric's eyes, I'd pack him up and take him home.

"Cain Smith, there you are!" a voice called out. I didn't think it was possible for me to tense any more.

But the impossible happened every damn day.

Kerry Winsor wanted to talk to me.

She spent her free time watching every corner of Strawberry Springs. She was in her late forties, but had a kid Eric's age from her second marriage. She loved talking to all of the teachers and parents.

And she loved talking about *me*.

I'd made local headlines many times since coming here, and she'd enjoyed discussing it each time it had happened.

"I bet Donny's rolling over in his freshly dug grave right now," she'd said. *"It's a shame that he sold that house."*

I'd heard it in the store of all places, and I'd left before I could hear any more about how much they hated me. I knew I was an outsider to everyone here but Bennie and Jackie. And though I'd accepted it, the reminders still hurt.

Kerry was nice to my face, which made what I heard worse. But the people of Strawberry Springs showed their colors when I wasn't around, and I knew better.

I would have avoided her like the plague, but of course, I *had* to be here.

"Kerry," I said.

"And little Eric! You look so handsome. Has anyone gotten a photo of you two?"

Absolutely not.

"Can we get one?" Eric asked.

Dammit.

"Sure," I said, and I handed her my phone, opened to the camera app. I knew she would snoop otherwise. I positioned Eric in front of me and let her snap a photo. When she handed me my phone back, her son, Tommy, was by her side.

"What teacher do you have?" she asked. "We have Ms. Rudder. Hard to believe she's old enough to be a teacher. I remember *her* first day of kindergarten!"

"We have the same," I replied.

Her eyes lit up. "How did I not know that? I guess we'll be seeing more of each other?"

Ah. Well. My day had gotten impossibly worse.

"I suppose so."

Out of the corner of my eye, Tommy peeked out from behind his mother's legs and waved at Eric.

He returned it with vigor, and the other boy moved out more.

"I bet Eric would like a friend," Kerry said to her son. "Then we could set up playdates!"

And I bet she would use that to get more information out of me. Absolutely not. I was not a part of the gossip machine of this town. I refused to be.

But Tommy listened and walked over to Eric to ask about his favorite TV show.

"He's got him talking about Bluey," she said. "They're best friends now."

Well, *fuck.*

I eyed the front door. A quick check of my watch told me we had three minutes.

"It's so hard dropping them off the first time," Kerry said. "But it gets easier."

My eyes slid to her. "I don't know if it will."

"Soon, you'll be wanting him to go. And then he'll start reading and writing. Then he'll be out of the house like my first is."

Yeah. I didn't want to think about that at all.

I was attached to Eric. He was possibly the only person other than Jackie and Bennie who genuinely liked me. And in return, I'd poured all the love I'd missed out on as a kid into him. When he grew up, I wasn't sure what would be left for me other than the chickens and cows on the farm.

"But that's not for a long time," Kerry reminded me. "And maybe by then, you'll have a nice woman to fill your time."

"That's not happening." I knew way too much about the women in this town, and they knew the same about me. A relationship with any of them was completely off the table. And besides, I didn't have time for romance when I was raising a child and running a farm.

Kerry opened her mouth to say something, but the doors opened and parents filtered in. I gave her a nod and took Eric to his classroom, eager to be away from her.

Nicole's hair was in a bun, and she welcomed every child with a tight hug. Eric wasn't excluded, but she wouldn't look me in the eye. I focused on my nephew, who nervously looked around. I knelt to get to his level.

"I'll be back in a few hours," I said.

"Okay."

"And I know this is scary, but you're gonna do great."

"How do you know?"

"Because you're smart. And kind. Way more than I am."

Eric hugged me tightly, and I returned it for far longer than I should have. When I let go, I ran out of the classroom before I stayed forever.

And thankfully, no tears fell until I was in my truck.

Strawberry Springs Neighborhood Watch
Kerry Winsor
First day down! We had a very fun time. Also **@Jackie Anne**, you should have told me Eric was in Tommy's class!

Comments:
Jackie Anne: Not my thing to tell.
Kerry Winsor: I had to make awkward conversation with Cain. Warn a girl!
Atticus Thompson: Ah, I need to ask him for eggs. Simone is going through a phase where she eats three a day.
Kerry Winsor: Scrambled or over easy?
Atticus Thompson: Hard-boiled.
Kerry Winsor: WHY?

———

"You HAVE A *HOUSE*?" Wren's green eyes were wide. Her strawberry-blonde hair was in a braid, and we were getting coffee in a quiet corner of town. I'd been shocked when she called me as I was walking out of the state building to get the house in my name. We'd hardly been able to talk in the last few weeks while she worked on her mystery project.

"Yep. An old farmhouse. It's probably abandoned."

Wren's jaw kept falling open. "Are you *serious*?"

"I'm serious."

"This is the greatest day of my life!" she nearly yelled. "I mean, your life. When you said you wanted a house that we could work on together, I thought it was a pipe dream. But you made it happen!"

"It might still be a pipe dream," I replied. "My parents and Trevor want me to sell it to developers."

I'd never seen a smile fall so quickly off someone's face. "Where is it again?"

"Strawberry Springs. It's three hours east of here and about an hour north of Knoxville, near the Kentucky border."

"What developer is going out there?" she asked. "And why would you sell beautiful farmland?"

"For money."

She pulled out her phone, presumably to bring up a map. "We're talking *history*."

"Right, but apparently, it's 'up-and-coming,'" I said. "It doesn't feel like an area that would appreciate that."

"Yeah, *no*." Wren shook her head. "There's nothing there. I'm sure some would love the quiet life, but the town isn't made for a subdivision."

She would know. She loved researching neighborhoods around Nashville. She bought the run-down, older houses no one wanted, often to keep them from getting demolished, and carefully remodeled and sold them. She was a local legend. People wanted her to buy a house in their neighborhood because it meant she would take care of what made Nashville special.

I knew she wouldn't like the idea of demolishing farmland for houses on principle. Still, hearing it made me feel better.

"How long would it have been abandoned?" she asked.

"Ten years, give or take. The letter he left said he had employees, but after this long, there's no way they would have stayed."

"If it's not in too bad of shape, it could be redone and sold." Her eyes met mine. "But judging by the look on your face, you don't like that idea."

"I thought it was gone," I said. "And now it's in my name. Shouldn't I do something with it? Papa Bennie was a cornerstone of Strawberry Springs. I could carry on his legacy."

"Maybe, but you'd have to see how the farm looks and probably do a lot of learning to get it there. It's not impossible, but you'd have to completely give up your life here. At least temporarily."

"And Trevor wouldn't like it."

She rolled her eyes. "If he really wants to marry you, then he should support whatever makes you happy."

He should. I wanted him to.

But I didn't know if he would.

There was an uncomfortable feeling simmering under my skin. Like if I turned stones over in my relationship, I would find cans of worms I wished I'd left alone.

"And if he doesn't?"

She smiled, her face a picture of serene calm, but then she leaned in and spoke. "Then we finally use our spot we picked out in high school to bury his body."

"Really, Wren? Murder?"

"I only want people surrounding you who invest in your happiness. The jury's been out for so long on Trevor that I'm pretty sure they escaped out the window."

I toyed with the sleeve of my floral shirt. I hadn't told

anyone, not even Wren, some of the things Trevor had asked of me, because I knew how they'd react. But she must have picked up on something from the sidelines.

Shaking my head, I said, "I'm sure he'll come around."

"Well, just let me know if he doesn't. I'm free until tomorrow."

"And what's happening tomorrow? This big project you've told me nothing about?"

Her smile grew. "That's actually why I asked you out for coffee. I finally can talk about it."

"What? Why didn't you lead with that?"

"Oh, I'm sorry. My best friend also had incredible news." She rolled her eyes again. "I can be happy about multiple things."

"Tell me everything," I said. "Are you renovating one of the old mansions or something?"

"Kinda. I was worried about capital, so I asked around to see if any investors wanted in. And one did."

"Really? You hate working with investors."

"I do, but if I want to up my game, I need to try. And I found a good one."

"Who is it?"

"It's the Home Repair TV Channel."

"*What?*" I gasped. "Like they're investing, or like . . . more?"

"More. It's a TV show alongside Jude Putman."

I slammed my hand on the table. "Your dream man?"

She nodded. "I've loved him ever since I saw him knocking out a wall on a rebuild. He's coming here, and we're filming starting tomorrow."

I squealed, ignoring the glares from onlookers, and climbed out of my seat to hug her. "I'm so happy for you!"

"It's a dream come true!" she said. "But it does mean I'll be busy pretty much nonstop while filming."

"Who cares? You're gonna be on TV!"

"They want us to have good chemistry. So, it's a mix of home reno and reality TV. It's called *Renovating with Love*. We're basically only going to see each other. And the producers said we can . . . *do* whatever we want."

"So, that means you'll do *whoever* you want. You're gonna climb him like a tree, aren't you?"

"Hell yes," she said.

I laughed and pulled her in for one last hug.

"So, if you do decide to renovate that old farmhouse, can you give me until spring?"

Spring was so far away. Plus, I wanted to do it how Papa Bennie had. He would plant in the fall and let them gather energy over winter.

But I was pretty sure it would take that long to convince Trevor to even go for it.

"Of course," I said. "You do what you need to. And I'll try to convince Trevor not to sell."

"I can help with that. Let me write up a market report. That man *loves* reports."

She pulled out her laptop and got to work while I returned to my side of the booth. I was so happy for her, and even though I'd miss her, I wanted her to get everything she wanted.

I only hoped I could have the same.

———

Instead of doing my weekend routine the next morning, which consisted of making coffee for Trevor and me before he would point out what needed to be cleaned, I was pacing around in front of our bedroom door.

I held all the research Wren had done on the area, sipping

on coffee I'd made for myself while working out exactly how to get him to see that selling the farmland wasn't the best idea.

Trevor knocked on the wall, his sign that he was up and ready for coffee. I took a deep breath before opening the door.

"That's not what I asked for," he said, eyeing the papers in my hand.

"We need to talk about something."

"And you couldn't bring coffee?"

I sighed. "If I make it for you, will you be in a better mood?"

"I would."

I pursed my lips, but turned to go to the kitchen. I made him a cup of coffee and then returned with it a few minutes later.

"Here," I said.

He took a slow sip. "Okay, go ahead."

"I don't want to sell the farm."

He didn't bother looking up at me. "Of course you don't."

"I'm just saying that I don't think that area is appropriate for a subdivision." I handed him the papers. "And neither does Wren."

He groaned and took them. "You told *her* of all people?"

My shoulders tensed. What was his deal with her? He always made little comments, either suggesting she didn't know enough about things to have an opinion, or that she was plain wrong. "She works in real estate too."

"She's anti-change. And biased."

"You're gonna say that before you even look at the research?"

"Let me guess, she told you it wasn't suitable because it's in the middle of nowhere and no one would want to move there."

"It's not near a neighboring big city," I reminded.

"There's a whole faction of people who work from home. We can build them farmhouses on an acre each and they'll move in droves. My dad did the research."

"And so did Wren," I replied. "Look at how many houses have been built there in the last few years. *Two.* And they took forever to sell. It's a small town, Trevor. Bulldozing farmland with a history to it and building a hundred houses isn't the way to do it."

"You're sentimental."

"And you're not listening to me." I let my desperation seep into my voice. I needed him to listen this time. Just this once.

"If you keep it, it'll just sit there forever."

"It's still good land. Maybe I could run it like Bennie used to and stay here."

He rolled his eyes. "You can't even focus in a meeting, Mollie."

"Because I'm thinking about things like this."

"There's nothing to think about. Sell it. Bulldoze it. Move *on.*"

"But that's not what I want to do." My voice climbed higher in pitch. I didn't fight him on *anything*. Why couldn't he let me have this? Just one compromise so I could remember that he cared about me.

"I don't care about what you *want*. Obviously, you can't see sense on this. I care about getting the money so we can buy our dream home."

His response hit me like a ton of bricks. "I never called it that."

"You don't know what your dream is."

"Actually, I do. And it's Papa Bennie's home."

His eyes cut to me, and he slowly stood. "Excuse me?"

"Trevor, the house was *beautiful*. The land was nearly endless. He made a living off of it for over fifty years. It has space, character, and—"

"Who cares? It's not in the place we want to be. You can't work in marketing and have a farm."

"What if I could?"

"You don't know the first thing about that kind of life."

"I could learn."

His voice grew deeper and louder. "And how would you keep your job? Working from home? In the middle of nowhere? You have a life here. A good one that people would kill for. And you want to add *farming* to it?"

"I do."

"Mollie, *no!*" he snapped. He took a step toward me. "We're selling that land, and it's final."

I retreated a step, but straightened my spine. "It's *my* land."

"And I'm gonna be your husband. Therefore, it'll be mine. And I know you better than you know yourself."

My voice shook as I let my rising frustration break free. "You don't know anything."

"I do. You're about to turn thirty, and you're flailing. You're scared to do anything, so you think running will help you. It won't. You think it's bad here? You won't fit in there either, because for some reason you have fancy ideas that *nobody wants.*"

"*I* want them."

"And you'll fail. And then you will have left behind your mom and dad, who care about you, to do something there's no way you can do."

His harsh words felt like a punch to the gut. "But what if it makes me happy?" I asked. "Don't you want that for me?"

"If it means you're covered in dirt and in the middle of nowhere? No, Mollie. I don't."

Why did I say yes to marrying you? The thought came unbidden. I wasn't sure if it was because I was truly having second thoughts, or if this was me reacting to him telling me no.

Mom told me that Dad pissed her off all the time. Sometimes, she said she regretted ever marrying him.

But sometimes didn't equal all the time, did it? I couldn't remember the last time I had felt excited about marrying Trevor.

"So, I just . . . what, assimilate into what you want?" I snapped.

"Eventually, you'll see that you want it too."

I shook my head, but he was done with the conversation. He rolled his eyes as if I were a petulant child and brushed past me.

"Where are you going?"

"Out."

"But we're not done."

"Oh, we're done. There isn't gonna be any more talk about this."

He pulled on his shoes and slammed the door behind him.

As soon as I was alone, I finally let myself feel all the emotions I had been trying so hard to suppress. *What am I doing here? Why am I marrying this man?*

I shook my head and looked down at my white-gold ring. All of a sudden, it felt like it shouldn't be on my finger.

He'd said I wanted to run, and maybe he was right. I couldn't be here anymore. I couldn't do this routine, and I couldn't keep looking at houses while pretending my heart wasn't in Strawberry Springs.

I slid the ring off my finger and set it on the side table. I already felt ten pounds lighter without it.

I knew Mom would be disappointed. Dad too. They probably wouldn't understand, and they would push me to get back with him.

My breath came out in stutters. I needed *out* of this life. Out of this relationship. But Trevor had inserted himself everywhere.

Well, everywhere except for *one* place.

On hour two of the drive, the calls started. At first, it was Mom. Then Dad. And eventually, Trevor. I turned off my phone, choosing to sit in silence as I tried to remember every single reason I was leaving.

But I was terrified that I was making a mistake.

There was only an hour left, and I wished it could go by faster. Buildings had turned into hills and fields, and I'd gotten off the two-lane interstate some time ago.

Instead of questioning every decision I'd just made, I tried to remember all the things I'd liked about Strawberry Springs when I was a kid.

I remembered a town square filled with people. There was a diner I'd begged Papa Bennie to take me to every day, along with an endless library and antique shop I would walk through when it was too hot to work in the fields.

Life moved slower there. People stopped to talk in the streets. They'd all known my name and asked how I was. It was the complete opposite of the life I knew.

And I needed it.

The Strawberry Springs welcome sign came up as I crested a hill. I slowed down to read it.

Strawberry Springs. Keeping the magic alive.

"Magic, huh?" I mused to myself. "I need some of that."

I could see the town square from the main road, and it was as cute as ever, with two-story buildings facing one another. A clock rose high over the library.

I was tempted to see the town up close, but my sights were set on the farm.

It was situated on hundreds of acres of land. Papa Bennie had split it between strawberry fields and livestock, which were situated on the back of the property. In front of the house were gorgeous displays of flowers he'd kept up with in his free time.

He'd told me his grand plans of adding different kinds of berries to increase his income in the warmer months.

I wish he'd gotten to do it. I'd loved the days when the farm was open to the public and people would pick their own berries.

I knew it would be different, but when I almost missed the driveway because I didn't see the wooden sign that announced its location, I saw firsthand how things had changed.

Papa Bennie had painted that himself, as well as built all the payment stands we would sell berries from. The sign was gone, and the fields where people would park were overgrown.

At least the gravel driveway was in surprisingly good shape. I turned onto it, eyeing the white home situated on the top of the hill.

It didn't look all that abandoned. The siding was in decent repair and the wraparound porch showed no age. No lights were on, and no cars were in the driveway, but the land was mowed and kept tidy.

My eyes swept over the rolling landscape and the clear skies. I parked and got out of the car, hearing nothing but the birds.

And when I took a deep breath, I smelled fresh air.

Holy *shit*, I'd missed this. The air was so clean, even with the animals close by. The sky was endless, dotted with clouds.

What would it be like to see this all the time? What was working in the fields like? Had Papa Bennie enjoyed seeing the sunset from his porch every night? Or had he come to resent it over time like Mom had?

I grabbed the key left in the letter from my pocket and approached the front door. It didn't fit into the lock, but I'd been locked out of dorms a lot. Maybe age had warped it somehow.

I knew how to use a credit card to get in. When the door was loosened, I took a long breath, preparing myself for dust and debris. I didn't know if I could even sleep in the house tonight, but even my car felt better than anywhere near Trevor.

Slowly, the door opened, and instead of an abandoned mess like I'd expected, I walked into a fully furnished living room.

It was exactly like Papa Bennie had left it, though the furniture was newer. A three-seater couch under the bright window. A small TV on a nightstand. A few jackets around. The walls were painted a serene blue, with photos of the fields adorning the free spaces.

It looked like someone had just been here *today*. But that wasn't possible. Surely, things would have aged. Surely, it should look worse than this.

Unless the magic of this town *was* real.

My thoughts were broken by the sound of footsteps, and I turned to the door to see a hulking figure staring at me.

All I could do was scream and grab the nearest weapon.

4

CAIN

Strawberry Springs Neighborhood Watch
Kerry Winsor
The group is SO quiet. What's up with that?

Comments:
Atticus Thompson: Simone got an A on her grad school final.
Kerry Winsor: That's not news. We all knew she would. (Congrats, though.) What about Gabriel?
Kerry Winsor: Has nothing else happened? Really? No offense, Atticus, but the Facebook group has been DEAD. Can't someone race down Main Street to give us something to talk about?
Jackie Anne: Do NOT wish that upon me. I need my beauty sleep in order to do your hair.
Kerry Winsor: Okay, fine. Maybe don't race down Main Street. But can someone do something interesting?
Jade Clark: I could try to make my zombie candle again.
Grace Day: You should add cinnamon this time.

Kerry Winsor: NO. The square STILL smells like a mix of coffee and jasmine sometimes.

Dale Garrett: I liked it, actually. Wanted to buy a few for the store.

Atticus Thompson: That's physically impossible, Kerry.

Kerry Winsor: Don't lecture me about physically impossible when your mother said her bones could predict the weather **@Atticus Thompson**

Jade Clark: Oooh, harsh.

SherriffMike Finch: I smell it too sometimes . . .

THERE WAS a woman in my house. One with wavy, golden-brown hair and hazel eyes with dark lashes. Her plush mouth hung open when she saw me, but then she screamed.

She was gorgeous. And I probably would have spent more time on that fact if she hadn't *broken into my fucking house.*

She grabbed the closest thing to her, a Jade's Goodies candle that I was saving for special occasions.

My favorite one too.

"Put that down," I snapped. My first words should have been *what the hell are you doing here?* or *get the hell out,* but dammit, the vanilla lavender scent was always sold out. And I wasn't going to let a woman who was obviously breaking and entering take that from me.

"No!" she snapped back. "Who are you? What are you doing here?"

"I think the better question is who are *you*? And what are you doing in my house?"

She slowly lowered the candle. "Your house? This isn't your house!"

"I've lived here for a decade."

"No. *No.* This place is abandoned. Nicely decorated. But abandoned."

"Does this look abandoned to you?" I asked. I mean, seriously. I'd put a lot of money into making my house feel like a home. "I'm the manager of Bennie Grove Farm, princess. I *live* here."

Now her eyes went wide. "You're the . . . You live here?"

"It's a perk of the job."

"But I'm . . . I own the farm. I'm Bennie's granddaughter."

I took another look at her. Bennie's granddaughter was nothing more than a ghost to me. He'd always said she would come back, but she never had.

And then he'd died, and she'd stayed gone.

I was sure he'd placed his trust in the wrong person, and looking at her now, I knew I had been right.

Her jeans were tailored to fit her perfectly. Her nails were done in a brown color that looked like a pumpkin spice fucking latte. She screamed class and money. Not a single flaw about her.

She wasn't from here—that much was for sure.

"The last I checked, the house was in a trust and none of his family cared about it."

She tilted her head. "It was, but it was supposed to go to me, and now it has."

It had been a decade of radio silence from Bennie's family. They'd abandoned the place. And now one of them was *here?*

Fuck.

"So, where the hell were you for the last fifteen years?"

"I was busy."

"Let me guess, in the city. Where you should be."

Her eyes narrowed. "Well, I'm here now. Whether you like it or not. I own this place."

"So, owned by a woman who has no idea that it was open or how to run it?"

She winced, and I knew the answer.

I opened my mouth to curse, but was interrupted.

"Begone, bad guy!" Eric yelled. He ran in with a large branch raised over his head. "This is our house and we're gonna defend it!"

The candle went back up and I glared again. "Do *not* use that." I looked to Eric next. "And stand down, Mr. Guard Dog. We're not getting robbed."

"B-but there's a stranger here," he said, looking at her. "You *are* a stranger, right?"

"No, this is Mollie. The owner of the farm."

"How do you know my name?" she asked.

"Bennie talked about you all the time. Said he wanted you to come back."

"I guess I'm a little late," she muttered.

"No kidding."

"Are you gonna tell me your name, or should I address you as whatever sounds fun?"

"Cain," I said through clenched teeth. "That's my name."

"I'm Eric!" He waved.

"Hi," she replied before her eyes met mine. "Is this the other worker? Do farms allow child labor?"

"No," I hissed, rolling my eyes before turning to Eric.

"How did you get in here anyway? I changed the locks years ago."

"Credit card."

"And how does someone like you know a trick like that?"

She crossed her arms. "I regularly rob people." Eric gasped. "Kidding. I had a sticky door in college."

"So, why are you here?"

"Uhhhh." She drew out the word. "That's a good question.

One I didn't realize I would have to answer." Mollie looked out the window and back to me. "So, the farm is open, right?"

"If by open you mean functioning, yes."

"Then where are the crops?"

I'd grown accustomed to never having to answer questions unless it was about when the next shipment of eggs and milk would be. "I manage the animals."

"The ones in the back of the farm? That's all you do?"

"All I do? I keep the farm running."

"Then it's less of a farm and more of a ranch."

I narrowed my eyes. "Seriously?"

"What? If your exports are only animal products, then it's a ranch. Papa Bennie ran a mixed-use farm and focused on crops."

"Bennie had far more employees and time. Crops require monitoring and people to pick them—"

"The farm was U-pick."

Oh, fuck how pretty she was. I was already starting to hate her.

"Still requires employees, princess." I was barely able to control my voice, and Eric winced. He knew how mad I was getting. I didn't ever use this tone with him, but he'd heard it once when Moosley, the resident diva cow, had tried to carry him into the barn to raise him better than I could.

"So, there's no one else working here?"

"The trust wouldn't let me hire anyone else. I only have permission to run the farm. Everything else went through the owner."

"Oh," she said. "Which is now me."

"Yep."

"So, I could just open the farm again?"

Fucking hell. "You would need to find the labor. And the money for the labor."

"Money. Does the farm have money?"

"What the—did you just come here on a dime? Did you not look into anything?"

"Not really, no. I thought I'd be fixing it to make it livable."

"Livable for who?" I asked slowly.

"Me."

My entire body tensed. *Her?* Living *here?*

"Listen, I'm not trying to cramp your style. And judging by the look on your face, I've stepped on some toes. I just want one of the four bedrooms to stay in for a bit. We can talk about running the farm once I figure out . . . anything more than I know now. But for the time being, I just need a place to sleep."

"The hay bales are free."

Eric elbowed me.

There was nothing more humbling than being told by a *child* that I was rude.

"Seriously? There's not one free room? What, do you have a hoard of kids? Or a wife that needs her own bed?"

"If I had a wife, she wouldn't sleep in a separate room."

She shrugged. "You look like the kind of guy who would snore."

Eric covered his mouth to hide a laugh.

He fucking liked her. I could tell. Despite how much I hated her, he likely never would.

"I'm gonna ignore that," I said slowly. "Or else you *will* be sleeping in the hay bales."

"You have a fragile ego, got it." This fucking woman. She didn't stop. "And for the record, I'm not usually this much of a nuisance, but . . . I don't know. Being out of the city makes me feel more like myself."

"So, you *are* a nuisance. Underneath all of that." I gestured to her clothes.

"*That?* What's wrong with what I'm wearing?"

"I can tell exactly who you are by looking at you."

"What, that I'm a city girl?"

"Yep."

"I'm not. Not entirely, at least. You'll have to explain how to look the part."

"There aren't enough words in the English language."

She rolled her eyes. "You could start with a few of them."

"I don't plan on talking to you, princess. So, no. I won't."

"Rude."

"I'll talk to you!" Eric said.

"Thank you." Her lips pulled into a grin. "At least someone's polite. It sucks you ended up with him."

"Turn the kid against me and you won't even get hay."

"What could be worse than hay?"

"Cow patties."

"Ew!" Eric said.

"Do you usually tell your boss to sleep in shi—" Her eyes moved to Eric. "Poop?"

"Do you usually show up to meet an employee and tell them everything they're doing wrong?"

"Fair," she said. "Which room is mine?"

My fists tightened. I didn't want to show her *any* room, but I couldn't kick her out of the damn place she owned.

"Bennie's. I'll show you."

"I know the way," she said before disappearing up the stairs.

I groaned the second she was gone.

"You have really bad manners," Eric said.

"What can you expect? I was basically raised in a barn."

"So was I, but I still know how to be nice."

I scrubbed my hand over my face. On a good day, Eric tested my limits like no one else.

But now, I had two people in this house to drive me up a wall, and I didn't know if I would survive.

5

MOLLIE

Strawberry Springs Neighborhood Watch
Tammy Jane
Did anyone hear those popping noises a few minutes ago? What was that?

Comments:
Kerry Winsor: Is everyone okay? **@SherriffMike Finch** got some info for us?
SherriffMike Finch: Hugh's car needs to go to a damn mechanic. It's backfiring like crazy.
Tammy Jane: At this point, I'll pay for it if I have to. That scared the bejeezus outta me.
Henrietta Brown: I heard that from miles away!
Kerry Winsor: It was THAT loud?
Marjorie Brown: Er, honey, that was me. Sorry. Got tired of the damn can opener and gave it a funeral with a baseball bat.
Henrietta Brown: We will be talking about this later.
Jade Clark: I'll be giving things baseball-bat funerals from now on. Great idea, Marjorie!
Kerry Winsor: JADE, NO!

Papa Bennie's room was mostly unchanged. The walls were still light green, and the bed was in the same spot I would run to when I'd had a nightmare so I could crawl into bed with him. I could tell this was a different bed, but the room held the same warmth that it had when I was a little girl.

There was a dresser in the corner and a small closet. I set my purse on the floor before falling onto the mattress.

My heart hadn't fully calmed down from when I'd heard someone walk in the front door, but instead of looking back on my conversation with Cain with a hint of regret, I felt proud of myself.

Sure, I had been annoying. He didn't like me, and I probably shouldn't have insulted what he'd done with the farm, but I'd said things that weren't simply placating agreements.

I didn't feel like Mollie, Trevor's fiancée. I felt like *Mollie*, the girl who used to spend hours running around here. I didn't know when I'd become a version of myself I didn't like, but this felt real.

I highly doubted Cain felt the same way. I could tell that every word I'd uttered had pissed him off.

He had obviously been here for a while. I closed my eyes, trying to think back to the time when Bennie was alive. His final years had been filled with fewer and fewer visits as his health had declined.

"There's a boy I work with," he'd said one Christmas. *"He's kinda like you."*

"I highly doubt that," Mom had said. *"And don't be trying to set her up with anyone. She's got school to worry about here."*

I wondered if that was Cain. I didn't know *how* he was like me, but Bennie had liked him. The kid seemed to like him too.

There must be some side of him that was nice. I'd probably never see it with the way I'd barged in here.

The window in the room looked out over the fields. They had been mowed short, but I remembered when they were filled with strawberries. It was a sight I wanted to see again.

I turned on my phone to Google how farms worked, but I was bombarded with messages.

> MOM
> Where are you?
>
> DAD
> Mollie, answer the phone.
>
> MOM
> That is enough! We are worried sick.
>
> MOM
> If you don't call us, we'll go to the police.

That had been only a few minutes ago, along with three more calls. I winced and knew I couldn't put this off any longer. They needed to know where I was.

"Thank God," Mom said when she answered on the first ring. "I've been worried *sick*. What's going on?"

"Where are you?" Dad asked. "We couldn't see your location since your phone was off."

"I'm fine. I just needed some space after Trevor and I got into a fight."

"A fight? You got into a fight?"

I opened my mouth to tell them about it, but another voice answered before me.

"Don't worry, Maribelle, it was nothing serious. I'll talk sense into her."

My stomach dropped. Was that Trevor? Was he at their house?

"Good," Dad said back. "Now we just need to know where Mollie is, and we can get this all sorted. Mollie, where are you?"

My throat closed up. Why was Trevor there? I'd *run*. I didn't want to hear his voice.

"Mollie?" Mom asked after I heard rustling on the phone and a sigh from Dad. "Are you okay? Why aren't you answering?"

"I'm fine," I said slowly. I closed my eyes and knew I'd have to get this out before it went any further. "I needed some space. I'm in Strawberry Springs."

"What?" Multiple voices asked loudly at the same time. I had to pull the phone away from my ear.

"You should have never gone," Mom said. "That's not—the farm is . . ."

"Being run by a farm manager? Yeah, I figured that out pretty quickly when I broke into his house. Or, my house, technically."

"This is why I didn't want you doing this," Trevor said. "You could have been hurt."

Did he really care if I was hurt? I wanted to ask him that, but my usual fear made its way into my stomach.

Apparently, I wasn't totally cured of being Trevor's Mollie.

"Nothing happened," I explained. "He was shocked to see me, and I had questions about the farm. Namely, where the profits went."

"The profits?" Dad asked. "Why would you worry about that?"

"Because the farm produces income. Where is it?"

"We used it to pay for your college," Mom said. "And the rest we saved for when you sold it."

"So I've had an income since I was eighteen and I didn't know?"

"It's a farm, Mollie," Trevor said. "It's not as much as you think."

It wasn't a kind thing to say, but it was far gentler than how he'd been when I was at the apartment this morning.

I squeezed my eyes shut. Sometimes, when I'd talk to my parents about Trevor, I didn't think we were talking about the same person. To them, he was kind, hardworking, and dedicated.

But to me? He was the exact opposite. And I wondered if I was somehow seeing it all wrong.

"Still," I said with a sigh. "I should have known it was here. There's so much I could have done—"

"On a farm?" Dad asked. "You have a much better job here."

Everyone kept telling me that. I wasn't sure it was true, but I also didn't want to quit either. It felt like giving in to something Trevor wanted.

"Why didn't you tell me someone lived here?"

"I didn't think you would disappear and go there, Mollie!" Mom snapped. "It's three hours away."

"I had to see it for myself," I said.

"And now you have. So leave and come home. We're worried."

"I need a break."

"From what?" Trevor asked.

"From everything," I said. *But mostly you*, I thought.

"Then come stay with us," Dad offered.

"I'm staying in Strawberry Springs."

"Where? There can't be any reputable hotels out there."

"I—in the farmhouse."

"What?" Mom's voice was climbing. "You can't—"

"I own it."

"Mollie, you're not living with a random man." Trevor's voice was firm. "As your fiancé, I forbid it."

"I left the ring behind," I said. "I thought that made it pretty clear that we *aren't* engaged anymore."

"I don't accept this."

I screwed my eyes shut. *Fuck.* I knew he would do this. It was why I hadn't wanted to talk to him ever again.

"Wha—what's going on, Mollie-bear?" Dad tried. "This isn't like you."

Nothing I was doing was like me. That was the problem.

"I need a change."

"What are you gonna do about work?"

"I could take a leave of absence."

"We need you here."

I winced. "I could also work remotely. I have my laptop."

"Absolutely not," Trevor protested.

Thankfully, Dad didn't immediately say no, and he was the one who'd make the final choice. "You know I don't usually allow that."

"Then I need to take the leave."

"Fine. You can work remotely. For a week. Maybe two."

Relief hit me like a truck. I could practically feel Trevor seething on the other end of the line.

"I don't understand," Mom moaned. "You have everything you could ever want. A caring partner, the potential to buy the perfect house. None of this makes sense."

And there it was. What I didn't need to hear.

I eyed my finger, which had a line of skin lighter than the rest. It felt good not to see the engagement ring there.

"I know it doesn't, but I need to figure this out."

"Mollie—"

"*Please.* I know you're all worried, but I need this."

"You want me to let my daughter live with a random man in the middle of nowhere?" Mom asked.

"Um . . . yes."

"Mollie—"

"Papa Bennie trusted him. I'm sure he's safe."

"This isn't—what the hell, Mollie," Dad cut in. "You're really doing this?"

"Yes."

"Then you call me if you need *anything*. And you lock your door. Is there a room for you?"

"There is."

"If that man does one thing to hurt you, you tell me. Understand?"

"I understand."

"I can't believe this," he muttered. "Stay safe. Please."

He told me they loved me before hanging up, and I reveled in the silence.

Then I got a text.

TREVOR

If you're staying with a random man, don't be angry when I do the same with another woman.

> We're not engaged anymore. Do what you want. I don't care.

And you'll be fine when the break is over?

> It's not a break. It's just over.

Big words for someone who couldn't say it to my face.

If I'd said it to his face, he would have strong-armed me into staying.

And as I looked back out over the fields, I knew I couldn't

have stayed in Nashville. I didn't feel *great*, but I did feel closer to who I was.

I was tempted to turn my phone back off, but I opened my text chain with Wren.

> So. I dumped Trevor.

WREN
WHAT

> And I went to Strawberry Springs.

OH MY GOD

> And found out there's a hot farmer working here, and I've chosen to live with him rather than stay miserable in the city.

I'M SCREAMING! If I wasn't going to film right this second, I would be calling you to get every fucking detail.

First off, FUCK yeah! Your single era. Second off, is the house livable?

> Very much so. All original. Kept in great shape.

YESSSS. SEND PICS!

I sent her pictures of the room I was in and the field outside. She screamed about how happy she was for me, and I couldn't resist the smile that bloomed on my face. At least someone was. Hopefully others would follow suit. Even if they didn't like it, maybe I could make them accept it.

I was finally brave enough to come out of the room and get my bags from my car an hour later. Cain was nowhere to be found in the dwindling sunlight, and I was grateful for it. I'd pissed *everyone* off today, and all I wanted to do was hide out for a while.

After getting my bags, I slowly unpacked. I'd grabbed my things in a mad dash to leave the apartment, but as I put everything away, I realized I had mostly Lululemon leggings and slacks.

That wasn't going to go over well on a farm.

But I didn't know where to get clothes, or if I would even be able to stay long enough to need them. I set aside a few of the pilling pairs to do the dirtiest of work in and hoped that would last me. After I was unpacked, I needed to use the bathroom.

I went out to the hall, watching for anyone. The door was only slightly down the hallway, and as I got close, I prepared myself to go inside.

I knew not all men were messy, but I also knew the one I'd lived with. If it hadn't been for me picking up after him, the bathroom would have been covered in clothes, and there would be water stains on every surface.

As far as I knew, Cain was a single man with a kid. Anything could be behind that door.

Slowly, I pushed it open. Instead of seeing clothes piled high, I saw . . . a bathroom.

A clean one.

The toilet was clear of any grime. The sink didn't have any either. The checkered black and white tile was nearly spotless, even behind the toilet.

I opened the curtain to the tub, and it was sparkling clean too.

"Are you looking for something?"

I yelped and turned. Cain stood in the doorway with his arms crossed. He leaned against the jamb and eyed me suspiciously.

Damn. He looked good in this light. His long, brown hair peeked out from under his baseball hat and fell to the nape of his neck. He was buff, way more so than Trevor, probably from all the time he spent working on the farm. His eyes were a shocking blue, like the sky on a warm summer day.

Now that the adrenaline had faded, he was hot. Kind of like the cowboy in my dreams.

I pushed away the thought. I wasn't even twenty-four hours out from running from my fiancé. I didn't need to be thinking of *anyone* at that moment.

"Do you have a maid?" I asked.

"What self-respecting maid would come this far? Sorry, princess, but you'll be cleaning up after yourself."

"So this"—I gestured to the bathroom— "is all you?"

"And Eric. Why?"

"No reason, it's just . . . nice."

He hummed. "Is the room to your liking? Or do you need fresh pillows with a mint on them?"

"Is that a dig at me being from the city? You do know that apartments don't have those things, right? It's normal living, but louder. And with less privacy."

"That sounds like my worst nightmare."

"And the streets are even worse."

"I've driven through Nashville. Eric likes the science center."

I tried to imagine him grumbling to himself as he navigated the endless bumper-to-bumper traffic on the roads. It would either be cute or terrifying.

"Stop looking at me," he ordered.

"What, do you hate being perceived?"

"Only by women who break into my house."

"Ah, well . . . sorry about that. Even if it is my house. I probably shouldn't have used a credit card on the door."

"Even better, you could have stayed in Nashville."

"Nope. Not that one." My voice came out harsher than I meant it to. He raised an eyebrow.

I stared him down, wondering if he was going to find some comment to dissolve whatever remaining confidence I had. Instead, he pushed himself off the jamb and turned.

"You're just walking away?" I asked.

"Yep. Whatever you've got going on is none of my business. Have fun in the bathroom. Don't make a mess. If you need anything . . ."

"Call for you?"

"Figure it out yourself."

And then he was gone.

"Grumpy," I muttered under my breath. "Would it kill him to smile?"

I shut the door before doing my business. It didn't hit me until I was done that while Cain was a total ass, I felt safer here than I had back in my apartment in Nashville.

6

CAIN

Strawberry Springs Neighborhood Watch
Tammy Jane
I'm closing up the diner early today, just so y'all know.

Comments:
Hu Gh: Better not be during my coffee time!!!!
Tammy Jane: Sorry, Hugh.
Hu Gh: You'd better explain yerself right now!!!
Jade Clark: Someone's feisty today.
Tammy Jane: Now listen here, old man, I don't have to tell you a darn thing.
Kerry Winsor: Something I should know about **@Tammy Jane**?
Kerry Winsor: **@Tammy Jane**???

WHEN I FINALLY GOT DRESSED THE next morning, the last thing I expected was to walk out of my room and fall on a fucking marble.

"Shi—Eric! What did I say about marbles in the hallway?"

"Mollie said it was okay!" He wasn't worried about me. I'd fallen many times before, which was why I had banned marbles in the first place.

My eyes shot to his room. His run was aimed right out the door, dropping marbles onto the wooden planks. Most of them ended up a few feet outside of my room.

Mollie was close to him, kneeling on the floor. Her hands paused as she added another part to the run.

She seemed lost in a stupor, but once she registered that I was now glaring at her, she turned to Eric. "Did you have to throw me under the bus like that?"

My molars clenched. It was too early in the morning for this.

Eric only had one adult. Me. But in my reading, I knew he was at an age where he'd try to break the rules by asking another authority figure to do things to see if he'd get a different answer. So far, he hadn't had that option.

"First of all, Mollie doesn't get to make any decisions regarding you. Got it?"

"But she's an adult. And she lives with us."

"She's not your guardian. I am."

"Guardian?" she asked.

"Yes. Eric's my nephew."

She slowly muttered, "That explains the two totally different personalities."

Eric smiled at her like she was the sun itself. "I'm the nice one."

"*No*," I said. "You two are *not* forming a friendship."

"Ms. Rudder says it's good to have friends," Eric challenged.

"*Other* friends. Not . . . this one."

"For your information," Mollie added, "I'm a great friend."

"And I'm already friends with her." Eric narrowed his eyes

at me. Since when did he have sass with me? Was this Mollie's bad influence?

"But," Mollie started. "As much as it pains me to admit it, we should be safe. What if we shot the marbles somewhere else?"

I blinked. She was backing me up?

"Out the window?" Eric asked.

"And then if they end up in the yard when I mow?" I countered.

"We could just set it up in Cain's room next time and shoot the marbles the other way."

I turned to her so quickly that I almost got whiplash. "N—"

"Yes!" Eric yelled, and he was already grabbing the run and moving it.

"Really?" I asked.

"Technically, if they go into his room, *he* has to face the consequences." She smiled and tilted her head to the side, revealing the smooth expanse of her neck.

I averted my eyes immediately. "Sleep in longer next time," I said, swiveling on my heel and walking out the door.

The animals needed their morning feed, and I didn't need to look at her. She was a thorn in my side. A gorgeous fucking thorn. She'd been in one of those fancy button-up sleep sets, but the buttons were undone down to the middle of her chest. That and her smile were burned into my memory, but I pushed them away. I didn't need lust on top of all the other shit with her.

My head felt screwed on better once I was done with the morning routine. Hennifer was kind today, and she got extra treats for not being the most annoying woman this morning. Even Moosley gave me a wide berth as I loaded up the cows with more hay.

When I got back, I worked on scrambled eggs and toast.

Mollie meandered into the kitchen around seven thirty.

She'd changed into some name-brand leggings Jackie had always wanted. The fruit-named ones.

And now her fucking hair was up. *Jesus.*

She had a laptop in her hands and sat at the dining-room table, which was one room away, still giving me a line of sight to her. Thankfully, she didn't seem to have the urge to talk, but after a few minutes, I felt her eyes on me.

"What?" I asked.

"Nothing. Just figuring out what work you do every day."

"I'm not working right now, I'm cooking breakfast. Have you ever done it?"

"Very funny. Yes. I usually cook it on weekends."

"And weekdays?"

"I . . . have a protein shake."

I shook my head and plated the food. "Eric! Time for breakfast!"

He came running down the stairs and grabbed the plate out of my hands. He wasted no time digging in.

"So, how does grocery sharing work around here?"

"You buy yours. I buy mine. Except for the eggs."

"Why's that an exception?"

"They're technically yours."

"Oh yeah. I've never had farm fresh . . . anything. Not in years, at least."

I hadn't bought eggs from the store since I was sixteen.

She stood and walked into the kitchen, eyes roaming over the counters. She was now within a foot of me, and *fuck.* She smelled like lavender and vanilla. Just like the candle she'd almost broken.

I jerked back.

"Food!" Eric yelled, pulling me out of her orbit.

"Yeah, yeah," I said, filling his plate again.

He worked on his second round of breakfast while Mollie grabbed the old Folger's tub. "That's . . ."

"I'll pay you back. Can you be nice this once and show me where the pot is?"

"Chicken grounds," I finished.

"They're *what*?"

"They're old coffee grounds from the diner near here. It's for the chickens to poop on."

She slammed the container on the counter. "*Poop coffee?*"

"They haven't pooped in it *yet*. I haven't taken it out to the coop."

She looked bewildered for all of a second before she restrained herself. "Do you have regular coffee?"

"Nope."

She let out a near cry. "Why?"

"Don't need it."

"That's so unfair," she grumbled and turned around. "Do you have Papa Bennie's coffee pot at the very least?"

"In the closet."

"All right, that's another thing on my list to do. Get that working. I didn't know people *tortured* themselves out here."

I eyed her up and down. No matter how many fucking times she opened her mouth and said something that pissed me off, I still found her fucking beautiful.

"Princess." I let my disdain slip into my voice. "You have no idea."

By the time Eric was loaded in the car, I knew there was no way Mollie would be unnoticeable in the house. Partially because Eric wanted to tell her every single part of his last two days of school up until we left. She listened with rapt attention while I wished she would vanish into thin air.

Whatever peace I'd had in the farmhouse was gone. She would be filling the space with her annoyingly bright smiles and happy voice.

"I want to show Mollie Hennifer. And Moosley!" Eric was saying as we got to the school. All he could talk about was her.

I didn't blame him. All I could *think* about was her.

"She might be nice, but it doesn't mean she's gonna love everything we do."

"Who doesn't love animals?"

"Some people don't."

Eric hummed. "I don't think she's like that."

We didn't know anything about her. Only that Bennie had liked her. But that had been over a decade ago. She had obviously changed since then.

I still walked Eric to class, even though I had a mountain of things to do at home. He gripped my hand tightly each time, but he was getting better and better about letting go when he saw his table.

"Morning, Eric," Ms. Rudder said. "How are you feeling?"

"Good!" he said, high-fiving her. "Hey, Tommy!"

And that was another thing. Every day, he ran to the boy who was quickly becoming his first friend.

Ms. Rudder turned to another kid, and I watched Eric, debating if he needed anything else from me.

Was I stalling so I didn't have to go back home to Mollie?

Yes.

"They're becoming best friends," a voice said.

My heart sank when I turned to see Kerry. This was not what I needed today.

"Of course they are," I muttered.

"Someone's in a bad mood. Did you wake up on the wrong side of the bed?"

More like I woke up with the wrong person in my damn house.

"No," I replied. "I'm fine."

Kerry hummed, and I wondered if she was using her powers of deduction to see straight into my soul.

I hadn't realized it until I was here, but Mollie being in town was going to be a *massive* story, especially once people found out where she was staying.

Fuck.

Once again, I would be in the news cycle. It had been bad enough when I'd gone after Donny and when I'd taken in Eric.

I couldn't take it again.

"I should get going," I said. "I have a lot to do."

She slowly nodded, her eyes still on me, and I ran out the door.

I hadn't even told *Jackie* yet. Much less the town. All I'd been focusing on was the woman in my house and the fact that my nephew had just started school.

But I was still avoiding home, so I checked the mirror in my truck and realized I could use a trim.

I changed course and headed for the town square, hoping that a refresh and some advice could get me out of this hole I'd fallen in.

Jackie was usually busy, but I must have caught her between clients. She was sitting in her chair, reading a magazine.

"Cain," she greeted. "Are you here to fill my free spot?"

"Yeah. Need a trim."

Her lips twisted. "Four words, huh? What's got you in a bad mood? Did Kerry try to talk to you? I heard Eric and Tommy are getting along."

Jackie knew I didn't like Kerry's gossip, and she had her own issues with it as well. She was a lifetime resident of the town, and had no problems with the smaller day-to-day things people talked about, but sometimes everyone went too far. Like they had with me. Like they could have with her if they knew her whole story.

"She did, but that's not even the half of it." I sat in the chair and Jackie put a protector over my shirt. "What do you remember of Bennie's family?"

She paused, her smile slipping from her face. "Bennie was the best of them. His daughter was . . . Well, she was smart. Sometimes thought she was smarter than us. Left right when she turned eighteen. And he didn't have any other kids. His granddaughter, though, was sweet. I think her name was . . ." She trailed off.

"Mollie," I supplied. "It was Mollie, wasn't it?"

"Yep." She nodded as she worked. "Bennie talked about her a lot, didn't he? Oh, he loved that little girl. And she loved him, but then her mom got all worked up about how much time she spent here and then she vanished. Now, why do you ask? Are you trying to get in contact with them again?"

"No," I said. "It's the other way around, actually."

Jackie's brow furrowed. "That doesn't sound right."

"Mollie was left the farm. She's . . . back."

"What? Why?"

"To check in? To make changes? No fucking clue. But she's mad that I wasn't able to do the strawberries, just like everyone else was—"

"You're one person," she said shortly. "You did what you could. If Mollie wants the berries back, then she can do it herself."

I laughed. "I doubt she'll do that. She has no idea what she's doing. She didn't even know the farm turned a profit."

"So, why now?"

"No idea, but she's staying at the farmhouse." I let out a harsh sigh. "It's awful."

Jackie completely stopped cutting my hair, and that's how I knew she was well and truly shocked.

"Do you wanna stay with me? Both you and Eric are welcome."

Still to this day, it baffled me when she offered help. When I had been struggling with running the entire farm myself, she'd worked on the berries as long as she could. And when I took custody of Eric, she'd bought every single thing I'd needed for him and refused any money from me to pay her back.

"No," I said. "But thank you. I'll handle it."

"And what does that mean?"

"Mostly hope she gets over whatever made her come out here."

"If it gets to be too much, let Eric come and stay with me. The last thing he needs is to have drama at home right now."

"That's unfortunately not a problem. He loves her."

"What?"

"She was up early playing marbles with him."

"Interesting." Jackie slowly returned to cutting my hair. "So, she's nice?"

"Too nice."

She hummed. "I wonder what she looks like after all these years."

Like an angel sent to fucking destroy me.

But then I caught the pensive look on Jackie's face. "*No*," I said. "Don't even go there."

"Sorry." She shrugged. "Just thinking of all the possibilities."

"That's not one of them."

Jackie nodded and finished my haircut, but her smile never waned.

And I knew I'd never hear the end of it.

7

MOLLIE

Strawberry Springs Neighborhood Watch
Kerry Winsor
Sometimes you try so hard but have to realize that others won't do the same.

Comments:
Jade Clark: ??? Are you vague-posting in the group?
Kerry Winsor: It's not illegal.
Tammy Jane: Doesn't look all that great.
Kerry Winsor: You do know you're supposed to ask what happened, right?
Kerry Winsor: Tammy??? Seriously? Why is this post getting no attention? **@everyone**
Marjorie Brown: Kerry, I love you, but I do not have time for your little drama fest.
Kerry Winsor: YOU'RE RETIRED! How could you not have time?

As I DROVE, I watched for the town welcome sign and the multicolored, two-story buildings of the town square again. I was technically on my lunch break from work, but I needed to get out of the house. I was in a new place. I wanted to *explore*, and while Dad and Trevor were in meetings, I knew no one would be looking.

The town square had always been incredible when I was a kid, but seeing it with adult eyes was different than the rose-tinted glasses of nostalgia. There was a lot of color, but more of the buildings were vacant than I remembered—including the once-massive library.

"No," I moaned. "It closed?"

I wasn't surprised. In small towns like this, things like recreation were the first things to lose tax funding. Still, I'd spent hours in there. It had been the largest in the area.

For a long moment, I bemoaned the loss of the library before surveying the rest of the square. The places that were open, like the grocery store, the diner, and the antique shop were all in good shape. The sidewalks were maintained, and impressive pots full of pansies and mums were on every corner. In the center of the square was a green space with paved walkways and a brick center courtyard. It felt so odd to be in the middle of downtown and see so much nature.

It was near lunchtime, and though I was mostly full from eating breakfast rather than having a protein shake, I wanted to check out the diner.

Center Point Diner was on the other side of the square and its neon sign flashed that it was open. When I walked in, I was greeted with white and black checkered tile and pink walls.

It was exactly how it had been when I was a kid.

"Oh! Hello," a woman with a rough voice said as she walked to the podium. She had dyed blonde hair with a pen in it. Her name tag read Geraldine, but I knew that wasn't who she was. "A table for one?"

"Yes, please." I smiled. "Tammy."

She nodded and walked away, but then froze. "Wait a second, I'm not wearing my real name tag."

"I know. You've done that for years."

She turned an appraising eye on me. "You're from here."

"It's nice to meet you again. I'm Mollie, Bennie's grand-daughter."

Her jaw fell to the floor as fast as the menus in her hand. "You're—you're back!"

"I am."

"My God, kid! You've grown. You're a knockout!" She walked a circle around me. "Where have you been all this time?"

"Unfortunately, working for the *other* family business. But I needed a break, and here I am."

"Well, let me be the first to welcome you." She pulled me into a tight hug. "Unless I'm not the first?"

"Ah, good catch. You're not. But we don't have to talk about that." I bent down to pick up my menu.

"First rule about small-town life, kid," she said as she walked me over to a table. "We talk about *everything*. Your mama owns the farmhouse, right? And I happen to know someone lives there."

I sat with an awkward laugh. My eyes widened when she followed suit and sat across from me.

I'd never met anyone so willing to talk before. Sure, there were friendly people in the city, but never someone so interested.

"My mom doesn't own the farm. I do. And I didn't know it until now. I thought it was abandoned, actually."

"It's certainly not."

"I figured that out when I walked in."

Tammy laughed. "So, you've met Cain Smith?"

"I did. And I did *not* make a good first impression, obviously."

She hummed sympathetically. "It's hard to with that one. Need some hotel recommendations?"

"Oh, no. It's my house. I'm staying there."

Tammy's eyebrows crept up to her hairline. "You're . . . what?"

"I'm staying in the house."

"W-with Cain?"

"Yes?"

Tammy looked like she was watching the finale of the best reality TV show on earth, and dimly, I realized that my telling her meant everyone in town would know.

I had a feeling Cain wouldn't be thrilled.

But was he ever thrilled with me?

"I can't believe this," she said. "And he let you?"

"Very begrudgingly. He hates me."

"He hates most people," Tammy reassured. "Don't take it personally."

"I don't know if that makes me feel better or worse, considering he's my roommate."

"Let me at least give you a warmer welcome than he gave you," she said. "I'm sure Eric was polite."

"Very polite. And cute."

Tammy stood and pulled out her pad. "Stick with the kid. And with me. Your first impression might have been a little rough, but we're far nicer."

"It'll take a lot worse than Cain to scare me off."

"Good." Her smile only widened. "I think you'll fit in here just fine."

Strawberry Springs Neighborhood Watch
Tammy Jane
Y'all remember Bennie's granddaughter? Mollie is back!

Comments:
Kerry Winsor: WHAT
Tammy Jane: AND SHE'S LIVING WITH CAIN AT THE FARM.
Kerry Winsor: WHAT!!! I KNEW HE WAS IN A BAD MOOD TODAY. Well, worse than usual of course.
Tammy Jane: It feels good to be the first to know.
Jackie Anne: Sorry to burst your bubble. I knew this morning.
Kerry Winsor: You're an insider. You don't count. AND WHERE WAS YOUR POST?
Jackie Anne: Cain was green in the face at the thought of everyone knowing. It was only a matter of time, but I couldn't betray him like that. At least not that bad. I think he thinks she's pretty, though.
Tammy Jane: She's fucking gorgeous, Jackie. Your boy is in trouble.

The food was incredible, and I was tempted to return to the house and fall into a food coma, but there was a whole town square to enjoy.

I walked around it once, taking it all in. There was an antique shop that had probably furnished Papa Bennie's decor, as well as a clinic and store. I passed by a bar that wasn't open yet, and tucked in a small corner was a shop that I'd never seen before. There was a crystal on the sign, and it was called Jade's Goodies. It was so out of place that I had to go in.

The inside smelled like lavender, and there were crystals on the shelves in the back of the store. In the middle was a mixture of incense and candles.

"Oh, hi!" a woman's voice said. "Sorry, I'm not used to new people coming in. Usually, I can ignore everyone until they come to the front."

When she walked out, the first thing I noticed was her bright pink hair. Her eyes were a deep brown and she had a nose ring.

"Hello," I said. "This place is so . . ."

"Weird? Yeah, that's what I was going for. You must be Mollie."

"You've heard of me?"

"There was a Facebook post," she said as she checked her phone. "Ten minutes ago. It's big news."

"So, you know everything I told Tammy?"

"You're Bennie's granddaughter and you live with the biggest grump in town. Well, second biggest."

"There's someone worse?"

"Hugh Jeffries. He owns the antique shop. The only reason he's first is because he's old as hell."

Hugh Jeffries. The name sounded familiar. I wonder if he—

"I'm Jade, by the way," she continued, interrupting my thought.

"Mollie, but you knew that."

"Sorry. I promise not everything makes it to the Facebook page. But this is just too good. I mean, a woman? Living with Cain Smith?"

"He has that big of a reputation?"

"Anyone who's as big of a recluse as he is? Yes. You're our

gateway into his life. Or at least what you'll share." She leaned forward with an eyebrow raised.

"I've only been here a day. So far, all I've seen is him stalking to the animal section of the farm and falling on marbles in the hallway."

"Oh, I wish I could have been there for that."

"And he keeps a very clean house," I said. "My . . . Someone I used to live with definitely did not."

"I'd find it hot if I didn't know him in his angsty teenage phase," she said. "But that's definitely good info."

"Will it be in the Facebook group in ten minutes?"

"I don't usually post there. That's mostly a thing for the older ladies in town. I just like to lurk. And annoy people with my comments."

I chuckled and let my eyes wander over the shop again.

"What brings you in?" Jade asked. "Sorry, I totally forgot to ask."

"I'm not sure. I'm wandering around to let the interesting things find me."

"I'm happy my shop made the cut."

"For one thing, it smells amazing in here." I browsed the candles, wondering if Cain would like one. He was extremely defensive over the one I'd almost hurled at him. "And it's different."

"I'm good at different," she said.

I picked up a candle and smelled it. It reminded me of spring, like the fields filled with ripe strawberries. "I'll get this one."

She looked at the scent. "Good choice. We all love strawberries here. It was a shame when the fields shut down. I loved going there in the summer."

"Yeah." I nodded. "I guess I should be happy the farm is even open, but those fields were Papa Bennie's favorite thing."

"Did you approve shutting it down?"

"I didn't get to approve anything. My family kept the farm in a trust until now."

"So this is a shock."

"I thought it was abandoned, so this is better than that." I walked over to the register and handed her the candle.

"We were all pretty mad when Cain shut it down. But he's the only one who works there. Bennie used to have a ton of employees."

And Mom hadn't approved any more. My jaw tightened. I hadn't begun to process how bitter I was about her not telling me, but it was hitting me like a ton of bricks regardless. Why did she hate this place so much? Maybe it wasn't her cup of tea, but everyone had been kind so far.

"Cain seems stretched thin," I said. "Especially if he's managing the animals by himself."

"Still, *you* could open the fields back up."

"I . . . could. But I probably shouldn't. I don't know how long I'll be here."

"Really? You're not here to stay?"

"I have a life I'll have to get back to eventually. I hope to split my time, but until I figure out finances and the logistics of hiring someone—"

"Good luck with that," she said. "It's hard to find people out here."

"I've heard." I let out a sigh. "I have no idea what I'm doing. My only hope is to wear Cain down into showing me the ropes."

She laughed. "He's not the kind of guy to be worn down. *Trust me.* Many have tried."

"How long has he been here?" I asked. "I never saw him before."

"A long time. We would all have been teens when he arrived."

So he was an outsider. That explained a lot.

But not everything.

"It's his sparkling personality, isn't it?"

Jade laughed. "Got it in one go." She handed me a bag. "But I do hope you like it here. I can't explain it, but there's something magical about this town."

"Like the sign says?"

She nodded. "The world is terrible, but it doesn't feel as terrible *here*. We all get along for the most part. We don't have the high rental prices or all the people clamoring to move here. It feels calm."

That calm could have been ruined if I'd let Trevor go through with his plans. Thank God I'd trusted my gut.

"I need calm," I said. "I think I was in the city for too long."

"Let me be the first to say, you should stay as long as you like. Enjoy the magic, Mollie."

8

CAIN

Strawberry Springs Neighborhood Watch
Henry Connor
I can't believe I have to say this, but please wash your hands. I just witnessed a very public rear-end scratching incident that makes me fear for people's health.

Comments:
Jade Clark: I SAW IT TOO.
Kerry Winsor: WHO?
Henry Connor: It doesn't matter. It's just a friendly reminder from your town doctor.
Kerry Winsor: Who do I need to avoid shaking hands with **@Henry Connor**? This will HAUNT ME.
Tammy Jane: You know, I haven't changed the men's bathroom soap in years.
Mark Bell: I haven't had to at the bar either.
Henry Connor: I wish I hadn't read this.

Strawberry Springs was so small that we only had one clinic with one doctor, and we were lucky to even have that. I wasn't sure how he made his money, but he saw nearly everyone in town for their regular visits and when they were sick.

I'd had an appointment scheduled months in advance to get Eric's checkup right when school started. Dr. Connor, otherwise known by his friends as Henry, got along well with Eric, and tolerated me.

That was as good as it was going to get.

Dr. Connor's office was right off of the square. Atticus, the local veterinarian, was the only other person in the waiting room, and he was reading a pamphlet about healthy eating.

"Guess I'm getting older," he said as he scratched at his close-cropped, curly black hair. "Apparently, I can't live off of a diet of only meat and potatoes."

Eric luckily did the talking for me. "But they're so good!"

"Still." He sighed. "I wanna see Simone graduate from college and have kids. Better fix it now."

Dr. Connor called us in next. The clinic was small enough that he didn't have a nurse and did all the work himself. He was a few years older than I was, with light brown hair that put half of the ladies' hair to shame, a lithe frame, and had apparently graduated from some fancy school before settling here. He had been welcomed with open arms.

I'd tried not to be jealous.

"Wow," Dr. Connor said as he looked at Eric. "You've grown. Can we check to see how much?"

Eric nodded and let himself be measured. Dr. Connor took his weight, too, before leading us to the exam room. It didn't take him long to check over his vision, his joints, and everything in between.

I was more than ready to get back home.

"So, he's officially in kindergarten." Dr. Connor looked at me. "How's that been going?"

"Good," I said.

"I like my teacher, Ms. Rudder."

"Ah, Nicole." Dr. Connor nodded. "She's nice."

To you, I thought unhelpfully.

Dr. Connor looked at me, expecting me to say something more, but I didn't have anything. I wondered if he tried to build a rapport with everyone. But we all knew it wouldn't work on me.

"Just know that a lot of kids who start school get a lot of illnesses. Feel free to call me if you have any concerns, especially when the weather cools. I'll work you in."

I only nodded.

"I never get sick! I have a strong immune system."

Dr. Connor laughed. "I bet you do, but we always like to plan for everything." He added after another pause, "I have nothing else. I hope you enjoy school, Eric."

He nodded happily and said his goodbyes before we walked out to the truck. I was more than ready to get home.

I had a bad feeling about the day that I couldn't shake. It followed me all the way back to the farm.

One text from Jackie and I knew why.

JACKIE

She came into town today. People know.

I tried to put it out of my mind, but the residents of Strawberry Springs were relentless. A few of them had my number for eggs, and they didn't take long to send me messages.

HUGH

I hear you have a pretty girl in the house. Must be a first.

TAMMY

You better not run her out of here. She's a sweet girl.

ATTICUS

Should have asked when I saw you. Can I get some eggs from you? (When you're over the issue of the woman, that is.)

Each time my phone went off, I became more irritated. I knew it was news, and I knew that these people thought I didn't know how to talk to women, which was true, and were worried I'd run her off. If only I were so lucky. But I didn't need to hear about it.

Mollie was at the dining-room table, completely unaware of the chaos she'd started. She was on her laptop, and the last thing I could handle was facing her when I was so angry.

But unfortunately, she didn't seem keen on leaving me alone.

"Hey!" she said, standing. "You didn't tell me the town square was so nice."

"Yeah. Nice." The front door slammed behind me and the smile quickly slid off her face.

"Who peed in your cereal?"

"Everyone on my phone lecturing me about what you told them."

"Was I not supposed to say where I live?" she asked.

"You weren't supposed to stay here long enough for them to ask." The words came out without warning.

"I never said how long I was staying." She crossed her arms over her chest. "I happen to like it here."

I shook my head and went to the kitchen to wash my hands.

She fucking followed.

"What's your problem? It's not a huge deal."

"Oh, it is to them. They've been blowing up my phone.

Tammy already told me not to run you off. Hugh made a joke about how I've never had a woman in my house in my life."

"I could see that," she said flatly. "Your attitude runs them off."

The words turned up the heat on my already flaming temper. "I would like it if my attitude would work on you."

Her eyes narrowed. "You're trying your best, aren't you?"

"Honestly? Yes. The farm was doing fine before you showed up. I don't need you crawling around trying to change things when I've run this place by my damn self for over a decade."

"And yet the main thing that people know it for isn't growing outside. This is a berry farm, Cain. There aren't any berries."

"Then it should have been managed better by its *owner*." I gave her a pointed look.

"For a man who doesn't want me here, you sure have a lot of complaints about how the farm was run. Sounds like you have things you want to change too."

There was a nugget of truth to that, which only pissed me off more.

"So, what's your deal?" she asked. "Tell me, and I can figure it out."

"I don't need a spoiled city girl who's never had to work a day in her *life* to figure it out," I snapped. "I'll do what I've always done. Run this while you do whatever the fuck you want to."

"Excuse me?" Her voice was low and she stepped forward. Most of the time I'd seen Mollie smiling, but there was no lick of joy on her face now.

Good. Maybe she finally knew how I felt.

"You heard me."

"No, say it again. And then explain it."

"You're a spoiled city girl." Now, I stepped forward. "The

luxury car. The fancy clothes. They all tell me you've lived a pretty privileged life back in the city. You haven't had to guess if you would be fed or not. Or work your ass off to impress the one person who would take a chance on you. I know your type, Mollie. And you don't belong here."

I expected tears or for her to run off and hide. What I didn't expect was for her to laugh. "You don't know a thing about me, Cain. So let's get one thing straight. I refuse to be talked down to by another man. You don't have to like me. Or even tolerate me. But you do have to respect me."

"Or what? You'll fire me? Good luck doing this on your own."

Her lips pursed. I had her there. "You know, all I wanna do is follow in my grandfather's footsteps. Papa Bennie took a chance on you a long time ago. But you're making it impossible for me to do the same."

Those words hurt. It looked like we had both scored a shot. "So then fire me, princess."

"Oh, I can do a lot worse than fire you." A slow smile spread on her face. "I know how much I piss you off, so it's time I see exactly what you do all day."

"What?"

"I'm gonna follow your every move. I'm gonna learn what you do. And then, if your attitude isn't in check, then I *will* take it over."

Fuck. "And what if I don't let you?"

"It's *my* farm, Cain. You should learn that you can't tell me what to do."

I thought she was bluffing until she was waiting for me by the chicken coops at six in the fucking morning.

"What the hell?" I muttered. She leaned against one of the fences, wearing those fruit leggings *again*, looking so out of place I thought she was pranking me.

"You know, I'm not usually a morning person. But I will be when I have a point to prove."

"You were up this early yesterday."

"That was a result of me being in a new place. I was looking forward to blissful sleep the next night, but you just *had* to open your mouth."

"You've made your point," I muttered. "I won't open it again."

"Good. But I'm still learning how to take care of the animals."

"One pile of poop and you'll run."

She rolled her eyes. "I've been in these fields since I could walk. I used to love finding cow patties. Trust me, I'll be fine."

"You'll ruin your fruit pants."

She opened her mouth and then paused. "My what?"

I gestured to her bottom half. "Those designer things."

"The—" She covered her mouth, and her voice came out choked. "You mean my Lululemon leggings?"

Son of a bitch. She was laughing at me. "I don't care to know the name."

"If my leggings are ruined, they're ruined. Now, come on."

I expected her to walk around to the gate with me, but she put one foot on the bottom post and then hiked her leg over the fence.

"What are you doing?"

"Going over."

"I installed a gate my first summer working here, princess."

She shrugged and hopped over anyway. "Oh well. Jumping fences will keep me young."

I paused. That wasn't the first time I'd heard those words.

I knew Mollie was his granddaughter, but I'd not seen any similarities until now.

"You coming?" she asked. "Or am I going in alone?"

I shook off my shock and went in through the gate. I gathered the feed and walked up to the door of the first coop. Mollie was already fiddling with it.

"You should wait."

"Why? Because I don't know what I'm doing? News flash, Mister I Can't Talk to a Woman to Save My Life: I can figure it out."

The real answer was that Hennifer would attack her. While most female chickens didn't get territorial, she did.

I was going to be nice and warn her. Now I wasn't.

Mollie got the latch open and Hennifer burst out of the coop.

"Aw, she's so cute."

That was all the time Hennifer needed to register the unfamiliar person, and she flew at Mollie.

"What the—Cain!"

"You said you wanted to figure it out." I shrugged. "So figure it out."

Mollie struggled for a bit as Hennifer tried to go for her eyes, but eventually, she grabbed the bird like a football. Her hair was mussed and her shirt ripped, but she was fine.

"You let that happen," she said as she glared at me.

"I absolutely did. You could have let her rough you up for a few more minutes, though."

"Scatter the feed, you dick."

I did as I was told, and Mollie let Hennifer go when she tried to get away. As brave as she was, she would give up on her guard-dog duties the second fresh food was on the ground.

"Nice hold on the chicken."

"I could have shown you that without getting attacked." She

crossed her arms, but watched as more birds came out of the coops.

Mollie said hello to the birds, watching them carefully. Hennifer made another go at her, but she ran out of the way.

"She's a good chicken," I said.

"She's an evil chicken," Mollie replied as she dodged another attack. I shook my head and went to collect my first round of eggs.

I heard her following me.

I didn't want her to figure out how to run all of this. I may have been brave the previous day, but the last thing I wanted was for her to fire me. I'd poured my blood, sweat, and tears into this place. And she could take it all away.

"I've never seen so many eggs in my life," she said. "Well, I've gotten close, but you've expanded the chicken farm."

"It's what I'm good at," I replied. I made the walk back to the house to unload and get more. By the time I returned, Hennifer was still chasing her.

"That chicken hates me," she muttered as I went to work on the cows.

"She doesn't like strangers."

"Then I'll work on not being a stranger." She smiled and jogged to catch up. The sun was now behind her, giving her an ethereal glow. "What's next?"

"Milking the cows."

"Lead the way."

She was still pretty. Even more so with mussed-up hair and a torn shirt.

Dammit. I was hoping I'd forgotten about the fact that I found her annoyingly attractive on top of it all.

No such luck.

9

MOLLIE

Strawberry Springs Neighborhood Watch
Atticus Thompson
Anyone know why the power flickered last night?

Comments:
Kerry Winsor: Probably was Cain blowing a fuse lol
Tammy Jane: This is a place for REAL info.
Henrietta Brown: Probably a squirrel in the transformer again.
Kerry Winsor: @SherriffMike Finch, info?
SherriffMike Finch: Do I look like an electrician to you?

As MUCH AS I wanted to pretend I could learn to do everything Cain did, I'd only taken in about twenty-five percent of everything I'd observed.

It seemed pointless to follow him around. He was a natural with animals. Even the evil chicken loved him. As well as every cow we'd seen. And he seemed to like them too. He almost *smiled* at them.

Until he had been reminded that I was there.

I liked animals, but I knew that there was no way I could be as efficient as he was, and I wasn't sure if I even wanted to. My passion was the berries. My passion was Papa Bennie's legacy.

Which laid to the front of the farm.

I didn't want to fire him in the first place. Firing him meant kicking him out of the home he'd lived in for a long time. And possibly the one that Eric had known for most of his life. I just wanted him to respect me, to know that I was serious about this. While coming out here might have been a last-second decision, working on the farm wasn't.

Cain left to get Eric at three, and I managed to check my laptop for the day. I hadn't planned on taking the day off, but I also didn't realize how much work went into washing and storing hundreds of eggs and getting milk ready to be shipped off for pasteurization.

Of course, Dad didn't understand that, and I'd already gotten multiple messages from him asking why I wasn't working. I messaged back that I was online now and would get everything done.

I got a few minutes of focusing in before I received a text.

WREN

Checking in. How is farm life? How is the town? HOW IS HOT FARMER?

> The town is great. Farm life is also great. As for the hot farmer . . . He hates me. I hate him.

Enemies to lovers?

> Enemies to enemies, really. How is hot costar?

I see your deflection. And I accept it. He is hotter in person. And flirtier.

YESSS! CLIMB HIM LIKE A TREE.

Working on my arm strength as we SPEAK.

I laughed and put down my phone, only to see a car pull into the driveway.

It was a fancy one I hadn't seen before. I was pretty sure Cain didn't take too kindly to guests, but I also didn't know him well enough to know who he had coming to the farmhouse.

There was a loud knock on the door. In the city, I'd avoided all door interactions if I could.

Did the same go for out here?

The knock sounded again, and I knew I couldn't delay it any longer.

"Hi," I said as I opened the door. "Can I help you?"

The man in front of me was older, with a graying mustache and a round belly shoved into a three-piece suit. He looked me up and down. "So, you're the wife, right?"

I nearly choked on air. "Wife of *who*?"

"Cain Smith. The man I'm looking for."

"Uh, no. I'm not his wife at all. I'm his . . . boss, technically. What can I do for you? Are you trying to place an order for eggs or something?"

"No," he said, but was interrupted by the sound of a vehicle coming down the driveway. This one I knew. It was Cain's white truck.

He pulled in behind my car and got out in seconds. "Who the hell are you?" he asked.

The man turned, but his eyes weren't on Cain. They were on the small child in the back of the truck. "There he is! Eric! Come here!"

Eric's eyes went wide, and he ducked in the back seat.

"I'm gonna ask again," Cain said dangerously. "Who are you, and how the hell do you know the kid's name?"

"I'm Waldren. Have you heard of me?"

"No."

He frowned. "I knew your sister."

"You probably knew her more than I did. We were separated when we were young."

"So then, how did you come to be the guardian of her son?"

"I was the only family member around."

"Wrong." The man crossed his arms. "I am. He's *my* son."

Cain's entire body went rigid. I probably shouldn't have been witnessing this, but it was like drama on reality TV. I couldn't look away.

"Then where were you when Olivia died?"

"None of your business."

"And I'm supposed to just take your word for it?"

Waldren laughed. "Come on. He looks just like me."

"Do you have functioning eyes?" I asked.

Both men turned to me. "Stay out of this, honey."

"Don't call me that," I snapped. "And I can get into whatever the hell I want to."

"You're not on his birth certificate," Cain said slowly. "Which I have."

"Yeah, it's one last slight from that *whore*."

"Watch it," Cain said. "That's my sister you're talking about."

"And gross. You could have said so many other things," I added.

"It doesn't matter. It's not like she's here to say anything back."

"No, but I am," Cain replied. "And you're not welcome here."

"I'm getting my kid."

"And I'm saying *no*," he said through clenched teeth.

"I have a DNA test from when she was pregnant." He waved a piece of paper around. "But I'll do as many as I need to. And when he comes back as mine, I'll be taking him."

"You do know Cain is his guardian, right?" I asked. "You can't just snatch him out of the home he knows."

He turned to me and got into my space. "I do what I want, *honey*."

This man was like Trevor, and I held a lot of anger for people like that. I felt like I was back in my apartment, getting trampled by the man I thought I would marry.

"She said not to call her that." Cain grabbed Waldren and dragged him down the stairs. "And stay the fuck away from her."

My heart pounded in my ears. I was used to him using that tone on me. Not *for* me.

"Get out of here," I said.

"I'm owed my child."

"You're owed nothing. Come back with a fucking lawsuit. Then I'll listen to you."

"Oh, I will." He sneered. "And I'll make you fucking pay." Waldren spun on his heel and stomped to his car.

When his car peeled out of the driveway, tires throwing rocks everywhere, I turned to Cain.

"Is he really Eric's dad?"

"No. There's no way he could come from a man like that."

"Maybe you should find a lawyer."

"He was just here to get a rise out of me."

"But—"

"Mollie, leave it."

"Seriously, Cain, this is—"

Eric poked his head out of the truck, eyes wide and shiny. "Is it safe now?"

Cain rushed over to Eric, his voice soft and kind as he told him things were safe, and he would be fine. I watched the sight with an achy heart. I hoped they would be fine, but something in my gut told me this wasn't over.

I gave Cain a wide berth for the night. I had a lot of work to do, and I knew he had a lot to do with Eric. I may have wanted to learn everything I could from him, but there were some things that he deserved privacy for.

As the day turned to night, my eyes burned, and I desperately needed a break. The house seemed quiet, so I snuck out the door and went outside.

In the city, I was used to seeing only the brightest stars in the sky. But I had remembered what it was like being on the farm and looking up. One of my favorite things to do as a child had been to sneak out past my bedtime and try to count all the stars.

I'd always thought I was sneaky, up until Papa Bennie brought me a glass of sweet tea and sat next to me.

The cicadas sang a tune, though quieter than they would in the height of summer. I sat on the front porch steps and looked up, getting lost in all the stars.

I didn't have any constellations memorized, but I made my own. It was easy to get lost in how many white dots were visible in the darkened sky.

My stargazing was interrupted by the screen door opening.

I turned to see Cain in a T-shirt and sweatpants.

"Need to go to your truck?" I asked. "I can move."

"No," he said, and he did the last thing I expected. He sat

next to me and let out a sigh. "Thank you for sticking up for me with Waldren. I didn't deserve that."

"Probably not," I replied. "But Eric does. You raised a good kid, which must mean that somewhere *deep down*, you're not so bad."

"I guess *deep down*, that's a compliment." His eyes looked up at the stars and we lapsed into silence.

"You must be really out of sorts if you're out here with me."

"You could say that," he muttered. "I mostly came out here to thank you."

"I appreciate it, but we're even. You got him out of my space."

"Do you really think I need a lawyer?"

"Depends on how serious he is. He knew your address."

"It's not that hard to find me. I made a website with my name on it for orders for the farm."

"Smart, but still. This may turn into nothing, but it can't hurt to have backup."

He slowly nodded. He didn't even look at me as he spoke. "I've lost a lot of people in my life. I won't let Eric be one of them."

I wasn't sure if he was talking to me or himself.

"My dad knows a lot of lawyers," I said. "Big ones. I could see who he knows."

"I'm not asking you for help."

"I know. I'm offering."

"I've been nothing but an ass to you since you got here."

"Yeah, you have. But you've not been an ass to Eric. And I think that matters more."

He looked over at me, and I wondered if we were having a moment. Everyone I'd talked to had said that Cain was impossible to get through to, but were they right? Or had I managed it?

But he must not have liked what he saw, because his gaze cut from me and he stood, going inside without another word.

I let out a sigh and dropped my elbows to my knees as I looked up at the sky again.

So much for that.

10

CAIN

Strawberry Springs Neighborhood Watch
Kerry Winsor
Has anyone heard about the house sharing situation on Bennie Grove Farm? I bet the drama is to die for.

Comments:
Kerry Winsor: @**Jackie Anne** you have to know something.
Jackie Anne: Nope. Nothing.
Kerry Winsor: Oh, come on. You can't hand me something like this and not expect me to ask! I bet the fights are legendary!
Nicole Rudder: They better not be. There's a kid in that house.

THE NEXT MORNING, I woke up with the feeling of regret sitting on my chest. I didn't know why I had gone out there to talk to her. I didn't know why she'd responded to a word I'd said.

But it was nice talking to an adult that didn't have a hand in raising me.

And *nice* didn't usually stick around.

She'd disappeared while I explained what had happened with Waldren to Eric, and I'd been grateful. I would never lie to him, but telling him who the man claimed to be and why he was there was hard. I knew he was aware that I wasn't his biological dad on a base level, but hearing about the man who claimed to be was different.

In another world, if Waldren hadn't demanded to take him, I might have worked with him. I would love for Eric to have more family. But the way he'd spoken about Olivia, and to Mollie, had told me what kind of person he was. And I'd be damned if that kind of man set foot anywhere near Eric.

He had stuck close until he went to bed. When he was finally ready to fall asleep, he'd insisted that I sit in his room on his too-small bed until he was out.

I'd scheduled a DNA test with the state out of an abundance of caution, so we would do that as soon as possible. Then I'd gotten up.

And that was when I had found Mollie outside.

Now, I wasn't sure what to think about things between us. Twenty-four hours ago, she was the bane of my existence, but now Waldren was.

When I got up to check on the animals, she wasn't waiting for me. I got peace and quiet as I did my normal routine. She was nowhere to be found when I made Eric breakfast. Her car was still outside, but she had seemingly vanished from my life.

I should have been relieved, but I needed to know if we still hated each other or not. I wasn't sure why, but I did.

By the time I had gotten Eric to school, I'd thought way too much about the woman sharing my house with me. The only distraction I had was when he looked at me as he fidgeted with his shirt and asked me to walk him in.

There was no way I was saying no to that face, no matter how miserable it made me.

"Mr. Smith," Nicole started. "I was hoping to see you."

"You were?"

She nodded, but there wasn't a smile on her face like there was with other parents. "I heard about your houseguest—" Son of a bitch. "And I'm concerned it's going to affect Eric at home."

"Mollie has nothing to do with Eric."

"But do you and her argue? Conflict at home can stunt a child's growth."

"It's not gonna," I said firmly.

"I know you have to be unhappy about this situation, and we all know how you can be when you're unhappy. How can I trust you to make good decisions when you live with a person you don't like? It didn't go well the first time."

I gritted my teeth. She wasn't wrong that I hadn't handled it well in the past, but I was a grown man now. A changed man. Someone who could take a comment like that and *not* get defensive. Besides, Eric already had issues with Waldren coming into his life. He didn't need to see mine with Mollie too.

"Mollie and Eric get along great, actually," I said in a low voice. "So she won't be a problem for him. As far as what she and I have issues with . . . We'll just have to discuss that when he's not around."

Nicole's eyebrows rose as if she were surprised I'd agreed to anything she'd said. "I'm glad you see it that way, Mr. Smith."

I nodded and walked out of the room without another word, more than ready to get into the truck.

But then I heard heels clicking, and a far-too-familiar voice called, "Cain, wait up!"

Shit. Kerry. It was tempting to keep walking.

"Yes?" I asked.

She stopped in front of me. "Why do you walk so fast?"

Because I don't wanna be here. Besides, Mollie had no issues keeping up with me. "Because I'm walking all the time. What do you need?"

"I heard what you said to Nicole. Very good parenting." Was that a compliment, or was that her talking down to me? Probably the latter. "But is it really bad with Mollie? I heard she was super sweet."

Now I knew what this was for. She wanted information. "Things are fine."

"Are they? I know how you are, Cain. You can't love having someone come into your house."

I only shrugged, and her frown grew.

"But still. How does it work? What room is she staying in? Is she as nice as she sounds? Are you trying to be nice to her?"

I blinked at the barrage of questions, surprised she was being so bold. Most of the time, people didn't have the balls to ask me things directly. But Jackie wouldn't talk, at least not about things that were deeply affecting me, which must have made me the last option.

"I'll let her tell you all of that if she wants to."

Kerry sighed. "Why are you such a locked book? It's so hard to crack you."

And it would stay that way. I wasn't interested in overhearing anything else about myself, and if I could put a pin in it by not telling everyone my business, then that was what I would do.

"I'm just quiet." It was the best answer I could give her.

I could tell she didn't love it. But she didn't stop me when I tried to walk away again, and I let out a sigh of relief when I got to the car. I was glad I could walk Eric to his classroom, but I hated every second of interaction thereafter.

It was going to be a long school year.

When I got back to the farm, Mollie was still nowhere to be found. I did more of my work in complete silence. It was nice, but I felt like I was on edge.

It was midday when I finished. I walked into the house to find her *finally* out of her room. She was on her laptop, looking at the screen closely. Her lips formed a pout as she typed.

"I thought you were gonna learn everything I do," I said when I walked in.

"You get a break from that. Work has my attention."

I frowned. "The farm *is* work."

"No, I know. But I also work for my dad in real estate. Apparently, there was something urgent that needed my attention."

"Urgent like a tornado?"

She laughed. "No. Just a can of worms I opened. It's an email thing."

"What email could be so important?"

"You know, I'm not sure." She sighed, but her eyes didn't move. "I still have to do this, though."

I didn't know how people could go into an office every day and work the daylight away. That kind of routine had to be miserable, and I wondered if she enjoyed it or hated it like I would.

Then I shook off the thought. I didn't need to wonder anything about the city girl who had invaded my home. She didn't get a pass for doing one nice thing for me.

A knock at the door broke my thought process. I turned, hoping Waldren wasn't back for more, but instead, saw a familiar brown braid.

"Jackie," I said when I opened the door. "What are you doing all the way out here?"

"I'm taking a late lunch and thought I'd check in on you."

Her gaze roamed the space and then caught on Mollie. She lowered her voice when she spoke again. "Oh, is that her?"

"Yes. She's working on emails or something."

I heard the laptop slam shut. "Not when there's a guest," Mollie said. I turned to see her walking toward the door. "Hi, I don't think we've met."

Jackie's eyes were as wide as the moon. "We haven't. Wow, you're as pretty as Tammy said."

Mollie's cheeks turned pink. "Thank you." She tucked a strand of hair behind her ear, and I couldn't help but agree.

"Don't you think so, Cain?" She elbowed me, and I glared.

"Not answering that."

My eyes snuck a glance at Mollie, only to find her already looking in my direction. I averted my gaze immediately.

"Telling," Jackie said. "How are you liking the farm?"

"I love it, though I miss the berries."

Jackie's smile fell a bit. "One person can only do so much, especially with no support."

Mollie didn't miss a beat. "Oh, I know. Cain's far too busy with the animals."

I didn't realize she'd thought that at all. I thought she'd wanted more out of me.

Jackie's smile was back now. "Exactly. At least you see sense."

"I'm trying to figure out the logistics of everything that bringing back the berries would take. Because unfortunately"— her eyes slid to her computer— "I can't stay forever."

"Why not?"

"I have a job back ho—" She stopped. "Um, back in Nashville. And I have to go back to that eventually."

I narrowed my eyes as she spoke. She didn't seem thrilled about the idea of going back, which didn't spell anything good for me.

"That's a shame, though I don't think Cain would be too upset if you did leave."

She laughed awkwardly. "Yeah, probably not. But now that I know the farm is open, I wanna do what I can."

I crossed my arms. There wasn't much for her to do, considering her knowledge level. I didn't know if she had the ability to be out in the fields for long periods of time like Bennie had.

"I can give you some privacy," she said. "I'm sure Cain has stuff to tell you."

"Stuff?" Jackie asked. "Did something else happen?"

"And why would you assume that I would tell *anyone* about yesterday?"

Mollie rolled her eyes. "Because you don't look like you want to throw up when she talks to you. So therefore, she's a friend. And you *should* tell a friend what happened."

She gave me a pointed look before disappearing down the hallway.

Damn her.

Jackie turned to me. "What happened? Did you piss her off or something?"

"What happened doesn't have anything to do with her. Someone else came by."

Jackie's brow furrowed. "Who?"

"A man claiming to be Eric's father."

Her jaw dropped and she gasped. "What? Since when is his father even in the picture?"

"If it's true, which I doubt it is, then just now."

"What did you do?"

"I kicked him out."

She winced. "Was that a good idea? What if he really is?"

"He was pushy."

"He could want to get to know Eric."

"There was something off about him."

"I could see how you would feel that way, considering you've raised him. But we can't judge based on feelings only."

"He called Olivia a whore and got way too close to Mollie."

"Excuse me? He called—" Her face went red, but then she paused. "Wait, he got too close to Mollie? And you were worried about that?"

"I might not like her, but she was uncomfortable. And so was I."

Jackie hummed, eyeing me. "Interesting."

"Back to the asshole who tried to take Eric," I said, refusing to think anything more about my defending Mollie.

"Right. He doesn't sound like a good person."

"It's like he wants Eric for a trophy. And I don't even know if he *is* his dad."

"That's a tough position," she said.

"He was angry at my sister. I bet that's all it was."

"And if it wasn't?"

If it wasn't, then he could sue me for custody. He could *win*.

"He won't," I said.

"You might wanna plan, just in case. Don't worry so much about Mollie—"

"It's a little hard not to."

"Hard to focus when there's a pretty woman in your house?" she teased.

"More like when a wrecking ball comes through my space in the form of a pretty woman."

Jackie hummed. "Now that people know she's here, I have a feeling she'll be busy. Or you'll get over it."

I didn't know if I could get over Mollie being here, but I needed to. Jackie was right: If Waldren did sue, then I needed to have a plan in place. Which meant depending on Mollie *more*.

And I would hate every second of it.

Jackie checked her watch. "Oh, I need to get back to the

salon, and you need to pick up Eric. But if this man comes back, let me know."

"He won't."

"Hopefully," she said. "Maybe he was just a blip."

My stomach churned at the thought of anything more, but I pushed it away, determined to go on with my day and survive Mollie's stay.

It was all I could do.

11

MOLLIE

Strawberry Springs Neighborhood Watch
Hu Gh
Where do I file a complaint? Tammy made my coffee wrong!
She gave me decaf!

Comments:
Tammy Jane: I told you that I was cutting you off, you old
coot. You're eighty years old. Chill on the damn caffeine! And
who brings a complaint like this to the group anyway? Post a
review online like everyone else!
Marjorie Brown: Now that you mention it, my toast was
burnt.
Tammy Jane: Now you're just egging it on. I'm telling your
wife.
Marjorie Brown: Please don't. I'm sorry!
Hu Gh: How to post a Goggle review.
Tammy Jane: It's called GOOGLE, Hugh!

I WAS in a post-work exhaustion coma when my door squeaked open.

"Psst," a little voice said. "Come outside."

"What?" I asked. "Eric? What are you doing?"

"I have a surprise!" He ran off without another word.

I didn't know what it could have been, but my mind flashed to either bubbles or something radioactive.

It was later in the afternoon. I'd heard the door shut, which meant Cain was probably finishing up the work with the animals that he hadn't done throughout the day. I thought Eric had been with him, but obviously not.

"I brought a chicken!"

True to his word, there *was* a chicken in his arms. And it was Hennifer, because of course it was.

She did *not* look happy to see me. She made a low noise at the mere sight.

"I've met Hennifer," I said, putting up my hands to appease her. "And she does *not* like me."

"What? She likes everyone."

"Not me."

"I'll show you." Eric put her down before I could beg him not to.

And she ran at me.

"No!" I put up my arms to meet the flurry of feathers. Luckily, her claws weren't as sharp as a rooster's would be, but they still hurt.

Then she settled on my shoulder.

"What the—" I stopped when I saw Eric giving her mealworms. "How did you do that?"

"She wants food," he explained. "Feed her, and she'll calm down."

He grabbed my hand and held out the worms. Hennifer pecked at them.

So Cain had simply let me get attacked.

Fucking dick.

"Should she be out of her run?" I asked.

"It's fine." He sounded unbothered.

"Are you sure Cain is okay with this?"

Eric winced, and I knew that Cain did not know what was going down.

"Okay," I said. "We need to get her back in—"

Hennifer jumped from my shoulder and *ran*. I gaped, wondering if she somehow knew what I was saying.

"Wait!" Eric said. "I need to catch her."

He burst into a run, and I realized that as the adult in this situation, I should probably help.

Hennifer yelled something in whatever language chickens spoke and flapped her wings as she saw me. She went over my head and onto the roof.

Eric gasped. "No. She's trying to perch."

We both looked up. "How mad will Cain be if she stays here?"

"Um, very?"

"All right," I muttered. "Guess I'm going on my own roof. Is there a ladder somewhere around here?"

"Yeah, in the shed behind the house."

Thankfully, the shed wasn't locked, and I was able to easily find a ladder to get up there. I checked to be sure it was stable like I'd seen Wren do many times before climbing up.

"Don't look down," I muttered to myself. "Or else you'll figure out really quickly if you have a fear of heights."

I made it to the top and reached out a hand to her. "Come here, Hennifer."

She glared at me, and I realized I hadn't brought any worms.

"You'll have to grab her!" Eric called.

"I have no food."

"I'll throw you some!"

I waited, and then realized that this five-year-old did *not* have the throwing skills of a future baseball star. Worms rained on the side of the house. One went into the gutter that was several feet away.

"Thanks, I got some," I lied as I climbed fully on the roof. Hennifer let me get close, but her glare told me I was on thin ice.

I tried to shuffle closer, but she flapped her wings and lunged at me. I yelped and lost my footing. My stomach went into my throat as I fell, and I was able to barely catch myself on the edge of the roof.

But that meant I was dangling.

"Fuck!" I finally looked and knew there was absolutely no way I could hop down. Not unless I wanted a broken ankle.

"That's a bad word!" Eric called out.

"I think I have bigger problems!"

My heart pounded in my ears and my problem-solving skills evaporated into nothingness.

"Cain!" Eric yelled. "Cain!"

Why was he yelling for him? That grumpy asshole wouldn't save me.

"What the hell is going on here?" His deep voice came only seconds later. "Mollie, what are you doing?"

"Hanging out," I said. "You know, just for fun."

My hands were tired, and I tried in vain to get back on the roof, but I had never been able to do a pull-up in my life, so it was no use.

"Just stay still," he said, and I heard the ladder move.

"Please tell me you have a plan." He sighed, and then an arm wrapped around my waist. "What the—"

"I'm grabbing you."

"You'll drop me!"

"No, I won't," he grumbled. "You're gonna have to trust me here."

"You don't even like me!"

"I don't, but that doesn't mean I'm gonna drop you."

I closed my eyes and felt his arm tighten.

"Now let go."

"No!"

"Goddammit, princess. I may be an asshole, but I'm also all you've got right now. Let *go*."

The words were not nice, but they were soft, and his arm *did* feel strong.

Slowly, my grip went lax, and he carried me down the ladder.

"The ground!" I said, lying on the grass face down. "Thank fuck."

"Bad word," Eric reminded me.

"Give me five minutes to recover and then I'll stop cursing."

Then I felt talons on my back.

Fucking Hennifer was now perched on me. This damn chicken.

"Why is Hennifer here?" Cain asked Eric.

"Er, I wanted to show her off?"

"I'm fine, everyone," I said, wanting to melt into the ground. "Thanks for asking."

"Come here," Cain said in a gentle voice. For a second, I thought he meant me.

But then he picked up Hennifer.

This was a new low for me.

"Eric, you can't do things like this when it's almost her bedtime. She's tired."

"I'm sorry," he said. "I just wanted Mollie to see her."

"Hennifer doesn't like her."

"Because I never have *food*," I said as I rolled over. "Which you never told me."

"A seasoned farm owner would know that." He shrugged like it was nothing.

"You're such a di—" I stopped myself just in time. "Giant pile of cow patties."

Eric laughed. Cain only rolled his eyes. I expected him to quip back. Even if it ended in a fight, I was used to it. It was nice dusting off my bantering skills.

"I'm getting Hennifer back to the run." He was gone before I could annoy him again.

I sat back on my heels. I was enjoying trading barbs with him. Why had he quit so easily? Was this a new thing?

"Be honest with me," I said. "Which one hates me more? Cain, or Hennifer?"

Eric tapped his chin. "Both don't like you." He patted my shoulder. "Sorry."

"Wanna go do marble runs in the hallway?"

"But Cain said no."

"Cain said I can't make decisions for you, which means I can't stop you if you start it."

A slow smile spread on Eric's face. "Race you to my room!"

Strawberry Springs Neighborhood Watch
Kerry Winsor
Can someone explain what gyatt means? Tommy just said it and I just can't understand these kids these days!

Comments:
Jade Clark: It refers to someone's figure. It's just a fun way to say it when you're giving a compliment. Try it in a sentence.
Kerry Winsor: Your gyatt looks great in that dress!
Jade Clark: Yep. You used it PERFECTLY.
Nicole Rudder: Jade . . . NO.
Jade Clark: I know. Got a nice screenshot, though.

BY THE END of the night, I was exhausted. Mollie was obviously still pissed, because I had to avoid marbles in the hallway when I put Eric to bed, but I'd ended a fight before it had broken out in front of him.

And that was what mattered.

I should have figured that it wasn't over, that she would seek me out. After getting Eric to bed, she was waiting for me in the kitchen.

"I didn't expect you to be the kind of man to pull out early."

I did a double take. "You wanna try rewording that sentence?" I asked. "Because I don't think that came out right."

Her bottom lip poked out as she considered it, and then her jaw dropped. "*Ew!* No!"

"You said it, princess. Not me."

"I meant in an argument. I feel so unsatisfied."

"Get used to it." I would *not* continue to go there. I didn't need to picture Mollie in any of this context. "I'm not arguing with you in front of Eric."

She blinked. "Why?"

"His teacher said it could negatively affect him." I looked outside. It was easier to say this when not facing her. "And after yesterday, I want him to feel as normal as possible."

"And you're just listening? Damn, you never do that with me."

"Let's get one thing clear. I will do anything for that kid."

Her lips curled into a smile. "That was always clear."

"Good."

"And I get it. No fighting when he's here."

"Just like that? You're agreeing?"

"Eric's a good kid. And contrary to what you might think, I'm not here to cause problems. That means I don't want my presence to ruin anything any more than you do."

"And how long are you staying for?" I asked.

Out of the corner of my eye, I saw her look down and then back at me. "No idea. I'll go back when I'm ready, I guess."

"You were raised there."

"That doesn't mean I liked it." Her voice was quiet. "I know you'll hate to hear this, but it's nice here. I'm glad that . . ." She trailed off and shook her head. "I'm glad I get to be here for now."

"You could've come at any time," I reminded her.

"I would've if I'd known." It was said under her breath.

I turned to her. "What does that mean?"

Her eyes went wide. "How did you hear that? Do you have the ears of an elephant?"

"Explain."

"Fine," she said as she crossed her arms. "I didn't know the farm was mine until the day before I came here."

"What do you mean you didn't know?"

"I *mean* that I was under eighteen when Papa Bennie died. It was in a trust for me, and my parents never took it out. Until now."

"Is *that* why I couldn't get in contact with anyone?"

She shrugged. "Probably. Legally, Mom had some sway, but she hates this place, so she left it to rot." When I raised an eyebrow, she rushed to explain. "It didn't rot, but I thought it had. In reality, you could've done whatever you wanted to."

"Not whatever. I couldn't make some decisions. Like hiring employees."

She winced. "Yeah . . . uh, sorry about that."

"So, you found out and came here?"

"Kinda. I was gonna wait, but then I needed to be here."

"*Needed?*"

"Yeah."

I didn't believe that for a second. "You're running from something, aren't you?"

Her shoulders tensed. "Why would you think that?"

"Why else would you stay?"

"Maybe because I like being here."

"Sure, but you're choosing to live with a man who completely hates you."

"It's not that hard," she said quietly. "I've done it before."

That had my attention. "You've done it before?"

She shook her head. "Do you really care about my life outside of this farm? Because I don't think you do."

I opened my mouth to . . . what? Ask her to open up to me? She was right. I didn't care about that.

Or I *shouldn't*.

But there was a part of me, one I needed to get control of, that did want to know why she was running. What had she seen here? And why had she left her cushy life? What was so bad about her past that she would endure all our fights and choose to stay?

"I'm going to bed," she said. "We can find time to annoy each other later."

"Were we annoying each other?"

Our eyes finally met, and I knew the truth. This was maybe the second time we *weren't* at each other's throats.

And I liked it.

"It won't be the norm," she said. "I'll probably be gone before this happens again."

I pursed my lips and let her walk away. I had no idea how long she would be here, but I also had no idea how long I could tolerate it without losing my damn mind.

Some of my anger dissipated in a cloud of smoke. She hadn't ignored the farm until now. She hadn't known.

That kind of information was dangerous for me to know, because it made me understand her. And I didn't need to be doing that.

She didn't leave.

Even as days turned to weeks, she was there. Sleeping in Bennie's room. At the breakfast table.

It was driving me up a wall.

She spent a lot of time in both places, working on a job she seemed to care so much about. I had no idea what she did, but she was busy at it.

The weather started to cool, which meant my work would be slowing down, at least with the chickens. I was looking forward to the break until it meant I would be in the house and in her orbit more.

Eric loved her. He followed her around whenever he wasn't in school, and the town quickly followed suit. I could tell by the way she went to Center Point Diner nearly every day that they'd welcomed her.

Of course they had. One look at her and I'd known.

I tried not to let her little smiles work on me. Most of our conversations were petty squabbles in the dark or somewhat-companionable silence when Eric was around. But I knew she was doing research on how to start the berry farm again, and the time to plant was soon.

I wondered if she would try to get me to do it, or if she would attempt it herself. Either way, the work was going to fall on me. She'd mentioned hiring employees, but school was in session and workers were hard to find.

She'd either figure it out or fuck something up trying.

My money was on the second one.

It was a crisp October day when egg production slowed to the point where I only needed to make one trip a day. This time of year, I would spend more time with the cows.

Mollie sometimes followed me to watch what I was doing, but the majority of her time was spent indoors on her computer. I didn't know how she managed to walk after sitting for so long.

Obviously, she'd decided to have a change of pace. When I

walked to the cow fields, I saw her in the distance. Moosley had taken an interest in her. The resident diva was following her.

I didn't know how, but Moosley knew what time of year it was, and she always demanded more attention on the cooler days.

Apparently, she thought Mollie was good for it.

Mollie didn't understand what was happening.

"Um, what?" she asked. "Listen, I promise I won't hurt you. I'm just going for a walk."

Moosley moved closer, and Mollie tripped over a cow patty.

"No, seriously! I can go."

Mollie walked backward, but Moosley followed. She sped up, and Moosley did the same.

Then she broke out into a full run.

Moosley kept up the pace.

"What do you want?" she called. "I swear, why do all animals hate me!"

I could have helped her.

I didn't.

She ran back and forth, only egging on Moosley, up until she finally got enough of a start to clear the fence and fall into a heap in front of me.

"You saw all of that, didn't you?" she muttered as she caught her breath.

"Yep."

"I could have been attacked, and you would have let it happen?"

"You weren't getting attacked." I walked up to the fence and pet Moosley. "She just wanted you to give her attention."

"Fuck," she groaned. "If I tried that with Hennifer, she'd peck my finger off."

"Every animal is different," I said. "But I thought you knew that."

"I have actual cow shit on my foot, and that's not the worst part of my day," she muttered before pointing at me. "You are."

"Happy to be of service."

She groaned and walked toward the house. I laughed, only for her to give me the middle finger.

I watched as she walked. She was, once again, in a ridiculous outfit.

She didn't seem to ever dress down. She had jeans, but they were branded, judging by the way they fit her perfectly and had a name written on the belt line. This morning she was wearing the loose pair with a flowy linen shirt and a massive hat.

Just the sight of her set me off some days. The more time went on, I couldn't decide which I hated more—her, or how much I looked at her.

I tore my eyes away and got my work done in record time. By the time I was back at the house, she was working again. I was tempted to piss her off once more today when I noticed a car pulling into the driveway.

I could recognize the sheriff car from a mile away. Mike was a good guy, but he didn't come out this way all that often. He preferred to stay in town near the diner or the bar.

"Shit," I muttered.

"What?"

"The sheriff's here."

"Did you do something illegal?" Mollie asked.

"Why would you ask that?"

"I'm trying to figure out if I should back you up or not."

"I didn't do anything," I said. "You're here all the fucking time. You'd know."

Mike's car rolled to a stop and my heart kicked into gear. I'd already gotten myself into trouble too many times in this town. These days, I didn't even speed.

"Cain," Mike called. "Good to see you." His eyes went to Mollie. "I don't believe we've met yet."

"I'm Mollie," she replied. "I own the house, and am generally a pain in his ass."

"Glad to see you're not too scared off by this one," Mike said. "Though that might change."

"I haven't done anything wrong, Mike."

He hummed and pulled a folder from his car.

"You're being sued, Cain."

"What?" Mollie and I asked at the same time.

"Here are the court documents. You might wanna read them. And make sure you have your ducks in a row."

I slowly opened the folder with shaking hands.

It was for custody of Eric.

"The DNA test was positive?"

"It was."

Shit. That asshole had actually done it. He was suing me for custody. Mollie peered over my shoulder.

"I—I don't—"

"I won't tell anyone," Mike said. "All I *will* say is . . . good luck, Cain."

And I knew what he meant.

To fight this, I was going to need all the help I could get. And for a guy who had never been a part of this town, I didn't have much of that waiting around.

Jackie would do it. But she was the only person I had on my side.

Mollie was walking away, and I turned to her.

"What? No 'I told you so'?"

"That feels like kicking a man when he's down," she said, grabbing her phone.

"What are you doing?"

"Just shut up for a second."

I blinked, about to tell her off, but she put the phone to her ear.

"Hey, Dad. Remember that thing I said I might need? I really need it now." She listened and then sighed. "No, Dad, I'm not coming back. This is unrelated." She paused. "This is that family lawyer thing. I know you said you would look into it, but I need it *now*." She paused again. "Okay, thank you. No, I haven't talked to Trevor. I'm sure he's fine. Love you, bye." When she put her phone down, she finally looked at me. "Give me your number."

"Why?"

"Because I'm sending you some information that should be here any second." Her phone jingled. "There it is."

Wordlessly, I did what she asked, and she put her number in mine. "There are the lawyers I promised you."

"I thought you'd forgotten."

"No, I just don't love calling my dad right now."

I stared at the message on my phone. She'd included three lawyers. I should thank her, or say *something*. But seeing it on my phone made it all the more real.

It had been a long time since I'd felt *fear*. Most of the time, I was able to push it away. But Eric was *mine*. He was everything to me, and I couldn't imagine my future without him.

"Cain?" Mollie asked. "You okay?"

I wasn't. Not in the slightest. I could have lied and said I was, but there was no pretending at that moment. There was only *fear*. Would I see him finish kindergarten? Would I be able to see him go to middle school? Teach him to drive?

My chest burned. My entire body was tight. This was my worst nightmare.

But then firm hands landed on my shoulders.

"Hey. You need to *breathe*."

"I-I can't."

Her hands tightened. "Yes, you can. Come on. Do it with me."

I didn't want to listen, but then Mollie's face appeared in front of mine. Even in my worst moment, it pulled me out of my thoughts, making me focus only on her.

Taking one breath and then two, I did what I was told.

"Good," she said. "You're gonna be able to fight this. You just need to call them."

"What if I lose?"

"You won't. Because I have a feeling you'll do whatever it takes to keep Eric."

She was right. Once again.

I nodded, but then caught on to how close she was. There were mere inches between us, and the only time we'd been this close was when we were fighting.

She must have picked up on it right when I had, because her eyes widened and she took a healthy step back.

"Good," she said. "I'll let you go call them."

She walked toward the front door.

"Mollie, wait."

She paused and looked back.

"Thank you."

Her eyes went wide. "You're welcome."

"Please keep this from the town."

"I already planned to," was all she said before walking through the door.

She'd asked me what would make me like her, and she had no idea that she'd just done it.

Hopefully, I could keep it that way.

13

MOLLIE

Strawberry Springs Neighborhood Watch
Kerry Winsor
Saw some fancy car on my way home. People better not start using the highway as some cut through to one of the cities.

Comments:
Tammy Jane: What city? Knoxville? That's over an hour away!
Kerry Winsor: People commute, Tammy.
Tammy Jane: Not from here, they don't!
Kerry Winsor: Either way. Just keep a lookout. **@Sherriff-Mike Finch**, I thought you should know.
SherriffMike Finch: Guys, I have a full-time job. Stop tagging me in everything.
Kerry Winsor: We just want to help as concerned citizens!

THE SUN WAS warm on my back as I walked to the tree line. I'd just left the former berry fields, trying to remember where they'd been. Though I lived on a farm, I didn't get outside nearly as much as I wanted to, so whenever work would slow down or Cain had a near meltdown in the living room, I made it my mission to explore.

So far, I'd made it to the cow fields, but the berries still nagged at me. I was deep in trying to remember how many fields Papa Bennie would plant when I received a message.

> **TREVOR**
>
> Dad is willing to negotiate the price of the land.

I gritted my teeth and didn't answer. I hadn't spoken to him about anything besides work, though I knew he'd been seeing Mom and Dad a lot. Every time they called to try and get me to come home, he would be there silently judging everything I said.

I opened my messages to Wren, needing to tell her everything before I chickened out.

> How did I not see what an ass Trevor was when he used to knock on the wall for coffee?

> **WREN**
>
> I'm sorry, he WHAT?

> And made me do all the cleaning.

> He's lucky I'm busy right now.

> Never let me go back.

> I'll drag you kicking and screaming away from him if I have to. ICK.

His anger was growing, and though he didn't say anything in meetings or in front of my parents, I knew the second I gave in and spoke to him, he wouldn't hold back. I told myself I would be safe if I didn't talk to him.

But the fact that I felt that way at all put my nearly five-year relationship into perspective.

Soon after, my phone rang. I almost ignored it, but I saw that this call was from Mom.

"Why did you call your father about a lawyer, Mollie?" Mom's voice was exasperated. "Just what is going on out there?"

"It was for a . . . friend." Cain definitely wasn't a friend, but was Eric? Either way, the less Mom knew, the better. "There's a child custody battle going on—"

"Don't get involved in the day-to-day there. It's all petty drama."

I knew for a fact that she loved petty drama in her neighborhood. Often, she was the cause of it when she went after people for having unapproved flowers in their garden.

"It's fine," I said. "I'm not too involved. I just wanted to help him."

She gasped. "*Him?*"

"His gender has nothing to do with this."

"It has everything to do with this. What does this help turn into? A date or two?"

"It's not like that," I said. It never would be. Did I think Cain was hot? Sure. He was a hot man who loved animals and was good with kids. Most women would melt for that.

But it was a problem when he opened his mouth. Or when *I* opened my mouth.

He'd seemed shocked that I'd done a nice thing for him. But I knew it wasn't going to change anything. Tomorrow, we would be back at each other's throats over nothing.

At least I didn't take shit from him. I felt like the same little girl who would say anything that was on her mind when I was here.

I needed to be her again.

"Well, what am I supposed to think? You're taking a break

from the healthiest relationship I've ever seen to go be in the middle of nowhere with a random ma—" She paused. "Please tell me this friend you helped isn't that farm manager who lives there."

"Uh, it's not?"

"You're lying. Why is this farm manager in a custody battle?"

"I thought you didn't want me to be involved in petty drama. Now you wanna know?"

She went silent for a long moment. "Fine. I don't want to know. What I do wanna know is when you're coming back."

Cotton made its way to my throat. "Not sure. Soon, maybe."

She let out a sigh. "I just don't understand why you're even there."

"You really can't see any reason why I'd like a quiet, small town over the city?"

"No, I can't."

"It's slower here. I can talk to the people who live here."

"Why would you want to do that?"

My frustration grew, and I had to bite my tongue to keep from saying something I'd regret.

"I need to go," I said. "I love you, and I'll talk with you later."

I hung up the phone, my mood even lower than usual. I didn't know why talking to my own family made me this way, but it was like I was back in Nashville, miserable with no way out.

Cain came outside not much later, presumably to get Eric from school, so I took that as a sign to get back to work at my computer. Marketing was the last thing I cared about, but I knew Dad would give me another lecture if I missed anything else.

Eric got home around four with Cain, and they started

dinner right after. Usually, I left to let them do it alone while I figured out what I would eat, but tonight I didn't have the energy to move.

Work was draining, especially since Trevor had sent me four emails with things to do, and one with another offer for the house. He wanted my answer and all of my tasks done same-day, or there would be *more* emails in my inbox complaining about my remote work. I finished what I could, but ignored the one about the house, knowing there was no amount of money that would make me sell.

I heard Eric talking to Cain about his day while they worked. Cain got a pot and let Eric watch it while it filled with water. After it was on the stove, Eric added salt. I was sure they were making pasta of some sort, which sounded delicious. I needed to get some at the store next time.

I was typing up another email when Eric ran over to me. I didn't expect it, and jumped when he asked, "What's your favorite sauce, Mollie?"

"Sauce?" I repeated, blinking the exhaustion out of my eyes. "For what?"

"For noodles! I like the white one, but Cain likes red."

"Oh, uh. Usually red."

"Aw, dang."

"But white is good too."

Eric seemed pleased and went back over to Cain. Now I was very hungry. Maybe I could go to the store and cook the same thing once everyone went to bed.

Cain hadn't so much as looked at me. When he wasn't actively cooking something, his arms were tightly crossed over his chest, his eyes only on Eric. Luckily, the five-year-old hadn't picked up on his sour mood, but I knew what was off.

Apparently, Cain was a decent cook, because it smelled

delicious. It was tomato rich with a hint of savory herbs. My stomach growled, begging me to have some.

Eric got his food first.

"Can I sit next to you?" he asked.

"Of course," I said as I eyed his food in jealousy. What brand of sauce was that? I needed to find it.

I dragged my eyes back to work, but the laptop shut in front of me.

Cain stared at me. "No working at the dinner table."

I glared. "I have things to do."

"They can wait."

"Do you have any other rules?" I asked as I rolled my eyes.

"We always eat at the table."

Was I seriously getting kicked out while they ate? Could he not let me be? I grabbed my laptop, wondering how I could get revenge.

But then the plate in his hand was set down in front of me.

"What is this?"

"Dinner," was all he said.

"I—what? You said we don't share food."

"I'm being nice tonight. As long as you put the laptop away."

The only reason I listened was because I was starving. I got up and tossed my computer over the back of the couch. When I returned, Cain had his own plate and sat across from me.

Eric was digging in, grabbing long noodles with his hands and shoving them into his mouth. I was tempted to do the same, but I used the fork instead.

It tasted as good as it looked. Better even. There were notes of garlic and onion, as well as perfectly al dente noodles.

When I looked up, Cain was watching me.

"Oh, uh. Thank you for the food."

"Were you hungry?"

More so than I wanted to admit. "It was a . . . weird day. I forgot to eat."

He knew it more than I did.

"It's so good," Eric said, his mouth full.

"It really is. What brand is this?"

"I make it myself and can it."

Damn. I didn't think he could get hotter.

"Let me guess, it's a family recipe that you share with no one."

"Not a family recipe, but I probably wouldn't share it with you."

"Because I'm annoying?"

"Got it in one go, princess."

I rolled my eyes, but the rudeness felt familiar, almost like a hug.

"I haven't had homemade food in forever."

"What did you eat in the city, Mollie?" Eric asked.

"Sometimes I went out to get food if my—if other people wanted to. And sometimes I cooked something basic, and we would eat on the couch."

"You didn't eat at the table?"

I shook my head. "Our apartment was too small for that."

"Too small for a dining table?" Cain asked.

"Yep."

"And let me guess, you paid an arm and a leg."

"Too much," I said. "We were sandwiched in between smaller buildings, and it was so loud. There was never silence. Not all of Nashville is like that, but where I lived was."

Trevor had wanted to be close to work. Trevor had wanted an apartment with luxuries.

Had I wanted *anything* about that place?

"It's changed," Cain said. "Before Jackie, I lived there most of my life. And now I see something totally different when I visit."

"Some people say change is a part of life, but it's . . . a lot. Going back will be an adjustment."

"How long are you staying?" Eric asked.

"I have no idea. Maybe for a while."

"Yay! We should eat dinner together as long as you're here."

I glanced at Cain, wondering if he would be staring at me like he usually was.

Instead, he was looking at his nephew.

And it hit me that I might be here longer than Eric was. That had to be what Cain was thinking.

Despite us not getting along, I couldn't help but feel the same way. Eric belonged with Cain. Hopefully, things would stay as they should.

"I won't impose," I said. "But maybe sometimes. I'd offer to cook, but I don't make anything as good as this."

"I'd try it!" Eric exclaimed before going back for another bite. I did the same, and we all ate in relative silence. Cain immediately started on cleaning up, another point in his favor.

"Need any help?" I asked.

He gave me a flat look, one that was a resounding no.

"Okay, maybe you don't *need* it. But do you want it? It's only fair since you offered dinner."

"That was a one-time thing. As a thank you for the lawyers."

I turned to see Eric playing with LEGO bricks in the living room. "Does he know?"

"Some of it. He knows that there's a lawsuit. I told him on the way home."

"He seems to be in a good mood regardless."

"He said he would tell the judge that he doesn't wanna go. As if it were that simple." He put a dish in the dishwasher. "I'll know more when I go to Nashville next week."

"I don't envy you, having to drive there. But I'm glad you called."

"There's no wasting time. Even if the traffic might send me to an early grave."

I laughed. "Don't let that happen. It's *my* job to do that to you."

He nodded, and I saw a ghost of a smile on his face. My heart skipped a beat. I didn't even think it was possible for him to do that, much less because of me.

"When we inevitably find something to fight about tomorrow," I said, "I'll remember this one good moment we had together."

"You could overachieve and find something new. What controversial topics do you have?"

I raised my hand. "I plead the Fifth. Unfortunately, I do have more work to do."

"Does it ever end?"

"Not where Trevor's concerned," I muttered. For a man who didn't want me working, he sure did have a lot for me to do now.

"Who's Trevor?" he asked. "I've heard that name before."

For a second, I froze. I'd barely told my best friend about some of the things Trevor had done. If Cain found out, he would never let me live it down for being with someone so awful.

I waved my hand. "Don't worry about it. You don't have to pretend to care."

I walked away before he could say anything else, going to my room to work.

But I could have sworn I felt his eyes follow me the entire way. I got to my room and opened my text messages with Wren.

Cain can cook. Who knew?

WREN

Cain???

Hot farmer.

Oh, you're using first names? Enemies to lovers confirmed!

I hate you.

Uh huh. Do you? Or do you wanna know when the first episode of the show airs?

TELL ME. I'm gnawing at the bars of my enclosure.

I appreciate your love. It's next Tuesday at seven.

14

CAIN

Strawberry Springs Neighborhood Watch
Kerry Winsor
I can't believe it's the last farmers market of the year next week!
Where does the time go?

Comments:
Marjorie Brown: Think they're selling melons?
Kerry Winsor: Marjorie, it's October.
Atticus Thompson: Pumpkins are a melon.
Kerry Winsor: Did you mean pumpkins? **@Marjorie
Brown**
Marjorie Brown: No.
Kerry Winsor: What is even happening here???
Marjorie Brown: Now who's blowing a fuse?
Henrietta Brown: Honey, we talked about this.

NASHVILLE WAS A FUCKING NIGHTMARE.

It had been years since I'd come here, and there was a

reason why. I hated the noise. I hated how everyone was constantly busy, never slowing down.

Mollie was like that, and it bothered me way too much.

But I had to be here to meet with the lawyer who could represent me in keeping Eric. I didn't know if I could since Waldren had been confirmed to be his biological dad, but I had to try.

Mollie had pulled me aside this morning and told me exactly where to park. It was a garage with spots big enough for my truck. I didn't want her help, but I appreciated it nonetheless. Nashville was stressful enough without the issue of parking. I had to walk to the lawyer's office, and the nerves only grew as I got closer.

The building was too fancy, and I felt out of place. But the receptionist was nice, and I didn't have to wait for long.

"Cain Smith?" the lawyer, a man by the name of Morgan, called.

"That's me."

He gestured for me to follow him, and we walked to a small office with a simple desk and chairs. Behind him, he had pictures of his family all over the walls. I sat across from him, and my leg wouldn't sit still.

"So, tell me about Eric."

"H-have you read what I sent in?"

"I have. But I want to hear it from you." He gave me a smile, and I wasn't sure if it was a good or bad thing.

"It started over three years ago, when I got a call from the state," I began. "Eric was in foster care after my sister died."

"Right. You didn't know her very well."

"We were separated when we were young."

"So, why did you take Eric?"

"I was a foster kid myself and I bounced around homes until I landed in Strawberry Springs. The whole time, I wondered if there was ever someone related to me who could step up. It never happened for me, but when I got the chance to do that for Eric . . . I couldn't say no."

"And how did taking him in go?"

"Rough, at first. I'd never been around a kid, but I bought books and whatever he needed. We had to figure it out, but I did whatever I could."

"How's it going now?"

"Fantastic. But at this moment? I'm terrified. I love Eric. I planned to . . ." I trailed off. "Well, it doesn't matter what I planned now, does it? I just need to keep him."

Morgan hummed. "He's only been in school for a semester, but his grades are slightly below average."

"He's behind, but he's working hard."

"I know. I see here that he's picking up reading faster than most. This is the sort of information we need."

"For fighting this?"

He nodded. "If we can prove that Eric would be better off with you, then you might get away with only giving this man visitation rights, or depending on how bad his lawyer is, nothing at all."

"He was in a suit when he came to the house to get Eric."

"He visited you unprovoked?" At my nod, he added, "Interesting. If Eric is happy with you, and is willing to tell a judge that, then we have a case. But it'll need to be airtight, especially if you get Judge Marlon."

"Who's that?"

"He's strict. And he wants families to be together. *Biological* families."

I let out a breath of air. "Even when they weren't around for five years?"

"Yes. Even then. You'll also need character letters from any friends you have. Ones that see how you are with Eric."

"Friends?"

"Friends, neighbors, anyone you know. The more the better."

Fuck. That was the one thing I couldn't do. "And they need to be positive?"

"They have to be. We want to build the best case we can. Will that be a problem?"

My entire body tensed. A problem? This was a death sentence.

But I had to fight this somehow. I couldn't let this asshole have my nephew.

"No. No problem. I'll figure it out."

I thought about it the whole way home.

In order for people to be able to do anything, they needed to see me with Eric. And in order for them to see me with Eric, I had to leave the house and be nice to them.

Which was going to be terrible.

As I pulled into the driveway, Mollie's shiny car sat innocently in the spot to the right. I sighed when I saw her, but knew I needed to start with her before anyone else.

If I hadn't been such an ass to her, she could have written a letter.

When I walked in, she was on the couch, laptop in hand. She didn't seem to be working. Instead, she was leaning forward and watching the TV intently.

"Is that reality TV?" I asked.

"Shh!" she snapped. "I'm watching my best friend and the man of her dreams."

I blinked. There were two people on the TV. One had

reddish-blonde hair falling over her shoulders in waves, while the other had dark hair and a permanent smirk.

"I didn't think very highly of you before, but this is worse than I thought."

She grabbed one of the throw pillows and hurled it at me. I caught it before it could hit my face.

"It's all fake, you know," I said.

"No, I happen to know this is real. That's my friend, Wren. On *TV*."

I turned. "Your friend renovates houses?"

"She's a Nashville legend. She finally got one of the abandoned mansions and is renovating it on live TV."

Where they were located had fallen victim to time. "She better not make it all gray."

"I'm offended that you even think that." She paused the show and grabbed her phone, scrolling for a minute. "Look at her work."

I took it with a roll of my eyes. I was more than likely going to see the typical beige or gray remodel with no character.

Instead, I saw old homes tastefully decorated. They had different color schemes, and all kept some of the original character of the home.

"And this is her show?"

"Yep." She pressed play and I turned, arms crossed. Wren was talking to the camera about her plans while the man next to her watched her intently. The scene changed, and he was knocking out a wall. "He's *so* hot."

"That man is a tool."

"*You're* a tool," she replied. "Besides, Wren has a huge crush on him."

"He's a TV personality."

"So?" She rolled her eyes. "Sit down if you're gonna watch. And shut your mouth."

I was tempted to walk away, but I used to live near that mansion. I'd explored it myself when I loved breaking rules. Slowly, I sat next to her and leaned back.

The place had been vandalized even when I had been there, but Wren talked about how much she wanted to make sure the community still loved it, and how she wanted to commission art on one of the garden walls by local artists.

This was obviously only the beginning of the show, but I could see where it was going. The camera kept panning to Wren and Jude while they talked, getting shots of them glancing at each other while they worked. They were probably going to get together.

I didn't care much for the romance. But I did care to see the mansion get restored to its former glory.

When the episode ended, Mollie nudged me with her leg. "So . . ."

"So what?"

"You watched the whole thing."

"It was . . . fine."

"Fine? It's gonna be a hit. I hope she gets a hundred seasons and gets to have just as many kids with Jude."

"A hundred kids?" I asked.

"Hey, if my best friend gets a shot with the man she's had eyes for since she was a teen, then yes. She can have as many kids as she wants."

"You're ridiculous."

She laughed. "I know. How did Nashville go?"

"It was as terrible as usual."

"And the meeting with the lawyer?"

My stomach churned as my problems came rushing back. "I . . . know what I need to do."

"Care to share?"

"Not exactly."

She rolled her eyes. "It's really one step forward and two steps back with you, isn't it?"

"There are no steps happening anywhere," I said as I walked off.

"You kinda like me, I can see it!" she called.

I rolled my eyes, determined not to tell her that she was exactly right.

But I didn't need to think about that. I needed help, and I only trusted one person when I needed that.

"All right, we're starting on Operation Get Cain Friends." Jackie's smile was wide.

"We're not calling it that," I said. "And they won't be friends."

"Yes, they will be. Once you get everyone in Strawberry Springs to see what I do, you'll have lots of friends. I was *waiting* for you to ask me for this."

The idea sounded terrible.

It was a chilly morning, but it would warm up by the middle of the day. Strawberry Springs was hosting its last farmers market of the year. Bennie used to be at every single one. I'd gone to a few, but they'd never gone well for me.

The eggs and milk sold without it, so I figured I'd never have to see the square covered in tents again.

"Now, while you're being a social butterfly, don't let me forget to get one of those rocking chairs from Hugh. I want it on my balcony."

I nodded along while I watched people—most of whom I knew—walk around and shop.

Eric was over at the playground nestled near the old library. Jackie told me he would be fine, and true to her word, he was already playing with Tommy and a few other kids who looked to be around the same age.

"Come on," she said. "The Nordic baker from the town over came today. I need to stock up."

Jackie looped her arm through mine and dragged me into the chaos. She bought bread. Then cake for Eric. Then talked to a bunch of people she knew. For a small town, it was so *busy*.

I stayed silent, even when Jackie tried to pull me into the conversations she easily held with the vendors. She was so friendly that talking came easy to her.

I wasn't as lucky.

"You'll have to open up if you want this," she said as we did one more lap around the square.

"Of course I want it, but all of these people . . . It's too much."

"I figured that one day of misery would be enough. You can get everyone at once."

"Maybe this is hopeless. The lawyer said I needed as many letters as I could get, but yours would be enough."

"Are you sure?"

And that was the issue. I could delude myself, but I knew the truth. I needed more.

My eyes drifted to Eric, who was still on the playground. I'd never felt like more of a failure.

But my nephew wasn't even looking at me. His eyes were on the road, and he took off suddenly.

"Mollie!" he yelled.

And there she was, in a striped sweater and jeans. I hadn't told her about this, and I was pretty sure she hadn't heard of the market.

Yet here she was.

"Son of a—I'll be right back." I raised my voice. "Eric! Don't run across roads!"

"But they're closed!" he said, pulling out of his tight hug with Mollie.

"I'm stealing him," she said. "Especially since *he* tells me about the farmers market."

"There are signs in the square," I replied.

She patted Eric's back before drawing a dick in the air and pointing at me.

"Jackie's here," I said with a roll of my eyes. "She might show you around."

"I think I want you to do it." She crossed her arms. "As penance for not telling me."

"I will *not* be doing that."

"Please?" Eric begged. "I'll go too."

"I thought you wanted to play with your friends," I said.

"Mollie's my friend."

"Two against one," she teased. "You're overruled."

I was hopeless against Eric's begging anyway—not that I would tell her that.

"Don't expect me to talk."

"That's my favorite side of you."

I opened my mouth, but she grabbed the front of my flannel and dragged me toward the people.

"What are you doing?"

"Making you do what you hate."

Jackie was waiting across the street, her eyebrows nearly at her hairline. "Hi!" Mollie greeted, letting me go. "I'm sorry to steal Cain, but I need to torture him. Can you believe I've been here for weeks and didn't know about the farmers market?"

"That's . . . He hates them anyway."

"Exactly," she said with a wink.

I groaned.

"Mind if I tag along?" Jackie asked. "I've already shopped, but I can show you all the good places."

"Absolutely," she said. "Come, Cain."

"I'm not a dog."

"Until you learn manners you are."

Jackie laughed but covered her mouth.

I cleared my throat and looked at Eric, then back at Jackie.

But Eric was laughing too. "It's like watching a funny show."

"And you get a front row seat every day. I'll have to come over more."

Jackie told Mollie about the baker, and she made a beeline for the booth. I was forced to look at the same woman I'd awkwardly smiled at while she talked about her process of bread making. I was many things, but a baker was not one of them.

"I'm getting two," Mollie said, pulling out her card.

"What are you even gonna do with that much bread?"

"Smother garlic and butter on it, of course."

"Yes!" Eric cheered.

"Oh, that sounds so good." The vendor clapped her hands together. "Especially with a homemade sauce."

"He may not look like much, but Mister Grump here"—she pointed to me— "makes an amazing homemade sauce."

The vendor laughed, but I shook my head. "What do I look like, then?"

"Like you'd burn water."

Now Jackie and Eric joined the laughter.

"You definitely know that's not true."

"You two are *so* cute together," the vendor said.

Both of us froze. Together? Us?

This was *bad*.

"Oh, we're not together. I'm his boss. Mostly of making his life terrible, but also of the farm he works on." Mollie was unbothered, so much so that it loosened the tightness in my chest.

"I'm so sorry!" The vendor's eyes went wide. "I thought . . . Ignore me. I don't know what I'm talking about."

"It's fine." Mollie waved her hand. "We just don't want to give this guy an aneurysm when he's finally out of the house."

The vendor smiled and handed Mollie the two loaves of bread before turning to me. "I've only seen you today. Do you live here?"

"Uh, yeah. I just don't get out much."

"It's nice to meet you. Maybe both of you will be back in the spring."

"I certainly will." Mollie shoved her haul into my arms. "And depending on how mad Cain's made me, I'll have him come to carry all the bags."

"Do that, and I won't share my sauce with you."

She sighed and started to take the bag back, but I held it out of her grip.

"Pick a side, Cain."

"I'm being nice while also being rude. It's my thing."

"Fine. I suppose of all the things to have," she said with a smile, "it's not the worst."

My heart nearly stopped, but she was on to the next vendor.

"I saw that," Jackie said.

"You saw nothing."

She was at the sweets vendor when I caught up to her.

"How many cookies can you and Cain eat in a week or so?" she asked Eric.

"Jackie already got us cake."

"That didn't answer my question."

"I have all kinds of flavors," the vendor said. "Even some that are less sweet, if you prefer!"

"I need some for a sweet treat after dinner. What do you think of the red velvet one, Cain?"

"Red velvet is just chocolate in a costume."

She gasped. "You take that back, you monster!"

I looked at the vendor. She nodded.

"Get the velvet," I said. "As more of a punishment for me."

"I was trying to get you something you'd actually eat. Do you have cookie opinions?"

"Get the cinnamon streusel," Jackie said with a wink.

Mollie turned and did exactly that, plus a few red velvets. Eric ordered a chocolate chip one, and by the time we were on to the next place, I had another bag in my hand.

I should have never let her shove her bag into my arms. Her shopping put Jackie's to shame.

And Jackie made it all worse by leading Mollie to the best vendors. Bags increased, as did the number of people in the square.

"Ooh, is that a coffee truck?" Mollie asked.

"Yep," I said.

"Finally, I can get a good latte."

I didn't know about *good*. The one thing Strawberry Springs didn't have was great coffee. Most people went to the diner for a cup, but it wasn't good.

Eric walked with Jackie, who was holding onto his hand tightly as she followed Mollie and me around. For some reason, I stuck close to the woman who'd made me carry all her stuff. She was easier than all the people around me.

Mollie got everyone a drink. Eric and I got something non-caffeinated while she got coffee-based drinks for herself and Jackie.

"Time for a taste test," she said, bouncing as she took a sip. She quickly stilled.

"Yeah," Jackie muttered. "Not great."

"We need a damn good coffee shop," another voice said. Mollie and I turned to see Theo, another one of the younger men in town, standing next to us. He had dark hair and tattoos, something he had gone to the next town over to get.

Theo had moved into town about eight years ago. He was always quiet, yet had been welcomed warmly since he did a lot of the handyman work that anyone needed.

"You like coffee," Jackie said. "You should do it."

"I'd need a lot of money for that."

"There's the grant," she offered.

Theo shrugged, grimacing as he took another sip. His eyes met mine, and he gave me a nod. I didn't get to see him much, but when I did, it was like he knew I shared his hesitance to speak to people.

If I could have called that a friendship, it would have been the best I'd ever had.

Theo's eyes then moved to Mollie. "Hi," she said with a bright smile. "I don't think we've met. I'm Mollie."

"Theo."

That was it. No double take. No checking her out.

Just the same as he did with every woman in town.

"You two should be friends," Mollie said, elbowing me. "You could sit in silence and enjoy it."

"Would be a good way to spend a Friday night," I said.

"Agreed." Theo took another sip and sighed. "I'm gonna go throw this away. I can't believe I spent ten dollars on this shit."

He walked off, still shaking his head, and Mollie dragged me to the next vendor in line.

It should have been a terrible experience, yet I didn't find myself hating it. Mollie was good at dragging me into conversations. She bought most of the food and told me I could use it to cook with for the rest of the week.

We stayed until the market dwindled, and finally, she announced she was done.

"Help me load all of this in the car and I'll free you," she said.

"At least I'll have my arms again."

"No quips about how much I spent?"

"It's your money."

"Or how terrible it was?"

"Not really."

"Interesting. Sounds like you enjoyed it."

"I have nothing to say about that."

"I have to go get the salon open for some afternoon appointments," Jackie said. "But I had *so* much fun. When this starts up next year, we'll have to go again." Then she turned to me. "Come talk to me after you help Mollie."

"Can't you just say it here?"

"Nope."

Well, *shit*. That didn't mean anything good.

"Come on," she said. "I won't keep you from whatever thing Jackie has to tell you."

"This time, you can keep me. I have a feeling I won't like it."

"Yeah!" Eric added as he skipped across the street. "We should stay with Mollie."

Mollie gave him a smile as we neared her car. I started to load the bread, cakes, and sauces she'd gotten, wondering what Jackie needed to tell me.

"There you are!" a loud voice called. "I've been dying to meet you!"

I sighed. *Kerry*.

I knew she'd been here. I'd figured as much when I had seen Tommy, but we'd been lucky enough not to run into her. Until now, it seemed.

"Hi," Mollie said, completely unbothered by the stranger currently running toward her. "You must have heard of me."

"Oh, I know everything that goes on in this town."

I dropped the last of Mollie's things in her SUV before closing the trunk.

That was when Kerry finally saw me. Her jaw dropped.

"Or not everything. Cain, is that you?"

"Yep," I said. "Just putting some stuff away. Nothing more."

Kerry hummed, appraising us. Eric was right next to Mollie, smiling away without a care in the world. That wasn't unusual. He didn't hate people like I did.

Thankfully, I had a healthy distance from her. Just minutes ago, when we were on the crowded street, that hadn't been the case. I'd gravitated to her like she was a source of comfort.

It was the candle thing. She smelled too much like my favorite one. It had to be that.

"Cain didn't tell me the farmers market was a thing, so I made him hang out with me as punishment."

Kerry laughed. "Is hanging out with you a punishment?"

"For him? It definitely is. We get along like two roosters fighting over the same hen."

"There'd be a lot more violence if that were the case," I corrected. The last thing Kerry needed to think was that. She already had a low enough opinion of me.

"Hm. Cats and dogs?"

"No. Those can get along."

"Oh, I've got it. Me and Hennifer."

"She doesn't hate you when you feed her."

"And I don't hate you as much when you feed me, but the feeling is mutual all of the other times."

"Well," Kerry said, "aren't you just two peas in a pod?"

I frowned. Did she not just hear that we fought all the time?

Fuck. I shouldn't have said anything. I had a feeling I would be hearing this from Nicole on Monday once Kerry told everyone we fought frequently.

"Tell me about you," Mollie said smoothly. "I don't even know your name!"

"Kerry," she said. "Otherwise known as the town's mom and gossip."

Mollie nodded, but her eyes flicked to me as if she knew exactly why I was so hesitant to talk to her.

"You'll have to catch me up on all of the gossip, then. I haven't heard much."

"I'd *love* that." She looked at me and then back at Mollie. "There's a lot you don't know."

Yeah, I should have seen that coming. I already knew Kerry would tell her everything I'd done as a teen. I'd be lucky if she didn't fire me, or worse, look at me the same way everyone else in this town did.

"Eric and I should go," I said, walking up to him. "We need to talk to Jackie."

"Of course," Mollie said. "Have fun being lectured."

"Yeah, right."

I walked away before I could hear anything else, and I tried my best *not* to turn around to see if I could guess if Kerry was talking about me or not.

I didn't need to know.

"You look annoyed," Jackie said when I walked in. "But less annoyed than I expected after all of that socializing Mollie put you through."

"I'm fine," I replied. "Ready to go home. What did you need to tell me?"

"Ah, well. I'll try to say this as gently as possible." She took a breath. "I can't help you."

"Can't help me?"

"With the town."

I blinked. Jackie wasn't usually the kind to not help unless I'd fucked up. *Badly.*

I hadn't tried hard enough. I should have forced myself to talk more.

"I understand."

"Now hang on. Don't get all broody until I explain."

"What's there to explain?"

"A lot." She handed Eric a coloring page, and he ran off to one of the extra stations. "First of all, I can't help you because I'm not the person for the job. I don't push you in the way you need. You hated every second of us going around the square. Until *Mollie* showed up."

"Mollie? What does she have to do with this?"

"She's the *one.*"

"No. *No.* Absolutely not. I'm not dating her. Ever—"

"Not for *that.*" Jackie rolled her eyes. "Though I do think there could be something there. I mean for helping you. You saw how she handled talking with the baker. And with the other people. You weren't as tense, and you even spoke."

"Because she kept dragging me into conversations."

"Exactly," Jackie said. "She knows how to get you to talk."

"She doesn't even like me."

"Well, whose fault is that?"

"It's mutual."

Jackie rolled her eyes again. "Really? Or were you grumpy with her?"

"Okay, *fine.* Maybe I could have been nicer when she broke into my house and critiqued my work. But the damage is done. We barely talk without fighting. She definitely wouldn't help me."

Again, I added mentally.

"You could offer her something in return. I'm sure there's something she wants to do."

The strawberries. She wanted to bring those back.

I thought about it. I could plant the roots as soon as possible for a field. It would make my days endless, but it could get done, and she would have them by spring, if she were even around.

"There . . . is something."

"Then offer it. I think she's the key to this."

"Can't you and I keep trying?"

"We could, but you're on borrowed time, and she got you to open up like *that*." She snapped her fingers. "Just ask her."

I groaned. "You know how much I hate asking for help."

"I do," she replied. "But you'll have to do it eventually. And I have a feeling she'll say yes."

"You haven't seen her when we're alone."

"She's a nice girl. She's Bennie's granddaughter. Kindness may have skipped over a generation of that family, but not her."

Even if I hated the idea, I knew Jackie was right.

But the timing couldn't be worse. If Kerry spilled everything I'd done, and I knew she would, then I had a feeling asking for help was going to be far more difficult than usual.

MOLLIE

Strawberry Springs Neighborhood Watch
Kerry Winsor
Since when does Cain go to the farmers market? I saw Mollie
dragging him around.

Comments:
Jackie Anne: Sometimes he gets out of the house.
Kerry Winsor: Uh, yeah. To maybe go to the diner. This was
way out of left field.
Tammy Jane: Damn. This was the one time I should have
closed the diner and gone.
Hu Gh: DON'T YOU DARE. THAT'S MY COFFEE
TIME.

As I UNLOADED everything I bought at the farmers market into
the cabinets of the house, I realized that I might have gotten too
much. I had no idea how fast I could go through all that I'd
bought, but I would try my best.

I'd told Cain I would share, so hopefully he would help.

But after dragging him around all morning? He definitely wasn't thrilled with me.

I still wasn't happy that I hadn't known about it. I loved to go as a kid. Papa Bennie would tell me I was his best salesman, but I figured it had been lost to time like the library.

It was fun, but I'd noticed there was a missing part of it. Bennie was the one who sold fresh berries in the spring and strawberry jam in the winter.

No one had taken his place.

I could see a future with not just berries, but other crops that went later into the season. Sometimes, Bennie had a surplus around the U-pick days, or he took the eggs to sell directly to people to catch up with them.

I wanted to do that.

But with my job and my uncertain future, I didn't know if I could.

Cain's truck pulled in right when I had just finished putting everything away.

"Welcome back," I greeted as they walked in. "Have fun with Jackie?"

"She let me color!" Eric said. He had a piece of paper in his hands that he showed me. I told him it looked amazing before letting my eyes fall on Cain, who was walking into the kitchen.

"Lunch time already?" I asked, trying to gauge how bad his mood was.

"Yep. If I push it any longer, Eric might eat one of us."

"I want pasta!" Eric called. "With sauce! And garlic bread!"

"I suppose the man has spoken," Cain replied. "If you'd still be willing to share."

"Do you think I'd change my mind that quickly? I'll share. As long as I get a plate."

He nodded, but his eyes lingered on me. "I thought you'd be more . . . mad."

"I thought *you'd* be more mad."

"About what?"

"Um, the farmers market? Me making you carry my bags while I shopped? How bad is your memory?"

"Oh, that." He shrugged. "Whatever."

"I'm sorry, what? You're just letting it go?"

"There's nothing to let go of. I didn't have that bad of a time."

"You didn't?"

"You did most of the talking anyway."

I crossed my arms. "Guess I need to come up with better punishments."

"I suppose you'd need more after what Kerry told you."

"I was talking about when you inevitably piss me off. What are *you* talking about?"

"What Kerry said after you left. You have to have feelings on it."

"She just told me to come to the diner more so we could chat. Was there something else she could say?"

The relief was evident on his face. His shoulders lowered, and he let out a breath.

"No, it's nothing."

"Try again. I didn't see you this worked up when I fell off the roof. Explain."

"Okay, *fine*. I don't have a great reputation around here."

"Oh, really? Is it your sparkling personality?"

"Yes, honestly." His voice was short, but then he looked away. "And . . . other things I did a long time ago."

I nodded. "I see."

"It was—"

I held up a hand. I could relate to your past making the

present hard. I still lay awake at night and thought about how I had let Trevor walk all over me. I was terrified that if Cain knew it, he would demand that I act like that here too.

"You don't have to tell me that part. You look like you might throw up just thinking about it."

He scrubbed his hand over his face. "You're gonna hear about it eventually. And I know it'll change things."

"It can't be worse than when you let Hennifer attack me."

"Yeah, it can be," he muttered as he started working on lunch. I watched him for far too long, seeing how tight his shoulders were and how every inch of his body screamed his tension.

But then I started to notice other things. The way his hair curled onto his neck. The way his ass looked in tight work jeans. I turned away before he could call me out on it.

A few minutes later, he summoned me to the dining-room table where food was sitting and waiting.

"So . . . what are you buttering me up for?" I asked.

"How did you know I was buttering you up?"

"You're being oddly nice." I took a bite of bread, but narrowed my eyes at him. "So, spill."

"I'll say this before I call Eric to the table." He sighed. "I need help."

I slowed my chewing. That was the last thing I'd expected, but I could tell he was miserable asking for it. Instead of letting my shock show on my face, I took pity.

"What do you need?"

He blinked as if that wasn't a response he'd expected. "The lawyer said I need character references from everyone I know saying that Eric is happy here."

Slowly, I nodded. "So you need me to write one."

"No—I mean, yes. But it's more than that. I need as many as I can get. Even if you and Jackie do it, I'd need more. From . . . the town."

"Is that why you were at the farmers market today?"

"Yes. Jackie thought it would help. But it was basically hopeless. Until you showed up."

"Me? What did I do?"

"Honestly? I don't know. But Jackie said I was more open with you there."

"But I was trying to annoy you."

He shrugged. "And it worked. In a lot of ways, actually."

I bit my lip. He and I might not get along, but if I could help, then I should. Eric was a good kid, and Cain was good with him.

Plus, Waldren seemed like a complete ass.

If I could prevent someone from being in the clutches of a man like Trevor, then I would.

I opened my mouth to say just that, but he said something else first.

"And I'd make sure this was worth your time."

"Worth my time?" My mind could go many places, but none of them made any sense.

"You want the strawberries back, right? Do this, and they'll be back by spring."

My jaw dropped. I could plant them? And he wouldn't complain?

"*Yes*," I said. "I was gonna help anyway, but now I'm really gonna help. Prepare to have the best social wingwoman of your *life*."

"Right," he said with a wince. "Because that'll be fun."

He gave me a nod and then called for Eric. I had more questions, like when we would start with social stuff and when I could start planting berries, but then Eric ran down the stairs and went straight for bread, and I knew that would have to wait.

"We should go out for brunch tomorrow," Cain told Eric. "Mollie, do you wanna come?"

I was shocked I'd even been addressed, but then I realized what it was for. Wingwoman time.

"Yes, of course. It'll be fun."

"Yeah, let's call it that."

The town square was busy on the weekend. I had come early to see Jade and get more candles. Cain and I were set to meet at ten, after he got all his work done at the farm.

Despite not having coffee, I was in a decent mood. Jade had watched the first episode of Wren's new show without me even asking her to, and we got to talk about it while I shopped. I still missed Wren a lot, but I was glad I'd found someone else in the meantime.

I had a decent spot in front of the library, so I walked over to the diner when I saw Cain's truck pull in. He eyed the bag in my hand.

"You got more?"

"Haven't you ever heard of supporting local?"

"Of course I have, but we have more than we can burn at this point."

We. I'd never been referred to as a part of a pair before, not even when I had been engaged. It sent a thrill up my spine. One that should *not* have been there.

"I'm getting pancakes!" Eric announced the second he was freed from his child seat.

"Hey, wait—" Cain tried to say, but he was next to me before the sentence was finished.

"Do you like pancakes or waffles?"

"I like both," I said. "But I'm getting French toast."

"That's what Cain gets!" Eric said.

"Great," he muttered. "People will talk about that."

"Why would they talk about what we're eating?"

"They'll notice the similarities. And that we live together. And we're a man and a woman."

"What if I'm gay?" I asked. "What if *you're* gay?"

"My high school history proves otherwise for me."

"The jury is still out on me."

He raised an eyebrow. "So you're . . ."

"Not really. I like men. A lot. But they don't know that."

"Give 'em a week. They'll figure it out, and then they'll want us to end up together."

"And then you'll kiss?" Eric asked. "Yuck."

I may not have had Eric's distaste for the idea, but I could pretend. "Don't worry. That's not happening. I'm banned from more relationships at the moment. Unless it's a relationship with plants."

"Don't remind me," he muttered as we walked to the door. He opened it and Eric darted through. Then he turned to me expectantly.

"What're you doing?"

"Do you really expect me to let the door slam in your face?"

"Well, if you're worried about how we *look*—"

"You're making more of a scene. Get in the diner, princess." His voice was near a growl.

I didn't like what that did to me.

I huffed and walked inside.

And everyone was looking at us.

"I told you so," he said close to my ear.

"Shut up," I hissed. "Don't you know it's rude to gloat?"

"I never said I was polite."

"Cain. Mollie." Tammy walked over to us. "What a surprise."

I laughed as I stepped away from Cain. "Hey, Tammy. Can we all get a table?"

"I didn't know you all were at a table-sharing level."

"There's only one in the farmhouse," I replied. "And to be clear, I'm on a table-sharing level with Eric. Not this one."

"Really?" Cain asked in a flat voice.

"She stole your kid," Tammy said. "I bet you're loving this."

"Yes. Love. *That's* the word I'm thinking of."

"Follow me," she said, still eyeing us like we were a TV show. "I'll get you the booth by the window."

"Thanks," I said when she put the menus down for us. I widened my eyes at Cain, trying to telepathically tell him to be polite.

"Yes, *thanks*," he repeated. When Tammy looked between us one more time and finally walked away, he spoke again. "Do you really think I don't say thank you to people?"

"You never leave the house. How am I supposed to know how you act in public?"

Cain moved to sit next to Eric, but the kid held out his hand. "I wanna sit next to Mollie!"

"*What?*" Cain asked.

"She's my friend. I get to sit next to you every day."

Cain gave me a death glare as he went to the other side. "Look at it this way. You get to look at him and make sure he eats everything on his plate."

Eric looked up. "Even the bacon?"

"Every. Bite."

Eric sighed. "I like you a little less now, Mollie. But I still like you."

"What are you all drinking?" Tammy reappeared. "And no, I can't add anything to your coffee to take the edge off. No matter how annoyed you are, Cain."

I stifled a laugh, but he looked genuinely insulted. I kicked his boot and shook my head.

"Just water for me," is all he said.

"I'll do coffee."

"Juice!" Eric yelled.

Tammy laughed in response. "You'll have to be a bit more specific, kid."

"Orange!" Cain and I looked at him with raised eyebrows. "Please," he eventually added.

"Be right up." Tammy's smile was bigger than usual, and I knew this was prime small-town talk.

And judging by the look on Cain's face, he knew it too.

"I don't drink, by the way. In case you had questions."

"I didn't. You can do what you want."

"It's not gonna be the first time you hear something like that about me, trust me."

"A lot of the parents think Cain is really quiet," Eric added. "I just say they don't know him. He talks a lot with me."

"You're the exception." Cain's voice was filled with a sadness that I couldn't explain. What exactly had happened in his past that was so bad? No one had said anything to me, and I wasn't sure I wanted them to.

He immediately returned to his quiet mode. I had been sure he hated me, but he still spoke to me more than he did when he was out in public. I eyed his tense jaw and rigid posture.

He hated being in town.

I opened my mouth to offer him an out, or to go take a break in the car, but then someone materialized at the table.

Next to me, Eric perked up. "Tommy!"

"Hey!" The other kid seemed just as excited.

Eric climbed over me to get out of the booth and went to talk to his friend.

"Cain!" Kerry said. "And Mollie. I get to see you two twice in a row!"

If it were possible, Cain looked even more tense. "Kerry. Hi."

"It's nice to see you again."

"I hate that we didn't get to chat much yesterday. I guess we're all getting a second chance."

"We are," I said with a smile. "And I can ask what your favorite dish is here. I'm not sure what to get."

"But—" Eric piped up.

"I'm not sure what to get," I repeated. Cain caught on to my meaning and shook his head at Eric.

"Oh, well let me tell you, the waffles are *so* good. I like them with extra whipped cream and maple syrup."

I was still getting French toast, but she was looking only at me and not the lump of anxiety across the table. "That sounds *so* good."

"This place is really a treat. Just like the rest of the town is. You liked the market yesterday, right?"

"Loved it, though I probably bought too much."

"Not after what happened yesterday," Cain said. I turned to him, and he looked as surprised as I was that he'd spoken at all.

"Oh? What happened yesterday?" Kerry asked.

"Eric gobbled up an entire loaf of garlic bread," I said. "I've never seen him eat so fast."

"So, living at the farm is going well?"

"Everything has been good," I said. "I love owning a house, and Eric is super sweet."

"I know it must have been a shock." Kerry looked at Cain. "You were in such a bad mood when she got here."

"You'll have to excuse the bad mood," I said. "I annoy him every day I'm there."

"Or nearly get yourself killed."

"That happened one time."

"You fell off a roof."

"Saving your chicken!"

Kerry laughed. "This is so interesting to see. Who knew a woman could get you to talk?"

She patted Cain's shoulder, and his jaw tightened again.

I would have said she were simply joking if not for the look on his face.

"You know what, while I have you, I might need a favor," Kerry said to Cain. "Did you hear that the school is looking for volunteers for the Fall Fun Run?"

He blinked. "They are?"

"Yes. You should come. We need all the help we can get."

I could have sworn Cain turned green, but he nodded.

"Can people without kids help?" I asked.

"If we know them. Why? Do you know someone?"

"Me!"

"Really?"

"I'd love to."

"Oh, great! We would love to have you both."

I winked at Cain, but his lips pursed as he looked pointedly at Kerry, who was watching the whole interaction.

"I think Tammy's coming with your drinks," Kerry said. "I won't keep you. Tommy, let's go to our table."

Tommy said goodbye to Eric and walked off.

"The whole Facebook group is gonna hear about this," Cain muttered.

"You were so nice!" Eric said. "I've never seen you say so many words."

Cain's eyes dragged over to me, and I tried to give him a reassuring smile. I could tell he wasn't thrilled to have opened up at all, but I also could see why Jackie thought I was the best option.

Even if he only spoke to argue with me, it was more than he'd ever done.

And hopefully, it would be enough.

CAIN

Strawberry Springs Neighborhood Watch
Kerry Winsor
Just saw a delivery truck of some sort. Who got something fun?

Comments:
Tammy Jane: Good Lord, Kerry. What do you do all day?
Kerry Winsor: Find all the info I can. It's a tough job, but someone has to do it. God forbid a woman has hobbies!
Marjorie Brown: I ordered a giant box of dildos.
Henrietta Brown: I took her phone. Can the admins delete that?

Two DAYS LATER, Mollie was calling, "They're here!" as she ran toward the door.

"What's here?"

"The roots!" she said, stepping out onto the porch.

I followed her, and true to her word, she had ordered a *ton*. Way more than a field's worth.

Shit. I should have told her I would order them so I could get an amount I could actually fucking handle.

"Mollie, what did you do?" I asked.

"I ordered berries."

"I don't have the capacity to plant all of these."

"What do you mean *you* don't have the capacity?" she asked. I glared, about to remind her that I didn't sit on my ass all day, but then she added, "I'm the one planting them."

"I'm sorry, what?"

"The deal was that I could plant the berries if I helped you."

"The deal was that *I* would do it." I shook my head. Why would she agree to help me and then plant the fields herself? She had a full-time job that kept her tied to her computer, and hadn't been here since she was a kid. "Do you even know how?"

"Um, mostly? I remember what Bennie did and how he took care of them. As far as *how* he got the fields ready from scratch? That I don't know."

"They weren't entirely from scratch. He used similar ones every year."

"Right," she said. "So I'll need a tiller at the very least. The rental will be astronomical, though."

"Hang on. I'm not past the fact that you agreed to help me when you thought you would be planting the fields. That's doubling the work on you."

She raised an eyebrow. "As opposed to doubling it on *you*?"

"Well, I'm getting the benefit."

"Yeah, by doing the thing *I* want to do. I'm not just here to sit in the house all day and watch you have all of the fun."

"Is playing in dirt fun for you?"

"It was when I was a kid." She shrugged. "And I have a feeling it would be now."

She was at least in workout clothes today, but they were

ones meant for a gym, not fields. I still saw her as the city girl. The one who was out of place here.

But the more I talked to her, the more I realized that she wasn't what she looked like.

"You have a tiller," I said.

"Don't tell me you're about to say you can be it."

"No, there's an actual tiller in the big barn." I pointed behind me.

"There's no way you still have Papa Bennie's farm equipment after all these years."

"And that's where you're wrong," I said. "Part of my contract was to keep them in shape in case . . ."

In case the farm started doing strawberries again. I wondered if this was the ending Bennie had always wanted. He'd always spoken so highly of Mollie, but I'd thought it had been a memory of a childhood version of her.

"Thank *fuck*," she said. "Those rentals were going to be so expensive that I was considering doing it by hand."

"It's impossible for you to plant a big enough field by hand in time, especially considering the number of roots you got. Come on, let's get the tractor out. We can attach the tiller to it."

We walked to the large red barn. It had become a victim of the elements as most barns did, but the painted structure was in decent shape.

"So, what all is in here?" she asked.

"I stored all of the farming stuff. The tractor, irrigation lines, and the machinery Bennie used. And the snakes."

"And *what*? Snakes? Why would you put snakes in here?"

"I didn't put them anywhere. They show up. Especially as it gets colder."

I heard her stop.

"I don't do snakes."

I turned. "Finally found the one thing you can't deal with?"

"They're unnatural," I said. "They slither and have weird tongues."

"They're not that much different than worms."

"Worms aren't venomous!"

"Most of the snakes in here aren't."

"Sure, until a damn cottonmouth is hiding. I did a research project on them in school. They're killers!"

I rolled my eyes and opened the doors. "Princess, I've been here a decade and a half, and I've never seen one."

"There's a first time for everything."

"Are you too scared to go in here?"

"I-I'm not too scared."

"Seems like you are."

"Now that sounds like a challenge."

I shrugged. "Could be."

She narrowed her eyes. "You *know* I can't back down when you challenge me."

"There's a first time for everything."

"I hate you," she said, but she stomped ahead of me and into the darkness of the barn.

Well. She won that round.

Luckily for both of us, the coast seemed clear.

"You have keys, right?" she asked as she got close to the massive green tractor.

"I keep them all on me," I replied, tossing them to her. "I'll get the tiller."

I dragged it out of the back and hooked it up. "Now to see if this works."

"Hang on," she said. "I wanna go through some of this. I had no idea there was so much."

"We can do that later."

"But what if the lines work? That'll save so much money." She walked to where they were sitting on a shelf and reached for them.

But one looked very off.

I reached out to grab her. "You shouldn't—"

It moved before she could touch it, and it fell to the floor.

"Snake!" she screamed. She jumped back and darted away, her feet barely touching the ground. I had no idea where she was going until she was behind me, her tight hands on my shoulders.

"Mollie, calm down!"

"No! It's a fucking—I almost touched it!" She urged me forward. "Do something."

"What am I supposed to do about it?"

"Be a man! Go to war!"

"With a snake?"

"Yes! Isn't that what you're good for?"

I turned to her, but she shoved me toward it with more force than I knew she possessed. Rolling my eyes, I inspected it, making sure it wasn't actually venomous. "It's a barn snake, princess. Totally harmless."

"Tell that to the heart attack it just gave me," she said. I gently coaxed it out of the barn while she went back outside.

"Am I just glorified snake removal to you?" I asked her.

"Today? Yes." She heaved out a breath and leaned on her knees. "Whew! That was scary."

"You've fallen off a roof."

"I'd take a broken ankle over dying of snake venom."

"It was a *barn* snake."

"Potato, po-tah-to." She waved me off, and I only had a second to wonder where the hell her logic had gone before she was climbing the tractor.

"All right. Time to make a fool of myself."

"Do you know how it works?"

"Nope. But I'll figure it out."

"Let me—" I reached to show her how to use it, but she stopped me.

"Don't you have something else to do?"

"Not till eleven."

"You're the one who said you *wanted* me to figure things out." She leaned forward. "Are you going back on that now?"

"I'm making sure you don't destroy the barn trying to get out of here."

"Hey, I'm an excellent driver. And *you're* hovering. It's starting to look like you want to spend time with me."

"Wrong," I said.

That was a lie. This was more fun than I had expected, even though I had no idea what went through her head at any given time.

"Sure," she said, putting it into gear. "You tell yourself that."

The tractor didn't move, mostly because she was hitting all the wrong buttons. She tried more, but to no avail.

Yep. This was going exactly how I'd expected.

"Need help?" I called.

"Fuck off!" she yelled back. "But yes."

I climbed up, hand on the back of her seat to keep my balance. She was a quick learner. I only had to tell her what everything was once before she understood. I hopped down, letting her take over.

Mollie wasted no time going to work on the fields. She must have been planning this, because she immediately got one field dug up and went to work on the next.

I watched her for way too long, marveling at how much she looked like Bennie as she worked. Then I pushed it away, knowing I needed to get to feeding all the animals for the day.

When I got back, the fields she'd made didn't look too bad. Sure, some of the edges were wavy, but they were in the spots Bennie used to grow things.

I was almost impressed.

Especially when I found her in the barn again.

"Okay, listen. I'm just gonna grab them from around you. Be very chill, Mister Not-Venomous Snake."

She slowly got the lines out, this time not running when the snakes moved.

"I thought you were scared of them."

"Terrified, but I'm being brave." She showed me the lines with a smile on her face. "Think they still work?"

"If you're lucky."

"Well, the welcome sign does say the magic is alive."

"That's just a tourist slogan."

She laughed. "What tourists?"

"Seriously, though. Nice work on the fields."

She gasped and turned to me. "A compliment? From *Cain*?"

"I'm just *saying* that you remembered a lot."

"I also looked up a lot of stuff." She rubbed the back of her neck. "Especially when I should have been working."

"For a city girl who works in an office, you don't seem to like it very much."

"Don't tell my dad that," she replied before walking up to the hose lines. "Now, did Papa Bennie hook these up here or to the main water line?"

"Main water line," I replied. "But you can test them here."

She nodded and hooked it up.

"Fair warning, you should start sl—"

She cranked the water on high and it sprayed *everywhere*.

"Fuck!" She gasped, fighting for the spigot. By the time the water was off, both of us were soaked.

"Slow drip, Mollie. You need a slow drip."

"What a rookie move," she muttered as she stood.

Her shirt stuck to her torso.

Her *white* shirt.

She wasn't wearing a bra, and I could see the outline of her—

I stopped myself. *Don't think about it. Don't think about it.*

"Oh my God," she yelled. "I need to . . . I've got to . . . bye!"

Mollie ran inside, slamming the door behind her.

I adjusted my jeans.

What the hell was this woman doing to me?

"What are the chances we can pretend that never happened?" Mollie asked as she came back out.

"High," I muttered. "But your lemon leggings aren't gonna help."

"These are Athleta."

"Fine. Your *athletic* leggings aren't gonna help."

She huffed. "Do you *have* to say it wrong?"

"There's no point in me remembering them."

"At least you're being annoying. It's distracting me from what happened."

"And you brought it up again."

"It's not every day I unwillingly enter a wet T-shirt contest with someone who looks like you."

"Looks like me?"

"You're also in a T-shirt. And you're surprisingly ripped."

This wasn't a good topic. In fact, it was a terrible one.

"I work on a farm."

"It's doing something for you. You would have won if the snakes weren't the only judge."

"That's definitely not true. Especially considering you were working in a field without a bra."

She sighed. "I was excited! Can you blame me?"

"Yes. It's probably not the safest."

"Oh, please. People used to work in fields in only overalls."

I considered it. Then I considered *her* in overalls and shook the thought from my head before my dick could catch on.

"Enough talk about . . . this." There were no other words for it. "Back to farming."

"You're no fun," she said, but motioned for me to continue.

"You got lucky." I looked at the irrigation lines, effectively changing the conversation. "It wasn't all that bad. I think they could still work. Bennie replaced them not long before he died."

"I'll take any luck I can get. Now, once I finish the fields, I can get the membrane and plant them all."

"How many fields are you planning?"

"Three."

"That is . . . a lot of work for one person who has another job."

I knew how this was going to end. She was going to get bored of playing farmer, and I would have to pick up the slack.

"I'll get it done."

"Will you?"

"Go get Eric from school," she said with a roll of her eyes. "And you'll see what I'm capable of by the time you're back."

"Or you'll see that you need help."

"One of us is wrong, and for once it should be you!" she called as I walked away.

I laughed. With her in a T-shirt and athletic leggings that

were thinner than anything I owned, I doubted she would get very far.

I quickly saw who was right. Mollie didn't stop on the fields, even when she ripped her nice clothes and came back coated in mud. While she did sleep in an hour later each day, she showed no signs of slowing down, even as she got the three fields ready for planting.

I was impressed, even if I knew she'd never let me live it down if I told her that.

The day of the school event snuck up on me. I was busy being tired by simply watching Mollie balance work on her laptop and all the things she was doing in the fields, but when the day came, Jackie reminded me with a simple text.

JACKIE

If you miss this, I think Kerry will come after you.

Wasn't planning on it. I'll be there.

Bring your best smile!

Ugh.

I wasn't sure if Mollie was still planning on going, but I didn't know if I could handle other people's kids *and* the parents in one day.

I found her at the dining-room table, eyebrows pinched over her laptop. Usually she worked at night, only taking meetings during the day.

"You busy?"

"Yes, but I can make time." She looked up at me. "If you're about to tell me I planted the first field wrong, I'll kick your ass."

"That race is today," I said.

She looked up, blinking slowly. "Race?"

"At Eric's school."

"Oh." She rubbed her eyes. "That's right. I said I would go to that."

"You sure you can handle it? You've been working hard."

"Yeah, I can," she said, standing. "And before you ask, I'm fine."

"You sure seem it," I said sarcastically. She rolled her eyes and went to her room. When she came out, she was wearing one of the few pairs of clean pants she had.

Her laptop dinged as we walked to the door, and she turned back to it, biting her lip.

"You can stay here if you want."

"And go back on our deal? No thanks. I can do it. Work will just have to wait."

"Is it something that can wait?"

She rolled her eyes again. "It's office stuff, as usual. It absolutely can."

Still, I saw the uncertainty in her gaze as we walked out the door. I was tempted to make her stay, but I doubted she would do that either.

Mollie was quiet on the drive. I liked the quiet, but she didn't. Usually, she was talking through every moment of silence.

When we pulled into the school parking lot, she hadn't said a word to me. I looked over to check on her, only to find that she was asleep against the window of the truck.

"Mollie?" I said. "Dammit, I knew you were working yourself too hard."

She didn't answer.

"Hey, come on. Wake up so I can tell you how dumb you're being."

I reached out to jostle her. The best place to touch her would have been a shoulder or an arm.

I let my palm rest on her cheek like a fucking idiot.

She jolted awake, sucking in a breath of air. I jerked back, not wanting to be caught acting like a creep.

"Shit, sorry." Her voice was thick as she stretched. "I'm ready to go."

"You're way too tired for this."

"I'm fine."

"*Mollie.*"

She didn't answer and went to open the door. I locked them so she couldn't leave.

"What the—Cain!"

"You need rest."

"I can get it when we're done here."

"I'm taking you back home."

"Absolutely not!"

"You can't stop me."

I shouldn't have said that, because she took it as a challenge. She ripped the keys out of the ignition. I tried to grab them from her, but she was way too fast.

She unbuckled her seat belt and tried to use the unlock button on her door, but it was busted. Never had I been more glad that I'd never fixed it. But then I quickly regretted everything when she reached over me to get to my unlock button. I tried to fight her off, which resulted in her tumbling into my lap and her ass hitting the horn on the truck.

She jerked forward, but there was nowhere for her to go but closer to me.

"What the *fuck*?" I hissed.

"You shouldn't have challenged me."

"So this is what you do?"

She hit the button and got off my lap, which immediately felt cold without her heat. I closed my eyes, trying to picture *anything* other than what had just happened.

I opened the door, only to see Nicole glaring at me with her arms crossed.

"Really? At the *school*?"

I gaped. "That wasn't . . . We weren't—"

"Sorry!" Mollie apologized, running over to Nicole. "That was just a little dispute over unlocking the door. One that Cain *lost*." She held her hand out. "I'm Mollie."

Nicole's glare was disarmed by Mollie stepping between us. For someone so tired, she still brightened wherever she went.

"Nicole. And what do you mean by dispute?"

"Oh, it was nothing. I'm tired. He wanted to take me back to the house to force me to get some rest. But I wanna be here, and he needs to be as well. How else will he see Eric's first race?"

"Still." She crossed her arms. "Watch how others perceive you."

"I didn't expect the people here to be watching."

"Someone is *always* watching."

Her gaze cut between us before she walked off to get us signed in.

"Did she mean for that to sound creepy?"

"Nicole's just like that." I shook my head. "Let's get this over with."

Kids were everywhere, wearing shirts with the school name on them. I spotted Eric talking with Tommy.

When he saw me, he jumped up and down and waved. I was taken aback by how excited he was to see me.

"You two will be counting laps," Nicole said as she handed Mollie a clipboard. "And no, you can't count your own kid's—"

"He's not my kid."

I always clarified that with people. I was his guardian, not his parent. And now I didn't know how much longer I would even be that.

Nicole didn't like that I'd interrupted her, and shoved another clipboard into my hands.

I looked at Mollie. "What did I do?"

"Maybe she didn't like you saying Eric isn't your kid."

"He's not."

"But you watch him. You care about him."

"Yes, I do. But he's not *my* kid."

"I think it's less about the fact that you're not his dad and more about how it sounds. I know this isn't true, but she might have taken that as you're saying he's not your kid because you don't want him to be."

"I would *never—*"

"Does she know that?"

"Dammit." I scrubbed my face. "People and their assumptions."

"You had them about me."

Fuck. "It's unfair that you're this tired and still right."

"I'm a multitasker," she said with a wink.

I didn't get a chance to say anything else to her because the race was about to begin. We all lined up and watched as kids ran laps around the field, and I counted each of the ones I was responsible for while also cheering on Eric. Across the field, Mollie did the same, but she was much more exuberant.

"You're running at the speed of light, Eric! You got this!" she yelled. It only egged him on, and though I wasn't counting his directly, I saw him lap most of the kids.

"You would be a nightmare at any sports event," I said after the race had ended.

"You can say it how it is." She turned to me. "I'm a nightmare everywhere."

The sun made her hair more golden, and her eyes were bright, despite how exhausted she must have been.

She wasn't a nightmare. She was a fucking dream.

"Let's go with that," I said.

She smiled at me, but then it faded. Her hand reached for my arm. "We have a problem."

I turned to see someone else walking up to the field. Someone I didn't want to see.

I hadn't recently considered the man who was suing me for custody of Eric, mostly because I was busy thinking about how I was going to stop him. I didn't think I would see him again until the court proceedings had started.

Obviously, I was wrong.

We both headed in his direction at the same time.

"What are you doing here?"

"I'm here to see my kid," he said coolly. "My girl is here too."

He gestured to a woman who couldn't have been any older than twenty-four. She was looking around eagerly, as if she had no idea what an imposition this was.

"How did you even know this was a thing?" Mollie asked.

"I'm his *dad*," Waldren said. "Of course I know everything going on with my son."

"And here I thought Waldren was a playboy." The girl-friend looked up at him adoringly. "Apparently he raised a son by himself?"

He raised?

Absolutely not.

"You don't even know him," I snapped. "What the hell is wrong with you?"

"And it's authorized visitors only," Mollie hissed.

People were glancing at us, and if Waldren walked away now, then it was possible that no one would know what was going on.

The last thing I needed was the whole town figuring it out. Their opinions of it would only make this worse.

"He's my son."

"The one you're suing over. I raised him. And he's never even met you."

"Wh-what?" the woman asked, eyes wide.

"Word of advice, woman to woman," Mollie started. "Find a new man."

"But he said—"

"He lied."

The woman's cheeks went red.

"That's only what they want you to think," Waldren said smoothly. "He's just an uncle who has a big head."

"You know what? Yeah," the woman said. "You do seem the jealous type."

"This will all be fixed once he's in the private school I've chosen," he told her. "And he's no longer out in the middle of nowhere."

"That's right," she said as she crossed her arms. "You did say you're moving."

"To Nashville," Waldren added. "Where he can get the education he deserves."

"You're not even from here," I hissed. "Do you really think you can lie and say you raised him?"

Waldren's eyes narrowed for a second as I poked a hole in his story, but then he wrapped an arm around his girlfriend. "Come on, babe. I'll let you meet Eric under much better circumstances."

They walked off, but I stared until they got into the car.

"How dumb is that woman?" I asked. "His story doesn't match up."

"Sometimes we believe what we want to," Mollie said quietly.

I turned to her. "We?"

"Ah, I mean her. Sorry. Tired brain." She shook her head and looked back at the field. "We should go say hi to Kerry. She's staring, and I bet she has questions."

I blinked past my curiosity and nodded. "We're not telling her who that was, right?"

"Absolutely not. We can make up some excuse."

"Tell her he was just lost, because that's exactly what he is."

MOLLIE

Strawberry Springs Neighborhood Watch
Kerry Winsor
Weird person at the school? Talking to Cain? What the heck happened today?

Comments:
Jackie Anne: That's between them.
Kerry Winsor: We all know you're weirdly protective of Cain, but this is NEWS.
Tammy Jane: I know nothing. So I don't know how much news there really is.
Kerry Winsor: Ugh. I knew I should have tried to talk to him and not Mollie.

———

WHEN WE WERE on the way back to the farmhouse, I started getting texts. For a while, I tried to ignore them, but when I saw it was my dad, I knew I was in trouble.

"You better go up to your room and sleep," Cain said as we pulled into the driveway.

"I'm all—"

He glared. "Don't even try."

The arms of exhaustion were still trying to pull me into sleep, but my anxiety over Dad being mad at me was winning.

"I have other things to do."

"Are you serious?"

I showed him my phone. "Work calls."

"This is your dad."

"Yep. And my boss. I'll rest later."

That wasn't the answer Cain wanted, but I darted out of the truck before he could lock me in and force me to sleep. I grabbed my laptop and went up to my room so Cain wouldn't witness my dad yelling at me.

Then I finally answered my phone.

"I knew I shouldn't have let you work remotely," he started before I could even say hello. "You're not focused, and I can never reach you!"

I winced and covered my cheeks. It took a lot to get Dad this angry.

"I'm sorry," I said. "I had something come up."

"And so have we. Multiple times, Mollie. You need to be focused on your job. Not prancing around in fields."

The embarrassment morphed into annoyance. I wasn't *prancing*. I was working my ass off to make something. And even though it wasn't perfect, I was proud of how it was coming along. Sure, some nights I fell into bed and passed out immediately, but it was more than what I'd had in Nashville.

But I did owe my dad eight hours a day too. I should have been reachable.

"I know," I said. "I'll do better."

I wasn't sure how. I was already working on something

every single hour I was awake. Sometimes, I had to take my dinner to my bedroom to catch up on work emails. Cain tried to argue with me that I was breaking the number one house rule, but I was too exhausted to even pretend like I cared. All I could do was survive until the berries were planted. In the darker months, I'd have less to do, but I wasn't sure if Dad was going to give me the leeway to make it that far.

"Trevor thinks I should fire you. He said this would happen when you went out there. If it were anyone else, they'd be gone."

I was sure Trevor wanted Dad to fire me for other reasons too, though I knew my work hadn't been top-notch.

"Dad, I'm trying. I promise."

"Are you?"

"Yes," I said. "You see how late I'm online."

"But you should be here during the *day*. Not when no one else is working."

"I'll try."

"You've been saying that this whole time. I need to see you *actually* be better. Or . . ." He trailed off.

"Okay," I said. "I'll be better."

He hung up not too long after, and I sighed. I had rows of strawberries to get done, and I'd planned on doing those in the morning, but with Dad's threat, I needed to be online at that time.

I thought about asking Cain for help, but he had enough on his plate as it was.

Shaking my head, I got to work, firing off emails and making sure everything was organized for the day.

I set up a tentative schedule and planned on bringing my laptop outside so I could hear it when I was contacted. It wasn't much, but it would have to do.

The sun was low in the sky by the time I had everything done with Dad's work.

But mine was just beginning.

Standing, I stretched and yawned, trying to find energy that wasn't there. I ignored the heaviness in my eyes and went outside.

I worked until long after the sun had sunk below the horizon. I didn't eat dinner, even though I saw Cain and Eric making it.

But I got another row done.

If the sun were out, I would have surveyed my work. I still had more to go, but at least I was getting somewhere.

I stood, ignoring the way I felt unsteady on my own feet, and went inside. My entire body ached, and I'd pay for this tomorrow.

"Are you done ignoring me when I tell you you're pushing yourself too hard?" Cain asked. He was finishing up dishes, the dinner already put away. My stomach panged, and I knew I needed to eat as soon as possible.

"Are you so mad that you won't share dinner?"

"And continue your torture? You're doing enough of that yourself."

He opened the microwave, which revealed a plate of chicken and vegetables. "This is for you."

"I don't care if you let Hennifer attack me. You're actually the best."

"Yeah, yeah."

"Thank you," I said.

Cain nodded and walked off. I had no idea what plans he had for the evening, but I had a feeling they didn't involve me. I wasn't sure why I was disappointed. Was I hoping for more of our back-and-forth?

I didn't look great anyway. I'd been in the dirt for hours, and

I knew I didn't smell good. I washed my hands thoroughly and grabbed my food.

Sitting at the dining-room table, I scarfed everything down faster than I ever had before. After that, I drank four glasses of water. My head pounded a little less, though it did nothing for my sore muscles.

Moments later, Cain walked in.

"You done?"

"Yes. I'll get out of your hair now."

"No, you're gonna take a bath."

My cheeks heated. "Yeah, that was the plan. It may not seem like it, but I *do* know how to take care of myself."

He rolled his eyes and gestured for me to follow him. I did, and my jaw dropped when I walked into the bathroom and found a bath had already been run for me.

"What is this?"

"Epsom salt, mainly. It'll help you not feel like garbage tomorrow. Rinse off in the shower first, then get in the tub."

"This is for me?"

"I'm not using Jade's nice stuff on Eric, that's for sure. He still tries to drink bathwater because he thinks it's funny. Besides, he hates the sunset scent."

I took in a deep breath. The air smelled fresh and clean. "That's what this is?"

"Yep. Enjoy."

"Why did you do this?"

He paused at the doorway before turning slowly. "You're doing too much. You know that, right?"

"But if I don't, then you would be in my boat."

He crossed his arms but nodded. "I know. And I can't fault you for putting in the work. But I *can* fault you for not being able to walk tomorrow."

"Because then you'd have to work on the fields?"

"Because you'd be miserable." His eyes were firm on mine. "Enjoy your bath, Mollie."

My jaw dropped as Cain left without another word. I was torn between being insulted and wanting to let him do whatever he wanted to do to take care of me.

The man that I'd planned on marrying had never done any of this. And I wasn't sure if I'd been with a complete dick, or if Cain was much more kind than any man I'd known.

Maybe both were true.

The bath didn't solve all my problems, but it fixed a lot of them. I was somewhat sore, but I felt alive after scrubbing all the dirt off myself in the standing shower and then sinking into hot water.

Life didn't feel like as big of a mess when I finally went to my room. Or at least *I* wasn't as big of a mess.

And I definitely owed Cain a thank you.

I flopped onto the bed, listening to nothing but silence until my phone rang. I groaned and grabbed it, but any frustration I felt vanished when I saw who it was.

"Wren!" I exclaimed. "Oh my God, I've missed you."

"Hey! I *finally* have a moment alone." She sounded good. Happy. "Figured we needed to catch up."

"We do. I've reached a new level of busy."

"Busy? Didn't you move to a small town to *not* be busy?"

"I still work for Dad." I let out a long sigh. "And it's strawberry-planting season. I've never been so tired in my life."

"Can't you take a leave of absence or something? Use PTO?"

"I tried. He said he needed me working, which I'm trying to do. I've definitely overstayed his two-week limit, though."

"Probably because you like it."

"I love it," I replied. "And even though I'm more tired than I've ever been, I'm having fun in the fields. Now I get how you feel when you're tearing up old tile."

"It's a feeling nothing else can compare to," she said. "Any reason you're not doing it full time?"

"I'm keeping doors open," I said, discomfort growing in my stomach. "I could plant all of this and immediately kill them. Which would be humbling."

"I somehow doubt that," she replied. "Do you really see yourself being happy back in Nashville?"

I wasn't sure. For so long, my life had been there. My future had been there. I had thought I'd go to college, get my degree, and work at Dad's company until I retired.

What I was doing now wasn't anything close to that. But it was hard to fully separate myself from what I'd planned on for so long, especially when Trevor seemed to want me fired.

"No idea," I replied. "I'm taking it one day at a time right now."

"All right, I won't push too much. You've done a lot of growing over the past few weeks. Literally and figuratively."

I huffed out a laugh, but then yawned. "Yeah. It's been *a lot*."

"You sound exhausted," she said. "Which means I'm on borrowed time."

"Tell me about the show. I watched the first episode with Cain."

"Wait, you're watching TV with him?"

"More like I was watching TV alone and he happened to walk in. He liked it, though. He apparently lived in Nashville for a bit."

"Interesting."

"What?"

"I don't know. You sound . . . happy . . . when you talk about him. I'm not used to hearing that about a guy you live with."

My cheeks heated. "First of all, it's not like that."

"I didn't say it was."

"And second of all, I'm happy because I'm in a better place. He has nothing to do with it."

"Even though he lives in the same house as you?"

"Well . . ."

"Right," she said. "Come on, you're single. You can do what you want!"

"Wren, he barely tolerates me. I'm not ruining that."

"Then go find someone else. Haven't you had a night to yourself at all?"

"I'll think about it. Once I survive a week of actually focusing on work."

"Try it now."

"Wren, I'm serious. My dad is thinking of firing me."

"He would never."

"He would if he had Trevor in his ear telling him to."

"Oh, of course Trevor's in his ear. He can suck a dick."

I rubbed my face. "Agreed, but I've put off work a lot. And gotten in trouble for it. Dad doesn't let people work from home. Nor does he give this much patience either. I need to lock in."

"You need to take care of yourself too."

"You sound like Cain."

"Do I now? Maybe he's not so bad."

"He's not, but I can take care of myself later."

"No, you need to now." Her voice was firm. "I know I said I won't push, but you have to see what's happening here."

"That I'm doing too much?"

"Yes, but you're also trying to make everyone happy. You always have, which is why you were locked in a job you didn't care about with a man whose only personality trait was how many hours he worked. And now you've finally done something for yourself, but you're still getting pulled in too many directions."

I stared at the ceiling. Leave it to Wren to go right for the kill. "I'm not gonna say you're wrong, but I also just *can't* leave my job like that."

"Why?" she asked.

I squeezed my eyes shut. "I don't know. It makes me so nervous."

"Anything worth doing is hard."

"What if I mess things up here, Wren?"

"I have a feeling you won't."

I had the same feeling, yet the worry nagged at me. "Mom left for a reason."

"You're not your mom. Nor are you your dad, or Trevor. What they love is different than what you love. I'm not saying to quit and leave your dad high and dry, but maybe consider what *you* want from life? And if it's to stay there, then stay there. Work on the farm. Be happy."

I let out a sigh. "I'll think about it when I'm not falling asleep on the phone."

"Fair enough," she said. "I'll let you go so you can get some sleep."

"But I wanna talk to you," I whined.

"We'll text," she promised. "But you should rest too. Text me when you see the next episode."

"Text me when you climb your man like a tree."

"Trust me. I'm working on it."

"How's it going?"

"Slowly but surely. I have one hell of an in right now."

"I hope it happens soon. And you get lots of orgasms."

"You should do the same. I'm sure you could find some hookup out there."

"The only man I talk to on a daily basis is Cain, and I think he would explode if I offered that."

"But would he give you orgasms?"

I closed my eyes, letting myself imagine it. "You know what? I think he would."

CAIN

Strawberry Springs Neighborhood Watch
Hu Gh
Goggle, why is my butt still itchy??

Comments:
Kerry Winsor: It was YOU!
Tammy Jane: This still isn't Google, Hugh.
Hu Gh: GODDAMMIT WHY IS EVERYBODY IN MY BUSINESS??
Jade Clark: **@Henry Connor** lol
Henry Connor: Hugh, stop trying to Google medical advice. I'm right here. Please just come into the clinic.
Marjorie Brown: Now THIS is what Facebook was invented for. **@Henrietta Brown** look at this.

WHEN MOLLIE SLEPT IN LATE, I knew she had to be exhausted. But the weather was cooling faster than she could plant, so she couldn't afford to lose a day.

"Hey, wanna come outside with me?" I asked Eric. "It's nice."

"Yes!" he said. "Are we gonna hang out with Hennifer?"

"Not this morning. Here. Put your jacket on."

Once we bundled up, we walked out into the fields. Mollie had gotten more done than I'd thought.

"What are we doing out here?"

"I'm helping Mollie get this done so she doesn't keel over."

"Can I help?"

"I was hoping you would. I'll dig and you plant."

"Yes!" He pumped his fist, but then stopped. "I thought you didn't like her."

"I—it's not that I don't like her."

"So you do."

I scratched the back of my head. "Kinda, but—"

"I knew it! She's so fun. And nice. Tommy's mom says you need nice."

My heart jumped into my throat. "Tommy's mom talks about me?"

"Only a little. I don't listen too much because I'm getting ready for class, but she tells Ms. Rudder things."

Fuck. I swallowed. "You know that you might hear something that's not true, right?"

"About what?"

"About me."

He frowned. "Why would someone lie about you?"

I knelt to his level. "Back when I was younger, I was different. Some people still see that side of me, even though I've changed."

"I can just tell them they're wrong."

I patted his shoulder. "That's very kind, but I don't know if that's enough."

Eric huffed and crossed his arms. "I don't like it."

"Neither do I, but I'm used to it. It's okay." He didn't answer, and I knew he needed a distraction. "Why don't we help Mollie out? Don't worry about those other people."

"Fine," he said. "But people need to know you're a good person."

"Maybe they will." I doubted it. "All I can do is be me and hope it shows. Now, come on. If we finish this before lunch, I'll make more garlic bread."

What Eric lacked in efficiency, he made up for with enthusiasm. We finished half of a field by the time he got tired. I stopped to make lunch before getting back to it. The chickens and cows were going to be angry by the time I got to them, but they would deal.

It was just after noon when I heard a door above us fly open. Seconds later, Mollie ran down the stairs.

She was in pajamas and a robe. Her wavy hair was particularly unruly, and she had a crease from her pillow etched across her face.

It was more adorable than I could take.

"I messed up." She talked fast, barely stopping to catch her breath. "I should have set an alarm. I should have turned my ringer on. Son of a *bitch*, I missed a whole day because I was too—"

She had to stop when I shoved garlic bread in her mouth.

"Good morning, princess."

She slowly chewed and grabbed the rest of the slice.

"It's not morning, which is the whole problem." She then realized what she was eating. "This is actually delicious."

"I'm making more."

She groaned. "Cain, I don't have *time*!"

"Look out the window," I ordered.

She rolled her eyes. "I know what I did last night. I still have—"

I put my hands on her head and moved her. She tried to fight it for all of two seconds before she saw what we had worked on.

"What the—did I sleep plant?"

"No. Eric and I did it."

Her eyes went wide. "But—"

"He wanted to, and I knew you needed sleep. It's not totally done, but the way I see it, I just have to work a little later with the animals, and you get sleep. It's not a huge deal."

"Of course it's a huge deal. I mean . . . you didn't have to . . . Why did you . . ." She trailed off, looking totally lost.

"Hasn't anyone ever done anything nice for you before?"

She blinked, cheeks going red. "Not as much as you'd think."

I stared at her, wondering what idiots she had been around back in the city, but before I could ask, Eric came running down the stairs.

"Mollie! Mollie! Did you see what we did?"

"I did," she said with a smile. "It looks great."

"And we have garlic bread. This is the best weekend ever!"

He ran to the kitchen to check on the progress of the pasta. I gave Mollie one last look before I went to plate everyone's food.

She was quiet as we ate, and out of the corner of my eye, I saw her sneaking glances at me. I could have called her out on it, but I had no idea how to tell her that helping out wasn't a huge deal.

Obviously, it was to her.

After lunch, she got dressed and went out to the fields to work.

She gave me a smile before running off. I let Eric play rather than help, though he came over to assist with planting when he felt like it. We were able to finish the second field and start on the third by the time the sun had begun to set.

"Okay, I have to stop," I said. "I need to go feed the animals and milk them. They're gonna kill me."

"I'll help," she said, getting up.

"No, I—"

"You spent all day helping me. So I'll do the same."

"Don't you have another job to do?"

"It's the weekend."

I wanted to argue, but she was heading to the hose to rinse her hands before I could stop her.

I grabbed extra treats for both animals before we went back.

The chickens were always first, and Hennifer swarmed me when she saw me.

"Hey, quit!" I called. "I have—"

But she was gone before I could finish the sentence.

"Wow," Mollie said as she threw worms down. "She really is not herself when she's hungry."

"I'm surprised you didn't let that attack go on for longer."

"I'm feeling nice after you helped me. But what I saw was enough too. You're not invincible," she said as she poked my chest.

And I knew I wasn't. Not by a long shot.

The cows grumbled about how late we were, but let me milk them while Mollie threw their favorite tubers on the ground.

"Okay," I said. "Now seriously, I don't need any more help. I've got it from here."

"I could cook dinner."

"No, you—" I checked the time. It *was* about the time I would normally start cooking.

"I make a mean burger."

"Really? You're gonna say that in front of the cows?"

She winced. "Sorry!" she whispered to them. Moosley was the only one who looked up, but merely flicked an ear in response.

"Fine," I replied. "Please start on dinner."

"We make a good team," she said with a smile.

I didn't want to admit it. "We do."

She laughed before running off, and I stared after her. It took a lot for me to get attached, but I was starting to like having her around, even when she drove me up the wall.

But things didn't go well for me when I started to get attached, and though she was a staple to everything now, I didn't know how long it was going to last.

I needed to distance myself and remember that all of this was temporary.

Yet I had no idea where to fucking start.

MOLLIE

Strawberry Springs Neighborhood Watch
Tammy Jane
When are we gonna talk about the elephant in the room?

Comments:
Marjorie Brown: Who, Kerry?
Kerry Winsor: MARJORIE, YOU TAKE THAT BACK!!!
Jade Clark: Shots fired.
Tammy Jane: NO, Mollie is gone.
Kerry Winsor: You're right! It's been a while since she's been spotted. Did Cain run her off?
Jackie Anne: Seriously? That's your first thought?
Kerry Winsor: Well, she DOES live with him!
Tammy Jane: Man, I hope she didn't go back to the city without saying goodbye. I liked her . . .

IT TOOK me another week to get the last field done, even with

Cain helping out when he could. When I wasn't doing that, I was trying to appear present at work.

The time I spent in front of my laptop was more boring than I could say. It was odd how I could work in fields for hours and love it, but answering emails felt impossible.

Once the fields were done and my day job was all that remained, I realized I desperately needed to do something fun before burnout set in.

But what even was *fun*?

I tried googling how to have fun in a small town and only got a ton of country songs that I didn't want to listen to. And though the animals and fields were fun, they were still technically work.

As far as anything else? I'd hit a wall.

Eventually, I knew there was no way I was going to figure this out on my own.

While working, I'd gotten bad about going into town. Trevor was on a warpath, giving me extra assignments to make up for my lack of office presence, and I had been spending most of the time I was awake tied to my computer. He'd also sent more emails about offers for the land, which I deleted every single time.

It was a few weekends later before I had the energy to even get out of the house, and the town square was as busy as usual. People who I was starting to get to know were everywhere, and most of them seemed shocked to see me. I'd said hello to everyone I could before going into Jade's shop.

"Oh my God!" Jade said. "I thought you'd gone back to the city!"

"What? Why would I do that?"

"You've been missing for weeks."

"I wasn't missing. I was working."

"On what? Cain handles the animals at the farm, and anything else doesn't need work now that it's cooling off."

"I also do marketing for my family's company."

"Oh, that sounds . . . fun."

"Trust me, it's not. That plus the farm keeps me busy."

"Are you taking it over?"

"Um, no. But I got some strawberries planted."

Her jaw dropped. "It's reopening?"

"If the berries look good next year. I got an everbearing kind that should produce a medium harvest its first year."

"You sound so professional when you talk like that. I *love* it. And strawberries. Oh! I should make more of the candles for the spring!"

"You should," I said. "But now I'm just working the day job, which is slowly killing any happiness I have."

"You sound like you need to do something fun."

"You took the words right out of my mouth."

"Are you open to suggestions?"

"Please," I said. "What does Strawberry Springs do for fun?"

"That's different depending on who you ask, but me? I go to the bar."

"A bar? Like, to drink?"

"Some do. I go on nights when my friend comes into town and plays. They set up a dance floor. It's so fun."

"I forgot there was a bar."

"Of course you would. You're hanging around Cain Smith all the time. Bell's Brews is the social center of the town. He's gonna avoid it like the plague."

It was unfortunately true. I couldn't see him at a bar.

"When's the next time the band plays?"

"Next week," she said. "They used to come more when they still had Gab—" She stopped herself. "When they had another local with them."

"Another local?"

She shook her head. "He moved away some time ago, saying he'd never come back. Small-town life wasn't for him, apparently."

I raised an eyebrow. There was more of a story there, but judging by the way her shoulders hunched, it was a tough thing for her to talk about.

Everyone here had a story, one that I didn't know. I wanted to know, though. They all knew everything about one another, and I felt left out just by being in their orbit.

"If you ever wanna talk about it, I'm here."

She looked up and sighed. "I forget that some people don't already know. He was my best friend, and the whole town thought we would be more, but . . . obviously not."

"Oh, I'm sorry."

"Don't be. He always talked about it. No one thought he would do it. Now he's happy in California. Made a successful video game too. He's living his dream. Who can be mad about that?"

"Mad might not be the right word. Sad?"

"Yeah. But it gets easier each year he's gone."

"And he'll never come back?"

She huffed out a laugh. "He hasn't even visited. He flies his family out occasionally. And with the way we ended things, he doesn't wanna see me."

"Have you found anyone else?"

"In town? God, no. I've known these people too long. Sometimes, I'll hook up with a stranger from the bar, but they all need a world map to find my clitoris."

I laughed. "That must be the female experience. My ex . . ." Now it was my turn to trail off. I hadn't mentioned Trevor since coming here.

"You have an ex?"

I thought about the five years we'd been together, and I'd

only ever had a real orgasm a few times. How he hadn't tried to get me back *once*, only sent me emails about work.

"I do, but I'll leave it at that. He doesn't deserve any more of my attention."

"Fair enough. So, the bar?"

"I'm definitely gonna be there. It's time for me to have fun."

———

I was tempted to go back to the farmhouse, but I walked around the square for a bit before running into Jackie. She was outside cleaning the glass door to her shop.

"Oh, hi!" she said with a smile. "I haven't heard from you in a while."

"Yeah, sorry."

"I guess Cain made you so mad you couldn't help him anymore?"

"No, not that. We were busy in the strawberry fields."

"*We?*" she asked with a raised eyebrow.

"Yeah, I started, but I couldn't finish it before it got cold." I pulled my sweater tighter around me. "So, he had to help."

"I thought he was gonna do it all."

"No, it's my project. Even if I did almost kill myself doing it."

"I'm glad it's done. But you do look like you could use a haircut."

I looked at my reflection in the window of the shop. My hair had been in a bun ever since I'd started working.

"You know what? I think you're right. Do you have an opening?"

"Yes," she said with a bright smile. "Come on in."

She sat me in a chair and bounced around the salon as if I'd told her I was paying off all her bills, not just letting her cut my hair.

"Maybe we can just cut a few inches off."

Jackie's mouth twisted. "We could. Or . . ." she mused as she grabbed my hair and pulled it back, leaving the length only to my collarbones. "We could do something bold."

I opened my mouth to tell her I didn't look good with short hair. Trevor had always hated it. But the second I thought of his name, I immediately wanted to cut it all off.

And the way Jackie held it told me I could look really good if I tried it.

"You're right. We should do it."

"It'll feel so much lighter," she said. "You don't need all that weight with the work you're doing."

She was right in more ways than one.

"So, what are you doing to celebrate now that you've got everything planted?"

"At first, I slept for an entire day," I replied as she started cutting. "But I just talked to Jade and was thinking about going to the bar."

"Really? There's a music night I think you would like."

"That's when I was planning on going."

"I wish Cain did things like that. Ever since he took Eric in, he's become a homebody. He needs a life."

"I doubt he'd want to go."

"I don't know. Maybe he would if you asked him."

Blinking, I asked, "Do you really think so?"

"It's always hard to predict what he'll do, but I do know that he acts differently around you. And he needs to get to know the people of the town. It's something he's avoided ever since he came here."

"He'll probably say no since the plan is for the town to see him and Eric together."

"Between you and me—" She leaned in close, as if she were about to tell me a secret. "I think the town needs to see him as he is. He's just as good without Eric as he is with him."

"You're right. He is."

"So, I think you should work your magic on him," she said with a wink. "And then let me know how it goes."

I returned to the farmhouse feeling better than when I'd left. I was sporting a fresh haircut, and it felt lighter on my shoulders compared to the long locks that had gone down my back.

When I walked in, Cain was helping Eric with his homework.

Cain did a double take when he saw me. I was sure he wasn't going to mention the shorter hair, but Eric wasn't like that.

"Your hair looks pretty!" he yelled.

"Thank you," I replied. "I needed to do some self-care."

"One time Cain made me a face mask to relax."

I looked at Cain, who was going red in the face. "That's so cute."

"It helped," he grumbled.

"And you already have very nice bath salts. You're a spa guy, aren't you?"

"He is!" Eric said. "And we have the biggest tub!"

It was true. The bath Cain had drawn for me after I'd spent a whole day in the fields was one of the best ones I'd ever had.

"Is there a reason you're torturing me today?" Cain asked.

"Of course. It's a special occasion."

"And what's that?"

"It's a day that ends in y."

His eyes narrowed, and I was pretty sure that if it were possible, smoke would be coming out of his ears.

Eric, as usual, thought it was hilarious.

Cain rolled his eyes and went back to the kitchen. I was tempted to follow him and ask about the bar, but figured that was a question for after Eric went to bed.

I kept myself busy by scrolling through forums on Wren's show until late into the evening. Once I didn't hear the ambient sound of Eric's voice, I went to find Cain.

Usually, he was in the living room or kitchen, but this time, he was nowhere to be seen. I eventually went to the door of his room, a place I usually avoided, and knocked.

"Cain?" I whispered.

It slowly opened, but only a crack. "What?"

"Can I talk to you for a second?"

"Don't tell me you're planning on bringing back some other crop," he said as he opened the door fully.

"I—" I stopped. Every part of my brain ground to a halt. "You're shirtless."

His golden skin was dotted with hair. Every muscle of his torso was on display, and his shoulders were even more impressive when not hidden.

"I was heading to bed. What do you need?"

I opened and closed my mouth, trying to remember any thought other than *how can a man be this hot?*

"Uh, plans. Questions! I have questions for you."

"Questions?"

"A single question. But a big ask. Kinda."

"Is it about crops? Because I have a feeling you have ideas that'll make us be outside more."

"I do, but it's way too late in the season. This is about our plan to make the entire town like you."

"Shit," he muttered. "Now I see why it's a big ask."

"And you haven't even heard what it is yet."

He sighed, but gestured for me to sit on the bed. I tried to play it cool, but my stomach tied itself into a knot as I took in everything about his room.

It was painted in the same green as mine, but it had pictures of Eric on the walls and a fluffy white rug on the floor over the hardwood. Two lamps illuminated the space, giving it a cozy and intimate feel.

Neither of which I needed.

"Your silence is terrifying." Cain's voice brought me out of my thoughts.

"Oh, sorry." I shook off my curiosity and focused on him. His face. Not his naked torso. "So, next week, I'm going out to the bar."

"What does this have to do with me?"

"I was thinking that it could be good for you to go as well."

"Why?" he asked slowly. I played with my hands in my lap. His eyes were already narrowed. This didn't mean anything good for me.

"I was talking to Jackie . . ."

"And?"

"And she was saying that you need to get out of the house more."

"I already am. With Eric. Like we agreed."

"Right," I replied. "But the people of this town need to know *you* too."

"They don't."

"Didn't you say the issue was with you?"

"They'll think I'm not a good parent if I'm out late at a bar."

"Say you're out . . . making sure I'm having a good time. That way, I'm not alone in a seedy bar—"

"The people aren't like that here."

"People could see you for who you are."

"And who am I, Mollie?"

"A grump with a heart of gold."

He rolled his eyes, but he didn't immediately say no. I counted it as a win. "You've obviously thought this through, except for the part where I have a child that can't go to the bar."

"No, I talked to someone about that."

"Jackie offered to watch him, didn't she?"

"You're good at deduction."

And good at looking like he wanted to murder me. "So, you two conspired?"

"A little bit."

"Son of a bitch," he muttered.

"What? She's close with you. Why wouldn't she want you to succeed?"

"She wants us to get together, princess."

"What?" I shook my head. "Not Jackie. She's seen us fight."

"And so has the town." He crossed his arms. "This is a terrible idea."

"Could be a good one." I crossed my legs and cocked my head to the side. "Why don't you prove me wrong?"

"Really? Now you're challenging me?"

"Is it working?"

"Unfortunately."

"Your stubbornness is your downfall."

"Fine. I'll go to the bar *once*, but only because I wanna see you eat your words."

"*You* might be the one eating *your* words."

"Get out of my room, princess." He gestured for me to leave.

My stomach tightened. I didn't want to go. There was something nice about being in this space with him, where he didn't wear his ball cap and could take a break from working hard.

I wanted to spend more time with him like this. Just us. In a room.

And that meant things I didn't want to think about. Things that weren't good for me.

CAIN

Strawberry Springs Neighborhood Watch
Jade Clark
Y'all better be ready for Lucas's show tonight!

Comments:
Kerry Winsor: I wish I could go! I need to find a babysitter that won't let Tommy plug the toilet again.
Jade Clark: Do I even wanna know?
Kerry Winsor: I'll gladly tell you.
Hu Gh: That damn music makes the bar way too loud! Tell 'em to turn it down or I'm sitting outside!
Mark Bell: I'll set up a table . . .

JACKIE WAS BOUNCING on her feet when I opened the door a week later.

"Don't say anything." My voice was firm.

"I won't then. But I'll *think* it." She walked in and saw Eric reading the book Nicole had given him to practice. It was hard to believe he was reading already, but once he'd started school, he had been learning so quickly that he'd been put into an advanced level with a few other classmates. "There's my favorite boy!"

"Jackie!" he yelled as he ran over to give her a hug. "I get to hang out with you all night?"

"Until bedtime. I even brought your favorite book for me to read to you while you fall asleep." She grabbed it out of her bag and showed it to him. Eric took it and opened the pages.

"Can I read it to you?"

Jackie's eyebrows rose and she turned to me. "Already?"

"That might be a little advanced," I said. "Are you sure, kid?"

"Yes!" Eric exclaimed. "I wanna try."

"Then we'll do it while Cain here has fun."

Tonight would be many things, but fun wasn't one of them.

"And where's the woman who's making you do this?" Jackie folded her arms over her chest. "I need to thank her again."

"I'm here!" Mollie came darting out of the hallway. "Sorry, work ran over, and I still had to get dressed."

I let my eyes linger on her, taking in the going-out version of Mollie versus the one I knew.

She still wore nice clothes, but these were different. Instead of her usual light-colored blouses and tailored jeans, she was in a dress. A floral one that hugged the curve of her waist but flowed out by her hips. It made her look like she was going on a date rather than to a bar.

This was bad for many reasons. The main one being that she looked incredible, and everyone would notice.

"Wow." Jackie whistled. "You look like you're ready for a night on the town."

"Is it too much?" she asked, twirling around. Her dress flowed with every movement.

"Yes," I said without thinking.

"Cain!" Jackie was affronted. "Were you raised in a barn?"

"Also yes. We've been over this."

"You don't say that to a lady. She looks amazing. She'll be the best dressed there."

Mollie's lips twisted as she considered it. "Most of my jeans are stained with mud."

That would fit in more than what she was wearing. But even though I should have told her to change, I couldn't bring myself to do it.

"We should go. I'm not staying out all night, and you should grab a jacket."

She shook her head. "I don't have one that matches. I'll be fine."

I grabbed one of mine. "Don't come crying to me when you're cold."

"Jesus," Jackie hissed. "How has she put up with you this long?"

"The beautiful sunsets and romantic dinners," Mollie said.

I turned to her. "What did you just say?"

"Oh, just what's going on. With a twist. Keep up the bad attitude, and I'll say it in the bar."

My jaw dropped.

Jackie and Eric laughed.

And I knew that I was going to fucking regret every second of this little adventure.

She smelled too good. And I couldn't extract myself from it because I was locked in the truck with her. Suddenly, the thirty-minute drive to the square was torture.

And that had to be the only reason for what I said next.

"Listen, when I said it was too much . . ."

"You were meaning it was too nice and that I overdressed. Don't worry, I get it."

I glanced over at her. "You shouldn't let me off the hook that easily."

"Probably not, but you're gonna hate every second of this, so I expect some grumbling."

"Call me out on it. Don't just take it."

It was her turn to glance at me. "O-okay. I will. But I'll give you a free pass for the first one."

"And I'm still gonna explain."

"And what is it? That you think I'm pretty or something?"

"That's exactly it, actually." The cab went silent, and I did the exact opposite of what I would usually do. I kept talking. "You're gonna be the best looking one there, though you usually are. And when people see you, they'll think it's a date."

"But it's not."

"Still. You just look . . ." I had a million words for it. Beautiful. Perfect. Like she was the fucking sun, and I was but a mere planet in her orbit. "Nice. Very nice."

"Huh. So Cain Smith *can* compliment people. Good to know. It's nice to know I don't only piss you off."

"Half the time you piss me off because you look like you do. How is it that you manage to make mud look good, princess?"

She let out a musical laugh. "No idea. But I've heard nicer things in the last ten minutes than I've heard in the last five years in Nashville, so thank you. You've more than made up for what you said earlier."

I clamped my jaw shut, unwilling to make myself look even more like a fool in front of her. Silence returned up until we were close to the town square.

"So, this bar . . ." she began. "Is it good?"

"I've only been a few times. I avoid drinking. I don't need to add any addictions to my roster of bad personality traits."

"That's pretty noble, actually. And if it makes you feel any better, I don't usually drink either. The hangovers aren't worth it."

"Most people do it anyway."

"I'm just smart."

"Not saying you're not, but there could be another reason."

"I suppose that'll stay a secret."

I raised an eyebrow at her. "You have a lot of those?"

"Yep."

"Like what? Your favorite color isn't pink?"

She rolled her eyes. "Did you mean to sound like an ass?"

"Not really. I just figured it was since I see you in it a lot."

"It's a great color, but not my favorite," she said. "My actual favorite is the color orange the sky turns when the sun sets."

I could picture it. The farm had a picturesque view of the setting sun nearly every night. When Mollie was working in the living room, sometimes I would catch her staring at it.

I glanced over at her, and her gaze had drifted out the window. The sun had set a long time ago, but its rays still changed the sky. The sunsets here were always indescribable, but I had a hard time enjoying them when I looked at them. All I could see were the empty fields.

"So, yeah. Not pink." She dragged her eyes away and blew out a breath. "You need to stop slipping into silence. I'm trying to distract myself from my nerves."

"You're nervous?" I asked. "I didn't think that was possible for you."

"I do mess up socially, thank you very much. And bars aren't really a *thing* I do."

"Yeah, working on your laptop seems to take up most of your time."

"I'm trying to change that."

"Don't worry. You will. The whole town will be talking about this tomorrow, and you'll have plenty of questions to answer."

"I share a house with you, and I wanted to hang out. I'll just tell them that."

"And you think that'll be enough? You know what this'll look like."

"We don't have that vibe, Cain."

"What kind of word is vibe?"

"You know, that *aura*."

"Aura is worse."

"We're purely friends," I said. "The town will see that."

"Bet you your first strawberry that they don't."

"My *first* strawberry?"

"The first one is always the most sentimental. I'm confident."

"You're cruel."

"Wanna take the bet?"

"Absolutely I do," she said.

"I'm sure we'll figure that out tomorrow, princess. But for now, you should look out your window."

She did, and her jaw dropped when she saw the square illuminated with fairy lights. Everything was warm and cozy, even the closed library.

"It's like Christmas. Do they decorate this early?"

"Nope. They're up year-round. No one wants to take them down."

"But they're all working. Someone has to maintain that."

"No one here cares enough."

"I think you and I both know you're wrong about that."

I resisted the urge to roll my eyes. She was right. People in this town cared about each other.

But only about the ones *in* the town.

We pulled up to the bar and saw people mingling inside, Hugh by the door.

"Here we go," I muttered. "Stay here."

I was *not* letting the crankiest old man in town see me act like a dick. I got out of the truck and started walking toward the passenger-side door.

"Am I dreaming?" Hugh called. "Or are you out of your house?"

"No. You're not."

"Since when do you go to bars?"

I tugged on the door handle. "Since *she* dragged me out to one."

Mollie slowly slid out, eyes on Hugh. She already had that damn smile on her face.

"No freakin' way. The new girl got Cain Smith too?"

"More like I dragged him here," she said. "Hi, I'm Mollie."

"You look familiar," he said. "Have I met you before?"

"She's Bennie's granddaughter," I mumbled.

"What brings you out to Strawberry Springs?"

"She owns the farm, Hugh."

"And you *like* her?"

"Somehow."

Hugh narrowed his eyes. "So, what's going on with you two, then?"

"Nothing," Mollie said. "Just two roommates having a friendly night out."

"I smell a whole lot of—"

"Don't make her uncomfortable," I cut in before he could call her out.

"Don't go all guard dog on me, Smith," Hugh said, rolling his eyes. "She's really got you wrapped around her little finger, huh?"

"It's more like I know what all this town does. And what they think. She doesn't, but I'll let her be delusional for a little longer."

A sharp elbow dug into my rib. "I'm right here."

"Ow, go easy, princess."

"When have you ever been easy?" she quipped back.

"Tell me again," Hugh interrupted. "You're friends?"

"Yep," Mollie said.

"I thought I'd seen delusional when Tammy thought she could do a 5k with no training. Now, I realize I didn't truly know what that was until I saw you two."

"Friends might be a strong word."

She thought Hugh was talking about friendship.

Dammit. She'd only proven him right.

"It's nice to run into you, Mr. . . . ." She trailed off.

"Don't remember me, huh?" He huffed. "Hugh Jeffries. Also known as the town grump. Well, at least I was until this guy came along." He jerked a finger in Cain's direction. "At least I socialize."

"What do you think he's doing now?" she asked.

Hugh harrumphed. "Still working on believing what I'm seeing. Pigs really do fly." He held up his flask, presumably full of whiskey.

My hand curled around her elbow. "Come on. Let's get this night over with."

"You could at least sound excited."

"Not on your life," I muttered.

We walked into the bar without another word. Lucas's band was playing country music, though with the rock twist he was known for. Most of the time, he was traveling to see Gabriel or playing in Nashville, so it was rare to see him back in town.

In high school, Lucas, Gabriel, and Jade had all been incredibly close. But then some sort of falling out had happened. Jade still talked to Lucas, but not Gabriel, and she'd become friends with Grace in Gabriel's absence.

Jade's pink hair was noticeable in the crowd. As well as more people from high school that I hadn't talked to since.

Most of them either ignored me or hated me. That didn't bode well for the evening.

Mollie's eyes were wide as she took it all in.

"That's Lucas up there," I said into her ear. "He's friends with Jade and Gabriel, who left some time ago."

"Jade had a thing with Gabriel!" she yelled.

"Keep your voice down."

"Sorry," she said. "But I do know *some* gossip."

"Good. Then you'll have fun being a part of it."

Mollie rolled her eyes before they landed back on Lucas. He was good-looking. Tall with blond hair. As far as I knew, he was a decent guy. He was someone I could see her with.

Lucas and I had never had an issue, but I'd never hated him more than when the thought of him and Mollie crossed my mind.

And with the way she stared, it might not have been all in my head.

"Let's go talk to Mark," I said, and grabbed her arm to get her to the bar. People turned as we walked, and I stared only at my destination, refusing to face the shock that had to be on their faces.

We made it to the bar, where the owner, Mark, was passing out drinks—mostly beers—to the people waiting. When he turned to us, he did a double take.

"What can I—holy *shit*. Cain?"

"Yep," I said.

"And . . ." His eyes slid next to me. "Wait, you're Mollie."

"Hi," she said brightly. "Nice to meet you."

"I've seen people talking about you in the Facebook group,"

he said, shaking her hand. "I'm Mark. The owner of this fine place. First drink's on the house."

"Oh, um, what do you recommend?"

"Hm, for a gal like you? Maybe a cosmo?"

"Can I get it without alcohol please?" she asked.

"Sure," he replied. "Cain, what about you?"

"Water," I said, and I caught another stray elbow from Mollie. Her pointed look was clear. "Please."

Mark turned and got our glasses.

"Do you always physically attack the man you're dragging to bars?" I asked as I rubbed my ribs.

"Only the ones who have no manners."

"I opened your car door."

"Next time, do it with a smile."

"So," Mark said as he put our drinks down. "Mollie, how are you liking it so far?"

"It's great here! Other than one individual"—she pointed at me— "everyone's been nice."

Mark laughed. "Yeah, he's like that."

I tensed. He was really going to say it right in front of me? Mollie caught it.

"Luckily he's not *all* bad," she added.

"Sure." Mark shrugged. "Already got her coming to your defense, huh?"

"Someone has to," she said, giving me an out. I was grateful for it.

But I wondered if she already regretted bringing me here.

Mark watched us with a smile. I knew that look. He was already planning a Facebook post about this.

And I could see it now. Everyone would say she's too good for me, that I had stolen her somehow from the hordes of other available men in town who could do better.

Like Lucas, for example.

Mollie's gaze had turned to the band, and she was smiling while looking at him.

God, I fucking hated this bar.

"This place is so cool. I hear that's a local artist."

"Not so much anymore," Mark said. "He moved out a year ago."

"I'm sure it's tough when someone leaves."

"Eh, he and Gabriel were always meant for bigger and better things. We felt worse for Jade, though. She'd rather die than admit it, but she had a crush on Gabriel."

"She doesn't need to admit it for people to know," Mollie said.

"Oh, we know all about that." Mark's eyes flashed to me. "Have you met Lucas yet? They're finishing up a set."

"I'll go say hi in a few." She smiled before taking a sip, and I tried not to let my annoyance get the better of me.

I finished my water before sliding it to Mark. Mollie was still working on her drink, searching for familiar faces.

Jade finally saw her and nearly bowled over the crowd to get to us.

"You made it!" she called, pulling Mollie into a tight hug. Then she saw me. "*And* you got Cain here. Did you take what I said as a challenge?"

"More like inspiration. He needs to get out."

Jade's eyes slid over to me. "That I can agree on. How are you? I haven't seen you in the shop in a while."

"I'm good," I said. "Happy to be out of the house."

The words came out stilted and were far from believable.

"You sure sound like it." She laughed and turned to the stage. "They've got a few songs to play still. Wanna join me on the dance floor?"

"No," I said immediately.

"Absolutely!" Mollie replied.

Jade laughed and dragged her off. I stayed by the bar. I wasn't sure where to look, but my eyes landed on Mollie anyway as the song started up.

She was following Jade, gearing up to dance. When the song reached its peak, she was fully moving without a care in the world.

Her smile was so much like Bennie's. Bright. Happy. Unburdened by the issues that mine had.

And despite it all, I couldn't help but return it.

Another glass slid in front of me, and I turned to see Mark. The song ended, replaced by something slightly quieter.

"You were smiling at her. I saw it."

"I wasn't," I replied. "I don't smile."

"You used to only smile at one person. Your kid. Now, we all need to add her to the list." He winked and walked off to serve someone else.

I had a sickly feeling in my stomach. I didn't want to agree with Mark.

But I'd been wanting to smile at Mollie for a long fucking time.

I watched her dance for a few songs before her eyes caught mine. She was running over to me the second they did.

"That was fun!" She grabbed my arm. "You should join."

"*What?*"

"It'll make you look good! And I don't like dancing alone."

I was shell-shocked. Completely baffled. That was the only explanation for the way I followed her.

The last time I'd danced was long before Eric came into the picture, so I had no idea what to do. Mollie didn't have such reservations, and her iron grip on my hands made it so I moved with her. The music was upbeat and most of the people around us were drunk.

The ones that weren't were staring at us.

Hard.

"Stop worrying about them!" she yelled in my direction. "Just have fun!"

I wasn't sure how to do that, but she spun, and my hand went with hers, turning it into a twirl. She laughed and did it the other direction, enjoying it just as much.

Slowly, and almost painfully, I started moving. Lucas's band was infectious, and so was she.

I focused on her, only her, and finally let go for the first time in a long time.

We danced for three songs, slowly growing closer. By the time it was over, we didn't have an inch between us.

The music ended as the band finished up the set. I caught on to how close we were and stepped back.

"You should go say hi to Lucas," I said before I could stop myself.

She blinked. "B-but—"

I walked off before she could say anything else, desperately needing space from her signature scent. When I came back, she would be talking to another man. Someone she probably would have far more in common with.

And I would be okay with that.

Or that's what I told myself. Even seeing her walk toward him filled me with rage I couldn't explain, and I had no idea how to stop it.

I found my place at the bar once again. I should have been thrilled that I was alone and that she was with someone else. But I wasn't.

I regretted my decision the first time she fucking smiled at him. I had no idea what they were even talking about, but her smile was the only thing I could see from across the room. Lucas was into her, without a shadow of a doubt. He had always leaned toward the women he planned to ask out, and he was no different even years later.

Mollie seemed to soak it up. She nodded along with what he was saying, talking back with enthusiasm that I wanted but didn't deserve.

"Jealous?" a voice asked from behind me.

"No," I said to Mark without even looking at him.

"You could be over there with her, you know."

Yeah, I could be. But being close to that would only fan the flame I felt deep in my gut. I looked away. By the time I looked back, she was walking toward me.

"What are you doing here?"

"Lucas just asked me out."

My molars clenched. Why the hell was she telling me? "Have fun."

I ground it out before walking away. It was tempting to leave. Lucas could drive her home for all I cared. But what I needed to do was get out of her sight so I could cool off.

"Cain!" she hissed as she followed.

"Go back to Lucas, princess. Send me a text if you leave with him."

We were walking down the hallway to the bathroom when she grabbed my arm hard enough to stop me.

"Stop," she nearly yelled. "Hang on. Why are you walking away?"

"Because I want to." The words came out harder than I meant them to, and her eyes widened.

"What the hell is wrong with you?"

"What the hell is wrong with *you*? Why are you talking to me when you have a man waiting?"

"Wait—"

"No, Mollie." I wrenched my arm out of her grip. "I need a minute alone."

"Then take me with you."

"No. It needs to be *from* you."

Her jaw fell. "What did I do?"

"Just go back out there."

"No," she said, stepping closer. "We've been getting along for weeks. You can't suddenly act like a caveman and expect me to let you get away with it!"

"I won't act like one if you walk away," I hissed back. I wanted to raise my voice, but I knew that if anyone heard a word of what I was saying, I would be in trouble.

"Not until I understand." Now she was even closer, invading all of my senses. All I could see was *her*. All I could smell was *her*.

And all I wanted to taste was *her*.

"Walk away."

"No," she said. "I'm not leaving until you tell me what's going on."

I couldn't think straight, and I knew I'd regret the words I would say next. "You wanna know what's going on? You're driving me up a wall, Mollie. With your damn dress and whatever the fuck you use to smell like that—I can't fucking think."

"W-well, fuck you. Get over it."

"I *can't*."

She stepped *closer*, dammit. "You're going to, because whether you like it or not, you're fucking stuck with me."

"You never back down, do you?"

"Not with you."

"You're gonna regret this."

She angled her head, glossy lips forming a smile. "Try me."

And that was when my control went out the window, and I grabbed her by the jaw and crashed my lips onto hers.

MOLLIE

Strawberry Springs Neighborhood Watch
Mark Bell
All right. I'm officially on the Cain and Mollie train. He
SMILED at her.

Comments:
Kerry Winsor: I didn't know he knew how to do that!!! Time
to start a bet.
Tammy Jane: Fifty bucks that it happens in a week.
Mark Bell: Fifty bucks something's already happened.
Kerry Winsor: Fifty bucks for it fizzling out within a few
months.

I THOUGHT I knew many things. How to drive a car. How to
pay bills.

How Cain Smith worked.

I was *very* wrong about one of them.

My mind was a confusing mix of *is this real?* And *I thought he hated me.* And finally, *shit, he's an incredible kisser.*

Just minutes ago, this was the last thing on my mind.

And now he was kissing me. He was in my space, filling my lungs with a scent I couldn't place. His hands cupped the back of my neck, and it hit me that this might have been the best kiss of my life.

All my kisses with Trevor had me molding into him. He wanted me pliant in all aspects of my life. But with Cain, I pushed against him with the same force he gave me. I was the one to run my tongue over his bottom lip. I was the one with my fists in his shirt to bring him closer.

But he was on the move too. A door opened, and instead of staying in the hallway where anyone could see us, we were now in a dark closet, the door shut firmly behind us.

That was when his tongue clashed with mine. That was when he hiked my leg up and fully pressed into me.

We needed to talk about this. We shared a *house.* Technically, he was my *employee,* but my brain was filled with an unhelpful mix of *more, please,* and *now.*

Cain's mouth left mine, but he placed a kiss on my jaw. "I told you that you would regret that."

"I regret nothing." My voice didn't sound like my own. I was out of breath. I went in for another kiss, but he pulled away.

"Don't you have a date with Lucas?"

"No," I hissed. "I was coming to ask you to help me out of it, you idiot. I guess this is one way to do it."

He narrowed his eyes, a sight barely visible in the dim light of the closet. "And you're—you kissed me back."

"Yes, I did."

"But—"

"We can talk it out later. Right now, I want you to kiss me again."

I hoped he wouldn't turn me down. I wasn't ready for the awkwardness to settle in. I didn't want to think too hard about this. For the first time in far too long, something felt *good*. I wanted more of that feeling.

Cain's lips returned to mine, and all tension left my body. I ran my hands through his hair, pulling him to where he fully pressed into me.

My weight settled against the wall behind us. I didn't feel crowded, but surrounded by something safe. Some*one* safe. I'd stood up to Cain, been myself, and he was still here kissing me.

This time, he pushed it further. His teeth sank into my bottom lip, and I let out a moan. Heat pooled in every part of my body, something I'd been missing for far too long. With Trevor, things like this had felt like a chore, something to get over with so we could say we had a healthy sex life and move on.

But this? This was *fun*.

Cain's hands roamed. Over the curve of my hip. Over the swell of my breast. Every part of me he touched, my attention followed like a lost puppy. I wanted more of his hands and less of the fabric between us.

My nails dug into his scalp. I wanted to beg for more, but didn't want to take my mouth off of his to do it.

He must have gotten the message, because his fingers slipped below my bra line. I sucked in a breath when he pulled my breast out of my dress and teased my sensitive peak.

I arched my hips into him, feeling his cock strain in his jeans.

"What are you doing?" he muttered against my mouth.

I gasped. "What I want to." His touch on my breast became firmer, and my mouth went dry.

"And what do you want?"

"Touch me. Anywhere. Everywhere."

He huffed out a breath, his mouth moving to my jaw and

neck. I leaned my head over, trying and failing to keep my composure.

Cain's hand left my breast, drifting lower and lower. I hiked my leg up again, giving him full access to what I hoped he wanted.

I already knew I was dripping. It had been far too long since I'd had good . . . anything in the company of another man. Trevor used to try until he'd gotten tired of it.

I doubted I would orgasm in a dark closet of a bar, but I could let him touch me.

His fingers brushed over the waistband of my underwear before moving between my legs.

"You're fucking soaked, princess."

I bit my lip. I thought I hated it when he called me that.

Not this time.

Cain slipped past the thin fabric. He found my clit so fast I jumped out of shock.

"Sensitive?"

"*Ah*, y-yes. It's been a while since a man could find it."

"Wha—do they need a map? Have you ever been with an actual man?"

I wanted to answer him, but I was a mess of gasps and pleasure. He traced the outline of my pussy so perfectly that heat shot out from his fingers and went straight to my core.

I had no concept of time, but my body responded to every one of his movements. My hips jerked, and I dimly realized that I wasn't struggling to build up to an orgasm this time. I was going to struggle with coming way too fast.

Blindly, I reached out to stroke his cock through his jeans, earning me a stuttered breath from him. I took in his hardness, imagining what that would be like inside of me, and I felt myself tighten around nothing.

Cain's mouth landed on my shoulder, and then came the brush of teeth on my skin.

My eyes slipped closed. I wasn't sure where I was any longer. All I knew was how I felt.

And it was incredible.

Cain's fingers were on my clit, teasing it with just enough pressure to have me on the edge, but not enough to where I was jerking away. He breathed as hard as I did, like he was just as turned on as I was—though I hadn't touched him like he had me.

"Come for me, Mollie. I need you to." He was more out of breath than when we'd been dancing, and I felt his words in every inch of my body.

It wasn't a habit of mine to do what he told me to, but this time, I wasn't in control. Pleasure was, and the words tipped me right over the edge of the cliff he'd brought me to.

Heat erupted from my core, spreading through every part of my body, up my spine and down to my toes. It was good. So good that I wanted more.

I wanted this to never end.

But it did, and though I was still catching my breath, the bar grew loud outside the door, bursting the bubble we'd found ourselves in.

Cain tensed before he moved away. "Shit," he said.

It must have been time for us to get back to reality. I tugged my dress back in place and waited for the regret to hit me.

It didn't.

But I was pretty sure I was alone in that.

"I shouldn't have done that," he said.

"You gave me the best orgasm of my life and *that's* what you say?"

He ran a hand through his hair. "Why were you so okay with that?"

"Did you forget the part where I said it was the best orgasm of my life?"

"Mollie, you're my *boss*. This is breaking so many rules."

A pinprick of reality broke through my post-orgasmic haze. He was right. What we'd just done complicated things a *lot*. I didn't regret it, but he had a lot more riding on this than me.

"I—yeah. I suppose we did break some rules."

He let out a sigh. "You should go."

"Of course. I'll just . . . go to the bathroom."

Cain nodded jerkily and I made a break for it before I could stop myself.

Bursting into the bathroom, I took off my smudged lipstick and made sure my dress was in the right place before I hunched over the sink.

I stared down at where my ring used to be, thinking of all the things Cain and I hadn't talked about. He barely knew me, and I barely knew him, and we'd gone at each other in the closet of a bar.

I would have laughed if this wasn't so *bad*.

Trevor and I were done, but I knew Mom and Dad expected us to get back together. They figured I would come home and settle into my old ways, including being with him.

But the truth was, every second I was here made me want to stay longer.

Until Cain and I eventually ruined the fragile peace we had.

My thoughts were a mess, and I still needed to turn down Lucas's invitation to dinner. The band stop playing, and I knew I needed to get that done before I completely lost my mind about what had just happened.

I walked out of the bathroom and right into a woman walking in. She jumped back, eyes roaming up and down my body. I hoped none of what I'd done showed anywhere on my face or neck.

"So, Mollie, right?" she asked.

"Yes, that's me."

She hummed as she appraised me. "You're actually kind of pretty. I'm surprised."

I blinked in shock. Was that an insult or a compliment? "Thanks?"

"Let me give you a word of advice then. That man you're hanging out with? Cain? You should stay away from him."

I stood up straighter, finally turning to her. "Why?"

She laughed. "Because he's a loser. And he's caused a lot of problems in this town. You're from Nashville, right? I bet you could find a lot of better guys there."

I'd tried my luck. And ended up with Trevor.

I may have messed things up with Cain, but I also knew I wouldn't take people talking shit about him. So far, I'd managed to avoid it. But the rising anger each time someone teetered on the edge of saying something bad about him was palpable.

And this woman was the tip of the iceberg.

"Can you remind me when I asked for your advice? Because as far as I know, I didn't."

"Excuse me?"

"You heard me. I only take advice I ask for, not petty words from someone who obviously doesn't know a damn thing about who Cain Smith is *now*. Not whatever you saw in the past."

Her eyes narrowed. "What do you see in him anyway?"

"I see the man who ran me a bath when I was sore from working in the fields. The man who danced with me even though he hated every second. I tried my luck in the city, and let me tell you, I did not find a man like Cain there."

"Then you're stupid," she said.

"Yeah. Maybe I am. Or maybe I'm making a move on a man who everyone else is missing out on."

I brushed past her, ignoring her glare, and was about to head outside when Lucas suddenly appeared in front of me.

"There you are," he said. "Have you thought about the date?"

I hadn't realized he wasn't still on the stage. That's how little attention I was paying.

"Um, listen, I'm really sorry but—"

His smile didn't falter. "You have a thing with Cain, right?"

"*What?* How did you—"

"I'm not completely stupid. But I still thought I'd shoot my shot."

"I'm sorry," I said. "About . . . saying no."

"Don't sweat it. You seem pretty happy here. And I travel, so it would be long distance anyway." He shrugged. "But I hope he tells you how pretty you are."

I thought back to the conversation in the truck. "He does."

"Good. Then I wish you the best."

I gave Lucas one last smile before I went outside. The cool night air hit me in the face.

"He already pissed you off, didn't he?" Hugh was still out there, eyeing me like he knew everything that had happened.

"*No,*" I snapped, my anger already rising again. "Cain didn't piss me off. Trust me, if he did, he would be the one hearing about it, and no one else."

"Oh, touchy. I see the protectiveness goes two ways, then."

I blew out a breath and crossed my arms. I needed to text Cain and tell him that I was outside. Or go back inside and face the consequences of my actions. Instead, I seethed.

Then a jacket landed on my shoulders.

"You really should have brought something to keep warm with," a deep voice said.

I let out a harsh breath. "Yeah, probably. Let's get out of here before I lose it."

"For once, I agree."

"Can I just say—" Hugh began, but Cain turned to him.

"She's already mad. Trust me, you don't wanna make this worse."

He huffed. "How do you know I'm gonna make it worse? All I was gonna say is that you should wipe the lipstick off your mouth before Jackie sees it."

I turned to Cain with wide eyes; there were smudges of pink on his lips. He wiped it away, but I could feel his tension from where I was standing.

Yeah, it was time to go.

When we climbed in the truck, I was working out what to say if he didn't talk the whole way home. Or what to do if he was so mad he started a fight.

He did neither.

"I'm sorry about Brooke."

"Who's that?" I asked.

"The woman you ran into outside of the bathroom."

"You heard?"

"Yeah, I was about to walk out."

I shrugged. "Don't worry about her. She was all talk and no bite."

"She wasn't wrong, though."

"About what?"

"About *me*."

I rolled my eyes. "She doesn't even know you. The real you."

"Mollie, *you* didn't know me years ago."

I would have argued, but I remembered the feeling I had in the bathroom. The one that I didn't know a damn thing about the man who'd just touched me. "Maybe you have a point."

He glanced at me and then back at the road. "I wasn't always like this. When I was younger, I was different."

"As we all are. I used to be platinum blonde."

Now he looked at me again. "I can't see it."

"For a reason. It was *so* bad for my coloring."

"I wish all I was worried about when I was younger was just hair dye." The words were bitter, but they weren't directed at me.

"Bad childhood?" I asked.

"I bounced around foster homes. Jackie was the first that stuck."

I blinked in shock. Jackie was his foster mom? That was how he knew her? "So, you were obviously going through a lot."

"Her husband didn't see it that way."

"She's married?" I tried to think back to when she'd done my hair. I hadn't seen a ring.

"She used to be. To a man named Donny. He hated that she took me in, but let her do it because it kept her busy. He made my life hell, and in turn, I did it back."

"Did anyone know?"

"He told everyone I was just an asshole." He shrugged. "And I was, but he left the part out where *he* was tormenting me. Jackie was mortified and tried to mitigate it, but in the end, he was a part of this town. I wasn't."

"So, he turned them against you."

"Part of it I did myself," he replied. "I was out of the house more when I started working for Bennie. It helped. I would stay late until I saw Jackie's car just so I didn't have to deal with his wrath alone. But then I came home to find her trying to hide a bruise on her face. And I *knew*."

"He hit her?"

"Apparently all the time. She begged me not to say anything, and I didn't. But I couldn't leave it at that. I found him at the bar, where he always fucking was. And I nearly killed him. That's who they see me as. A punk kid who went after his foster parent."

"But you were protecting someone."

"They didn't know that. And they probably never will. Jackie can't even *talk* about that asshole, even though he died years ago."

"No one knew?"

He pursed his lips and let out a long sigh. "I think Bennie did. Or he had an idea. He tried to talk about it with me, but I didn't know what to say without outing Jackie."

"He always had a way of seeing things others couldn't." Like how I belonged here. "And like I said when we met, he trusted you with the farm. Which means I do too."

"That trust isn't gonna do anything if it ruins your reputation here. We can't keep doing this."

"Hang on, *what*?"

"Mollie, think about it."

"I *am*. We're changing their minds. And I'm helping you with it, whether you like it or not."

"But you have a chance here to have a good reputation—"

"My reputation is mine to do what I want with it. I've spent years being so polite and perfect, and you know what it got me? Nothing. I'm doing what feels right. And *you* feel right."

Cain's grip on the steering wheel was tight as he stared at me.

"You're impossible, princess."

My skin erupted in gooseflesh. I wanted to blame it on the weather, but I knew it wasn't that. "I do like defying expectations," I replied.

He huffed out a laugh before we lapsed into silence. My mind went back to that closet, and I wondered if I'd get the chance to feel that again.

Minutes later, we pulled up to the house. It was late and all the lights were off. I toyed with the hem of my dress, wondering how I could ask about *us*. But I didn't need to.

Cain moved first, and suddenly, his lips were on mine.

This wasn't like the rough kiss in the closet. This was tender and full of a promise that I couldn't name yet.

"I thought you said this was a bad idea," I whispered.

"It might be," he said. "But it feels right."

His thumb brushed over my cheek, and I leaned into it.

"Is Jackie staying the night?" I asked.

He blinked, but answered quickly. "Probably. I bet she's asleep."

"In your room?"

"Probably the guest room. Why?"

I shrugged, heart kicking into gear. "If you *need* a room, you could always share mine."

Now he nodded, getting the full meaning of what I was saying.

"Well," he replied, "she *does* hate the mattress in the guest room. So maybe she did sleep in mine." His thumb moved again, sending sparks over every inch of me he touched.

"I think we're just being nice."

"I didn't know we knew how to do that."

Letting out a laugh, I got out of the truck, hoping he would follow to continue what we'd started.

To do what felt *right*.

Strawberry Springs Neighborhood Watch
Mark Bell
My supply closet is NOT a make-out closet! Keep your kissin'
in your own places!

Comments:
Jade Clark: But I saw Mollie follow Cain there.
Kerry Winsor: NO.
Mark Bell: YES! Gimme my winnings!
Tammy Jane: DANG IT.

SHE WAS EVERYWHERE the second we were in her room. In my
head. In my arms. In my mouth. She was relentless as she kissed
me, just like she had been at the bar.

And I was hopelessly addicted to it.

Just feeling her wetness rush onto my hand when she'd
orgasmed had almost made me come in my pants. I didn't know

how I was going to last and make sure she was a fucking puddle on the floor before I let myself take anything from her.

Mollie dragged me to the bed, her hands once again fisted into my shirt. All that work in the fields had made her stronger than she realized, and I'd caught myself letting my eyes trace the subtle definition in her arms more times than I could count.

We fell onto the bed in a mess of limbs, her on top of me. She went to grab at my aching cock again, but I knew that was a recipe for disaster.

"Hang on," I said. "Slow down."

"Do you not want me to return the favor?" she asked, one eyebrow raised.

"Oh, I do. But I'm not done with you."

"I already came earlier," she said with a laugh. "I'm good."

"You're not just gonna be *good* when you're with me. Do you understand?"

Her jaw went slack. "What else could you have planned?"

"I wanna taste you." I pressed a kiss to the skin behind her ear. "And make you come on my mouth."

"You're into that?"

"Of course I am. Why wouldn't I be?"

She'd mentioned something about this before, about a man not being able to make her feel good.

And I wondered if it was connected to what she was running from.

"I've never had that done to me before. Do I just . . . lie back?"

"I want you to sit on my face."

Her eyes widened, but I was serious.

"I'm definitely heavier than you think I am." She shook her head. "I would crush you."

"And what a way to go. I know what I want, princess. And

the only way I'm changing my mind is if you look me in the eye and tell me you don't want the same thing."

Her cheeks were a perfect shade of pink, and her teeth had sunk into her lip.

"I'll try," she said. "But you have to tell me if I'm too heavy."

"I will." I definitely wouldn't be doing that. "We need to get these panties off."

I hooked a hand under her dress, pulling her underwear down her thighs. Mollie wasted no time throwing them across the room.

Still red cheeked, she crawled to me, which was a sight I'd never get over, and straddled my face. I reached up and circled her clit with my tongue before I pulled her to fully sit on me.

She gasped, but I got to work as her weight settled fully onto my face. Her pussy grew slippery as I circled and licked her core.

She was moaning and gasping, and I tapped her leg twice.

"Was it too much?" she asked.

"Absolutely not. But you're gonna have to be quiet, princess. Unless you want the whole house to hear what we're up to."

"Sorry," she said. "It's too bad you can't be in two places at once, or you could shut me up."

"I'll do that later."

I dragged her pussy back down. Mollie must have covered her mouth, because her moans were muffled, so hopefully only I could hear them. Her hips began to jerk, and she became impossibly wetter as she rode my face, chasing the pleasure she deserved. Her whole body stuttered as she came, and I enjoyed every second.

She fell onto the bed next to me, momentarily catching her breath. I did the same. I'd not even been touched and yet I was worked up.

"Be right back," she said suddenly.

"Don't tell me you think we're done."

"We're definitely not done."

My mouth went dry at the curve of her breasts, now fully exposed, and the shape of her body, as I watched her stand and grab a condom from her purse.

But I didn't get nearly long enough to stare at her because she was raising an eyebrow at me again. I threw off my pants before rolling the condom down my hard length, and then she was on top of me again. The taste of her mouth was second only to that of her cum, and her tongue brushing against my lip had me worked up immediately.

I rolled us over until I was on top of her. I traced her clit with the head of my cock, earning a shudder, and then made my way to her entrance.

Biting the side of my cheek, I pushed in an inch. And that was almost too much. Her fingers went to my hair, and I checked on her to make sure her face wasn't twisted in pain, but her head was pressed into the mattress, eyes squeezed shut as she moaned.

I went in deeper. One movement at a time. When I was fully seated, I saw *stars*.

She gasped. "Cain." Her pussy fluttered around me, and *fuck*.

My hand gripped the side of her neck. Not too hard, but enough to get her to stop before I spilled my load. "Stay still, princess," I hissed. "For once in your *life*, stay still."

Mollie whined, but did as she was told. I moved my hand, but she dragged it back.

This woman was going to be the death of me.

I pressed a kiss on her cheek before I finally thrust in once. Then twice. Then three times.

She felt so perfect. Tight. Hot. Like she was made for me.

Her legs tightened around my waist, using all of their

strength to squeeze me. Mollie arched into the bed, fingers twisted into the sheets, and I picked up the pace.

I was going to get addicted. Every day, I would look at her and think of *this*. The way her tits looked when I pushed inside of her. The way her face twisted as she was getting close again.

I wanted to hold out forever, to stay in this moment of pure bliss before life trickled back in. But I couldn't. She felt too good, and my own orgasm was building.

"Cain," she said. "I'm gonna—"

I kept up the pace, but only a few more movements in, my cock exploded as I bottomed out in her one last time.

My vision whited out and my hand tightened on her neck. It took me far too long to come back into myself, but when I did, her hips were jerking against mine. She hadn't come yet.

"Let me help with that, princess." I snaked a hand down between us, rubbing my thumb on her sensitive clit. Mollie let out a sigh of relief as I took over, tracing patterns into her. It didn't take long to make her shatter around me.

There was only silence between us as we caught our breaths.

She broke it first. "Holy *shit*."

"Yeah," I said.

I finally lifted my body off her, and my cock slipped from her pussy. I already wanted to do it again, even if I was far too tired to.

Standing, I made my way to the door, grabbing my clothes. "Where are you going?" Mollie asked.

"To clean up."

"And are you coming back? Please tell me you're not the kind of guy to sleep with someone and then not offer cuddles at least."

That was exactly the kind of man I was when it came to one-night stands.

Then again, this wasn't that. In fact, I didn't know what this was at all.

"I'll be back," I said. "Just give me a few minutes."

I went to the bathroom and changed. By the time I was done, she had changed as well.

The second I laid down, her head curled on my chest and my arms wrapped around her. I'd grown used to sleeping alone despite never being fond of it, and I had a feeling this, too, would be something I would remember.

Mollie was still asleep when the sun woke me up. I delicately moved my arm from under her head before sneaking out, hoping no one would see me.

That was when I ran into Jackie in the hall.

Her mouth dropped open before pulling into the biggest smirk I'd ever seen.

Fuck.

I shut the door before she woke up Mollie and headed downstairs.

Jackie followed. "I knew it! *I knew it! I knew it!* You *do* like her!"

I sighed. "Yeah, yeah."

"How did it happen? I can't believe she even went for you."

"Hey, I'm not that mean."

"You very much are."

I rolled my eyes. "Not *all* the time. Whatever. It's nothing official anyway."

She groaned. "But this is the kind of woman you *should* be official with. Tell me she's not one of your one-night stands."

"I don't know."

"You need a partner, and she could be it!"

"Jackie, it only *just* happened. We haven't talked about anything else. I have no idea where this is going. And there's the whole issue of her owning the farm."

"But would you be willing to make it official if you could work all of that out?"

Normally I'd say no. But not this time.

"We'll see."

Jackie gasped. "Yes!"

I scrubbed my face, knowing that Jackie would follow up, and I needed to figure out where Mollie and I stood. I had no idea about her opinions on relationships or anything about her life in the city. Usually, none of that mattered. I was a one-and-done kind of guy.

But this time, it did.

"Okay, I'll leave you alone to get your work done," Jackie said with a smile. "But I can't wait to see where this ends up."

The uncomfortable feeling in my stomach grew. "I might end up disappointing you."

"You could never," she said, giving me a hug before leaving.

When she was gone, I got a few minutes of silence while I grabbed a flannel and shoes before there was a knock at the door.

My mood fell even further. The last time I heard that sound, it hadn't ended well for me.

I opened the door to see a man with blond hair pushed back on his head. He had piercing blue eyes, and was dressed in an expensive suit.

"Who are you and what do you want?"

"Wow, no manners." The man rolled his eyes. "I guess that's what I should expect from a place like this. I bet you don't get too many visitors."

"You'd be surprised," I replied.

"I need to speak with the owner of the house."

"She's asleep."

The man's lips pursed. "Of course she is. And I assume you're the farm manager?"

"I am."

"And you two get along?"

"We manage." I crossed my arms. "Do you want something from her?"

"In a way."

"Then you'll have to go through me."

His eyes narrowed before searching me up and down, as if scrutinizing me.

I didn't give a shit what he thought.

"Fine, I have no problem doing that." He reached into his briefcase and pulled out a stack of papers. "Can you give this to Mollie? Tell her it's from Trevor, and it's the final offer for the farm."

"For the farm?" I repeated slowly.

"Selling it." He stepped back and let his eyes trace over the land. "She's been sitting on a gold mine here. I told her that we could build hundreds of houses on this lot. Maybe more."

I could only stare. She was talking to someone about *selling*? And now she had a final offer?

When the fuck was she planning to tell me this?

"Tell her that I expect an answer tomorrow." As he started to leave, he gave me a smile, one that didn't reach his eyes. He climbed into his car and drove away without another word.

I looked down at the papers and saw a number so large my jaw dropped. It was labeled as the final offer, with multiple others attached.

She'd been *bidding* for this.

Goddammit. I thought I knew her. I thought I could *trust* her.

I should have known she was going to let me down.

MOLLIE

Strawberry Springs Neighborhood Watch
Kerry Winsor
Look at my little Brussels sprouts! I need Strawberry Springs to have a fair so I can enter them!

Comments:
Atticus Thompson: Nice.
Kerry Winsor: Nice?! Do you know how much work I put into these? They're more than nice!
Kerry Winsor: @everyone HELLO? LOOK AT MY HARD WORK!

I wasn't surprised when I woke up alone. Cain was always up way before me, and though this was still early by my standards, I was sure he was already halfway through his morning routine.

I got out of bed slowly, feeling the pleasurable ache from everything that had happened the night before. I couldn't wait to see him after Eric went to school, when we could talk about everything that we could be. I wasn't sure if I was ready to date, but I was willing to consider it if he offered.

We meshed well, and when we didn't, I stood up to him. I knew, without a shadow of a doubt, that this was nothing like what I'd had with Trevor.

Throwing clothes on, I went downstairs to start coffee. I was expecting to be alone, but I wasn't.

The second I was by the coffee pot, papers were slapped onto the counter. I jumped and turned, only to see Cain glowering at me like he had been when I had talked to Lucas. His arms were crossed, and underneath his hat, his eyes were sharp.

No, this was *worse*.

"You okay?" I asked slowly. Did I piss him off in my sleep? Did he regret sleeping with me?

Neither of those were good options.

"Your final offer for the farm came in. Hand delivered by whoever the fuck you were talking to." He shook his head. "And to think, I almost didn't hate you."

He stormed away before I could say anything, slamming the door behind him. My jaw was on the floor.

What the hell? An offer for the farm? I looked at the papers he'd left behind.

I saw a number way too high for the value of the land, written on the header of Trevor's parents' company. They'd listed it as the final offer based on my demands—like I'd fucking had any.

I flipped through, horror only growing as I saw their list of plans. Houses, houses, and more houses. I hadn't even seen it in person, and I knew it was wrong.

And on the last page, I saw a note. One that made it all so much worse.

You know the right choice, Mollie. This is more than enough money. Say yes.

Had Trevor been the one to deliver these? Had he come *here*?

My stomach roiled. I didn't think he cared enough, but then again, his emails had become increasingly insistent.

I darted out the door after Cain. He was halfway across the field by the time I followed him.

"Cain!" I yelled, pushing my legs as fast as they would go. "Wait!"

I didn't know if he would even bother. I wouldn't if I were in his position.

But he stopped, and a minute later, I caught up.

"I don't wanna hear your apologies," he said slowly.

"I-it's not that." I struggled to catch my breath while he fully turned to me.

"What else could you possibly say? You looked me in the eye and pretended to care about this place while you were trying to *sell* it. I don't even wanna look at you."

"I wasn't trying to—"

"I saw the paperwork. It mentioned *offers*. It mentioned that you had *demands*. And I guess they met them."

He turned to walk away. "Hey!" I grabbed his arm and dragged him back.

"Let me go." His voice was barely controlled.

"No!" I snapped. "You need to at least hear my side of it before you make your call. Admittedly, I should have told you that I'd gotten emails about offers, but I thought ignoring them was enough!"

"According to the paperwork, you had demands."

"It's how Trevor negotiates," I said. "He takes silence and makes it into something it isn't. Cain, I'm not selling the land. He just wants me to."

"Why?"

"I—" My mouth closed. I knew why. He wanted me to sever

ties with this part of myself, to completely be what he wanted me to be. But try as I might, I couldn't say it. "It was just a money thing."

Cain let out a humorless laugh. "Somehow, I doubt that. I know how much this land is worth. That was double it."

"He was trying to get a rise out of me."

His eyes narrowed. "Sure. Whatever you say." He turned to walk away again, but I heard him mutter, "This is why I don't fucking do this."

I grabbed his arm again. "Do what? Sleep with people?"

"No! *This.*" He gestured between me and him. "Us. Getting close to people never fucking goes well for me."

"It's not going *that* poorly."

"Really? I told you about my past last night, which involves one of the biggest screwups in my life. But you won't do the same."

"It's not . . . You haven't done anything wrong."

"It doesn't matter," he replied, pulling his arm out of my grip. "At the end of the day, I care about you more than you do me. It's why I told you what I did. One day I thought I'd get used to that sort of shit. Whether it be with Jackie or with Er—" He stopped himself. "But it never gets easier."

"I . . . care about you," I managed to say.

"Sure. But this isn't how it should work. I might be shit at relationships, but I do know that it's a two-way street. You have a whole life you lived in Nashville that you're telling me nothing about." He sighed. "And that's your choice to make. But if you're asking me to *trust* you, to *know* you, then it's gonna take a little more than promises."

I opened my mouth, but no words came out. I wasn't sure why I couldn't say it. Why I couldn't tell him about Trevor. About the way I'd folded myself into him until I had been nothing. It wasn't like I didn't trust Cain.

But I couldn't say it.

"All right," he said. "I get it."

"You have to know that I won't betray you by selling the farm . . . Right?" My words came out hoarse, nearly blocked by what I *should* have been saying.

"Yeah. I get it. You're saying you won't betray me."

I wanted to feel relieved, but I knew this had fundamentally blown up whatever we'd had. "I *won't*."

"You want me to trust you. Sure. Just let me know when you're ready to trust *me*."

Cain walked away then, leaving me standing in a field to gape after him, regret burning my insides.

And then I thought about Trevor, and the regret turned to rage.

I walked back to the house and threw the offer in the garbage, right where it belonged. I had thought I was safe from him all the way out here in Strawberry Springs.

Apparently not.

I pulled out my phone and typed out a message.

> Got your offer. The answer is no. Do not come here again.

TREVOR

> I drove three hours to deliver that to you, and you didn't even consider it?

> The only thing I considered is burning it. My answer is and always will be NO.

He said something else, but I blocked his number. I'd have to deal with him at work, but I was done dealing with him now.

I only got a moment to pour coffee before my phone rang. At first, I thought Trevor had somehow gotten through. Instead, it was Mom.

We hadn't talked all that much, but I'd thought about her as I fell asleep. Usually we spoke every day, and this was the longest we'd gone without regular communication.

I was still mad, but maybe I could get some answers from her.

"Mom," I said when I answered. "Were you a part of Trevor's plan to offer way too much for the farmland?"

"Hello to you too," she said. "And I knew he was offering more, but not the details."

"He came here today to hand deliver it."

"Aw!" she said. "That's so romantic."

I almost screamed. "He handed it to *Cain*. It caused a major issue."

"Who cares? You won't see him again after you sell it."

"This is his *job*!"

"He could always find something else."

"Mom, *no*. I'm not selling the farm. No matter how much money is offered."

"He's working so hard on this," Mom defended. "He came all that way just to try and work with you. Doesn't that make you feel something?"

I gritted my teeth. It made me want to shove *him* in a trash can. To hide him from Cain and everyone here. I didn't want them to know what kind of man I'd almost married. I didn't want them to know anything about me other than who I really was.

And then it hit me. I was embarrassed of him. Of Trevor.

"Hello? Are you there?"

"I don't want Trevor coming here with any more offers. Actually, I don't want any talk of selling the farm, or of me getting back together with him. It's not happening. Ever."

There was silence on the line. I'd never been this firm with Mom before, but it felt right.

"I don't understand," she said. "And I'm so worried about you, out there all alone."

"I'm not alone."

"You're not with us. I haven't seen you in weeks! I was just hoping you would be back in time for my birthday, and now you seem to be staying."

Her birthday? I checked my calendar and cursed. That was in *days*, and I'd totally forgotten.

"I might not be back in town, but I can come visit."

"But that's a three-hour drive."

"I can make it work," I told her. "I can come for your party if you want me to."

"Yes, *please*. It's been too long. I need to see my baby girl. I need to *see* that you're okay."

My heart warmed. Despite being upset, it was nice to be reminded that she wanted time with me.

"Tell me all about the party," I said. "I'll be there."

She told me every detail, down to what color scheme she was using. I listened intently, happy to hear her voice, happy to talk about anything other than Trevor or land selling.

"Now, what if you came a day early?" she asked, her voice hopeful. "We could see each other even more!"

"I have to work, unfortunately."

"You could go to the office. Your dad would love that."

I sure wouldn't. "It's fine," I said. "I . . . sometimes have to help with the animals, so I can't leave for too long."

"Help with the animals?" She scoffed. "Then why do you even have a farm manager?"

"It's . . . a deal we made. Don't worry about it. I'll be there for the party."

She let out a long sigh. "I just wish—"

"Mom," I said gently. "I'll be there. Can't we just be excited for that?"

"Yes, sorry. I can't wait."

She told me she loved me before hanging up, and I let out a sigh of relief. That had gone better than most of our conversations before.

But then I'd remembered everything with Trevor, and my mood plummeted again.

I needed to tell Cain who he was and what he'd done. Embarrassment wasn't enough of a reason to hide it. Besides, he'd told me everything about himself, even though he wasn't proud of it.

It was time I did the same.

I went outside to find him, only to see his truck was gone. It wasn't unusual for him to leave during the day to either drop off milk at the processing plants or to get more hay for the animals, but I still wondered if he was avoiding me.

When he finally came home, it was after school had let out, and Eric was in tow.

"Mollie!" Eric called when he walked in. "I got a book from school to read! It's for the second-grade level!"

"What?" I said with a gasp. "That's so amazing."

"Can I read it to you? Please?"

I may have needed to talk to Cain, but I also wouldn't ignore Eric when he wanted to spend time with me.

After he was done with his book, he wanted to go to his room to play with his toys, so I went to find Cain. I checked the back of the farm and then the front before I realized that the barn door was open.

"Hey, can we talk?" I asked.

"I think we did that earlier." He was moving things around, taking tools and racking them on the wall.

"We did, but there's more for me to say." I took a breath, fighting against the feeling of heat in my cheeks. "Trevor was my fiancé."

Cain paused his work and slowly turned to me.

"What?"

"Yeah. Before I came here, I was different. A shell of myself, even. I think Trevor liked that, and he thought that if he bullied me enough, I would give in. I always did before."

Cain only stared, and I didn't know if I should stop or keep going.

But now the words were flowing, and I couldn't stop them.

"Even the day I got here I was just . . . what he wanted me to be. When I was a kid, I wasn't like that. And then I met him and it all changed. I didn't know one person could break me down into someone I didn't even recognize. I didn't know how to escape it until I got here. I'm sorry I didn't tell you. At first, I thought you'd hear that I could be pliant and want that version of me—"

"I would never want that." His voice was hard.

"I know that now," I said. "Which is why even I was confused when I couldn't tell you who Trevor was and why he offered so much money for this place. But I think I'm . . . embarrassed. Mortified, even. Who you've seen is who I am. I feel like *me* now, and I look back and wonder how I even survived."

My eyes were on my feet and heat had crept from my cheeks throughout my whole body despite the chill in the air. I had no idea what Cain was thinking. Or if he was still angry about earlier. I could only get the words out before I stopped myself.

"So, I'm sorry I didn't tell you. It really wasn't a trust thing, but a *me* thing. If you're still mad, take all the time you need. I'll be ready to talk when you are."

It was time to make my great escape. I needed to hide out and try to get my racing heart in order. I had needed to tell him, but it was still so *hard*.

I was halfway across the barn before a hand clamped down on my wrist and I was pulled into a broad, warm chest.

"You have nothing to be embarrassed about, Mollie." Cain's arms wrapped around me, giving me solace I wasn't sure I deserved. "Only he does."

Now I was feeling emotions. Big emotions. Ones that swirled together and made my eyes water. "I should have left before it got that bad."

His hold tightened. "Leaving is the hardest part. I know that for a fact. And you did it. Instead of being embarrassed that it happened, you can be proud that you're *free.*"

I'd expected him to be annoyed I'd waited this long. I didn't expect *compassion*, and somehow, his kind words made everything I felt even stronger.

"It wasn't like it was that bad. I don't know why I'm reacting like this."

He pulled away and made me look him in the eye, a gentle hand on my chin. "It may not have been that bad *yet*, but things escalate. They did for Jackie. It started with him slowly driving wedges between her and her friends. Then, he made sure she never had enough income to leave. And maybe he was just an asshole, but in the off chance he was planning something bigger, I'm glad you're here instead."

"I know he blindsided you this morning, but I'm glad you saw him and not me. I don't even know what I would say to him if I saw him in person."

"Well, if *I* see him again, I'll tell him he looks like a little rat, and no amount of fancy suits is gonna hide it."

I laughed. "I might steal that."

He stared at me, his hand now gently tracing my cheek. And I could *feel* how much he cared this time.

"Thank you. For understanding."

"You're welcome, but I need you to know one more thing."

"What is it?"

"I will *never* try to control you. Or take you from the people who care about you. I might not be liked. I may have made mistakes. But if I ever do a damn thing like he does, you can kick my ass."

"With you . . . I would. But I don't think I'll have to." I wiped at my eyes, finally feeling like a human again after my meltdown. "Hopefully I don't see him next week when I go to Nashville."

"You're going to Nashville?"

"My mom's birthday. I'm mad at her for keeping the farm from me, but this is the longest I've gone without seeing her. I wanna go, but I have a feeling he'll be there." I shrugged. "I'll avoid him the best I can. But honestly, I'm dreading it."

"If he's there, you don't have to go."

"I can't keep pushing my parents away. I really miss them, and it's her birthday. I'll be fine."

His jaw tightened, and I thought he would argue, but he let out a breath instead. "Okay," he said. "But if he does *anything*—"

"I'll leave."

"Or you can kick his ass. Either way is fine with me."

"I'll have to make a plan." I smiled at him before it faded as all the things that had happened today hit me again. "Are we okay?"

"We're okay, Mollie."

His confirmation made my whole body loosen. "Thank God. I think I exhausted myself worrying about it. I'm probably gonna need to sleep this off."

I was halfway to the barn doors before he spoke. "One question, before you go?"

"Yeah?"

"What are you gonna do when you go back to Nashville?"

When.

Not if.

I'd never hated a word more.

"I'm working on figuring that out."

"When you do, will you let me know?"

I nodded. "I have a feeling you'll be the *first* to know."

We were interrupted by Eric calling for Cain to ask about dinner. It was late, and I stayed outside, hoping to work through all the emotions today had brought up.

I wound up on the porch, watching the sunset. Pinks, oranges, and purples painted a scene in the sky, and though I was sure I was missing dinner, I couldn't find it in me to regret it.

The door squeaked open not long after I sat.

"Dinner's ready," Cain said.

"Oh, thank you. I'm gonna stay out here for a bit." I gestured to the sky. He followed my hand and slowly nodded in understanding.

"All right, then."

He went back inside, leaving me alone. I'd miss hanging out with him and Eric for dinner, but at least I'd get to see one of the most gorgeous sunsets I'd ever seen in my life.

Then the door opened again.

"It's so pretty!" Eric said. He sat right next to me, a bowl of chili in his hand.

"Does Cain know you're out here? I thought you ate at the . . ." I trailed off when a bowl was handed to me, but it wasn't from Eric.

It was from Cain.

I turned, jaw agape.

"Change of plans," he said as he sat a few steps behind me. "We're eating out here."

"Why?" I asked.

"Because someone stubborn likes to." He nodded at the sky. "Now why are you looking at me? I thought you loved sunsets."

My cheeks were on fire as I looked back at the vibrant sky. It was hard not to look at the man who was breaking his own rule of eating at the table to make sure I could have dinner in front of the sunset. I'd never been with someone who forgave so quickly.

Cain's leg brushed against my back.

"Thank you," I said.

"Rule one of the house: We eat at the dining-room table, but it can only be broken by rule two, which is dinner together is more important than location."

"I'm a part of the house now?"

"Duh," Eric said as he took a massive bite.

I teared up again, but for an entirely different reason now.

The sunset didn't last as long as I'd wanted it to, but we'd finished with our meal by the time the sky was turning navy blue. Cain grabbed our bowls before we went inside, and I watched as he washed dishes.

It was things like this that showed he cared. Cooking dinner. Cleaning up after himself and others. And it was one of the hottest things I'd ever seen.

"So, how do I con you into watching more of *Renovating with Love*?"

"Mind putting the dishes up?"

"Not at all."

We lapsed into an easy silence after we cleaned up from dinner. Eric went up to his room to play while we caught up on the few episodes that had dropped.

Eric was in and out of the living room, asking questions or simply wanting to see that we were still there. So I kept my distance, despite wanting to touch Cain again.

When we were finally caught up on the show, I texted Wren.

The show is so awesome! Finally caught up! And the chemistry is SO good.

WREN

Thankssss. It's been a work in progress but I'm making it work. How are things? Are they perfect and magical yet?

Haha, no. Definitely not.

Are you okay?

Trevor came to the farm. Cain and I fought. Well, not really fought. More like he thought I betrayed him.

I fucking hate him.

Cain?

No, Trevor.

First off, if I catch Trevor, he's dead meat. Second, I'm glad you worked it out with Cain. Sometimes I got the vibe you let stuff go with Trevor.

It's easy to stand up for myself when it's Cain.

Interesting. When are you two gonna be together?

Honestly? No idea. We did hook up, though.

WHAT? LEAD WITH THAT NEXT TIME, MOLLIE!!!

Strawberry Springs Neighborhood Watch
Hu Gh
Can someone tell me if this is infected?

Comments:
Jade Clark: Your entire ass?? ON MAIN?????
Kerry Winsor: **@Henry Connor** !!!!!!
Henry Connor: Come to the clinic. Now.
Atticus Thompson: You ruined my breakfast. Gross, man.
Marjorie Brown: **@Henrietta Brown** IT HAPPENED AGAIN.
Henrietta Brown: Do you hate me? WHY would you tag me in this?

———

"I MET Wren right before high school," Mollie said as she fished out another cookie dough piece from the tub of ice cream. "And we instantly connected. She was working on the playground of my mom's neighborhood, and I followed her around like a lost puppy under the guise that I was helping. She's the kind of girl who can figure out *anything*, so I doubt she needed me. She's the thing I miss most about Nashville. She's so busy, though, that I'd probably miss her even if I was there."

Mollie handed me the ice cream tub, and I took a bite of the vanilla that she was avoiding. "Is she different than she is on TV?"

"Not really," she replied. "But I've hardly seen her date, so getting to see her fall in love is really nice."

I bit down on my reply as I handed the ice cream back over. There was something about the romance in the show that was either forced or fake. But maybe that was my cynicism getting to me.

I was up way too late, but once Mollie had opened the doors of her past, she'd been giving me little details of who she was, and I finally got to see the whole picture. It was a stark contrast to where we'd been this morning, where I'd thought she'd pulled the wool over my eyes for money.

"Aw, man." Her bottom lip poked out. "Is there no more cookie dough?"

"I'll get the kind with extra pieces next time," I replied, and took the container from her.

"Sorry that I didn't save any for you."

I hadn't had a single piece of cookie dough since we'd gotten it out. I'd left them all for her.

"It's fine." I got off the couch and went to the kitchen to wash our spoons.

She followed me. "I'm not bothering you with how much I'm talking, right?"

"No." I tried to keep my expression level, but I knew my own downfalls. "I asked to know more about you. You also have to remember I'm terrible at talking, but I'm good at listening. I promise."

"You're not *that* bad at conversation," she said. "But I'm also not used to guys wanting to know much about me."

"Is that something Trevor taught you?" I swallowed the instinctual feeling of rage. I'd worked on that over the years, especially since Eric had come into my life. It hadn't worked out well for me to go after Donny when I'd found out what a piece of shit he was, yet I knew I would pummel Trevor if I saw him.

But Mollie didn't need that. She needed someone to be here with her. To listen without making it about how *I* felt.

It was another thing Jackie had taught me in the years since Donny had no longer been in our lives.

"Unfortunately, yes. He would play the part of listening, but I think he really wanted a girlfriend who never had problems. Who could be a trophy with no feelings or emotions."

Fuck that guy. "Then he should get a blow-up doll as a girlfriend."

Mollie laughed. "Now there's an idea."

I set the clean spoons aside and turned to find Mollie looking at me, eyes bright with hope. People usually didn't look at me that way, and my mind immediately flashed to when she would be looking at me like everyone else did.

I tried to push it away, but I was too used to being let down.

"Actually, Mollie, there's one thing we *should* talk about."

She nodded. "What is it?"

"It's the whole boss and employee thing. If this doesn't work out . . . We should talk about what happens with my employment."

"O-oh, right. I mean, should we really be worrying about if this doesn't work out? We don't even know what *this* is."

"I don't know about you, but if I'm sleeping with someone, there's only one person involved. And it's you."

"There's no one else for me either."

"So, this is an exclusive partnership . . . where you also pay me."

"The farm pays you."

"You own the farm."

"Ah, right." She ran a hand through her hair.

"I'm not trying to say you *would* do anything, but you have the power here."

"Right, which I'm not used to having." She bit her lip as she considered it. "I mean, be honest, does this really feel like I'm your boss? We both tend to make decisions."

"It doesn't change the facts, princess."

"What I'm trying to say is, Papa Bennie hired you. So you're a part of this. I'm not interested in dismantling anything he had a part in. Even if . . . even if this doesn't work out. Emotions"— she gestured between us— "have nothing to do with whether or not you have a job."

It was hard to take her at her word, just like it would be with anyone else.

But her word carried weight. I'd already seen the offer thrown into the trash. She'd done everything she said she would since her arrival.

And if I was doing *this* with her? I needed to trust her.

Even if I felt like things were too good to be true.

"Okay," I said. "That makes me feel better."

"Oh! I have an idea to make it even better." She ran out of the room, coming back in with a piece of paper and a pencil. She leaned on the counter, scribbling something down. She then turned and handed it to me. "Here's a contract of employment. As long as you want it, you have at least five years at the farm. I can't rescind it unless there's fraud."

I read the words, which matched what she'd said. "Is this legally binding? It's written in pencil."

"It still counts. I'll file it away with everything else. If I break my end of the deal, you can take me to court."

"I've got enough court dates coming up."

"Still, it gives you recourse. Which I think you need."

A knot loosened in my chest. She was right. "Thank you, Mollie."

She smiled. "Sometimes I have good ideas."

"You have them a lot of the time." I took the paper from her and signed my name. "They just come with a lot of work."

"Well, at least I'm willing to get my hands dirty."

"That you are," I replied.

"So, now that all of the legal shit is out of the way . . ." She took the paper and set it on the kitchen counter. "Can I finally kiss you?"

"You feel the need to ask?"

"Eric was awake earlier, and I don't wanna make you have to explain anything you're not ready to." Dammit. She was thinking way ahead of me. It only made me like her more. "And I wanted to be sure all of this was cleared up before making a move. So, now I'm making a move."

She looked through her lashes at me and I couldn't take it anymore. I pulled her to me and kissed her.

A giggle escaped her as I did, and her hands slid up my chest and around my neck.

As her sweet scent invaded my nose, I had to remind myself that there was no rush. We could do this whenever we wanted to. This kiss was simple, gentle brushes over her lips, just like the ones in the truck had been.

It was an intimacy that I didn't usually allow myself. I kept emotions and longing away from anyone, not willing to be let down in the end. But there was something about Mollie that made me want to try.

There was no one else that I would kiss in the kitchen of my

home. No one else I would let get so close to Eric. No one else
that I'd opened up to. I was bad at words, so I tried to convey all
of my thoughts in the slow and steady kisses we shared in our
quiet intimacy.

"Come back to my room," I murmured into her lips. We
didn't have to sleep together. We didn't have to do anything. I
just didn't want to let her go.

"Gladly," she replied.

We walked upstairs, yet I kept a hand on her, whether it was
the small of her back or the space between her shoulder blades.

I sat on my bed, expecting her to find space next to me.

But then my heart skipped a beat when she sat on my lap.

"Too much?" she asked, her voice quiet.

"No, princess." I grabbed her hips and pulled her closer,
making sure she couldn't fall off. "You're never too much."

I had only a second to notice the reddening of her cheeks
before her lips were on mine again. Now that she was secure in
my lap, one of my hands slid from her hips to the warm skin of
her back, hidden beneath her blouse.

Mollie was soft, yet firm, and the muscles of her back tensed
as I touched the area near the band of her bra.

"If you want me to stop, say the word." It was a reminder
she shouldn't have needed. An attempt to give her the power
she should have had all along. I knew how men could take and
take and take.

I refused to be like that.

"No, keep going," she said breathlessly. "I think I'm just
losing my mind a little bit."

"Why?"

"Because you're way too good at this. I wanna keep kissing
you. But I also want you to throw me on this bed."

Her words sent liquid heat through every part of me. "We'll

have to make both happen," I said, reaching to unhook her bra and tug off her blouse.

"*Yes*," she murmured with a gasp as I trailed my kisses from her mouth down to her jaw and neck. She let out a soft moan every time I dragged my teeth lightly over her sensitive skin, and I filed that away for future use.

Her breasts were hot and heavy in my hand, and I couldn't get the image of them out of my mind. It started the day she'd sprayed herself with water and had only gotten stronger when we'd fucked, and made them all the more mouthwatering now.

Mollie was responsive like this. I knew what I was doing was making her feel good, judging by her tiny noises and the way she arched into me. I knew her. Even before I knew everything about her.

I wanted to make her come again. Multiple times, in many different ways. I loved feeling her slippery wetness on my fingers and on my tongue. I just didn't know which one to do first.

But then her hips ground down onto mine, and I knew where I wanted to feel her.

Putting my hand between us, I worked at the button of her jeans. She got the message and slid from my lap to take off her pants and then helped me do the same. I was ready for her to get back on top of me, but she palmed at my cock through my underwear, sinking to her knees.

"What are you doing?" I asked.

She smirked. "Isn't it obvious?"

I grabbed at her jaw and pulled her back up to me. "If you do that, this is gonna be over very quickly. And I have a rule about this."

"A rule?"

"You come first. Every time. And multiple times."

Her eyes widened. "R-really? Every time?"

"Yes," I said as I freed my cock from my boxers and brought her back into my lap. Both of us sucked in a sharp breath when I rubbed against her already wet folds. My hands went to her hips and slid her up and down the length of my cock. It was tempting to push inside of her, but the way she started moving when she realized how good this felt told me all I needed to know.

I let her have all the power to chase her own orgasm. Her hips were the ones moving, her body pressing into mine, and judging by the sounds she made, she was enjoying herself.

I bit my tongue, trying not to let myself come just from this. Her pleasure was contagious, infecting me even though I wasn't inside of her.

Mollie's movements grew jerky, and her hands tightened on my shoulders. Her mouth hung open, and I knew she was close.

My hands moved to the back of her neck and into her hair, where I grabbed and gently pulled.

The second I did, she let out a broken moan as she came.

It was one of the hottest things I'd seen in my life. Her pussy still moved up and down my cock until she was sensitive, and then she finally stilled, catching her breath.

"You like it a little rough, don't you, princess?" My voice was low as I tried to keep myself from pushing inside of her right then and there.

"I've never even considered it before," she said. "But fuck yes I do."

"Let me make you come again," I whispered.

"I know there's a rule and all, but I don't know if I can."

She could. I knew she could. "Will you let me try?"

"Yes," she said. "But I'm so fucking sensitive."

"I can work with that." I coaxed her off my lap and onto the bed, laying her out on her back. I kissed her lips, her jaw, and then made my way down to her core.

"Again?" she asked. "You must really enjoy that."

"It's the best thing I've ever tasted," I said. "But we'll work our way to that."

I took a finger and slowly parted her pussy, pressing one inside of her. When she didn't jerk away, I curved it, going right for her G-spot.

"*Ah*," she murmured.

"You okay?"

"Yes," she said. "So good."

I resumed my movements, pushing one finger in and out. I let her get used to it before adding a second, and was rewarded with her arching off the bed, pressing into me deeper.

That was when I brought my mouth to her clit and gently lapped at it.

"Fuck." Her fingers ran through my hair. I waited a few seconds to be sure she wasn't going to push me away, but her palms kept me pressed right at her wet pussy.

I flicked my tongue out while inside of her. She preened at every one of my movements, unable to speak.

"C-Cain," she said. "Fuck, I'm gonna come again."

I increased the pace, and her thighs wrapped around my head as she came once more.

"You . . . owe me an 'I told you so,'" she managed to say a few moments later.

"I got all I needed. No 'I told you so' required."

I pulled out a condom and before I knew it, it was out of my hands and in Mollie's. She was the one who opened it, having fully recovered from her two orgasms, and she slid it on my hardness, eyes on me the whole time. I bit the inside of my cheek as I felt every one of her movements, but then she pumped up and down, and I growled and tossed her back onto the bed.

"You're killing me," I said into her mouth.

"Good."

My hips lined up with hers and I sank inside of her in one thrust. Her fingers twisted in the sheets, her cheeks red.

"*Cain*," she said, eyes closed. "You feel so . . ."

"At a loss for words?"

"Y-yeah."

My lips pressed to her hot cheeks. "Welcome to my world."

"Start moving," she finally settled on. "*Please*."

I did as I was told, pulling all the way out before slamming back in. Her entire body moved with each thrust, her breasts bouncing and her jaw dropping open.

Finding a rhythm, I kept the movements up. Her thighs tightened around my back, and the waves in her hair grew messier as I rocked her against the bed.

She was gorgeous like this. Totally and completely gorgeous. I wanted to come, but I also wanted this moment to last forever, to never end so I could bask in this bliss.

But her tightness was barreling me toward an orgasm. My balls ached. My cock was on fire, and I caught myself losing rhythm as I tried to get as deep inside of her as possible.

"Fuck," I muttered as I finally exploded, like a tightly coiled spring being released. I came harder than I ever had in my life, buried to the hilt inside of her.

Mollie's hands were in my hair when I came back online, and she was as out of breath as I was.

"I think I came again," she said as she gulped in air. "Which I didn't think I could do."

"You absolutely could," I said, "if someone gave you the time to."

Her eyes met mine, and a small smile made its way onto her face.

"You're still up for post-sex cuddles, right?" she asked.

"Always." I kissed her on the cheek.

We both cleaned up before bed. This time, she grabbed my hand as we went back to my room. I wrapped my arms around her midsection as I brought her to me, reveling in how warm she was. I felt complete for once in my life.

This is good, I thought as I fell asleep. *Too good.*

I wonder when it'll end.

MOLLIE

Strawberry Springs Neighborhood Watch
Kerry Winsor
@everyone A TRAGEDY has befallen our little town!

Comments:
Jade Clark: Is it another ass on main?
Kerry Winsor: My Brussels sprouts! They were eaten by DEER!
Atticus Thompson: No way. Deer in Tennessee? Say it ain't so.
Kerry Winsor: Thanks for the sarcasm, Atticus. As the resident veterinarian, do you have any tips on how to keep them from my yard, or are you just determined to kick me while I'm down?
Atticus Thompson: Your house is in a field. Build a fence.
Kerry Winsor: Easy for you to say! I'll just chase them off next time.
Henry Connor: Do NOT chase deer. That's a one-way ticket to the hospital.

A FEELING of dread settled into the pit of my stomach as I saw the Nashville skyline in the distance. I'd driven three hours, and the closer I got, the less like myself I felt. I'd gotten used to Strawberry Springs, and it was obvious my worst day there was far better than my best day here.

It wasn't like I had a lot of bad days anyway. Ever since Cain and I had first slept together, they were good. Great, even. It had only been a week, but we'd settled into a rhythm of sharing the house that I could only have dreamed of.

He would either come to my room or I would go to his. Rarely did either of us sleep alone. It was completely different than the last time I'd shared a living space with someone I was with.

Which made the drive to Nashville all the more difficult.

Cain had tried to hide it, but I knew he wasn't thrilled that I was coming. I'd considered backing out, but then I remembered Mom's hopeful voice on the phone.

I was telling myself it would be fine when I pulled into the driveway that was full of cars.

But then I saw one I recognized all too well.

Trevor's.

"Fuck," I groaned once my car was in park. I closed my eyes and tried to channel *calm*. Instead, I got a mix of rage and fear.

Slowly, one inch at a time, I fought my body and got out of the car.

Trevor was waiting for me.

"I'm surprised you showed," he said, and his eyes dragged over my body. "You don't look as bad as I thought you would."

"As bad as—excuse me?"

"You're . . . *feisty*." He laughed. He'd used that word on me a lot early in our relationship, and it had always felt like an insult. "We'll see how long that lasts. Welcome back home, Mollie."

"Some welcome. You immediately gave me a backhanded compliment."

He smiled, but it wasn't kind. "It's all you deserve."

I remembered Cain's words about Trevor, about how all of this was so dangerous, and I steeled myself.

"Don't you have people to suck up to?" I asked.

"I'm trying to check on my ex-fiancée who left me for a dump in the middle of nowhere."

I hummed. "It really says a lot about your relationship skills, doesn't it?"

He stepped close, making my heart jump into my throat. "Let's get one thing clear, you don't—"

"Mollie!" My mom's voice interrupted us as she bounded out of the house. "It's so good to see you!"

I was pulled into a tight hug, one that gave me much-needed breathing room from Trevor. "Hey," I said, hugging her back.

"Was your drive okay?"

"Yeah, it was good."

She pulled away and looked between Trevor and me. "Oh, I was excited for this reunion. What were you two talking about?"

I should have told her what he'd said. I needed to be open about it, but the same ball of cotton that had stopped me with Cain made its way into my throat.

Trevor used that to answer first.

"Just pleasantries," he said. "I think the people of Strawberry Springs have few manners. She forgot a few of them."

"Oh, trust me. They have *no* manners." Mom rolled her eyes. "The only thing that matters to them is gossip." She turned to me. "Which is why I'm glad you're here."

My body still buzzed with nerves, and all I could do was nod. She pulled me inside, ready to show me off to all her friends. Trevor smirked at me as he followed, and though he disappeared after a few moments, I knew this wasn't over.

Mom introduced me to a bunch of people who all smiled and fawned over me being in town. They also gave me some version of what Trevor had said.

Wow! Is that dress new? I didn't know you could find something like that out there.

You're in such good shape! Who knew farm life would make you lose weight?

I thought you'd be dressed down! And then Maribelle would have to fine you like she did me for my flowers!

My annoyance rose, but I kept it together as I hung out with Mom. Her smile was *so* big now that I was home, her laugh brighter than ever before.

It made me feel terrible for leaving.

As we caught up with everyone, I kept an eye out for Trevor. He was mostly talking to our coworkers, but I knew he was watching me too.

How had I not noticed the evil glint in his eye?

"I know things are hard right now," Mom said when we were alone. I didn't realize she had followed my gaze. "But I hope you guys can talk. You always had such a nice relationship."

"You know what?" I said. "I need some water."

"Okay!" Mom replied. "I also have your favorite ice cream waiting for you. Cookie dough!"

My heart panged. I didn't think cookie dough ice cream would ever taste the same without Cain sharing it with me.

I went to the kitchen and took a deep breath before pulling out my phone to text him.

The walking red flag is here. I regret everything.

I barely had time to send it before someone walked up behind me.

"Don't think I haven't seen you staring." Trevor's voice was like sandpaper on my nerves. "Have you finally realized you miss me?"

"I'm making sure I know where you are so I can avoid you."

"You're feeling very bold for a woman who dropped her ring on the table and left."

"I'm taking a page from someone else's book today." I went to leave, but he caught me by the arm.

"I told your mom I'd talk to you, and that's what I'm gonna do."

"We've exchanged words. That's talking."

"Mollie." His voice was a hiss. "We're gonna talk. That's final."

His order was my last straw. I would *not* be letting this happen.

"It's funny that you think you can talk to me like that, but you and I know damn well your balls aren't big enough for that. Nothing about you is."

I wrenched my arm out of his grip and stormed off. My breath came in heaves as I sat in the den, finally alone.

> God, FUCK Trevor.

Cain didn't answer either text I'd sent him, and I tried to fight the disappointment. I waited for a few minutes before I meandered around the party, talking to a few of my coworkers while I avoided Trevor. It worked, mostly. It was easier to tolerate their curious questions about what I was up to rather than Trevor's straight disdain.

I didn't look him in the eye, but I could feel his rage about my words.

Eventually, I finally found myself next to Dad. He nursed a glass of whiskey and smiled when he saw me.

"There you are, Mollie-bear."

"Here I am," I said.

"It's nice to see you catching up with everyone. I bet you miss them out in Strawberry Springs."

I actually didn't. I barely thought about these people. "Yeah, kinda."

"Come outside with me, Mollie. We need to talk."

A pinprick of nervousness made its way back into my stomach, but I followed him to the backyard. It was a cool night. Cars rushed by on the nearby road, creating a white noise that Strawberry Springs didn't have.

"It's been a few months now," Dad started. "Longer than we expected."

"I know, but I've been working hard."

"You have. But it's not the same as being in the office. You're missing out on a lot."

I crossed my arms. "Is this where you tell me to come back?"

"You need to," he said. "I don't know everything that happened with you and Trevor other than what he's told me—"

"He's told you things?"

"Yes. And I want you to know that I understand how scary it is to commit."

I blinked. "He said I left because I wasn't ready to commit?"

"Yes. And what you two had was real. And you're scared."

"I . . . I didn't—"

"Fear can take on many forms, Mollie. But you two have been together so long." Dad patted his pocket and pulled out something shiny.

"Is that Trevor's ring?"

"It's *your* ring." He grabbed my palm and turned it over. "He and I have talked long and hard about this. Despite *every-*

thing, he would be willing to take you back and pick up where you left off."

"I'm seeing someone else," I said, shaking my head.

"Even so. Hang on to that. You need a reminder of the life you have here. You've basically moved there while telling us this is temporary."

I looked at my feet. Was that what I was doing? Even Cain had asked me when I was going back. And I never had an answer.

"But still—"

"Mollie," Dad said, "it's time to choose."

"Choose between what?"

"The farm or here. I didn't want to do this, but Trevor thinks it'll work. And I'm inclined to believe him."

"Are you giving me an ultimatum?"

"Yes. Come back to work. To Nashville. *Now.* You can keep your job and get your fiancé back. Or, you can return to fields and an old house."

"Dad, come on."

"We've tried being nice. You're trying to balance two lives here, Mollie. Pick one and stick with it. If you walk out that door and go back to the farm, I'll have my answer. Then you can mail that ring back to Trevor. I just hope you're happy with whatever you choose."

He gave me a small smile before he went inside, and I was left with a cold ring in my hand. I was tempted to throw it, but knowing Trevor, he'd sue me for it.

"It's time for cake and singing!" Mom called from the door.

"Coming," I said as I shoved the ring deep in my pocket.

"Everything okay?" she asked as I passed by.

"Yeah. I just have a lot to think about." I could tell she wanted to know more, but I walked to their expansive dining room, where everyone had gathered. Dad and Trevor had the cake, and they called for her to join. As everyone sang happy birthday, I considered my options. I watched everyone Mom knew. I watched the way Trevor acted so nicely to her by clapping and hugging her after.

And I realized I didn't like most of these people.

I was going to leave at the end of the night. And go home. To the farm. To Cain.

I grabbed one slice of cake and nibbled at it in the corner. As time went on, the decision only felt more right.

As the first guests left for the night, I figured it was my turn. I'd brought my laptop, so I grabbed it out of my car, taking it to my dad's office. After leaving it on the desk, I walked back outside.

"Mollie!" a voice called after me. "Did your dad not talk to you?"

I paused and turned toward Trevor.

"He did. I've made my choice."

"You're throwing it *all* away," he said incredulously. "Everything you have here."

"I have things back in Strawberry Springs."

"What, like that guy you live with? You're a fool."

The words hit me hard. I *did* feel like a fool.

But only when I thought about how much time I'd wasted with him.

"Or maybe I'm taking control of my life. Which obviously pisses you off."

"Only because you don't know what to do with your life."

"And you do?"

"Yes. I do." He took a step closer, and I took one back. "I saw the finances for that farm. You'll barely have enough to live off of. You'll be in the middle of nowhere, and I'm not gonna come back for you."

"I'm fine with all of that. In case I haven't made it clear, I don't want you in any capacity."

"Fine," he said. "But you're also leaving your parents behind. They've been a mess without you. I've been picking up the pieces."

My heart ached, and he knew it.

"I sincerely doubt they'll talk to you after this," he said as he stepped far too close. "You don't know the things they've confided in me, the worry they have that you're destroying your life. And you're proving them right."

This was the real ultimatum, and I knew it. The job wasn't enough, so he was bringing my parents into this.

"Walk away, and you'll lose everything," he warned.

"I lose everything if I stay," I replied.

"Not from my perspective."

I gritted my teeth. That wasn't the answer I needed, but I'd never once had a conversation with Trevor where he hadn't told me he was right.

"Then I'll do what feels right," I said. "I'm going *home*."

"I'll make sure they never talk to you again, Mollie! Do you understand me?" He was screaming at me, which was my cue to leave.

I blinked back tears as I stormed to my car and drove away. I didn't know if he really could convince my parents not to talk to me or if he was talking out of his ass.

My hands shook as I drove; I was in no place to deal with the traffic of Nashville. I needed to leave, but I also needed to calm down.

The second the car was in park, the tears started. Trevor had shaken me in ways I hadn't known he could. What Dad had given me felt heavy in my pocket. I fished out Trevor's stupid ring and regretted that I hadn't shoved it up his ass where it belonged.

Then again, he had been too busy threatening me. I bet he wouldn't have even taken it back.

What if Trevor did have the kind of power to make my parents leave me?

Should I go back? Did I want to lose my parents over my happiness?

I was torn. So torn that I didn't know what to do.

Then my phone rang.

It wasn't Mom or Dad. It was Cain.

I answered the second I saw his name.

"Mollie." His deep voice interrupted the second ring, and I let out a breath, snapped out of my contemplation. I threw the ring in my glove compartment, unable to look at it anymore. "Where are you right now?"

"A gas station in Nashville."

"Are you okay?"

"No," I muttered. "Not really."

"I just saw your text. Trevor was there."

"Y-yeah. And it was bad."

"Which gas station?"

"Does it matter?"

"Princess." His voice was firm. "Please tell me which gas station."

I read off the name and what street I was on, confused, but needing to hear his voice.

"Thank you," he said. He took a second before he spoke again. "What happened?"

"It started out fine. Well, mostly fine. Trevor was an ass from the second I arrived, but then when I saw Mom, she was so happy to see me."

"But it got worse?"

"Dad made me choose. I either stay in Nashville or go back to Strawberry Springs and lose my job."

"*What?*"

"He said Trevor convinced him I needed an ultimatum. I thought I was free of him, but now he's going after my *parents*. And Dad believes him." My voice went high as emotions hit me again. I leaned against my steering wheel, hoping no one pulled in next to me to witness my meltdown.

He was quiet for a second, but then finally spoke. "Do they know?"

"No," I managed to get out. "B-because I still can't fucking talk about it. What if they don't believe me, Cain?"

"Baby, they will."

"And if they don't?"

"Then you'll have me. You'll always have me."

Headlights pulled up next to me and I tensed. The last thing I needed was a random person asking if I was okay. I didn't want anyone to see me.

I wished I was home in the fields. Those were far more private.

A shadow approached the car, and I knew I had to tell them I was fine and to leave me alone. However, when I turned to do just that, I didn't see a stranger.

I saw Cain.

He had his ball cap on. His phone to his ear. He slowly pulled it down and ended the call.

My jaw fell open and I rolled the window down. "What the—"

"Hey, princess." He leaned forward on the side of the car.

"You're . . . you came . . . here?"

"You might have needed me. So here I am."

"But Nashville is three hours away."

He rubbed the back of his neck. "I asked Jackie to watch Eric the second you left. You seemed really torn up about this ex. If you didn't need me, then it would have just been a drive to clear my head. But if you did . . . I'd be here."

I could only stare at him.

Tears gathered in my eyes again.

"That bad, huh?"

"No. I mean, yes. God, you . . . *thank you.*"

"I've seen what happens when someone faces a man like Trevor alone. Never again will I let that happen."

"So I do have you," I said, leaning out of the window to bury my face in the crook of his neck. Even with all the chaos of the city, being near him still made me feel safe. Cain's hand curled around the side of my head, fingers running through my hair.

"Always," he replied.

I sniffed as I pulled away. My life was a mess, but I wanted to make sure I didn't mess his up either.

"It's getting late," I said. "I imagine you wanna head back."

"I'm actually under strict orders from Jackie to at least take you out to dinner. The punishment is pretty severe."

"That's sweet, but you can't want to stay in Nashville longer than you have to."

"I may not like the city, but we're here. You have to know somewhere good to eat, and I have a feeling you're hungry. Unless the shit birthday party fed you."

"All I've had is cake."

"That's not dinner. Tell me where you wanna go."

"I want a burger," I said. "And I have the perfect place."

He looked down at his flannel. "Will I be underdressed?"

I laughed. "No. Not at all. This is *not* a fancy place."

Cain met me at Riverside Burger Shack, a tiny hole-in-the-wall joint with only outdoor seating.

"You chose an outdoor eatery in late fall?"

I shrugged. "I'll live."

He rolled his eyes, but peeled off his flannel and placed it on my shoulders. "It'll be even better now."

How much could he do for me in one night? My tears had dried, but they were already threatening to fall again.

We walked up to the counter and ordered before grabbing one of the wooden picnic tables.

"Not too bad of a place," he said. "I expected something more . . . uppity."

"There's a time and a place for that. And after the night I've had, I'd rather eat a burger on the side of the road."

"Fair enough. Now, about this ex . . ."

"I can give you the address to find him, but it's a shitty high-rise apartment."

"I'm tempted, but no."

"You're gonna tell me I need to talk to my parents, aren't you?"

"In a perfect world, you should." He sighed. "But the reality is that he did a number on you. Jackie *still* can't talk about what happened."

"Hers was worse."

"It doesn't matter whose is worse. It matters that it happened."

"It feels like my family is falling apart all because I came to Strawberry Springs. They hate that I'm there. They don't understand it, and I don't know if they ever will."

"A family shouldn't fall apart because you're making one choice they don't understand. Jackie makes a lot of choices I don't get, but I still care about her. And it doesn't help that they have a shithead in their ear telling them lies." He paused and then winced. "Sorry, I'm trying to be mature here. I just . . . hate it when someone I care about gets hurt, but the last time I did anything about it, it didn't go well."

"Trevor isn't even worth your time," I said. "But it's nice to know someone cares."

Our order number was called and he grabbed our plates. I watched as he took a bite of the greasy burger and considered it.

"What do you think?"

"It's good but . . . have you been to Center Point for lunch yet?"

"I've only gotten breakfast food."

"Theirs is a little better," he admitted.

I gasped. "Cain, are you admitting you like something in town?"

He chuckled. "I'll happily admit that I like things in town. It's the people who don't like *me*."

"I'm sure if they knew the whole story they would."

Cain shrugged. "It's not my secret to tell. It's Jackie's."

"Would she ever—"

"No," he cut me off. "Unfortunately, everything you felt is multiplied with her. And it doesn't help that once it's out, everyone would know."

"They would tell everyone?"

"Some people have no decorum. I've made my peace with it. Mostly. I just have to get people to like me in spite of it."

"We could have another meal at the diner. I can be your full-time helper now."

"Maybe we should," he replied. "Because you need to try one of their burgers."

Plans were laid, and though the food was great, I couldn't wait to get back home. I had no idea what was going to happen with Trevor and my parents, but when Cain was in front of me, everything felt okay.

And that meant more than I could say.

Strawberry Springs Neighborhood Watch
Dale Garrett
The storms are a comin' this week, people! This might not be the week for sleeping naked.

Comments:
Atticus Thompson: It's these temperature changes! Damn Tennessee weather.
Hu Gh: I'll go out of this world the same way I came into it! If the world sees me naked, then they see me naked!
Tammy Jane: You already posted your whole rear end in here, Hugh. It's nothing we ain't seen before.
Jade Clark: Think Hugh's ass will scare off the storms?
Marjorie Brown: Don't forget your wigs either! I'll warn Henrietta.
Henrietta Brown: Don't make me take your phone again.

———

"You look cozy."

I jumped at the sound of Mollie's voice. She was sitting at the dining-room table with a steaming cup of coffee in her hands.

"Why are you awake? It's barely seven."

"I couldn't sleep." She shrugged, but I could see the way yesterday's events weighed heavily on her shoulders. "I kept thinking about what Trevor could be telling my mom and dad. I don't suppose I could speed run getting over my embarrassment and be able to talk about it tomorrow?"

"It doesn't work that way, princess."

She sighed. "Then I suppose I'll have to slowly work on it. But on the bright side, now that I don't have a job, I can join you in taking care of the animals."

"You already did that a few times."

"Yeah, but then I got in trouble. Now I won't get in trouble at all. I'm a free woman. One who wants to charm Hennifer."

"She's probably already forgotten you."

"But I haven't forgotten her."

"Wear a thick jacket," I said. "If you have one."

"Um, can I borrow one of yours?"

I let out a sigh. "You need *actual* work clothes if you're gonna be doing this full time, not whatever you brought from the city."

"I hate shopping by myself. Who am I supposed to go with to get opinions on how I look? The only person I know who wears work clothes is currently filming a TV show."

"I'll take you."

She blinked. "What?"

"Come on, princess. I can tolerate a little bit of shopping."

She raised her eyebrow. "And food?"

"We're supposed to be seen together, aren't we?"

"Fine, but I'm helping you this morning."

I opened the door for her. "And once you feel how cold it is, you'll regret it."

───────

Mollie didn't complain, but I could tell she was freezing. Fall was giving way to winter, and even with her jacket, it wasn't enough. Hennifer immediately jumped at her when the coop opened, which resulted in one hell of a rip on the shoulder of her cheap hoodie.

"What do I need to do to make her like me?"

"It might just be you."

"Unfair," she pouted, but focused her attention on the other hens. "S-see?" she said when she was able to pick up a chicken, one that Eric had named Jumpy. "N-not all hate me."

"Usually, she's a runner."

"I must have an aura."

"The only aura you have is cold. Your lips are turning blue."

"No one asked you to look."

I rolled my eyes and unzipped my jacket as I pulled her to me. "Get over here."

"But s-shouldn't we do our usual banter?" Her cold nose pressed into my neck. "Damn, you're so warm."

"We're going to the square right after this," I said, rubbing my arms up and down her back. "It was originally cute when you were underprepared. Now it's dangerous."

"You think I'm cute?"

I hid a smile as I pressed a kiss to her forehead. "Some days."

"Who knew that just a little bit of time would turn you into a softie?"

"I'm many things, but I'm not that."

"You are where it counts." Her hands fisted in my shirt again. "The town will see it soon."

My entire face flushed, and I wondered if it would help her warm up faster. I was having thoughts I didn't know what to do with, like taking her back to either one of our bedrooms and completely forgetting any plans we had for the day.

But the moment was broken by the sound of her stomach rumbling. "Sorry," she said as she pulled away. "I didn't eat much yesterday."

"Let me go milk the cows and wash up. Then we'll get breakfast and clothes."

"Really?"

"Yes. And if you don't wanna be alone, Eric's up. I bet he'll bother you as much as you want."

"He's never a bother," she said, rolling her eyes. "But I'll take you up on that."

"Welcome in," Tammy said as the door jingled closed. "I'd say this is a surprise, but with all the rumors flying around, I'm surprised I didn't see you in here sooner."

"It took him having a burger in Nashville to tell me how good the ones here were," Mollie replied.

"Nashville?" Tammy's eyebrows rose and she looked at me expectantly.

I froze. Most people didn't even try to talk to me these days.

"Yeah," I replied. "Mollie needs to see the way a real burger's cooked."

"You're a little early, but I can make something happen."

Tammy smiled at Mollie, but the expression carried over to me.

I didn't know what to do. Was Tammy finally warming up to me?

"Glad you tried something new. A change of pace is good for you, right, Cain?"

I blinked. "Yeah. I guess it is."

Tammy grabbed three menus. Mollie elbowed me.

"Did you see that?" she asked. "It's working!"

I waved for her to walk in front of me, but I was as excited as she was. I didn't think it would ever be possible for the town to see me as anything other than the punk kid who'd gone at Donny.

But maybe I was wrong.

"I'm guessing a coffee, a water, and an orange juice for Eric," Tammy said as we sat.

"You would guess right," Mollie replied.

"I always do. Be right back."

"Everyone seems to be in a good mood today," Eric noticed.

"As they should," Mollie said. "Things are looking up."

I usually didn't agree with that sentiment, but Tammy warming up to me meant something. Someone who might be willing to say Eric was better off with me than Waldren. One more person on my side.

"So, do I get to hear why you two were in Nashville, or is that a secret?" Tammy asked as she put the drinks down.

"Jackie said it was a *date*," Eric said.

"That wasn't the intent," I said. "And Mollie gets to decide if it's a secret or not."

She obviously didn't like to tell people about her past, and I'd keep it quiet if she wanted me to.

Mollie dumped creamer into her coffee. "I have this ex in Nashville. Cain knew I was gonna be seeing him at my mom's birthday party and drove up just in case I needed him . . . which I did."

"You drove three hours *just in case* she needed you?" Tammy set her hands on her hips.

"I-it was nothing."

"You and I have a very different definition of nothing."

"He's not a man of many words," Mollie said, smiling over at me. "But his actions count."

"That's what I always say," Tammy agreed. "You two are cute together."

I had no fucking clue what to say. I was busy trying to decide if this was even real.

Thankfully, Tammy didn't compliment us much more. I wasn't sure if I could handle it if she did. Instead, she took our orders and walked away to help other customers.

Mollie nudged me with her foot. "You should ask her."

"Ask her about what?"

She pointedly looked at Eric.

My entire back tensed. "I don't know if she'll say yes."

"You've come in here with him before, and she seems to like you."

"Just say please," Eric said, looking up from his coloring page. "It always works for me."

I blew out a breath. Saying please sounded so easy, but nothing worked like that for me.

Mollie reached out and grabbed my hand. "You've got this."

Nodding, I stood before I could talk myself out of it. Tammy was by the front, checking her phone in a rare moment of quiet.

"Hey," I said. "Can I talk to you about something?"

"Did I forget straws again?" she asked with a sigh. "They're normally in my apron, but I keep running out—"

"No, it's not that. It's . . . something else."

She crossed her arms. "You look like you're about to give me bad news."

"Hopefully not. It's not bad for you. Probably. I, uh, need something."

Both of her eyebrows rose.

God, I hated this. I hated every second of it.

"There's . . . something going on. And I need people who have seen me with Eric to write a letter talking about what they've seen."

"For a custody battle or something?"

I closed my eyes. "Yeah."

"Okay," she said.

"Okay?"

"I'll write it."

"You will?"

"You're many things, Cain Smith, but bad with kids is not one of them. I may not know the whole story, but I do know you dropped everything for that child sitting in the booth over there. I'm happy to help."

My shoulders slumped in relief. "Thank God."

"And I'll keep this between us," she added with a wink. "I know how you like your secrets."

"I wasn't aware anyone else kept secrets," I said.

"Not all of us run to the Facebook group with everything. At least not when it's serious like this. I can tell by all of *this*," she said as she gestured to me, "that you're not having a fun time."

"Thank you," I said. "I didn't expect you to be so nice about this."

"I can be nice when I wanna be. I also don't just believe what I hear. You know what I mean?"

"I don't think I do."

"Some people listen. Others watch. You've got a good thing going over there."

"Mollie's helped a lot."

"She has, but you had it before. With Eric." She smiled. "When do you need the letter?"

"As soon as you can."

"It'll be in the mailbox tomorrow."

"Thank you," I said.

"You won't thank me when you see my next egg order. I hope you have a good stock."

"I have plenty, but trust me, I won't complain about a large order."

She nodded. "Good. Now get back to your table. I think Mollie's stared at us long enough."

I turned, and true to Tammy's word, Mollie was looking over at us while she drank her coffee. She didn't even look away once she saw we'd both noticed.

"Did that go well?" she asked after I rejoined them at the table.

"For once, yes. She agreed. And it's not gonna be front-page news in the Facebook group."

"Yes! One down, more to go."

"Hopefully they'll be as easy," I said.

Tammy brought our food out only minutes later. As she set it down, Mollie spoke up.

"Thank you for being so nice about the *thing* you're writing."

Tammy looked at me. "She knows?"

"She knows basically everything."

She hummed. "Interesting. But you're welcome. It's not a big deal. Anything for that cutie." Tammy pointed at Eric, who currently had two pancakes shoved into his mouth.

"Eric, manners."

"I wike da food!" he said as he kept eating.

"You know, I sometimes eat like that too," Mollie said.

"So," Tammy started as she leaned on the table. "Any fun plans?"

"We're heading over to Treasure Trove," I said. "Mollie needs clothes that don't fall apart when she's working outside."

It was one of the few surviving original shops, and it was now owned by Grace, who'd taken it over when the last owner retired. It had tougher clothes as well as a new section of trendier items. Most of the younger women in town went there.

"A whole new wardrobe, huh?" Tammy asked. "You plan on doing a lot of farming?"

"Yep," she replied. "I'm officially staying. Probably for good."

Tammy's eyes lit up. "Oh, if only Bennie were here. He'd be thrilled. What about you, Cain? Are you thrilled?"

I only looked at Mollie. "Very much so."

Her rewarding blush and smile were worth the possibility that Tammy would go back on her word—at least regarding news about us.

Hugh called Tammy over before she could tease me any more.

Mollie took a bite of her burger. "Yeah, you're right. This is so much better."

"Told you."

She rolled her eyes, but was too busy eating as fast as Eric was. Tammy came over to check on us a few times, but seemed just as friendly every time she saw me.

I didn't know how to react.

After lunch, we walked over to the boutique, and she went straight for the florals.

"Nope," I said. "Farm clothes."

"But there's a strawberry shirt!"

"Work clothes. Then fun clothes."

She muttered a curse, but followed. Eric immediately found the kids' boots and begged to try them on.

"Hi, Cain!" Grace said with a smile when she saw us. "Need new jeans?"

"I'm here with her." I gestured to Mollie, who waved from behind a rack of overalls.

"Mollie!" Grace's eyes lit up. "It's so nice to finally meet you. I've heard so much about you!"

"I'm still getting used to it. Hopefully it's only good things. I can only think of one person I've pissed off."

"Do you mean me?" I asked.

"That's a given," she replied. "I mean someone not you."

"Brooke," Grace said. "Yeah, I've heard all about that since she's my sister."

Mollie paused with wide eyes. "Oh, um. Sorry about that?"

"Don't be. She loves to start things she can't finish." Grace waved her hand. "I get along with everyone."

Mollie's eyes cut to me, and I knew what she was thinking. Grace could be another contender. If this hadn't happened this morning, I would have disagreed, but now I had hope.

"How has business been?" I asked her.

It was out of character and we all knew it. Grace's eyes were wide when she finally responded.

"Good. Kinda steady. I'm just glad for cheaper rent for the shop, you know?"

I nodded.

"Small-town life has its benefits," Mollie added.

"Rent prices and everything else actually went up for a while," she replied. "Kinda like everything in the world seemed to, but we got some sort of small-town grant that stabilized things, which was just in time. We only lost the library and the town hall."

"A small-town grant?" Mollie narrowed her eyes. "I haven't heard of anything like that."

"Something about the preservation of historical towns." She shrugged. "None of us complained."

"It's how Jackie can afford rent in the square," I added.

"And how Jade and I can stay open."

"Does the farm have it?"

"Never needed it," I said. "But it's always there if we do."

"I'll have to look into that in case the weather ever messes with anything."

"Jade told me you were only here temporarily. But it kinda sounds like you plan to stay."

"I do," Mollie said. "So you'll all have to get used to me."

I knew this. But hearing her admit it twice to other people made it feel real. Mollie was a permanent part of my life. She was here. Living with *me*, of all people.

"And how do you feel about that?" Grace asked with a teasing smile.

I could have said something smart. Or I could tell the truth.

"A little like I won the lottery."

Mollie dropped a hanger, looking at me with dark pink cheeks.

Grace laughed. "All right, then. Now I see all the rumors were true."

Normally, that sentence would have made me bristle. Instead, I nodded at Mollie before walking to help Eric take off a shoe that was stuck on his foot.

After we had multiple bags of new clothes for both Mollie and Eric, we walked back to the truck.

And I opened the door for her before she got in.

MOLLIE

Strawberry Springs Neighborhood Watch
Grace Day
Okay, Mollie and Cain are kind of cute.

Comments:
Kerry Winsor: Oh, a post from the resident lurker!
Grace Day: Hey, Jade lurks too.
Kerry Winsor: She comments more than you.
Grace Day: ANYWAY, I ran into Cain and Mollie at the store. She's really brought out a different side of him.
Kerry Winsor: Seriously. She whipped him into shape. He needed it!
Nicole Rudder: She could probably do better, though. But the options are pretty slim, I guess.

MOM CALLED TWO DAYS LATER. My heart sank as I tried to decide whether to pick it up or not. Finally, I couldn't take it anymore and did.

"Mollie! Thank God. I wasn't sure if you would answer."

Neither was I. "Hey," I said, trying to keep my voice level. "How are you?"

"How am I? Not great, honestly. Your father told me he gave you an ultimatum at my party."

"Yeah, he did."

She scoffed. "I told him it wasn't the time. I had a whole plan ready to make you feel comfortable at home, and both he and Trevor got impatient!"

I winced at the mention of Trevor. "Listen, it's fine. I don't think it would have changed my decision."

"Come on, Mollie. Something has to."

"I like it here, Mom. It's charming and nice—"

"It's a hellhole."

"What? No, it's not. Are *you* okay? You don't sound like yourself."

"I'm worried about my daughter! You know how much I hate where I came from. You know how hard I worked to get out of there, and you go *willingly*?"

"And I'm happy that you're happy where you are. I need you to understand that I'm happy where I am."

"There is no understanding it because it makes no sense!" she snapped.

"Mom—"

"Listen, if you come back now, I bet your dad will go back on everything he said."

I'm sure he would. One puppy-dog-eyed look from me and everything would be back to normal.

But that wasn't what I wanted.

"I'll be fine here. The farm earns money—"

"Not enough!"

"There's enough to live off of. Prices aren't that high thanks to some small-town grant, and I already have ideas to make the farm bigger and better."

"And is that boy gonna go along with it?"

"Cain? Why wouldn't he?"

"I know a thing or two about him. He has a record."

"Papa Bennie—wait, how do you know that?"

"Trevor did some digging on this Cain Smith."

I closed my eyes, holding back a groan. If *Trevor* had found this out about Cain, then he would have twisted the truth and made it sound far worse than it really was.

"Papa Bennie trusted him," I repeated.

"My father had a habit of trusting anyone with a sob story."

"Mom, *I* trust him. A lot, actually. We can make it work."

"You're not at all concerned that you're sharing a house with a man who was in jail for battery?"

"I know about that, and honestly, while I don't agree with the methods, it was justified."

She scoffed. "Are you *that* blinded by that town?"

"Mom, I'm safe."

"God, I can't do this!" she wailed, and my eyes widened at her tone. She sounded like I had when I'd left after the party, like she was losing everything. "I can't watch you waltz into a place that will eat you alive."

"But—"

"Mollie, no. You don't know that town like I do. And you don't know what you're in for. Just come home!"

I was silent for a long time. I would be lying if I said I wasn't tempted, but I knew exactly where I wanted to be.

"No," I said. "I won't be doing that."

"Then I can't talk to you," she said with a sob. "I'm putting my foot down."

"So, you're just never talking to me again?" I replied. Now my voice was high.

"I'll always be here for you. Call me if you need anything, but I can't continue to reach for you when you're so stubborn about this choice. I hope you see sense before it's too late, Mollie. For your sake."

And then she hung up.

I had to sit in silence to process. Had she just . . . cut me off? Just like Trevor had said he would make sure of?

Fuck. He'd won. He'd taken my parents and gotten them on his side.

And I'd let him. Like a fucking idiot.

The fields were still barren when I went outside, and there was nothing to do. Cain probably had a handle on the animals, but I didn't want to take him away from his work while I was dealing with the consequences of my own actions.

I meandered to the cow fields where they grazed for food. Most of them paid me no mind as I leaned on the fence.

With my new jacket, I could stay in the cold for a while. Maybe I needed to, considering the wind wouldn't judge me for crying about what Mom had said.

Behind me, I heard a huff, and I turned to see Moosley had found me.

"Hi," I sniffed. "Having a good day?"

She looked at the field and then back at me.

"I'm not," I said, wiping at my eyes. "I think my ex has ruined my relationship with my parents. And I let him when I came here, like an idiot."

She looked back out at the field.

"At least you won't judge me."

Then she turned, giving me a side-eye that looked *very* judgmental.

"Or you will," I said with a laugh. "That's fine."

I figured she would wander off in search of more food, but her large head leaned against my arm.

The tears came harder, and I let them fall. I didn't regret my decision to come here. Even now, when I was crying in a field, I still felt something. Back in the city, I hadn't.

But I wished I'd done it differently. I wished that I'd never dated Trevor in the first fucking place.

Moosley was patient and leaned on me while I cried, even though I caught her side-eyeing me a few more times. I was calming down, but was still wiping my eyes when I heard footsteps.

"What are you doing crying on a cow, princess?" Cain's deep voice washed over me. Normally, I would hate that anyone had caught me, but he always had a way of finding me when I needed him.

"My mom called. She cut me off. She doesn't wanna talk to me anymore."

"Son of a bitch," he muttered. "I was hoping she was smarter than that."

"She's obviously not," I replied.

His footsteps got closer. Moosley huffed protectively. "I'm gonna make her feel better," he said to the glaring cow.

"It's okay," I told her. "He will."

If I thought I was getting side-eye, it was nothing compared to the one Cain got. Thankfully, she walked off, but still watched us warily.

"She's protective of you."

"You have Hennifer. I have Moosley." I tried to smile, but it didn't reach my eyes.

Cain was now in front of me and I leaned into him, hoping he could work his magic on me and make me feel better.

"I still feel *so* dumb."

"People fall for manipulation sometimes, princess. It's way too easy to do."

"But I didn't want to lose them."

"He'll show his true colors eventually."

"And if he doesn't?"

"Remember what I said when I came to Nashville?"

"I have you," I repeated.

"And Jackie. And Eric."

"And Moosley."

"For some reason, yes. You also have a cow."

She must have heard her name, as she was making a return. She slowly trotted over, and I thought she was coming to check on me.

Then she got to the fence and turned around.

Both of us jumped away, but the spray was powerful.

"Moosley!" Cain yelled. "Dammit, cow!"

I felt shock for all of one second before I burst into laughter. I didn't know who it had been aimed at since it had gotten us both, but Moosley glared at Cain before she walked away.

"Yeah, yeah," Cain said. "Laugh it up. Now I need a damn shower."

"Hey, I need one too," I replied. "At least the farmhouse has two bathrooms."

"It's an old house, princess. We can't run two at the same time."

"We could share," I offered.

He turned to me, eyebrow raised. "Really?"

"What better way to save water?"

We could have gotten out of the shower once the grime was

washed off of us, but the second I saw his naked body under the spray of water, I had other plans.

The bathroom was a humid mix of both of our body washes, and I'd been watching him clean up like it was my favorite TV show.

"Do you need a picture?" he asked as he rinsed the conditioner out of his hair.

"I wouldn't say no," I replied. "But there's something else I could use instead."

"Get over here."

Cain tugged me into the spray, pressing his lips to mine. He tried to take it slow, to drag out our first kiss like he always did, but I'd spent the last fifteen minutes watching his broad shoulders and his rippling muscles. I was more than ready.

I nipped at his tongue, earning a groan from him as I deepened the kiss. His fingers dug into my ass as he brought me closer.

I wasn't sure if I should rush this or take my time, but my body told me I needed a release as soon as possible. Some nights when we fell into bed, we were too exhausted to do anything but wrap each other in our arms.

The memory of what he could do to me always simmered under the surface, begging to be brought to life.

I bit his bottom lip. His erection was pressed to my stomach, nothing in between us.

After what had happened with Trevor, I didn't think anything could feel like this. I wasn't used to heat under my skin, or even being wanted in the same way I wanted someone else. This was a puzzle piece clicking together easily after being forced to try and fit somewhere that it didn't belong.

Nothing in the past mattered anymore. It was all compounded until it was flat and empty. In this moment, he was perfect, and that was all that mattered.

My nipples were hard, begging to be kissed. My clit was on fire as it asked for attention too. I wanted him everywhere. No, I *needed* him.

But Cain's attention was on my mouth. His hands sliding on my wet body weren't enough, yet I lingered on every movement.

"Goddammit, if you don't touch me right now . . ." I trailed off as his hands brushed over my ass.

"You'll what? Keep making those noises?" Now his hand moved to my breast. "I like torturing you."

"You asshole."

He huffed out a laugh and then pushed me against the tile wall. I didn't feel the cold on my back, only the feeling of my heart jumping into my throat.

God, I loved being manhandled.

"What do you need?" His voice was low.

"Everything," I whispered back.

"Then let's find a way to give you that," he murmured into the shell of my ear as his mouth trailed downward.

I arched into him the second he took my nipple into his mouth. His tongue swirled the sensitive bud, and I had to quiet my moans to keep myself contained.

"No need for that," he said. "We're alone this time. Let me hear you."

Fuck. I slowly lowered my arm. I was used to keeping quiet. There had always been someone around in Nashville. Trevor had never made me scream anyway, but I'd pretended for his sake.

This time, I let go.

A finger teased me open, slowly pushing in. I clenched around him as he hooked and went right to my G-spot, a near-mythical thing. I hadn't known I could come this way until Cain had showed me I could.

His teeth grazed my nipple and I pressed my head back into the tile, already gasping for breath.

"*Yes*," I rasped out.

"Is this everything?" he asked, his words rumbling against my nipple. "Or do you want more?"

Another finger teased my opening and my knees went wide.

It was euphoric to get exactly what I needed when I needed it. To have a man put me first and make me feel good time and time again. Was this what Wren had been talking about? It had to be, because there was nothing that could be better than this.

I was gasping for breath, not sure where to focus my attention because everything felt so fucking good. My pussy was hot as he fucked me with his fingers. My nipples were only adding to the sensation that thrummed through every cell in my body.

His thumb moved to my clit, and that shoved me toward the edge. I tried to hold out, to keep a hold on the rising pleasure as long as I could, but it was inevitable. Cain's mouth and hand were too perfect.

I tumbled over, every part of me alight with the feeling of my orgasm. My vision went black, and I might have floated off out of the shower and into the sky.

It took a while for my body to come back online.

I knew that I wanted to taste him. Cain might have had other plans as he pressed a kiss to my mouth, but I fell to my knees.

"What—"

My mouth covered his cock, silencing him. I paused for only a second to feel its heavy weight in my hand, then I took him as deep as he would go.

He pressed on my tongue and the back of my throat, and I bobbed up and down, hearing him gasp as his hands ran through my hair and cupped my head.

I got a few minutes with him in my mouth before his hold tightened.

"You're way too good at this." My stomach flipped at the praise, and I kept up the pace. I was determined to continue making him groan as he fucked my mouth.

But then his hand grabbed my neck gently. "As tempting as it is to come down your throat," he said, his voice soft yet unyielding, "I have other plans."

"Other plans?" I asked.

"Your mouth is great, but there's another place I wanna come."

The water turned off and he hauled me up.

His lips pressed to my wet cheek for all of a second before he said the hottest thing I could have ever imagined.

"Bend over the sink, princess. And then we both get to watch what I do to you."

"What about your rule?"

"I'll make you come on my cock. Don't worry about that."

Impossibly, my cheeks only grew redder, but I nodded. Nothing else sounded better. I scrambled to get to the sink, ready to feel him inside of me.

But then logic made its way into my mind.

"We don't have a condom," I said, turning back to him.

"Fuck."

"I could get back down on my knees."

His eyes met mine in the mirror and I knew he wanted me like *this*. No other way.

"I'll be right back," he said, and then he was gone.

In the seconds that he retreated to his room, I felt a stab of disappointment. I didn't want him to go, and I hated that we had to wait for a condom of all things.

For the first time in a long time, I wished hormonal birth control had worked for me. I wished I could feel him *bare*.

Maybe I could get over my fear of IUDs. Maybe I could figure something out to make sure that next time, we could do whatever we wanted to without worrying about a condom.

Cain didn't take long, and the second he was back, he tore open the wrapper with his teeth and had it on in seconds. When he lined himself up with me, my body broke out in chills.

I knew that when he'd fucked me the first time, he'd broken me for all other men. And as he pushed inside of my pussy, inch by agonizing inch, I knew that was still true. He filled my body, stretching me in ways I wasn't used to. I was addicted to it and all I wanted was more.

"Look," he said, grabbing my hair and tipping my head back to make me look into the mirror. My mouth was agape. My nipples were hard. "You're so fucking perfect all the time, but even more so when I'm inside of you."

My body heated at the words. He pulled out and thrust in, jerking me forward. I both saw and heard my moan as he picked up the pace.

I didn't usually think about fucking in front of a mirror, but it was the hottest and dirtiest moment of my life. Cain was already unfairly attractive, his chiseled body coated with a sheen of sweat, the bit of hair he had on his chest only adding to his beauty. But now I saw exactly what I felt written all over my face, and it sent me to new heights.

Trevor used to complain when I wouldn't come from penetration alone, since it meant he'd had to put in more work. I'd simply thought it just wasn't a thing I could do. The last time Cain and I were together, I finally had.

With the right man, it was *very* possible.

I was working myself up again, purely from the feeling of his cock inside of me. But as I started to approach the edge, he stopped and leaned forward, teeth sinking into the crook of my neck.

"Wh-what are you doing?"

"We're gonna take this nice and slow," he said. "Until we're both begging to come."

"I already am," I managed to say.

"Not as much as you could be."

He finally moved again. He pulled all the way out of me, leaving me aching and empty, and then slammed back in. He was rough, yet gentle. Hard, yet soft.

And minutes later, I was about to come again.

Only for him to stop.

He was going to make us both lose our minds, and yet I would let him. As he worked both of us up and then paused, I reached new feelings of need that I didn't know I had.

Looking in the mirror, I thought I'd been red before, but now my whole body was flushed. Now I was barely breathing properly. Now my whole body ached.

"C-Cain,"

"Y-yes, princess?"

"You have to—"

"I don't have to do anything." He marked his sentence with a rough thrust.

"I . . ." Another thrust. "Need." Another. "To—ahh!" This one hit depths I didn't know were possible. "*Cain.*"

"Fuck it," he said, and he didn't stop his pace. His hips pumped into me and my pussy tightened around him.

"*Yes!*" I yelled as I returned to the edge. I had no idea what I said as I was driven over it. All I could feel was an electric heat shooting from my core down to my toes and up to my fingertips.

It kept going, even as I felt him jerking inside of me, cum erupting from his buried cock.

I had no idea how much time I lost while floating through the stars. All I knew was that neither of us were able to stand when we were done, and I had to use the sink cabinet to support myself.

"I . . . I can't tell if I'm mad at you for that, or if I'm grateful."

"I saw your face as you came, princess." He pressed a kiss on my sweaty cheek. "I'd say the second one."

Eric was quiet when Cain picked him up from school, but told the both of us he'd just had a long day. Judging by the crease in Cain's brow, he was worried about it, especially after Eric went to bed early.

I hoped he was just tired like he said he was.

Quickly, I figured out I was wrong.

I was snuggled up in my fuzzy blanket with Cain when he suddenly bolted out of bed. For a second, I was confused, but then I heard the sound of a child's cry and knew exactly why he'd run.

Throwing a robe on, I went out in the hallway. Cain was kneeling in front of Eric, who had tear-stained cheeks.

"You're burning up," Cain said, his hand on Eric's forehead.

"I don't feel good. I threw up."

I could sense tension from every inch of Cain's body, and suddenly, I was feeling the same as he was.

Suddenly, I wished I knew more about kids and sickness.

"Dr. Connor warned me about this," Cain said. "I need to call him. And clean up the—"

"I'll call him," I offered. "Hand me your phone."

I thought Cain was going to turn me down, but he looked between Eric and me and then passed me his unlocked phone, and I found the contact.

"Hello?" a man's voice answered. He sounded sleep ruffled and I felt bad for waking him up.

Then I heard Eric sob, and I no longer felt bad. Still, I'd never called a doctor in the middle of the night, but I also had never lived in a place like Strawberry Springs before.

"Hi," I said. "I'm Mollie, a friend of Cain's. Eric is really sick and he wanted me to call you."

"Eric's sick?" There was movement on the other end of the line. "Well, it's not unusual. Kindergarteners get a lot of things. What are the symptoms?"

"He threw up and has a pretty high fever. Oh, and Cain is very panicked."

"He's serious about Eric, so I'm not surprised. I'll be over in a few minutes. I can test to rule out a few things and bring some Pedialyte."

"Wow, do all doctors in small towns do house calls?"

Dr. Connor laughed. "No, but I'd do it for Cain and Eric. See you soon."

He hung up after that and I blinked in shock at the phone. Did Cain know that Dr. Connor was making a house call specifically because he was asking?

Cain was running Eric a bath when I found him. "Dr. Connor is on his way."

"What?" he asked. "I thought he would just tell me what to do over the phone."

I shrugged. "He offered. He said he could rule out a few things."

"I don't feel good," Eric muttered, and Cain's attention was back on him. I made sure the washer and dryer were ready to clean Eric's bedding before pulling up what to do for a sick kid on my phone.

Headlights appeared in the driveway twenty-five minutes later, and I opened the door to a tall man with light brown hair.

If I wasn't already smitten with the man upstairs, he would have turned my head. He was over six feet with a lithe figure and an unfairly sharp jawline. His hair was longer, going past his ears, with a middle part that he pushed back when he saw me. He had on black-rimmed glasses that did nothing but accentuate his handsome features.

"Hi," I said. "Are you Dr. Connor?"

"Call me Henry," he said. "Where's Eric?"

"Upstairs. I think I just heard Cain get him out of the bath."

I motioned for him to follow me. Eric was dressed, but still looked miserable.

"Hey, kiddo. Not feeling well?"

Eric only shook his head. Henry grabbed his thermometer and got right to work. Cain hovered, unable to sit still.

After running all of the swab tests, Henry finally looked at Cain. "I think it's a stomach bug. Thankfully not the flu or anything else."

"What do I need to do?"

"Support, mostly. Try to have him take smalls sips of the Pedialyte I brought. If he can't keep anything down, take him to the hospital."

"Will do. Thank you for coming all the way out here, by the way. You could have just told me this on the phone."

"I think ruling things out does amazing things for panicked parents." Henry smiled.

"I'm not—"

"Guardians count," Henry said. "At least in my book."

Cain nodded, and Eric asked to go lie down. I watched as Cain took him to his room and got him settled.

"Is there anything else you need?" Henry asked.

"No, not really." I shook my head. As Cain stepped back out into the hallway, I gave him a purposeful look and pointed between Henry and Eric's closed door.

"Not right now," he muttered as he joined me.

"Then when?" I asked.

"Is there something else going on?" Henry asked, an eyebrow raised.

Cain sighed and scrubbed a hand over his face.

"Not about the sickness, but there's one other thing."

"What is it?"

"I need a letter. Saying Eric is well taken care of here."

Henry frowned. "Does the school need it or something? I've never heard of them asking for such a thing."

I didn't know how Cain's conversation with Tammy had gone, but I had a feeling he hadn't admitted everything that was happening. He could barely talk about it with me, so I wasn't sure what he would say.

"Eric's biological father is suing for custody. I need to prove that Eric's happy here."

Henry's eyes widened. "I didn't know his biological father was in the picture."

"He never was. He wasn't even on the birth certificate. But the DNA doesn't lie. And he supposedly has a right to do this . . . even if both Mollie and I think he's not fit for it."

Henry looked between us, but his gaze settled on Cain. "Thank you for telling me. I know something like this is sensitive. You probably don't want people knowing."

"No, I don't. But I need these letters, so everyone will know eventually."

"It won't be from me," Henry reassured. "And I'll help. I have plenty to go off of."

"You do?"

"You've taken him to every appointment since you brought him home. He always seems so happy when I see him. And I just saw how worried you were when he was sick." Henry smiled. "Do you want me to keep going?"

"N-no," he said. "I got it. Thank you, Dr. Connor."

Henry blinked. "Dr. Connor? I thought all of my friends called me Henry."

"Are we friends?"

Henry winced. "Ah, well. Maybe we're not. I'd like to be, though."

If it weren't such a serious moment, I would have laughed at the shocked expression on his face.

"The answer is yes," I said for him. "And I'm sure he's always wanted the same. He's just awkward."

"Really?" Henry asked.

"Yeah," Cain replied. "I don't do . . . people all that well."

Henry laughed. "Neither do I, but in different ways. I thought you hated me."

"He's like that with everyone," I said. "Even me, until I made him admit it."

"Yeah, yeah, I'm gruff." Cain rolled his eyes. "But can we continue the teasing when it's not three in the morning?"

"Maybe at the next appointment. Bring Mollie along for the full effect."

"Definitely."

Henry laughed. "I'm glad I came out here. Even if it did make me lose a little bit of sleep."

"Still, sorry for making you come all the way."

Henry waved it off as if it were nothing before he turned toward the door. He paused and looked back at us. "Oh, and you two are good for each other. If I can say that."

Cain spoke before I could. "You can. And I know. Life got better when she showed up."

"I'm glad you found your person," Henry said. "If only we could all be so lucky."

Strawberry Springs Neighborhood Watch
Henry Connor
It's sickness season! Wash your hands and stay safe.

Comments:
Nicole Rudder: I am not ready.
Kerry Winsor: Please tell me there's been an uptick in hand washing since your last post.
Henry Connor: Eh, stay away from handshakes for the time being.
Kerry Winsor: What is with the people in this town?

———

AFTER HENRY LEFT, I stared at the door, trying to make sense of what had just happened.

I didn't know how to process what went down. All I knew was that my body was buzzing, begging me to go lay down with Eric to make sure that he was okay.

But I also didn't want to leave the woman next to me.

"I'm gonna go check to see if we have yogurt and rice for when Eric's feeling better," she said. "And *you* should go be with him."

"You're not upset?"

She rolled her eyes. "Why would I be upset that you wanna be with Eric? I'm not that selfish."

"I didn't think you were. It's just . . . after everything—"

"He's sick. And he needs you. That's all I need to know."

"Thank you," I said before I could forget. "For all of your help."

"You're thanking a lot of people tonight," she replied. "How are you feeling?"

"Not as bad as one would think. I do owe you and Henry, so it's easy."

"And to think, you could have had a friend this whole time."

"I didn't think . . . I don't know."

"What if . . ." She bit her lip while she considered her words. "What if you have it wrong? What if the town *does* care about you?"

I thought about it. I almost wanted her to be right, but there were signs to the contrary.

Nicole's words when Mollie first got here, telling me that I should make sure nothing affected Eric.

What I'd heard Kerry say in the store.

What Brooke had said to Mollie in the bar.

The wounds were still there, and I honestly hoped that I could get enough letters without any of those people knowing. Without most of the town knowing. Sure, there were people I'd formed tentative trust with, but there were others who didn't deserve it.

"I think I got some people wrong," I said. "But not all of them."

"Who?"

I opened my mouth, but heard Eric whine from his room. "I need to—"

"Go," she said. "Take care of him. We can talk about this some other time."

That was all I needed to hear. I walked into the room and put my hand on Eric's hot forehead. He leaned into me.

"It hurts, Dad."

I froze at the words.

I would have been lying if I said I hadn't thought about Eric calling me that, but it was under very different circumstances, before Waldren was ever in the picture.

Now that our future was in flux, I didn't know what would come of this. I wanted to be his dad in every way, which made me consider adoption. My plans had been ruined by the fact that I needed a lawyer on retainer, and if Waldren somehow won this case and got custody, I had a feeling he wouldn't take kindly to Eric calling me his dad.

But I wanted it. So, *so* badly.

"I know," I eventually said. "I'm here."

Eric burrowed against my chest, holding me as if I could float away at any second.

I tried not to think about what could happen if this case didn't go my way, but as I sat in the dark room, holding the child I'd raised as my own, I knew I couldn't lose him.

No matter what the cost was to my pride, he was staying with me.

And I would make sure it happened, even if I had to beg for it to the people who hated me.

Eric was better a few days later. I was sure he didn't remember what he'd called me while he was half asleep, and I didn't know if that made it easier or harder to make it through each day.

He knew I wasn't his dad, but I wanted to hear him call me that.

Even if I shouldn't.

I was focusing on who to ask next. Jackie was monitoring the Facebook group, but most people were asking about the sounds they heard in the night, not talking about my custody battle. I thought I was in the clear until she showed up at the house one day.

She wore that worried expression, biting her lip and shuffling her feet. I knew this wasn't good news. I was on the way to milk the cows, but when I saw her, I decided it would have to wait.

"They know, don't they?"

"Not about what you're expecting. I was looking through some of the posts I missed while I've been busy, and I found this one from a few days ago." She got her phone out and showed me. It started out fine. Grace had made a rare post saying Mollie and I were cute.

But then I got to Kerry's and Nicole's comments.

When I was done reading, my stomach sank in the same way it had when I'd heard Kerry talking about me in the grocery store.

"Well, at least I know who not to ask." I handed the phone back to her. "Though his teacher would have been a helpful addition."

"To say these kinds of things in a group that *I'm* a part of—" She shook her head. "They have no shame."

They never had. It was why she'd never wanted me to talk about Donny in front of anyone.

"I'll find other people. I have two already."

"Three, including me. And Mollie."

"Yeah," I said. "I'll make it work."

Jackie rubbed my back. "Should we tell her? I don't think she's in the group. Maybe it'll show her who not to trust."

I thought about it. Mollie liked the townsfolk, and most of them liked her. The last thing I wanted to do was pop her bubble while she still had it.

"No," I said. "I'm sure she'll figure it out."

Jackie narrowed her eyes. "You're protecting her from it, aren't you?"

"For a little while. She'll see it eventually."

"She might just return the favor."

"I don't need any protection."

"That's where you're wrong." Jackie gave me a smile. "One day you'll see it."

I didn't know about that, but I shrugged. "Are you busy at the salon?"

"A little. I could help with the animals, though. To take the sting off what you just read."

"I'm fine without help. I know this town. This isn't news to me."

"But it's still not okay."

"No, but it is what it is. I know who not to ask. Now, if you'll excuse me, I have to take care of some spoiled cows before Mollie tries to again."

"Is she not good with them?"

"No, she's great with the animals. But she spends more time talking than working."

Especially with Moosley. How she'd gotten that cow to like her, I'd never know.

Jackie offered to help one last time before I convinced her I was okay. When she drove off, I mentally filed away Nicole and Kerry as people who couldn't help.

And now I had to figure out who remained.

MOLLIE

Strawberry Springs Neighborhood Watch
Mark Bell
Need a plumber. Bathroom. Can't explain more than that.

Comments:
Jade Clark: Sounds like a . . . shitty situation
Jade Clark: A shituation, if you will
Kerry Winsor: Oh, you've got jokes. Funny, coming from the woman who told me the wrong definition of gyatt.
Jade Clark: You JUST figured it out?
Kerry Winsor: I SAID IT AT CHURCH, JADE.
Mark Bell: PLUMBER, GUYS!
Hu Gh: Doesn't goggle do that?
Marjorie Brown: @Theo Murf can you help?
Kerry Winsor: You're actually being helpful?? Has hell frozen over?
Theo Murf: Dammit, Marj. Poop? Really?
Theo Murf: @Mark Bell Yes, I can help.
Henry Connor: Please just wash your hands afterward.

WINTER SETTLED IN, then turned to spring. Our already busy days grew even more hectic as the chickens ramped up egg production and I had to monitor the strawberries.

It hadn't been a hard winter, but I'd gone out every day to check on them in case something went wrong. Cain had told me I couldn't control everything with the farm, but I wanted this so badly that I'd felt like I'd needed to.

And as the sun stayed in the sky longer, I grew more and more nervous.

I wanted to open the farm this year. When Cain and I went into town for breakfast, people asked about it, and I wanted to deliver.

"They'll get over it if you can't," he told me every single time.

"I know, but this is exciting. I'm making it happen."

Keeping up with the farm and sneaking into each other's rooms every night was almost enough of a distraction from our problems, but not totally. As the court date loomed, both Cain and Eric had grown more and more restless.

"Who all do you have who's willing to help?" I asked over breakfast. It was the first somewhat-warm day, and we were eating on the porch to enjoy the beautiful weather.

"Tammy and Ron, Jackie, Henry, and you."

Tammy's husband was the only recent addition, and we were both pretty sure it was because they went home at night together and he'd figured out some of it.

"That's it?"

He shrugged. "It's been hard to figure out who wouldn't tell the whole town."

"But they'll know eventually."

"I'm hoping to keep *some* of it under wraps."

I narrowed my eyes. Cain had started backsliding into some of his old ways a few months ago. I didn't know why he was worried about everyone knowing.

I was half tempted to beg Kerry to let me into the Facebook group so I could see if anyone else knew. We'd discussed it when we'd run into each other at the square, but I'd never gotten to talk to her for long before Cain would interrupt.

There was obviously some sort of bad blood, something that Cain didn't want to share.

"What's the worst that can happen if you don't?" I asked. "Sure, being in the center of gossip isn't fun, but it's better than . . . the alternative."

His lips pressed together. I'd caught him staying up late at night, more than likely thinking about Eric.

"Theo might be a good choice," he said. "He's the guy who fixed the heat at Center Point the other week."

I nodded. "Yeah, and he talked to Eric for a bit. Seemed pretty open-minded."

Cain nodded. "That's one more down."

"What about his teacher?" I asked.

"Nope. Not an option."

"But she would be—"

"Mollie, I'm telling you she's not an option."

It was rare that he got so firm with me these days. The last time it had happened was when I'd tried to feed Hennifer for the third time in a day to get her to like me.

"Would you like to tell me why?" I asked.

"Not really."

"Fine," I huffed. I didn't know why he was keeping secrets, but I knew that getting him to open up before he was ready was like trying to take down a brick wall with a thumbtack. "What about Jade?"

"She . . . might work."

"Grace seems to like you."

"Yeah, her too."

"And Kerry—"

"Not her," he cut in again.

"Lemme guess, you won't tell me why?"

"You don't wanna know why. Trust me."

"Okay." I stood. "Keep your secrets. When you're ready to tell me everything so I can help you, I'll be around."

"Mollie . . ."

"We'll talk later." The last thing I wanted to do was fight, especially when stress was so high for him. I may not have known everything going on, but I did know that sticking around when I was already annoyed would do me no good.

I went to my room and opened the window to get some fresh air. I was ready for the strawberries to come up so the air would smell sweet like it had when I was a kid, but we were a few months away from that. I reached for my strawberry candle from Jade's shop, only to find I'd burned through it.

Well, a little shopping wouldn't hurt. And it would probably make my mood better.

Grabbing my purse, I got into my car and drove to the square. There were people all around enjoying the weather, most of whom I knew.

"Hey," I greeted as I walked into Jade's shop. "Got any more strawberry and vanilla candles?"

"Duh," she said. "I know you love them."

"I'll get two. Then I'll be out of your hair."

"Please don't be. It's so slow today that I'm dying of boredom."

"I suppose we *could* catch up. I'm giving Cain some space and I don't need to be home."

"Space? Is everything okay?"

"Everything is fine. Mostly. He's just stubborn about things."

"Don't I know it. Though, you can get through to him like no one else."

"When he chooses to tell me everything." I muttered it under my breath, but regretted it once it left my lips. "You didn't hear that, though."

"Seems like you're pretty annoyed at him. Welcome to my daily life."

"You're annoyed at Cain all the time?"

"No, just men in general. Especially *one*." She rolled her eyes. "You're right, though. Space is good. And you could get even more."

"I'm not going back to Nashville or anything like that."

"Um, no. I was thinking a girls' night."

"Where?"

"At the bar. I'm going tonight."

"But—"

"Grace will be there. Come on. You'll love it."

I bit my lip. I'd had fun the last time I was there, but that was because Cain had gone with me.

Then again, I did want to get closer to Jade. Wren was still filming, especially since the show paused due to the holidays and a burst pipe, and I was feeling her absence more and more as time went on.

"Okay, I'll go," I said. "Sounds fun."

"Yes! I can't wait."

We talked about other things going on in town, mostly petty gossip about who Brooke had been seeing, before I went back to the house. Cain was still working, so I went upstairs to look through my closet.

I didn't usually reach for my nicer outfits since I worked outside so much. Cain had been right when he'd said I needed the work clothes—my existing collection had been ruined over time.

Still, I had a few dresses to choose from. And I knew just the person to help me pick.

> Are you around to help me pick a dress?

WREN

> For like ten seconds. What's the occasion?

> Girls' night. I have three options.

> Ugh, I'm so jealous. I need girl time.

> Definitely the red one.

> We'll have girl time when you're done filming. Maybe here in town?

> I'm counting down the DAYS.

When I walked downstairs, about to leave, Eric was home and working on his homework.

"You look pretty!" he said with a smile.

Cain turned, eyes wide. "Are you going out?"

"With Jade," I said. "I figured I should do a girls' night."

He stared at me, and I could see all the questions he wanted to ask, so I went to the front door and gestured for him to follow me.

"Is this because of what I said earlier?"

"Not entirely," I said.

"You've avoided me all day."

"You've been busy."

He sighed. "Come on, princess. You never care if I'm busy."

I pressed my lips together. "I just wish you trusted me."

"I do trust you. It's others I don't."

"And why not?"

He sighed and rubbed the back of his neck. "Let's just say . . . people are nicer to you than they are me. Especially when they're talking among each other."

"Seriously? But you've been so friendly."

He shrugged. "The past is the past. But they're good to *you*."

I opened my mouth to ask who was so two-faced, but my phone went off with a text. Grace had offered to be the designated driver, saying I shouldn't be burdened with it on my first girls' night, and they were outside.

I usually didn't drink, but there had been a few girls' nights where I'd let loose with Wren. Each time was hilariously fun. Maybe I'd try with Jade and Grace too.

"I wanna know who, but I have to go."

"I'll tell you what Jackie showed me when you get back."

"It's not Grace and Jade, right?"

He shook his head. "No. They don't really post in the town group."

I nodded. "Good. But you better not go back on telling me everything."

"I won't," he said, and he pressed a kiss to my mouth. "Have fun."

I was tempted to stay and hear about everything, but I went out and got into Grace's tiny sedan.

"Girls' night!" she cheered the second I was in the car. She wore a blue dress and her curly hair was tied back. Jade had on a green top and her hair was freshly dyed to match.

"Wow," I said as I looked at them both. "I feel underdressed."

"Stop, you look amazing." Grace rolled her eyes. "And you've been to the bar before. Half of the people never wear anything nice."

"I'm only looking like this because I hear it's packed with

people from other towns." Jade winked. "I'm gonna try not to go home alone."

"And don't worry," Grace added. "Even if she bails, you'll have me to bring you back."

"Thank you for coming all the way out here," I said.

"It's not much farther than the nearest Walmart," she said. "Don't worry about it."

Jade caught me up on what they were talking about. Apparently, Brooke had decided she wanted to be a country singer and was considering auditioning in Nashville. Grace wanted her to do well, but wasn't sure that singing was the career for her, especially since she'd heard how her sister sounded in the shower. No one wanted to be the one to break that news to Brooke, however.

The town square was packed when we finally pulled in, and the inside of the bar was even worse.

"Wow," I said loudly. "It's busy."

"When Tammy volunteers to run it for Mark, she makes special drinks. Everyone wants one."

Tammy was behind the bar, hands busily pouring and shaking drinks. She had on blue eyeliner and laughed with all the women waiting for their order. Some of them I didn't recognize.

"Are they from Strawberry Springs?"

"No, some of these ladies travel to be here. Karaoke night gets *really* wild."

"Please tell me we're not singing," I begged.

"It's not in the plans." Jade shook her head. "Unless we get drunk enough to not care about our pride. You *are* trying one of Tammy's drinks, right?"

I thought about turning them down, but I trusted these people. I liked it here. I could let loose just this once.

Between the strong cocktail and me being a lightweight, I

felt the effects immediately. I was laughing louder at the ladies singing their hearts out on stage, and by the second one, Jade and I were on the stage singing a country song about killing cheating exes.

By the third, I was telling people how I never enjoyed my life back in the city, and everything started going blurry by the time I was on my fourth.

I must have really been out of it, because I thought I saw someone hanging out by the bar I didn't expect.

"Kerry?" I asked. "Are you really here?"

She turned with a laugh. "Oh, you look drunk. I bet Cain's gonna *love* this. And yes, I'm here. I might be a mom, but I can have fun too."

"Good," I said. "You deserve to have fun. *All* the fun in the world."

"What did you do to her, Jade?" Kerry asked.

"Girls' night!" she exclaimed. I blinked, wondering if there were enough words there for Kerry to understand. Jade then grabbed my shoulders. "Come sing another song with me."

"I want another drink."

She pouted. "Fine, but I'm inviting the cute guy to join me."

"Have fun!" I yelled at her as she ran off. Slowly, I made my way to the bar.

Kerry followed me.

"It's nice to see you out and about," she said. "I was worried Cain was keeping you hostage."

"Nah. I like being there. It's fun most of the time."

"Most people don't associate Cain with anything having to do with fun. You must have put some kind of spell on him."

"I wore him down. Plus, I help with a lot."

"Like what? I thought he was too stubborn for that."

Tammy put down another drink, which I grabbed immediately. I took a sip before answering. "Secret stuff."

Kerry's eyebrows went up. "Secret stuff? I *love* secret stuff."

"I'm not supposed to tell you."

"Hey, in this town, we're all like a family. You can trust me with anything."

My mouth twisted as I thought about it. If I had been sober, I might have remembered that Cain didn't trust her. It didn't matter if *I* did.

But I wasn't sober at all, and I took Kerry at her word.

"Stuff about a stupid biological dad. Stuff where he could lose Eric. He needs help, but he would never ask."

Kerry stared at me while I took another drink. "Wow. Is that why he's been so nice to everyone lately?"

"Yeah." I nodded enthusiastically.

"Interesting." Her voice was sharp and her eyes were narrow.

I was too drunk to think about what that could have meant.

But then Grace found me, saying it was near midnight and that I needed to get home. I followed her blindly, stumbling through the crowd and nearly falling asleep in the car.

I wouldn't know what I'd done until the next morning.

When it all fell apart.

CAIN

Strawberry Springs Neighborhood Watch
Kerry Winsor
So, you know how Cain's been all nice lately? Apparently, he's in a lawsuit for custody of Eric and needs our help. THAT'S why he's being nice. Mollie finally spilled the beans.

Comments:
Nicole Rudder: Knew it.
Hu Gh: Should've seen this coming.
SherriffMike Finch: Oh, damn. Knew about the lawsuit. Didn't know he was playing everyone with being nice, though.
Kerry Winsor: You KNEW? Why didn't you tell us?
Tammy Jane: Some things don't need to end up on Facebook, Kerry.
Kerry Winsor: This DEFINITELY needed to be here! And everyone agrees with me!
Nicole Rudder: Seriously. At least I didn't fall for his act.

HEADLIGHTS CAME DOWN the driveway and I had to stop myself from bolting out the door. Had Mollie had fun? Was she happy? I wanted to know everything about her night out.

I was as patient as I could be, though I opened the front door the second Grace's car stopped.

The passenger door opened next. "Cain!" Mollie yelled before stumbling into my arms.

"Whoa there, princess." I grabbed hold of her to keep her steady. "Are you drunk?"

"Just a little." Her arms went around me and she squeezed. "You smell so good. Has anyone ever told you that?"

There was a laugh, and I saw Grace watching us from where she stood next to the car.

Normally, I'd be embarrassed, but this time, I didn't really care.

"She had a few of Tammy's drinks. Jade's in the back seat cursing me out for not letting her go home with anyone else."

"Thanks for getting them home safely."

She brightened at the words. "You *do* know manners."

"I have to be on my best behavior." I pointed to the woman in my arms, who was putting more and more of her weight on me.

"I'm happy for you both. And I bet Jade will say the same thing when she's sober." Grace waved and got back into the car before driving off. I opened the door and led Mollie inside.

"That was so fun," she said. "But it would have been even more fun if you were there."

"Defeats the purpose of a girls' night."

"Who cares about rules?" she asked. "Why can't the man I love join in on everything I do?"

I paused. Did she just say . . .

But then I shook it off. What she said while her inhibitions were lowered could easily be something she wasn't ready to fully admit. I wouldn't address it until she was ready.

Unless I said it first.

"We'll talk to the girls about it. But right now, I'm getting you in bed."

"You better join me," she pouted.

"Not when you're drunk," I replied.

"No, for *sleep*. Please? I love it when you're there."

"And I love being next to you," I replied. "But you always grumble when I'm getting up and moving."

"No, I don't."

"You definitely do."

Carefully, we climbed up the stairs and into her room. She threw off her dress and then fell into bed while I turned to give her some sense of privacy.

"Get some sleep, princess," I said softly.

"Stay."

"You know I'll be here in the morning."

"But I want you here *now*."

I sighed, but I knew I wanted to be with her just as much as she wanted to be with me. I was determined to give her space, especially after I'd annoyed her this morning, but it seemed like she was already past it. "Fine. I'll go get changed and be back."

Mollie was drifting in and out by the time I opened the door, but the second I climbed into bed and wrapped my arms around her, her breathing evened out, and she was sound asleep.

And I followed her within minutes.

———

Both Jackie and Henry sent me screenshots of the Facebook group at six the next morning, but only Jackie sent me some of the comments. I knew even without seeing them that people were pissed.

And now, so was I.

Kerry had made it clear who she'd found out from, and I didn't understand how this could have happened. Mollie had been on my side since the day she got here. Why would she tell Kerry, the woman who loved to talk about me behind my back, the worst thing that was happening to me?

Now everything was ruined.

I only had the few letters I did. And now, because of what Kerry was saying, they all thought I only cared about them when I needed something from them. And I could admit that it looked that way, but I also knew that it had been nice feeling like a part of this town for once.

That hadn't lasted for long.

As Mollie came downstairs, my entire body tightened.

"I couldn't even sleep in because of this headache," she muttered. "I'm never drinking again."

"Probably a good idea," I said. My voice was short, and she froze when she heard it.

"What's wrong?"

I wanted to snap at her. I wanted to tell her just how wrong she was for telling *Kerry*, of all people, what was going on.

"Take some ibuprofen." I put the pill bottle on the counter before walking off, jaw still clenched. I needed to get work done and be away from her before I said something I would regret while she was still hungover.

I stayed outside for as long as I could, but she eventually found me while I washed eggs.

"Please tell me you're not mad because I went out last night. I thought you said you wouldn't try to keep me from friends."

I stopped, and all of the tension I was trying to avoid came rushing back. "You really think that's what I'm mad about?"

"It's the only thing I could have possibly done."

"It's not, actually." I pulled out my phone and handed it to her.

Mollie's eyes went wide.

"Shit."

"Yeah, that's one word for it."

She screwed her eyes shut. "A lot of last night is blurry. I remember her talking to me and asking questions . . ." She trailed off. "Fuck, I told her everything."

"And now everyone knows."

"Maybe some of them wanna help?"

I scrolled to the pictures of the comments where people did *not* want anything to do with me.

"Cain, I'm sorry."

"Of all the people," I said. "You had to tell *her*?"

"She's only been nice to me!"

"Yeah, that's how she is. Nice to your face and then does *this* when your back is turned."

"Has she done this before?"

"Yes. She has. When I sold Donny's house, I caught her telling the cashier that he would be rolling over in his grave if he knew I even had it, and recently she and Nicole had a lovely time in the Facebook group talking about how you were too good for me."

Her jaw dropped. "Oh. She was who you were gonna warn me about, wasn't she?"

"She was." I crossed my arms. "I wasn't making it up when I said people in this town don't like me."

"What about Tammy and Henry?"

"They're exceptions. Everyone has always seen me as the punk kid who came in and beat up his foster dad."

"But he was a terrible person! Didn't they have any idea—"

"No, and they never will. Jackie asked me to keep secrets, and I *do*. Unlike some people."

There it was. Her eyes fell to her feet. I almost wanted to take it back, but I still couldn't get over the fact that she'd done this.

"I'm sorry," she said again. "I was drunk, and she was asking questions. I thought it might help you be a part of everything. Now I see that I was wrong."

Being drunk wasn't an adequate excuse.

"You were."

"How do I fix it?"

"Right now? I have no idea. I'm just surprised that everyone isn't here with pitchforks and after my head." I ran a hand over my face. "I'll have to tell my lawyer that I have all I can get. And if I lose this case . . . then I lose the case."

"You can't—"

"It's always been a possibility," I said. "Now it's just more of one."

"Cain—"

"Give me some space. I'm way too angry to talk to you right now, and I don't wanna say something I'll regret."

Her eyes were wide, but she nodded. "Yeah, okay. I'm . . . really sorry."

She went into the house, grabbed her purse, and hastily left. Normally, I would tell her not to leave, but I didn't know if I could say a damn word to her.

I didn't let the weight of losing Eric hit me until she was gone.

MOLLIE

Strawberry Springs Neighborhood Watch
Kerry Winsor
I feel so much better now that I know the whole story. We're all in agreement that we're NOT talking to Cain, right?

Comments:
Jade Clark: He lives here. We kinda can't not talk to him.
Kerry Winsor: We could boycott the farm.
Tammy Jane: Are you serious?
Kerry Winsor: He needs to know he was wrong!

I KNEW I needed to make myself scarce. I didn't know *where* I was going, just that I needed to leave.

And out of habit, I was heading toward Nashville.

Was that where I wanted to be? Maybe not.

But the entirety of Strawberry Springs was mad. Rumors were swirling, and I had caused it. Cain didn't need me at the farmhouse.

What other choice did I have?

I struggled not to cry as I got closer and closer. I was terrified of what my parents would do when they saw me, but they were the only ones who didn't hate me. Or at least I hoped they didn't.

But I needed them. Desperately.

When I pulled into the driveway, I completely broke down. I felt terrible. Both for leaving and for causing such a mess back in the place that had started to feel like home. My chest ached as I thought about the way Cain had looked at me, like I'd broken everything.

And I had.

The door to my car opened. "Mollie?" Mom's voice asked. "Honey, are you okay?"

I silently shook my head.

She opened her arms without explanation. I fell into her, still feeling the regret of *everything*.

"Come inside." Her voice was soft. "You need some tea and a listening ear."

I followed her without another word.

Minutes later, I had a warm drink in my hand and my tears had slowed to sniffles.

"Tell me everything."

"I doubt you wanna know. It's Strawberry Springs drama."

"If it upset you this much, then I want to." She grabbed my arm. "So, start from the beginning."

I wiped my eyes and did as she asked. I told her how Cain had been in the beginning and how we'd finally made a truce. And then how it had all fallen apart. She listened intently, but her eyes narrowed as I got to the night prior where Kerry had tricked me.

"This is almost exactly what happened to me," she

muttered. "I'm telling you, that town sees everything one way. And nothing will change their mind."

"I really hurt Cain."

"No, *they* did. Honestly, asking questions while you were drunk?" She shook her head. "Of course they did."

"Did you know Kerry?"

"She was younger than me, so not really. But trust me, there were plenty of people like that when I lived there."

"What happened when you were there?" I asked.

"It was years ago." She shook her head.

"It still seems to affect you."

"Oh no, don't turn this around on me."

"But maybe it'll help me understand," I said. "Please?"

Her lips thinned, but then she nodded. "Fine. I had a friend once. A close friend. And we did the kind of things friends do—be honest with one another. She was dating this man who wasn't good for her. I kept trying to tell her, but she never listened. Eventually, I told her I couldn't watch it happen, and that she needed to dump him or I would walk away. Of course, she told everyone, and you know who they sided with? *Her.*"

"Really?"

"Yes. They tried to shame me into submission, tried to tell me I was jealous of her perfect little boyfriend." She crossed her arms. "No one spoke to me up until I left for college. And I never looked back."

I looked down at my tea, stomach roiling. "That's terrible."

"It's not the kind of place for you," she said. "I just hate that you had to see it this way."

My shoulders slumped, but not out of relief. I didn't want to be done with the town; I only needed a break to think things through.

But would I even be welcomed if I *did* go back?

Maybe Cain would only grow angrier over time. Maybe the town would too. And I would come back to Nashville.

The thought made me want to cry all over again.

The front door opened, and I looked up. Dad was walking in, a concerned expression on his face. For half a second, I was happy to see him. Then I realized he wasn't alone.

Trevor was with him.

Fuck.

"Your mom texted me that something happened," Dad said. "We came right away, Mollie-bear."

"We're worried," Trevor added, smiling down at me.

It felt more like a smirk.

"I'll catch you two up while I refill Mollie's tea," Mom said. "Come on."

Dad nodded and headed toward the kitchen.

"Actually, I'll stay here," Trevor said. "Mollie doesn't need to be alone through this."

Mom put a hand on her heart. "You are so sweet."

He was a fucking liar. My fists tightened as they walked away.

"Seems like you learned your lesson," Trevor said.

"Fuck off," I hissed.

"Not entirely, I suppose. You still have that damn attitude. You know, I really had you trained until you went and whored yourself out to some lowly farmer."

For a second, all I could do was gape. Had he really said that?

But then, all my sadness vanished, replaced with the white-hot fire of rage.

Trevor smirked. "We'll just have to work on getting you back up to my standards."

Yeah, that was it. I was Mollie fucking Wilson. I'd gone off on Cain for far less.

I wasn't taking this from him. Not on the best day of my life. And definitely not on my worst.

"How *fucking* dare you!" I snapped, slowly rising from my chair. "Let's get one thing straight. I will *never* let you talk to me like that again, no matter if I'm here or not. You will *never* make me feel small again. You will never be able to turn me into whatever fucking wife you wanted because I will fight you every step of the way. Do you understand me?"

"Mollie?" Mom's voice sounded panicked. "What happened?"

"What's wrong?" Dad asked.

"*What's wrong?*" I laughed and looked at Trevor. "Repeat what you just said to me."

"I said nothing," Trevor hissed. "You've lost your mind."

"Oh, you're scared the second they're in the room? Funny." I turned to my parents. "Because when you two are gone? He's a completely different person."

Mom's eyes went wide. "Wh—Mollie, what do you mean?"

"I told you she would do this. She's blaming it all on me." Trevor laughed. "Don't believe a word she says."

I was too far gone to feel fear. I'd lost everything.

Except for myself.

"If you believe *him* over me, then that's fine. But you should know the whole story. Like how he never cleaned and put it all on me. Or how he would knock on the wall to summon coffee every morning. Or how he lied about the farm and then tried to force me to sell. How he made snide comments about Wren to try to isolate me from my friends, and how he talked a big story to you so you would cut me off. He's emotionally manipulative at his best. Emotionally abusive at his worst. And I'm not taking it anymore."

"Oh come on, she's lying!" Trevor snapped. "I've never emotionally manipulated anyone in my life!"

"Really? Then why did you never let me make any choices for myself? Why did you constantly say you were *training* me to be your wife? Was I a dog to you? Or just a trophy you wanted to show off?"

Mom covered her mouth, but Dad spoke first. "When did you feel this way, Mollie?"

"I felt this more and more every single day until I left."

"Is he why you left?"

"Yes. I got out before it could get so much worse."

"What did he say?" Mom's voice was shaky, but I hadn't seen her this mad in a long time.

"Come on—"

"No," Mom said. "If someone uses the word *abuse*, I listen. Honey, tell me what he said."

"He said he had me trained well before I whored myself out. Despite the fact that he said he would be seeing other people."

Mom turned to Trevor, jaw on the floor. "How *dare* you."

"No, I didn't!" Trevor snapped. "She's lying like she always fucking does! She's nothing but a spoiled princess who cares only about herself."

"Is that all you have to say about me? Because you've said a lot worse in the past. Or are you too much of a fucking chicken-shit to try it now?"

"You little *bitch*." He sneered. "I don't know what sort of inbred bullshit that town taught you, but you should learn your place!"

He stepped forward, and I wondered how hard it would be to punch him in the face.

Someone else did it for me.

"You fucking asshole," Dad said. "Don't you ever talk like that to my daughter."

"Get out!" Mom yelled, pointing at the door. "Before I call the damn police."

"Wh-what?" Trevor asked.

"Leave," he boomed. "Now!"

"But she—"

"OUT!"

Trevor was red in the face, but stomped out the door. Dad cursed and got out his phone.

"I'm calling HR. A man like that isn't working for me." He left the room in a rush, his footsteps echoing throughout the house. "And I should probably cover my ass for hitting him. Honestly, how *dare he*—"

Mom grabbed my shoulders and pulled my attention from what Dad was muttering. "When did it start?"

"When did what start?"

"This behavior."

"I . . . I'm not sure. It was just a lot of little things. Comments here and there. Him always seeming to get what he wanted. Then he got bolder, and I just felt . . . trapped. So, I left."

"Why didn't you tell me?"

"You said that it was normal to fight with your partner. I thought it was all fine. Until it wasn't."

"But *still*. If you said what was happening, I could have told you—"

"When did I have a chance? He was *always* here when I saw you, saying the things you wanted to hear. He did it even after I was gone! And every time we've spoken since, you've pressured me to get back together with him."

I was ready to continue to defend myself, to tell her I wasn't in the wrong for falling victim to Trevor's tricks. To say that I'd done my best, even if it had taken me a while to say it.

But then she let out a loud sob and started crying.

"M-Mom?" I asked slowly.

"I fucking *fell* for it!" she said, her voice thick with emotion. Another sob escaped her before she continued. "Like a fool. I thought he was so *perfect*."

"Mom. He's smart. He knows how to trick people. How could you have known?"

"Because I've *seen* it! God, and to let it happen to my own daughter? What kind of a mother am I?"

"We're all human here. We can't help that he said what he did. What matters is that you're on my side now."

"How are you not more upset by this? I mean, he said such mean things—"

"I've processed my pain over time. Trust me, it was messy and hard but . . . I'm okay. At least with the stuff from him. Running was the best thing I ever did."

"Oh, honey." She pulled me into a tight hug. "You never have to run again."

Her words washed over me, and I went stiff. She was right. I didn't need to run.

So why had I run from Strawberry Springs?

Was it because I was unsafe?

Or was it because I was too scared to face what I'd done?

Hell, I'd faced Trevor. *Finally*. And I'd gotten my parents to believe me. Couldn't I also do the same back home?

"I-I can't stay."

"What?" Mom asked. "But you're supposed to move back."

"No, I can't. I have unfinished business at home."

"Home?" she scoffed. "But this is your home."

The anger was back. "Mom, I'm not gonna run anymore. I'm fixing what I broke in Strawberry Springs."

"It's not your fault, it's theirs!"

"I had a part in it. I hurt people I care about."

"But I don't *understand*. Why do you care so much about that place?"

"Because even when people aren't perfect, they're still *people*. I might not like what they did, but I have to give them a chance to do better."

"They're not worth that."

"I think they are."

Her face turned red and she shook her head. "No. *No.* I won't let you."

"Mom, I'm not asking for permission. I get now that you don't understand why I like the town. That's fair, after what you went through. But my experience isn't yours."

"But—"

"You don't have to understand my choices. All I need is for you to *respect* them."

Her jaw dropped, and she shook her head, ready to argue more.

"I love you, and I'll call you later. But I have to fix this." I gave her a kiss on the cheek and ran off.

"So, you're gonna run again?"

"I'm not running from you. Nor am I running from my problems. I'll always be a runner, Mom. But it's time I ran *to* them."

Tammy didn't even smile when I walked into Center Point Diner.

"Here to wallow?" she asked.

"No, I'm here to talk to you. You know this town better than anyone."

"Debatable."

"And you were on Cain's side. I need to know how to fix this."

Tammy's lips thinned. "And why should I help you? You're the one who blabbed to Kerry and set all of this off."

"I was drunk and stupid. And wrong. But I need to do something. Even if it means facing who I hurt."

"It wasn't me that you hurt. Haven't you talked to Cain?"

"He needs a break from me."

"Then I suppose you can start with the one closest to him." She pointed to where Jackie was sitting. The woman sitting in the window wasn't the one I knew. Her eyes were downturned and her hair was a mess. "You're not the only one wallowing today."

The guilt in my stomach only multiplied, and I made a beeline for her.

"Jackie, I am so sorry," I said as I approached her table.

She looked up briefly and then down again. "I don't speak to traitors."

"And you still speak to Kerry? Did you forget that she's the one who told everyone?"

Jackie's shoulders tensed, but she finally looked at me. "I do it for peace, which I suppose I should extend to you. But I'm *not* happy."

"I understand."

"Neither am I," Tammy said. I jumped, not realizing she had followed me over. "What the *hell*, Mollie?"

"I know," I muttered.

"There's one rule in this town. If Kerry knows, everyone knows."

My shoulders slumped. "I've figured that out."

"There's a reason some things stay private," Jackie said.

"Is there anyone who wouldn't believe this at face value?"

"Me," Tammy said. "Maybe Mike. He can be smart."

"That's *it*?"

"Kerry's job is to inform everyone of everything," Tammy explained. "She's the reigning queen of drama and the others eat it up like fish. She's a—" Her words were cut off as she stared at the door. "Speak of the devil."

I followed her gaze and saw Kerry walking in. She was in a good mood.

Probably because she had gotten to tell everyone everything.

For the second time that day, I understood why Mom had left. Was this how it had always been? Had there been some queen bee running things in town while they were in high school?

Kerry didn't seem to pick up on everyone's ire. She waltzed over as if nothing was wrong.

"Hello, everyone," she said with a smile. "Nice day outside, right?"

Jackie looked down at the table and didn't answer. Tammy's fists clenched, but she did the same.

Were they serious? They were just going to let it happen?

"The weather might be nice," I said. "But my day isn't. What I told you last night wasn't exactly Facebook material."

"But everything goes on Facebook."

"Not everything," I replied. "Some things are personal. And now the whole town is on a witch hunt."

"Well, maybe he should have talked to us before he needed something. Did you ever consider that?"

"Maybe you could have tried to make him feel included."

"I've done nothing but *try*," Kerry snapped. Obviously, I'd hit a nerve. "I'm not rude to him every time I see him. I treat him like every other person in this town, despite the fact that he's done terrible things to us."

"He has not."

"Oh yeah? Then let me give you some information. He beat Jackie's husband here in the town square. In front of *everyone*."

"Keep it down," Jackie hissed.

"No, I won't keep it down." Kerry shook her head. "You've defended him until your face is blue, and for what? He went after your husband and then sold your house!"

"You don't know him."

"You know what? I'd love to!" She threw her hands in the air. "But he won't talk to *any* of us."

"He was trying to," I defended.

"Not without a reason. And, in case you didn't notice, I'm not included in that."

"I wonder why he didn't want to talk to you," I said. "Maybe it's the stuff you said behind his back?"

"What stuff?"

"Mollie," Jackie began, "you don't have to—"

"No," I said. "I'm not backing down this time. I heard about what you and Nicole said on Facebook. That was public, Kerry. And I also know you said Donny would roll over in his grave if he knew Cain sold his house."

"Am I wrong?" she asked with a scoff. "I don't understand why Jackie defends Cain after everything. Donny was her *husband*!"

I wanted to say something, but I couldn't. I knew why. Jackie knew why.

But she didn't want anyone else to know.

"Even I don't know, but that's her business." Tammy's voice was quiet, but I was glad she spoke at all. "Come on, Kerry."

"You could tell me," Kerry asked. "Ever thought of that?"

"Kerry, *please*." Jackie's face was red, and I wondered if this was how she looked when she'd begged Cain to not tell anyone why he went after Donny. "I don't wanna talk about this."

"If you don't talk about it, how am I supposed to get what the hell you're thinking!" Kerry snapped.

I looked at Jackie.

Tell them, I urged with my expression.

She shook her head.

"Whatever," Kerry said. "The only reason he's nice is because he's been using us. If I don't know all the information, then I only know what I see. And what I've seen is that he's a selfish asshole. Maybe Eric is better off with someone else."

"Absolutely not!"

I was about to say the same thing, but the words didn't come from me.

Jackie looked different. Hearing Kerry's thoughts on Cain had morphed her shame into anger. She was standing now, breathing heavily as she regarded the other woman.

"Then tell me how you know that," Kerry said. "Tell me what happened! I've been your friend for years. Can't you trust me?"

"After you just told the whole town that Cain was about to lose his child? And *encouraged* it? No, honestly, I can't."

"This town is a family," she said. "The Facebook group is how we communicate!"

"Then this is one fucking dysfunctional family," Tammy said. "Not all of us signed up to have our shit plastered online."

"It's not to be mean! *My* stuff is everywhere. Look at what the group said when my husband was deployed!"

"Just because something is fine with you doesn't mean it's okay with everyone else," I said sharply. "If you really want this town to be like a family, then it means you respect what *they* want, even if you don't understand."

"Okay, that might make a little bit of sense. For some things. But with Cain, that was a warning for everyone. Not just gossip."

"Cain is a good person," Jackie said.

"And how do you know that? Because I haven't seen it!"

"I'm still not telling you!"

"I won't tell anyone, but I need to *understand*."

"Kerry, do you have eyes?" Tammy asked. "Do you really think Donny was a good fucking person?"

"I mean . . . I thought he was decent. He kept to himself. He certainly wanted to keep *Jackie* to himself. She would disappear for we—" She froze. "Wait a second."

"Dammit." Jackie looked out the window. "Now everyone's gonna know."

"Did he hurt you?" When Kerry realized Jackie wouldn't answer, she turned to us. "Did he?"

"I don't know, but why else would Cain have done that?" Tammy answered.

"You know," Kerry said as she looked at me.

"Yes, I do. He told me why everyone saw him as the villain." I looked over at Jackie. "And he was fine staying that way if it meant protecting someone he loved."

Jackie's eyes were closed, but she turned to us. "Yes, he would do anything for someone he cares about. Even at great cost to himself."

"He would still keep it even if it meant he lost Eric."

The words made Jackie sigh and she slumped over. "Everyone will know anyway. At least Cain might get something from this." Jackie took one breath to steel herself. Then she looked at Kerry. "Donny hit me, Kerry. Every day of our marriage. I had to disappear whenever he left a mark I couldn't hide."

The diner was silent. Kerry covered her mouth, eyes wide. Tammy looked to be in a similar state of shock.

"It was *that* bad?" Tammy asked. "I knew you fought, but not . . ."

"It got better when Cain was around. And I felt better having someone to care for, but then . . . then Donny wanted me to get rid of him. I said no, and Cain saw the bruises that came of it."

"Oh my *God*," Kerry said. "No wonder you didn't want the house."

"Yes."

"No wonder Cain went at him. But why didn't he say anything?"

"I asked him not to. I didn't want everyone to look at me like I was the victim. Because in a way, I wasn't."

"How were you not the victim?" I asked.

"I stayed," she replied with a sad shrug. "I never felt like I could afford to leave. Not until Cain figured it out. And then we got the grant that made rent cheaper. But I still stayed. Even when people offered me outs."

"Who offered you an out?" Tammy asked. "I would've if I'd known more."

"Me too," Kerry added.

Jackie sighed and looked at me. "Your mom did."

"M-my mom?"

"Yeah. Before we got married. She saw it before it got bad. And she stood by me up until she couldn't anymore. I bet she'd love to know she was right."

I blinked, remembering what Mom had told me.

Was *Jackie* the friend that had betrayed her?

"Did you . . . tell the town she didn't want to be your friend anymore, by chance?"

"I told *two* people," she said, shaking her head. "Which meant everyone knew. I learned my lesson after that, but the damage was done. And technically, it was my fault. Donny swooped in, told me I didn't need friends if I had him and . . . then we got married."

I winced. That had almost happened to me. I could have ended up with Trevor in the end and he'd been planting the seeds of doubt about Wren, even if I didn't listen.

"Shit," Tammy said. "I remembered that drama. We all thought we finally had something on the girl destined to be in the city who thought she was better than us. Turns out, she was smarter."

"*That's* what happened with Mirabelle?" Kerry asked. "God, I didn't know so much of what went down."

"You were ten when it happened," Tammy said. "And besides, you can't know everything."

I thought Kerry would fight us on it, but she let out a long breath. "You're right. I can't. I guess I should have trusted that Jackie knew what she was doing. You always liked Cain."

"He's sweet under that gruff exterior," she said. "Like with Eric—"

"*That* I've seen," Kerry interrupted. "He'd do anything for the kid."

"Including talking to people he was sure hated him," I added. "He didn't think anyone would give him the time of day, but he did it anyway."

"And he really needs these letters?" Kerry asked.

"He does," I replied.

"Well, we could tell them what Jackie told me," Kerry said. "Then I bet people would understand."

"I'm not about to go waving my abusive ex-husband story around town to get sympathy. That's staying in this diner," Jackie said firmly.

"I suppose that's fair." Kerry sighed. "I kinda wish I hadn't told everyone what I did. I sure look dumb now."

"No fucking kidding," Tammy added.

"I'm sure between the four of us, we can figure out some way to help," I said.

"Isn't he mad at you?" Jackie asked. "I thought you two had broken up over this."

"We're not at a full breakup, but he *is* mad. Maybe he won't see past this, but I want him to keep Eric either way."

"Me too. Somehow, I like the kid with him." Tammy shrugged. "Who knew?"

"I do too," Kerry admitted. "I'm in for fixing this."

"Good," I said. "Because I'm pretty sure most people will listen to the gossip queen if she clarifies some things."

"Do people really call me that?"

"Yes," we all answered.

"And it's *not* a compliment," Tammy added.

"Okay, okay. I now know to have better boundaries." She smiled. "But it *is* a pretty cool title."

"You just need to use it for good," I replied, and gestured to the table.

Kerry sat and looked at us expectantly. "All right, I will. Now, where do we begin?"

CAIN

Strawberry Springs Neighborhood Watch
Mark Bell
All that drama and now everyone's silent. What happened?

Comments:
Atticus Thompson: I don't know. I kinda just want it to go back to normal.
Jade Clark: Seriously. I'm not here for petty stuff like that.
Marjorie Brown: Kerry is quiet for the first time in her life, and you're COMPLAINING?

I DIDN'T WANT to have to go into the school, but there was a message to all of the parents saying the kids needed help bringing home an art project, so I begrudgingly walked in.

The last thing I wanted to do was see anyone. Especially Nicole. And especially Kerry.

I was hoping I could keep my head down and leave, but of

course, Kerry was in the classroom, whispering to Nicole in the back corner.

"Hey," I said to Eric. "Where's your project?"

"Back there." He pointed to the one corner I wanted to avoid. *Fuck.*

I gritted my teeth and walked over.

Kerry jumped when she saw me. "Oh, Cain! Hi!"

It wasn't like her to act nervous. She usually walked through life without a care in the world, especially when she'd found a new nugget of information to share.

"Hi. I'm just here to grab Eric's project. You guys can go back to talking about . . . whatever it was you were talking about."

I searched for his name, feeling both women's eyes on me.

"Cain," Nicole said. "I have a question to ask you."

Great. *Perfect.*

I grabbed Eric's project and tried to keep my face neutral. "Yes?"

"Let's say you're driving down the road one day and see a cold kitten. You're allergic to cats and hate them, but you spot it. What do you do?"

What kind of test was this? "I take the kitten home and make sure it's okay. Why?"

"Okay, and now Eric wants to keep it."

"Is there a kitten outside or something?"

She shrugged. "It's just a hypothetical."

Kerry watched intently, and I wasn't sure why she wasn't throwing what she'd learned in my face.

Unless this was some roundabout way to do it.

Still, I knew I needed to play along.

"First of all, I don't hate cats, but if I did . . . Well, I would keep it. I missed out on a lot as a kid when I was bouncing around homes. Eric gets what he wants."

"See?" Kerry said. "I told you."

Nicole ignored her and slowly nodded.

Kerry gave a thumbs-up, but she wasn't looking at me. She was looking out the window. I followed her line of sight and saw a flash of golden-brown hair.

Had everyone lost their minds?

"I hope that clarifies things," I said slowly.

"Yes. It does."

I looked back out the window again, but there was nothing. "I'm . . . gonna go. Nice talking to you."

"You too," Nicole said.

"Are you sure there's not a cat?" I asked. "If it's outside, I could get it."

"No cat," Nicole said. "But at least I know who to call if there ever is one."

I blinked, still unable to make sense of the purpose of that question. I walked over to Eric.

"Are you friends with my teacher now?" he asked as he grabbed my hand.

"No, I think this entire town has finally lost their collective minds," I muttered. "Don't worry about me. I'm fine."

"You seemed mad this morning."

I had been. The betrayal was fresh. It still hurt to think about, though I was more worried about how people would act.

It turned out the answer was far weirder than I expected.

I could deal with weird.

"I'm fine," I said. "Let's get you home and get you a snack."

"Will Mollie be there?"

I hadn't seen her since this morning. I wasn't sure if I could handle it. "I don't think so. It's just the two of us."

Eric sighed. "Fine. But I wanna show her my art."

I didn't blame him. Even while mad, I still thought about her throughout the day. I didn't think I knew how to stop.

Which meant she and I needed to talk as soon as she got back from wherever she'd gone.

When Mollie didn't come home, I grew worried. I'd asked for space, but she didn't need to leave the house. Or worse, the town.

As time ticked by, I thought back to everything I had said to her. In my anger, I knew I hadn't been the nicest, but I hoped there was nothing that would have made her leave permanently. Eric was attached.

So was I.

I sat on the couch as the night grew into the morning, hoping to see her come back. If she hadn't by the next day, I would start asking people if they'd seen her.

I must have dozed off at some point, because my eyes flew open when I heard the front door shut. I was lying down when she walked in, a massive folder in her hand.

"Where were you?"

She yelped and dropped the folder on the ground before turning to me. "Cain! You scared the shit outta me."

"Likewise, princess." I eyed her. She was in the same clothes as yesterday. "Where the hell were you?"

She knelt and picked up the papers. "I was giving you space. Among other things."

"And you were out all night?"

"Well, it took a while to get everyone—I mean, every*thing*, done." She stood. "Here you go."

"What's this?"

"Papers. Ones you should read. I don't expect this to fix everything between us, but I wanted you to have them." She gave me a smile and then stepped away. "Once you see what they are, I'll go back to giving you space."

"And space means what exactly? Because I thought you were gone."

"I wasn't gone. Just busy. But if you want me to leave—"

"No," I cut her off. "I didn't ... next time I say I need space, just let me go outside. You don't have to run."

"Funny. That's not the first time I've heard that in the last twenty-four hours."

"When did you hear it the first time?"

"Don't worry about me," she said, shaking her head. "You should open the folder."

"But—"

"Cain," she said firmly. "Open it, and things will make sense."

I wanted to work this out, but she seemed oddly focused on whatever this was. Slowly, I flipped open the folder and saw a handwritten note stacked on top of a *ton* of other handwritten notes. I picked up the first one.

To whoever,

Cain is a grade-A asshole, but not about that kid of his. Or his girl. In fact, to those who don't piss him off (not me) he's a really good guy. You should definitely let him keep Eric.

Hugh Jeffries

I blinked. Was Hugh complimenting me? At the bottom of the page was another note in different handwriting.

.   .   .

Cain, this one is for your eyes only. Do NOT send this to your lawyer—Mollie

"What did you do?" I asked slowly.

"Keep going," she urged.

To Judge Marlon,

As a father myself, it was shocking to hear that Cain had taken in a child three years ago, but it shouldn't have been. I admit that I missed it, but he is truly a kind soul. He's dedicated to Eric and always has been. He's more dedicated to the success of his child than many biological parents are. I see Eric growing into a fine gentleman, especially with Cain as his father. Please accept this as my formal recommendation of his character.

Atticus Thompson

Judge Marlon,

I may not have been in town as long as some other letters you'll get, but I've seen a lot of Cain around town. I know his type. He's guarded and takes a long time to warm up to people. But I do know that once someone has his trust, he'll do anything for them. And Eric is the one person that has that. I know terrible parents. Cain isn't one of those. He's the kind of parent I wish I had. Don't take Eric from a good home based on biology alone. Keep Eric where he's happy.

Theo Murf

Judge Marlon,

I've known Cain since he was an angsty high schooler who hated us all. To say that he's grown is an understatement. He's a dad. Through and through. It's honestly kind of cute, and it's a reminder that anyone can be the kind of parent a kid needs. He comes into my store all the time to get the candles and soaps that Eric loves. Every time, Eric is so happy to spend time with him.

I may not have kids, but I know when they're well taken care of. And Eric is. There is no better place for him to be than with Cain.

Sincerely, Jade Clark

To Judge Marlon,

I'm currently Eric's teacher in kindergarten and have also known Cain since high school. I wasn't sure what to expect when I saw I would be teaching the boy Cain is raising, but I can't lie and say I was excited. Once upon a time, Cain was a very difficult man to get along with. I expected the same from Eric.

I couldn't have been more wrong. Eric is bright, kind, and so willing to learn. He's progressed more than any other student in my class, and not just because of his own dedication. Cain has been willing to do <u>anything</u> for Eric since day one. That includes talking to moms he doesn't get along with. Volunteering for events when he doesn't have the time. Eric has done everything a child can do and more with Cain helping him every step of the way.

I urge you to consider this in your decision. In all the ways that matter, Cain is Eric's father.

Sincerely, Nicole Rudder

"Wha—I don't understand. Nicole hates me."

"She changed her mind."

"*How?*"

Mollie stepped forward and pulled out another letter. "This is how."

Dear Cain,

I would say this myself, but Mollie warned me you might still be angry and need space. She's a real voice of reason! Though, I couldn't let myself not say anything to you, even if it's a letter.

I'm sorry I said what I did. I shouldn't have gone to Facebook with your information. To me, we're all a family. I want us all to talk about everything, but Mollie made me see that what I want isn't what everyone else wants. That means respecting each other's boundaries.

And beyond that, I had the wrong idea about you. Apparently, you protected Jackie when she needed it (and no, that will not be in the Facebook group!) and you also make her smile. For that, I owe you a thank you. And an apology.

It's clear to me that you're a key part of this town. And I wish I hadn't made you feel excluded. I hope seeing that everyone can see sense and help you is enough to prove that you are <u>welcome</u> here. Even when you're kind of a jerk!

Love, Kerry.

PS: I sent my letter directly to the judge. It's more of what you've already read, but it's really shitting on whatever guy is coming after Eric. Did you know he littered?!?!?! Heard it from Mark. I hope you beat his ass in court. (And in real life? Is that illegal to say?)

· · ·

"Cain," Mollie asked gently. "Are you okay?"

I flipped through the rest of the letters with shaking hands. "Everyone is here. Everyone wrote one."

"Yes. They did. It took all night, and Kerry wrangling some people into shape, but they all care."

"You and Kerry spent all night getting these?"

"Jackie and Tammy too. Though they crashed about halfway through and are probably still asleep. I imagine the Facebook group is mad that the diner's closed, but they can deal."

I wanted to answer, but all I could do was put the papers down on the couch and pull her into the tightest hug of my life.

"Whoa!" she said. "Is this a good hug or a strangling hug? Because—"

"Mollie." My voice was shaky. "I don't deserve you."

She was finally quiet, and her hands moved to rest on my back. "Actually, you do. Or did you forget you drove three hours just in case I needed you?"

"It's not enough. You did all of this, even after I was mad at you."

"But it was mostly my fault."

"You got *Kerry and Nicole* to write one. I don't even know how you did it."

"The same way I got you to see sense. I yelled until they listened. And Jackie helped. She . . . told Kerry everything."

"She said something about that in her letter. Did she really?"

"Yes. And she promised not to tell anyone. Between Tammy, Jackie, and me, we made her realize that not everything is gossip. She learned her lesson."

I could only stare at this marvel of a woman and wonder how she'd managed the impossible.

"You're incredible. Amazing."

She pulled away, cheeks pink. "You can do a lot when you stop running. When I was back in Nashville—"

"You were in Nashville?"

"Yeah," she said. "When you said you needed space, I figured I would get out of your way."

"Not there. Not where you could have run into Trevor."

"Yeah, not my finest moment. But it worked out. I finally stood up to him too."

"You did?"

"Told my parents everything. They sided with me. He did say that he almost had me *trained* until I whored myself out, but it got me out of my funk."

My hands tightened on her. "Are you fucking kidding me?"

"I'm not."

"He's basically *admitting*—"

"It was bad, but he's getting what he deserves. I'm pretty sure my dad fired him. I bet he'll have to use the ring he proposed with for money once I send it back to him. I'm tempted to throw it away, but he would definitely sue me, so I'm gonna do the right thing."

Through my anger, an idea formed. I'd come a long way in my need for revenge, but I loved Mollie. No one was going to get away with talking to her like that. "You still have the ring?"

"My dad thought I needed a reminder of my life there when I went for my mom's birthday." She shook her head. "It's buried in my glove compartment. It means nothing to me."

"No, I'm glad you still have it."

"Why?"

"Because I think we should send it back with a gift. Can you watch Eric tonight?"

"Yes," she said slowly. "Why?"

"Because I need to take a little road trip."

I banged on the door of the address Mollie had given me. I'd told her I would give the ring back, and she'd told me not to get my ass in trouble with whatever I did.

What I was doing wasn't exactly *legal*, but it was what he deserved.

I stepped back as the door opened. Trevor peeked out, his eyes catching me. He looked like he was ready to punch me, and his face turned bright red. "*You.* You have a lot of nerve coming—"

That was when he stepped out of his apartment and into a pile of shit. Actual shit.

Because there was a massive pile of it from Moosley right under his feet.

"What the—"

"Thought I would hand deliver this to you for what you told my girlfriend yesterday. You should enjoy it. Breathe it in."

"This is disgusting! What's wrong with you?"

"Oh, you don't like it? I thought you wanted the land. This would be what you'd find there." He glared, and I started down the stairs, only to remember the actual delivery I was planning. "And here's this back."

I tossed the ring to him, but it landed in the cow patty. "You're demented," Trevor growled.

"Yeah, probably. But hopefully, you'll learn your lesson."

"And what's that? Never come to your shitty-ass town?"

"No." My voice darkened. "Never mess with Mollie again, or next time, you'll be *eating* the shit."

Trevor's eyes went wide, and I took the opportunity to walk away. He screamed obscenities after me, but I didn't engage. He would be busy cleaning for a while.

I couldn't stay too long. Mollie had only gotten a short nap after being out all night. She woke up to watch Eric, but I'd promised her she could get rest the second I got back. The six-hour round-trip drive was worth it, though.

Still, I pushed my truck and got back a few minutes early. The lights were on, though it was past Eric's bedtime.

"Hey," I said when I walked in. "Is Eric up?"

"What kind of babysitter do you think I am?" Mollie asked as she fought a yawn. She was on the couch and sat up when I walked in. "He's out. Right on time too."

"You're exhausted," I said. "I'd give you a pass."

"Don't need it." She yawned again. "Who needs sleep anyway?"

She slowly stood and made her way over to me, but stopped as she got close. "Is that . . . cow shit I smell?"

"Yep."

"What did you do?"

"Gave Trevor a present. One to match his personality."

Her eyes widened. "You didn't."

"I did."

"Oh my *God*." She laughed. "I probably should tell you how mean that was, but he deserves it."

"He does." I was about to go to the bathroom to shower, but I had one other thing to say. "No one messes with the woman I love."

Mollie's jaw dropped. "The woman you *what*?"

"Love. In case you hadn't figured it out, I love you."

"But I just messed up a lot of things."

"And then fixed it. Even made the town see things no one else could. Mistakes are gonna happen. It's what you do after that matters."

Her cheeks went red. "For the record, I love you too. And I'd show you how much if you didn't smell like shit."

"Give me fifteen. I can fix it."

"If I can stay awake," she said. "Though the smell is pungent."

"We have plenty of time to do that tomorrow. Get some rest."

"Will you come and find me after your shower?"

"Every time, princess."

MOLLIE

Strawberry Springs Neighborhood Watch
Kerry Winsor
Since when do deer hang out on porches? Damn thing scared the bejeezus out of me and made me spill my coffee! I think my neighbor a mile away heard me yell at it!

Comments:
Jade Clark: Channel your inner Disney princess, Kerry. You don't have to go to war with them.
Kerry Winsor: THEY'RE INVADING MY LAND, JADE! THEY TOOK MY BRUSSELS SPROUTS AND NOW MY MORNING PEACE? WHEN WILL IT END?
Henry Connor: Kerry, just checking in. How are you feeling emotionally these days?
Hu Gh: I know you're young, Henry, so you might not know, but when women hit a certain age, they start to lose it like this.
Jade Clark: WHOA.
Kerry Winsor: I can fight you **@Hu Gh** AND I WILL WIN.

SherriffMike Finch: Please keep this off Facebook and away from me . . . I don't wanna have to fill out an incident report . . .

I'D CHEWED through all my nails by the day of the decision date. Every single time we drove to Nashville to see the judge, my nerves only grew. Cain's lawyer hadn't been kidding when he'd said Cain would need all the evidence he could get, because the judge seemed hell-bent on moving Eric in with his biological father.

Eric had been questioned. Cain had been questioned. And so had I, since I was the owner of the house.

But neither of us knew if it would be enough.

Judge Marlon walked out and sat at his desk, his gaze on some papers. He was an older man with a balding spot. I could feel Cain holding his breath from where I sat in the back. I didn't blame him. I was doing the same.

I couldn't tell when I'd gotten so invested in Cain and Eric. It might have been the first day I saw them, when I'd watched the rock-hard heart of the man melt for a kid he'd taken in years ago.

Either way, I felt every single ounce of stress Cain did.

"Thank you all for being here," Judge Marlon said. "I won't make you wait. We're discussing the custody case of Eric Smith."

"His last name should be Pines," Waldren said. "Considering he's my kid and all."

Judge Marlon's lips thinned. "I'm going off the name on the birth certificate, sir, as I've said each time we've met."

Waldren scoffed.

"I've reviewed all the files. It's my goal to always reunite biological parents, especially when they were not aware of the child."

Fuck. That didn't bode well.

"But considering the . . . extensive evidence of Mr. Smith's involvement with Eric, and all of the character references I've received, I believe I've made the decision that will benefit both parties. I assign joint custody, with Eric spending his weeks with Mr. Smith and weekends with Mr. Pines."

"What?" Waldren asked. "But I'm his *father.*"

Judge Marlon held up a hand. "You are, but Eric is settled in his current home. And I believe it's not beneficial to him to have him move schools at this point in time. And speaking of your fatherhood, I'm also going to be opening a case involving child support for you, Mr. Pines."

"Are you *serious?*" Waldren complained.

"I-I don't need child support," Cain said.

"It's not about needing it. Waldren has a responsibility to you. We'll also be considering back child support, considering you've funded Eric's needs for most of his life."

"Absolutely not!" Waldren snapped.

"You're the one who established paternity and wanted contact with your child. If you refuse to follow the court orders, then I'm sure Mr. Smith would be happy to continue providing *all* of Eric's care."

Waldren glared. Cain kept his gaze on Judge Marlon, but the tension in his shoulders was obvious. This wasn't the worst-case scenario, but neither of us trusted Eric's biological father. I knew it was going to be next to impossible for Cain to let Eric go with Waldren.

"The first weekend with Waldren will be in two weeks," Judge Marlon said. "I'll be watching closely to ensure this does not negatively affect the child in any way, and if it does, we will further review."

As the session was called to a close, I opened my phone to message Jackie, who was anxiously waiting for an update.

> Cain kept primary custody. But he does have to let Eric go with Waldren for the weekends.

JACKIE

> Oh no.

> Well, I had a celebratory cake and an I'm sorry cake. I suppose we'll eat both. I'll let him break it to Eric, even though he's asked me a hundred times.

As people filtered out, I caught up with Cain.

"Are you okay?"

He only let out a long breath in response. I winced and rubbed his back. We passed by Waldren, who was loudly complaining about the outcome, and got in the truck to go home.

"I don't like this," he said as we drove. "Olivia had to have a reason she didn't want him in Eric's life."

"I agree. We can hope he's more than he seems, but on the bright side, the letters worked. You keep primary custody."

"I owe the town a thank you . . . or *something*. Once I get through letting him go with that fucking idiot."

"Jackie said we'll have both cakes tonight after you explain everything to Eric."

"After I explain it to Eric," he repeated in a wilted murmur. "*Fuck*."

"Need help figuring out what to say?"

"Please."

He looked at me with the same awed expression he always had when I jumped in to help. I only hoped that one day this wouldn't be so hard for him, and that everything would turn out okay.

But I had a terrible feeling about all of this.

"After everything he's done, now *this*?" Jackie shook her head.

I looked up the stairs. Cain had come home and gone right to Eric to explain what had happened. I was giving them space when Jackie found me. She seemed as torn up as Cain was, and I didn't blame her.

"I'm glad it wasn't the worst it could be," I said. "Still. He's been the only caregiver for Eric for years."

"He barely let me watch him before you came around," she said. "He's such a good kid. He doesn't deserve this."

"He's not alone," I said. "He has us."

"You're definitely good for him. Me? I don't know."

"What do you mean? You were the only one on his side for years."

She shook her head again. "After I asked him to keep a secret that alienated him. All of it because of a man who didn't treat me like I was worth anything. God, I should have listened to Mirabelle when she told me who he was. Maybe then I could have . . ." She trailed off, eyes back on the ground.

"Could have what?"

"Given Cain the family he needed."

"But *you're* family to him."

"Not the kind he deserves. I hurt him in the end."

"You made a choice that hurt him, yes. But you've also done good things. Like standing up for him in front of Kerry. Watching Eric when he asked you to. Being here for him when *he* needed it."

"But—"

"No, Jackie." I turned to her and grabbed her hands.

"Family isn't being perfect all the time. Family is messy. We hurt each other. We make stupid choices, but in the end, we're here for one another. And that's what you do."

"I . . . You're right. Mirabelle must have taught you that."

"Not in words. She's a good mom, but . . . she's not perfect. None of us are. But if you're here and supporting Cain and Eric when they come down those stairs, you're doing exactly what you should be."

She smiled at me, her eyes watery. "You are one smart girl, you know that?"

"You should have seen me when climbing on the roof to get Hennifer. I was *not* smart then."

"Still." She pulled me into a tight hug. "I'm happy Cain has you."

"He always will," I said, and I meant it. More than he could ever know.

"Have you talked to her? Your mom?"

My stomach fell. "Not really. She said she didn't wanna watch me make a choice she couldn't support. And I'm obviously still making that choice."

"A choice she couldn't support? It's not like you're staying with your abusive ex."

"I think Strawberry Springs feels similar to an abusive ex to her. She doesn't see it like I do."

Jackie's shoulders drooped. "I suppose I'm a bit at fault for that."

"She'll come around." I tried to smile, but it didn't reach my eyes. "Hopefully."

"You have me if she doesn't." Jackie's hand landed on my shoulder. "She might be stubborn, but you're her daughter. She has to still care."

I opened my mouth to say I hoped she did, but Cain came

down the stairs carrying Eric, who had tear-stained cheeks. Both Jackie and I jumped into action, trying to offer support.

Eric was a resilient kid, and by the end of the night, he was smiling again. He said he didn't want to go, but he would if he had to.

Cain, on the other hand? He was miserable, and I hated to see it.

Hated it more than anything.

Strawberry Springs Neighborhood Watch
Jackie Anne
Can we all just agree to be nice to Cain this weekend?

Comments:
Kerry Winsor: Oh no. Is it time?
Jackie Anne: Can't confirm or deny.
Kerry Winsor: Well, there's my answer.
Mollie Wilson: This is not the weekend for drama. That's all
I'll say.

———

THE FRIDAY that I'd been dreading came far too soon. When I
wasn't busy with the animals, I was working out how to get Eric
to Waldren. He had been demanding, trying to get me to come
all the way to where he'd just moved to in Nashville. He'd also
asked questions that told me he had no idea what he was doing.

I warned Eric that it might be hectic, and every part of me
wanted to take him and run.

According to my lawyer, that was a bad idea. I needed to let this happen and see if it caused any issues. He said I was lucky Judge Marlon had sided with me at all. I needed to stay in his good graces.

Mollie had been extra helpful, and I still didn't know how to thank her. She'd been cooking meals and not complaining when I spent extra time with Eric. Some nights, I fell asleep in his room, worried that he would be gone when I woke up. Each time, she smiled and told me things would be okay.

I owed her. And when this weekend was over, and Eric was back with me, I would figure out some way to repay her.

In the end, Waldren won when he told me he didn't have a car seat for Eric, and I prepared to be in the car for six fucking hours.

But when I walked out of the house, Mollie was leaning on my truck.

"What are you doing?"

"We're taking my car."

"We? And why your car?"

"Mine is comfortable for long trips, and it has some features that make highway driving easier."

"You still didn't say why you're going with me."

"I'm not leaving you to deal with dropping Eric off on your own," she said. "This is hard. For both of you."

She looked at Eric, who was pressed against my side. "I want Mollie to go," he said softly.

I sighed. "Are you sure about this?"

"I wouldn't offer if I wasn't sure," she replied. "Let's go."

I put Eric's seat into her car and we headed out. She even offered to drive. I was grateful, because I wasn't sure if I should be behind the wheel of a car while so nervous. I dreaded every second as we got closer to Nashville, and I could tell Eric did too.

Waldren lived in a high-rise apartment, one that screamed money. The lobby was all marble and the doorman gave me an odd look when we walked in.

"There he is!" Waldren announced when he saw Eric. "My kid."

"Hi," Eric said quietly.

"Why so bored? You're gonna have a blast here! And I can finally invite my girlfriend over." He muttered the last part, and I knew he was still lying to her about raising Eric.

"Maybe this weekend should be for the two of you."

Waldren ignored me. "I have games and movies. I bet you've never seen any of that."

"He has," I replied dryly. "But he prefers to play outside or with his toys."

Waldren glanced at me, his smile dropping. "I bet *you* taught him that."

"It just came naturally to him." I crossed my arms. "Now, I brought his car seat. You want it?"

"No, I don't plan on leaving the house with him."

"You need to order one, at the very least."

"I'll do it when he's playing games." Waldren waved me off, and my fists clenched. Why was he brushing off anything to do with *my* kid?

I pushed the thought back. I'd never let myself think about him as mine, but those letters from the town had gotten to me.

"You should do that, considering Judge Marlon is watching this *closely*," Mollie said.

"Fine. Fine. You two worry too much. Come on, Eric, let's go play."

Eric looked between me and Waldren, and my heart broke.

I knelt to his level. "It'll be okay. I'll be back Sunday."

Eric nodded. We'd already been over the details of the situation time and time again. He knew he had to do this, just like I did.

But damn if his wide eyes didn't kill me.

I hugged him tight, trying to keep myself together before letting him go. Waldren walked off with him and up the stairs.

"I fucking hate that guy."

"Me too," Mollie muttered. She glared up until her phone went off.

"Who was that?"

"It was Tammy. She texted me to ask if we could come by the diner."

"We, as in both of us?"

Everyone in town knew that Eric wasn't going to be with me for some weekends. I'd told everyone the court battle results myself, including the split custody. But I hadn't told anyone when, mostly because I didn't want them to ask me questions while I was adjusting to the change.

"It seems so. Want me to tell her it's not a good time?"

I let out a sigh. Tammy was one of the first people I'd trusted, and though it was typical for me to hide when things were rough, I didn't want to turn her down when she was obviously trying. "We'll go. No promises on how social I'll be."

"You'll do better than you think," she said with a smile. "I'll tell her."

"I regret this," I said when we pulled in. There were cars everywhere, filling up almost every space available. "Since when is Center Point packed on a Friday night?"

She laughed. "I did give you an out, but I think it'll be fine. You might need the distraction."

Tammy was waiting for us. "Welcome, you two. Whatever you get is on the house."

"Really?" Mollie asked.

"What do you know?" I added.

"Yes really, and I know a few things." She gave me a sad smile. "But I'll ignore it if you don't wanna talk about it."

"Who talked?"

"No one," Tammy said. "But we're not dumb. Jackie told us to be nice to you this weekend, and I knew they would start the whole split custody nonsense within weeks."

"They did," I said. "Thank you for offering free food, but I'll still pay."

"Nope. I won't let you."

"But—"

"Do you think I won't shred a card if you hand it to me?" She raised an eyebrow, and Mollie laughed.

"She's not the one you try to out-stubborn, Cain."

"No one in this town is," I muttered as I sat.

Tammy smirked before getting our drink order. While she was gone, I only had a few minutes to check my phone for an update on Eric before someone else was at our table.

"Hey, Cain." Atticus gave me a half smile. "You know how I like to cook. I made extra of my bread with the eggs I buy from you." He set down a loaf on the table. "You should have it."

"Oh, uh, thanks? But if you want it—"

He waved his hand and disappeared before I could finish my sentence.

"What was that?"

"Not sure, but this bread looks so good."

"Everyone is acting—"

"Cain!" a high-pitched voice called, and Kerry waltzed up to the table. "I brought cookies!"

"You too?" I asked. "I mean, I appreciate it, but—"

"Well, we're trying to be nice since this is the weekend—" She stopped herself. "I mean, uh, this is a completely and totally normal weekend."

"You know."

"I do. Sorry. But it's *not* in the Facebook group."

"Then how did Atticus know?"

"I think we all figured it out, so you better prepare yourself."

"To be in the gossip mill again?"

"To get taken care of. Don't you know how we do that?"

"Not really."

"We give *food*, silly. We did for Donny's funeral, though now I regret that." Her face morphed into disgust as she talked about Jackie's ex. "And we'll check in."

"But I don't need all of this."

"It's not about what you *need*. It's about us caring to help where we can. Obviously, we all wanted you to keep sole custody, but Judge Asshole decided not to do that."

"Judge *Asshole*?" I laughed. "Interesting name."

"Our letters were very clear." She crossed her arms. "But whatever. We can do other things to support you."

I had no idea what to say, but the heat creeping up my cheeks was unmistakable.

"Look at his *face*," Mollie said as she laughed. "You're gonna break him."

"Between you and me, that's the goal. We have a *lot* of time to make up for. Enjoy the cookies."

I took them numbly, wondering if this was what I'd been missing out on. If this was what Mollie had seen in Strawberry Springs.

People came up to us one by one, dropping off different things for no reason. They didn't mention why, but as the pile of stuff on our table grew, so did my gratefulness.

"I'm glad we brought your car," I said as we left. I'd tried to pay, and Tammy had brought out the shredder and let it run until I'd put it away. "I don't think all of this would have fit in the truck."

"Definitely not. How are you feeling?"

"Like I'm not alone. I see why you like it here so much."

Mollie gave me a smile before walking over to the driver's seat.

It took us a while to get everything put up, but once we were done, the silence of the house got to me. I hated not having Eric here to play with his toys or talk to, so Mollie put on her friend's show in order to pass the time.

It helped.

By the time we were caught up, she was texting Wren to tell her how much she loved it, and I felt like things were okay, like I could do this if I had to.

I only hoped Eric was fine too.

We went to bed early, as if that would pass the time just a little faster. My nightly routine felt empty without me putting Eric into bed, but Mollie pulled me into her room and held me tight.

"Are you okay?" she asked in the dark of the night.

"No, but I don't feel alone. And that's close enough."

Her arms squeezed and I fell asleep within minutes.

My phone rang before the sun was up. I was in a deep sleep, but the second I heard it, I was wide awake.

"Hello?" I answered, trying to get the sleep out of my voice.

"Cain?" Eric asked.

I sat up in a second. "Eric. What's wrong?"

"I . . . I need help. You know how you said there were adult drinks I should never have?"

My stomach sank. "Yes."

"Waldren had some. And then he drove me to some weird place in Nashville. It's called a club."

"*What?*" I ground out. I was going to *kill him.* "Is he in the car?"

"No, he's inside. He left his phone. And he drove weird."

"Hang up and call 911. Tell them what you told me. Do not let him drive you anywhere."

"O-okay."

"Good job calling me," I said.

"I don't like him, Cain." His voice was quiet. "I wanna come home."

"Yeah, I don't like him either. Call who I told you to call, and I'll be there as soon as I can."

"You're coming to get me?"

"I'll *always* come and get you."

When I hung up, Mollie was rubbing her eyes. "Is something wrong?"

"Very. I'm gonna go get Eric. Waldren drove drunk with him in the car." I threw my clothes on, trying to keep a handle on the rage I felt.

"What the fuck?" she said, getting up to do the same thing. "Obviously, I'm coming with you."

"I can't promise this is gonna be the safest ride you've ever been on. I'm not wasting time."

"You should call Mike," she said. "I bet he could give you a sheriff's escort."

I didn't want to do anything but get to Eric, but she had a point. Mike sounded annoyed that he'd been woken up, but when I asked, he said he would escort us. He even sounded as angry as I felt when I told him what had happened.

Eric obviously had done what he was told, because the police called me minutes later to tell me he was safely in their custody, and I needed to come get him. Mollie got in touch with my lawyer to let him know what had happened, and to file for sole custody since Eric had been in danger.

I was seeing red by the time we arrived in Nashville, and neither Mike nor Mollie could stop me from getting to Eric the second I was in the police station. Neither tried, but my heart had been pounding from the second I'd gotten the first phone call, and I needed to see him with my own two eyes.

Eric was in a waiting room, looking downtrodden but otherwise fine. When he saw me, his entire face brightened, and I wrapped him in the tightest hug of his life.

"Are you okay?" I asked, pulling away to check every inch of his skin.

"The police got him. Was what he did bad?"

"Very bad," I said. "You could have been hurt."

"Oh my God," Mollie said. "It's so good to see you."

"Mollie's here?" Eric asked.

I nodded. "And the sheriff from home. He's the reason I could get here so fast." I looked over at Mollie. "Where is he?"

"Getting the details from the officers who picked Eric up," she said. "And asking if he can cuss out Waldren."

"He can get in fucking line," I muttered.

"Bad word," Eric said.

"Yeah, but when someone does something like this to my kid? I can't hold it back."

Eric stared for a long time before hugging me tightly again, and I took a second to revel in having him back.

"Dang city cops won't let me at him," Mike muttered. "But good news, they called Judge Marlon and he granted temporary sole custody."

"Temporary?" I growled.

"That's just what it's called," he explained. "But I asked if it would be made permanent, and more than likely yes. Waldren's gonna be lucky not to be in *jail*."

"He should be," I muttered. "What was going through his mind?"

"He was mad the whole time I was there because his girlfriend did something."

"Did she dump him?" I asked.

"Yeah, that. He was really mad. He barely even talked to me. He almost left me by myself, but I told him he couldn't do that."

It would have been better for him to have been alone, but I didn't want to make him feel any worse.

"Still," Mike said. "You're good to take him home . . . though you probably would have done that anyway, and I wouldn't blame you."

"Thanks," I said.

"Glad I could help. And I'm glad you're back where you belong, little man."

"Me too," Eric said. I let him go, only for Mollie to hug him the second I did.

Mike smiled. "Some little family you have here."

"Yeah," I said, watching Mollie fuss over every little part of Eric. "But I'm happy to have it."

MOLLIE

Strawberry Springs Neighborhood Watch
Mollie Wilson
TWO WEEKS UNTIL STRAWBERRY SEASON!

Comments:
Kerry Winsor: GIMME!
Mollie Wilson: They're SO close.
Tammy Jane: You better save some for me . . .
Henrietta Brown: Finally! Something new to do that I don't have to drive an hour for!

"Jesus Christ, princess. Gimme that." Cain took the saw out of my hand. "You're gonna cut a finger off."

"Technically, that would require *moving* the saw." I'd been trying to cut a piece of wood, but with no luck. All I'd managed to do was make a scratch on the side of it.

"You're putting too much pressure on it at first." His arm

moved back, cutting a perfect line, and I got an incredible view of his arms bulging as he moved. "See how I'm doing it?"

"No. Can I see it again?"

"Fine. You move like this." His arm went back and forth. "You wanna try?"

"I'm good."

"But you wanted to build the payment stand yourself."

"I did, but I like what I'm looking at more." I didn't even look in his eyes, only at his arms.

Cain smiled in my direction, and I thought he was about to flirt back.

Instead, I got a face full of feathers.

"Ack! Hennifer!" I wrestled with her before I held her away from me. "Come on. We let you out to get cicadas and you repay me with this? It was my idea!"

"I told you she would do this," he replied.

"All of the other chickens are having a feast!"

"She's not like other chickens."

I glared at her, and I could have sworn she glared back. But then one of the massive bugs flew by and distracted her. She wriggled to get out of my grip and chased it around the yard. It was one of those years when the cicadas were everywhere, and no matter how much time I spent outside, I still didn't like the way they flew at me every few seconds. The chickens wouldn't do much, but it was fun to watch the few we'd brought out chase and try to eat them.

"I should have brought Moosley out here. She would have eaten some."

"She would have chased me around until I went inside," Cain said.

I walked over and grabbed the saw. "Okay, let me try again."

Following what Cain had demonstrated, it was much easier to get a cut through the tough wood.

"Did you know you look hot as hell doing that?"

"Not as much as you. I don't have your muscle."

He laughed. "You've gotten a lot stronger since you arrived. And it's hot as hell."

I wanted to disagree, but he was right. In more ways than one. I was a completely different person—one I wanted to be.

"Your compliments have gotten better too. I'd keep it up, but we can't open in time if I don't finish this."

"I need to give the cows some hay anyway." He kissed me on the cheek before walking away, but he didn't leave my mind, even as I put together my rough stand.

The second I wasn't in crunch time, I would reward myself with jumping my hot farmer's bones.

But unfortunately, I had to be responsible for now.

I got a good thirty minutes of work in before my phone rang. I let out a groan and hoped it wasn't someone else from town asking when I'd be open.

Instead, it was Mom.

My annoyance turned into anxiety as I answered immediately.

"Hey," I said. "Is everything okay?"

"I was just about to ask you the same question," she said. "Your dad is here too."

Both of them? Oh no. I was in trouble. "Hi, Dad."

"Hey, Mollie-bear. Feeling okay?"

"At this very moment my arms feel like noodles, but overall, I'm great."

"Even after *you-know-who*?"

"You mean Trevor? You can say his name."

"Speak for yourself," Dad muttered.

"Last time we talked, you were going back to deal with the drama," Mom said. "And I didn't hear from you after that."

"I thought you didn't wanna watch me make this choice."

She let out a sigh. "Well, yes, but I still want to know."

"That's not what you said."

"I told you we could have called her at any time," Dad said.

Mom shushed him. "So, what happened?"

"I yelled at everyone and they saw sense," I replied.

"What *really* happened?"

"That is what really happened. I told Kerry she was wrong. She tried to argue about Cain. And then me and a few other people told her she was out of line and needed to respect people's boundaries."

"And that *worked?*"

"In the end, everyone here wants to be there for others. That's sometimes enough."

"Wow," Dad said. "I didn't know people still cared about each other these days."

"I wish it had happened like that for me," Mom added.

"About that . . . the people involved feel bad, if that helps."

"It's fine. I'm over it," Mom said. She didn't sound over it at all. "So, what have you been doing?"

"Finishing up a custody battle, driving to Nashville because a child was in danger—"

"*What?*"

"What kind of town is that?" Dad asked.

"This happened in Nashville," I reminded him. "And trust me, everyone was mad about it."

"Is the kid okay?"

"You mean Eric? He's great. Better than that, even. And since all of that got fixed, I've been getting ready to open."

"To open the farm? Already?" Mom asked.

"When did you have the time?" Dad added.

"I planted the strawberries last fall. That's what I was so busy with. I have three fields made. Next year, I'll have more. Right now, I'm making a new payment stand."

"And it's going well?" Dad asked. "You like it?"

"I do."

"Then I'm happy for you," he said.

"I know this might be a stretch, but I'd love if you guys could come on my opening weekend."

"Me? Come to Strawberry Springs?" Mom laughed. "I don't think I could."

"I wasn't kidding when I said that people feel bad. Things are different now. You might be surprised."

"Still, honey. I don't think it's for me."

My stomach sank in disappointment. "Okay," I said. "But all the information will be on Facebook if you change your mind."

"Thank you, Mollie-bear," Dad said. "I bet it'll do great."

"Yeah, I think so too."

I told them I loved them before saying goodbye. I wished Mom had been open to at least seeing the farm, but I wouldn't push. I could show her pictures the next time I visited.

I worked late into the afternoon as I painted the new stand and sign. Cain had told me I needed to be done by dinner so we could all eat together, and I was determined to make it happen.

The sunset was a mix of gorgeous colors as I walked to the road to hang the new sign for the farm. It was brightly colored, just as it used to be.

I found Cain in the main barn. He'd been slowly reorganizing it for more farming use since I kept having a lot of ideas about things to do when I had the time. I didn't want to stop at just more fields of strawberries. I wanted blueberries, raspberries, and fields of flowers for people to visit. All of my marketing experience would finally get put to good use.

"It's done!" I announced. "We're ready to open next week. As long as the berries cooperate, of course."

"You're not as covered in paint as I expected you to be."

"I'm great with a paintbrush," I said with an eyeroll. "And I'll be even better once we add more stuff."

Cain sighed. "You'll never stop, will you?"

"What, making the farm better?"

"Challenging me," he replied as he put down the pile of tools he was holding and walked over to place his hands on my hips. "Driving me up a wall."

"What did I do now? I was on my best behavior today. I couldn't have made you mad."

His lips came close to my ear. "Not *that* kind of driving me up the wall."

My skin heated. We slept next to each other every night, and most of Cain's clothes were in my room. Some of those nights, we were intimate. Unless I had exhausted myself and I'd passed out the second my head hit the pillow.

That had been the norm lately.

But I never stopped wanting Cain. And at this point, I wasn't sure I ever would.

"Tonight, I'll make sure I drive you up the wall in the way you want then," I whispered. "We only have a few hours."

"Fuck waiting. We could do it *right* here."

"But Eric could—"

"Kerry picked Eric up to let him play with Tommy. I don't have to go pick him up for an hour."

His hand went to my jaw as he pulled me in for a kiss. In the back of my mind, I was so proud of him for how far he'd come. How he'd not only let Eric have time with his friend, but also trusted Kerry to watch his child.

But then his tongue slid across my bottom lip, and I didn't have any more thoughts.

I wasn't sure how it happened, but suddenly, I was on one of the tables. It had once been filled with tools, but space had been made, and Cain was in between my legs. I hooked my ankles around his back, trapping him against my body.

The sun sank in the sky and the light coming in from the open barn door barely illuminated us. Cain's hand deftly unbuttoned the top of my flannel and slid behind the fabric of my bra to palm my breast.

"Look at you," he hummed as his mouth moved from my cheek to my jaw, every word punctuated with a brush of his lips. "You're beautiful like this."

"L-like what?"

"Getting touched in a barn."

My eyes closed. I didn't give a shit where we were, but maybe I should have. I didn't know how he was able to do it, but whenever he was this close with his mouth on me, I was able to forget about everything that worried me.

"We can go back to the house."

"Absolutely fucking not." His teeth nipped at the delicate skin of my neck. "We're doing this right here. Right now."

"Fuck yes." The words tumbled out of me as I opened my legs wider for him.

The sun disappeared behind the horizon as he peeled off every layer of my clothes. My flannel was first, tossed somewhere in the barn. My paint-splattered jeans followed, and then my underwear.

His fingers went to my clit, slowly circling it. The feeling was incredible, but I knew I had to have more.

"I need you," I gasped. "Like right this second."

My core begged for him. Just the feeling of him being inside of me, stretching me open as he pressed in, would be enough to tip me over the edge.

"I can't, princess." His words echoed into the shell of my ear. "We don't have a condom."

"Why didn't you prepare?" I moaned.

"I *was* trying to get stuff done and wait until tonight. But then I saw you in those fields, looking as fuckin' amazing as you always do." He pressed a kiss to my collarbone. "I couldn't help myself."

I *also* couldn't help myself. I knew what I wanted, and I didn't want to stop.

"I've been tested, ever since I was with Trevor."

He paused. "Please tell me you didn't go to Henry for that."

"No, it was in Nashville. Before we broke up, but we didn't do anything after that."

"He's a fucking idiot."

"The point is, we can just . . . not worry about the condom."

"There's another consequence you might be forgetting about, princess."

Right. *That* one.

I tried to let the thought wash over me and fill me with the same fear it used to. But then I imagined Cain with a tiny baby, and *fuck*. It didn't have the desired effect.

"I don't care." The words slipped out of me and Cain pulled back, eyes wide.

"What?" he asked.

"I mean, you're it for me. And I hope I am for you."

"You are."

"So if *that* happened, then it would be okay. At least with me."

Cain's lips tilted up into a smirk. "So . . . you're saying . . . fuck it?"

"I am."

I wondered if he would pull away and talk some sense into me. I probably needed it.

But instead, he crashed his lips against mine. I ran my hands through his hair, feeling like I was levitating.

"Is that a yes?" I asked, needing confirmation.

"You have no idea how fucking hot that offer is. And yes." His teeth nipped at my bottom lip. "I bet Eric would like a sibling."

If I weren't so far gone, it would have dawned on me that he'd finally been the one to hint at what we all had known for a long time. He was Eric's dad. But I was too wrapped up in him to think about anything other than how good he felt.

Cain's belt hit the floor, taking his pants with it. His bare cock pressed into my core, and I sucked in a sharp breath of air.

"*Fuck*," I hissed.

"Yeah, I'm getting to that."

I'd never been with anyone bare, too worried about the consequences if I let it happen. But now, with the man I planned to spend forever with, I could only feel the pleasure of him parting me as he pushed in.

Cain made it in an inch before he pulled out. I whined, even though I knew it would feel just as good when he returned to his task. Still, my hips chased his.

And his hand wrapped around my neck. Gently, but with enough force that it sent shock waves through my whole body.

"What did I say about staying still, princess?" His cock entered me again, getting deeper.

Every part of me was sensitive, and I swore that feeling him with nothing between us made it even better. I was on the edge as he rocked in and out of me, slowly working up to burying his full length.

His fingers circled my erect nipples.

"I wonder how hot you would look while pregnant with my baby."

That did it.

With a cry, I orgasmed again. Heat surged from my pussy, traveling through every inch of me. For a second, I wasn't a person, only this feeling of pleasure that was earth-shattering.

"Fuck," he said. "I felt that."

"Sorry," I said as my vision returned.

"Don't apologize for coming. Just do it again."

Cain pulled out and then slammed back in, all the way to the hilt. My body was sensitive, but instead of making me want to pull away, I leaned into the feeling. My nails dragged down his back while his hand moved from my neck to my collarbone as he thrust with an incredible rhythm.

Another orgasm built impossibly quick. But this was how my body was when it was him. It could come almost from a simple order.

"Cain?"

"Yes, princess."

"I . . . think I'm gonna come again."

"This soon?"

I could only nod.

His hand on my shoulder tightened. "Good."

This time when I came, my entire body convulsed, my pussy gripping onto every single inch of him that was inside of me. Dimly, I heard him curse, but I was too busy following every bolt of lightning coming from my core, feeling it for as long as it graced me with its presence.

Cain slammed into me one last time, pulling me as close as humanly possible, and I was pretty sure I heard my name on his lips as he came too. I wasn't sure where I ended and he began, but I loved every second that we were intertwined.

He started to pull out, and I let out a whimper. Cain's eyes traced over me. His hand moved from my shoulder down to my core, and he pushed his come back inside of me.

"The sunsets are hard to beat, but this might be my new favorite view."

"I think . . . we may have unearthed some things."

Cain's head dropped on my shoulder. "You're lucky the house is big."

"We might wanna talk about some of this more . . . but that was so fucking good."

"It was." He kissed my cheek. "And I'd love to be here all night, but it's now dark and we need to shower before I go get Eric."

"Agreed," I said. "Not only did I work my ass off, but this table is dusty as hell."

He chuckled and pulled away. I immediately felt cold, but he reached out to grab my hand. "Come on."

"Where are my clothes?"

"I'll find them later."

"You want me to walk to the house naked?"

"Perks of living in the middle of nowhere," he said before pulling me out of the barn and into the house.

It hit me as we both showered and made plans for dinner how *right* all of this felt. What we'd done might have been an impulse decision, but I didn't regret it.

I didn't regret anything in Strawberry Springs.

"When is the next episode of *Renovating with Love*?" Cain asked when we were setting the table for dinner.

"I think in a few days," I said. "Which reminds me . . . I need to catch up with Wren. I haven't heard from her in a bit."

"I wanna meet Wren and make a new friend!" Eric said from his place on the couch. He'd been all about meeting new people ever since he realized things were different between Cain and the town.

"Hopefully you will soon," I told him. "I just need her to be here for a bit."

I pulled out my phone and went to my text chain with Wren.

I am SO sorry. I've been a bad friend and haven't texted.

WREN

It's okay. I have too. Been so busy with Jude and then planning the next season.

How's it going?

It's going well. I think. I need life to slow down for a bit after this. Sometimes I feel like I can't think straight.

CAIN

Strawberry Springs Neighborhood Watch
Kerry Winsor
Did anyone hear that big boom?

Comments:
Kerry Winsor: @SherriffMike Finch have any info?
SherriffMike Finch: I'm gonna turn my damn tags off.
Hu Gh: Type it into Goggle
Kerry Winsor: That's not how it works!
Tammy Jane: For the last time, old man. It's Google!
Hu Gh: Google. Goggle. What's the difference?

JUDGE MARLON MADE his decision quickly.

I was made the sole caregiver of Eric, and Waldren was given time in jail for what he'd done. He'd paid to get out on bail, which I hated, but I knew he had no interest in finding Eric again. Apparently, according to Mike, he'd muttered something about hating being a parent anyway.

Now he never would be. Not to *my* kid anyway.

Kerry had spread the news like the town crier of positivity. With my permission this time. Everyone had congratulated me, and I took it in as well as I could. I still wasn't used to everyone being on my side, but I'd figured out how to do some small talk whenever someone found me at the square.

And I enjoyed it. I finally belonged somewhere. I refused to take it for granted.

All our focus was on opening the farm and making sure Eric was okay after everything. Henry had referred us to a child psychologist, and they'd been working together once a week at the school.

But I still saw Eric glance at me when he thought I wasn't looking. I didn't know what was going on in his head, but there was something he hadn't told me.

I wasn't sure if he was sparing my feelings or if he didn't want to talk about it, but I'd told him he could any time he needed to. I assumed that he would eventually get there.

Even Mollie noticed it, and she brought it up while I was getting the mail one day.

"I still don't know what it is," I told her. "But I'm trying to be patient."

"Has he told his therapist?" she asked.

"I want him to tell Dr. White whatever he wants to, so I don't ask. Not that they'd tell me anyway. All I can do is wait."

Her hand landed on my shoulder. "It's killing you, isn't it?"

"I hate that he dealt with *any* of this. Even if it was only for twelve hours." I shook my head and opened the mailbox. "But it happened. And it got me sole custody."

"He'll open up eventually."

"I hope so," I said as I went through the mail. "Because—" I paused when I saw a blank letter with my lawyer's address on the top. "Shit. Please tell me this isn't another bill."

I still had savings, but not as much as I wanted to. Mollie and I had discussed making me a co-owner of the farm now that we were together and building a life with each other, but even with the extra money that would offer, it would take time to build it back up.

The last thing I wanted was to have to pay more for this custody battle that was over.

Tearing open the letter, my heartbeat kicked up a notch.

But then I saw it. And it was the opposite of a bill.

"Is that a check?" Mollie asked, peering over my shoulder. "Holy *shit*. How much is that?"

"That is . . ." I did the math in my head, my breathing shaky. "Every dollar I paid him."

"What?" she asked. "But how?"

I flipped the page, noticing a letter with his signature on it.

Hi Cain,

The town of Strawberry Springs is under the STM grant. Your bill was covered by donation, so I'm refunding you what you paid. It was a pleasure working with you.

Morgan Thompson

"The STM grant?"

"That's the one that lowers the rent," I said. "Why would it pay my lawyer bill?"

"And on that note, why would one lower rent?" Mollie shook her head. "None of it makes sense."

"Do you think it's fake?"

"Is the grant fake?"

"No, it always pays out. Always has. For about five years."

Her lips pressed together and she grabbed the check,

holding it up to the light. "It has the watermarks of a business check." She looked at it closer. "And no typos. This might be real."

"It doesn't make sense," I replied as she handed it back. "But with this, I could . . ." I trailed off.

"You were saving that for a reason, weren't you?"

"I was. And if this goes through, then I could still do it."

"Wanna share with the class?" she asked.

I hadn't voiced these plans. I was never sure if they would happen, but now there was something in my hands that could bring it to fruition.

"I want to adopt Eric."

Mollie's eyes widened for only a fraction of a second before her head tilted to the side. "You do?"

"I always have. I may have had guardianship of him, but he's always felt like more than just my nephew. He's more like my son. I want to make it real."

A slow smile spread on her face. "Then you should cash that check."

The cashier at the bank had taken one look at the check and then over at me, and I knew she had a ton of questions.

She didn't ask them. And I didn't offer up the information.

I should have known others would know within minutes.

"Hello, rich guy," Kerry said as I pulled in next to her at school.

"Let me guess. Facebook."

"Yep. But I didn't post it."

"I'm pretty sure that this violates some kind of privacy law, even if you didn't post it."

"One, Amber's sleeping with the owner of that bank, and two, I don't know how much it was. But it was a lot."

I shook my head. "It's not a huge deal. It was a refund from my lawyer. My expenses were covered."

Kerry's eyebrows raised. "By *who*?"

"The STM grant."

"What? That covers lawyer fees too?"

"I guess so. If the check clears. The bank placed a hold on it."

"Not surprised," she said. "But hopefully it does. Never look a gift horse in the mouth."

"I'm trying not to."

"What are you going to buy with it? Maybe a ring?" Kerry wiggled her eyebrows.

That wasn't a terrible idea, if I had enough left over. "Probably not a physical item, but I have plans."

"I'm on the edge of my seat."

"I need to talk to the person about it first."

Kerry sighed. "That's so mature. But also boring."

"Sorry." I shrugged. "But you'll be like the . . . fourth to know."

She gasped. "How could you be so cruel? I thought we were getting along."

Kids filtered out of the school, heading to their parents.

"I suppose I'll have to get over it so we can schedule their next playdate. Tommy's begging for it."

"He and Eric can play this weekend when the farm opens."

"Yes!" she said. "Oh, I can't wait to get fresh berries again."

"Me either. I'm gonna try to master Bennie's iced tea he used to make."

"You better share."

"Keep any talks of rings and plans a secret and I might."

"You drive a hard bargain, but my silence *can* be bought."

Eric ran up to me, hair flying in the wind. "Hi!"

"Hey, kid. Ready to go?"

He nodded happily and I said goodbye to Kerry as I loaded him into the truck. While we drove back to the farm, I glanced at him in the mirror. He played with his hands, looking unnerved.

"You know," I said softly, "if cars bother you now, we can work on that."

"Why would cars bother me?" he asked.

"It's normal to feel differently about things after something bad happens. And I know you've been working on feeling better."

"I do," he said. "I'm okay."

"But if you weren't, you can tell me, remember?"

"Yeah, I know."

We lapsed into silence and my stomach sank. I wanted to know what he was thinking so badly it hurt, but I knew I couldn't pressure him.

Eric didn't sit still, even when we pulled into the farmhouse.

"Are you sure you're okay?" I asked, fully turning to him.

"Um . . . actually, can we talk about something?"

"Do you wanna go inside?"

He shook his head. "Can you unbuckle me?"

I reached back and got him out of the seat. He climbed to the front.

"I'm staying with you forever, right?" he asked.

"Yeah, of course. The judge said I had sole custody."

"And no one else can take me?"

"Nope."

"I know Waldren is my dad or whatever." Eric looked down at his hands, and I resisted the urge to forcefully correct him. Waldren was a sperm donor. Not a dad. "But I don't see him like that."

"He was never around, and he did something bad. You don't have to see him that way."

"Dr. White said something the other day, about how kids who lose parents might miss them. Or have questions. I know what happened to my mom, but I never cared about my dad."

"You didn't?"

He shook his head. "To *me*, I have one." His brown eyes moved up to meet my gaze. "It's you."

My heart stopped. People had alluded to me being a parent. Some had mistaken me for it.

I tried to keep Eric away from all of that. And yet . . . he'd seen it anyway.

"Dr. White told me I have a biologic. . . bio—something dad. And that's Waldren. But that doesn't mean he's my actual dad. And I wanted to know if I could . . . If it was okay to . . ." He looked back down, color on his cheeks.

"If you could *what?*" My voice was raw from emotions I couldn't name. I didn't want Eric to notice how my heart was pounding, but I knew what I wanted him to say.

"Can I call you Dad?"

For a second, I didn't think he'd really said it. Because it was *exactly* what I had hoped would come out of his mouth. His wide eyes looked at me with so much hope, and I couldn't leave him hanging.

"Eric, yes. You absolutely can."

"Even if you never call me your son?"

"You *are* my son. In every way that matters. I didn't say it before because I wanted to make it official before I asked."

"Official? What does that mean?"

"Before this whole mess with Waldren, I wanted to adopt you, kid. To become your dad in the eyes of the law. I'd been saving for it for years."

Eric's eyes widened. "Really? Can you do it now?"

A day ago, I would have had a different answer. But now it was very possible. "I might be able to. I'll try my best."

Eric jumped to hug me, his little arms wrapped tightly around my neck. My heart was full as I returned the gesture. It used to be that I would never have let myself hope for anything because I was always let down.

Now I saw that I was wrong. Life was good.

Especially when everything was perfect as it was.

MOLLIE

Strawberry Springs Neighborhood Watch
Mollie Wilson
Good news, everyone! The berries are ripe and ready! Bennie Grove Farm reopens today!

Comments:
Kerry Winsor: I'm getting to the farm first.
Atticus Thompson: Do we bring our own baskets?
Kerry Winsor: This year, yes. Mollie is working on getting the branding together.
Mollie Wilson: How are you faster than me?
Kerry Winsor: Oh, these thumbs can MOVE!

OPENING day of the strawberry patches dawned so vibrantly that it felt like fate. I'd transformed the front field to be a parking lot, posted on every social media I could, and even ran a few ads to make sure people knew about us.

We had plenty of berries to go around, and I could only hope that my plan worked.

Early that morning, I did my usual walk of the fields, making sure there were enough ripened for everyone to enjoy.

Massive red berries dotted each field. It was obvious my work had paid off. They looked delicious, and while I was pretty sure Eric had snuck some, I hadn't tried one myself.

I knew I couldn't until someone else got the first one.

"Eric!" I called. "I know you're out here!"

"I'm not doing anything!" he said. "I was just moving the flags."

He'd "moved" the flags that would tell people where to pick four times yesterday.

"Sure." I put my hands on my hips. "I won't call you out if you go get your dad for me."

A bright smile bloomed on his face, the same one that always did when someone used Cain's new title. The check had gone through, and he'd officially started the adoption process, but Eric had called him his dad from the second he could.

Cain didn't know it, but Kerry had taken to calling him Eric's dad on every social media platform. He was aware the town knew, but I'd seen his new title more than his name.

Which was a lot, considering we were both in the town news frequently since the farm was opening again.

"You rang, princess?" Cain made his way to me. "I can't stay long. I need to collect all the eggs before this place is swamped."

"I won't keep you." I bent down and picked a berry. "Just making true on my promise."

"The first berry, huh? I was so right about us."

"Technically, the town was."

He rolled his eyes. "Don't ruin the moment."

I handed the ripened berry to him and watched as he took a bite.

"Dammit," he said. "These are as good as I remember."

"Yes! Now it's my turn."

I grabbed my own and ate everything but the leaves in one bite. Sweet flavor exploded on my tongue, and I was transported to my childhood. I hadn't had berries this good in years.

"I see why you ate a bunch," I said to Eric.

He gasped dramatically. "I didn't!"

"Lying doesn't suit you," Cain added.

"Fine, Dad." He rolled his eyes in the same way Cain did. "I'm gonna go *not* steal more." He winked and then ran off.

"That kid," Cain said, but he was smiling as he watched.

"Are you ever gonna get used to being called Dad?"

"No."

I wanted to tease him about it more, but the first car pulled into the farm, even though we weren't opening for an hour.

"There's Jackie. Ready to help."

"She doesn't have to do anything," I replied.

"But she will." He kissed me on the forehead. "Show her how to use the card reader. I need to go finish with the eggs."

Jackie looked ready for a day outside. She had a wide-brimmed hat and a strawberry-printed linen shirt on.

"It looks so great!" she called. "Just like it did when Bennie was alive."

"I'm pretty sure he had more fields for picking. And he had tulips. But I'll get there next year."

"Don't get down on yourself." She pointed at me. "You've done so much since you got here."

"Sorry," I said as I held up my hands in mock defense. "We open in about an hour, so I'm about to get the card machine up and running."

"That's so fancy."

"I figured it would make it easier for customers, especially the ones who don't carry cash anymore."

"I bet it will. Now, come on and show me how to run it. I want you out talking to everyone."

"Because I'm so friendly?"

"No, so you can enjoy your moment."

The moment was currently a ball of nerves, but I knew she was right. Jackie quickly picked up how everything worked, and by the time I was done, cars were filtering in.

Kerry and Tommy were the first to arrive. Tommy wanted Eric to show him his room, so they went inside to play while Kerry picked berries.

"These look delicious," she told me as she grabbed a particularly red one. "Though judging by how excited Tommy was to be here, I suppose I'll have to make a ton of strawberry jam."

"You don't have to buy something every time you come here."

"Nonsense. I wanna support someone local."

I had just enough time to tell her thank you before Atticus arrived and asked a ton of questions about where I'd sourced them. Mark was next, and then Tammy, and then Mike. Just from them alone, I'd made a decent amount. When the town came together to support someone, they did amazing things.

But as the sun climbed higher in the sky, more people came, driving in from different places. Some were neighboring towns. Some were passing through and happened to see the sign. One had even come all the way from Nashville.

I'd been shocked at the woman with curly blonde hair when she told me.

"It wasn't that bad," she said with a laugh. "My husband did most of the driving."

She pointed to a man with dark hair who was busy picking berries.

"I've driven there more times than I could count in the last few months, so thank you for making it all this way."

"Did you need to get supplies or something?"

"No, I'm from there. And it's the hub of other court-related things that my boyfriend would kill me for if I mentioned."

"A former local? Damn, I was hoping to be the one to tell you about hot chicken."

"I haven't been."

She gaped. "You *have* to go to Prince's. Next time you're in town, of course."

I didn't know when I would be in town, especially since I hadn't heard from my parents. My heart ached thinking about it, but I knew I didn't want to be the only one driving three hours to visit. If they stood their ground, I would have to make time near the holidays and birthdays, but not too much more. I had a lot of work to do here.

"Did I step on a nerve?" the woman asked. "I'm sorry if I did."

"No, you didn't. My family's there, and it's complicated. They don't like that I moved out here to run a farm, so . . . I don't know when I'll be back."

"I think this is amazing. I grow some food in my backyard, but it's nothing like this. If I didn't have a family home, I'd probably move out here too."

"A family home? That's funny. That's what this is."

"Hang on to it," she said. "And I might not know you all that well, but this suits you."

"I'm Mollie, by the way. Maybe I'll catch you at a hot chicken restaurant."

"As long as it's Prince's, you definitely will." She held a hand out to shake. "I'm Amy, and my husband is Levi. You'll probably see us again when I drag my two friends out here."

"You'd drag your friends three hours out of town for *straw-berries*?"

"Duh. They'd get food out of it. I bet there's a cute small-town diner near here."

"There is," I said. "Center Point. You should try it."

"Oh, I will. Now, let me grab Levi before he picks all the berries you have and puts you out of business for the day."

I laughed as she waved goodbye, and I considered adding more advertisements near Nashville. If she was willing to drive all this way, then others might too.

A hand landed on my shoulder, and I turned to see Cain. "We're down to the last field," he said. "Looks like our first day was a success."

"It was. And I have ideas for more."

"You're gonna keep us busy, aren't you?"

I laughed. "You know it."

Most of the ripe berries were gone by the time we neared closing for the day. I was walking the fields when one last car pulled in. I checked how many we had, and it was barely enough, but I could serve one last customer.

But then I saw *who* it was and my jaw dropped.

Mom and Dad were getting out of the car, a basket in hand. Dad made his way straight to me while Mom looked at every detail of the farm, jaw agape.

"You guys made it!" I said, running to them both and pulling them into a tight hug. "Thank you."

"Mollie-bear, this is really nice," Dad said. "And I saw the fancy website and posts you made about it. Glad to see you're using that marketing brain of yours."

"It worked. I've been busy all day."

"This is . . ." Mom's voice was quiet. "It looks like it did when I was a kid."

"Cain kept up on the house, but the fields were me. I have *so* many plans. Like adding blueberries and orchards. There's so much land here that I could work with."

Her eyes cut to me. "You sound so . . . happy. Like you were when you were a kid."

"I *am* happy," I said. "I love it here."

"Are there any berries left?" Dad asked. "I can barely see anything from here."

"The farthest field has a few. I'll walk you over there."

I gestured for them to follow me, but we all went slow so Mom could see everything. Dad grabbed a full basket, which wound up being almost everything that was ripe before we walked to the stand.

I'd completely forgotten who was manning the stand until Mom stopped dead in her tracks.

Jackie looked up, her eyes going wide for a second before a smile made its way onto her face.

"Maribelle," she said. "It's nice to see you."

"I didn't . . ." Mom cleared her throat. "You're working here?"

"I'm helping out. I wanted Mollie to enjoy talking to people on her first day. I got to learn a *lot* about payment processing."

"Sounds fun," Mom said. "I suppose it makes sense that you would have met Mollie, considering you're next door."

"Oh . . . that old house." She shook her head. "It was sold a long time ago. I live in the square now. Above my shop."

"But didn't you marry that ass . . ." She shook her head. "I mean, Donny?"

"I did," Jackie said. "And . . . he turned out exactly like you told me he would. It was a long time of misery. But . . . he passed many years ago."

Mom nodded. And I looked at Jackie. "Do you . . . maybe have anything else you wanna say, Jackie?"

"Right. Um, Maribelle, I'm sorry about what I told the town. You were always right, and I should have listened rather than letting my pride get in the way. The gossip here can be fun, but not about certain things. I learned that the hard way . . . especially when I hid what Donny was doing. I ruined this place for you, and it's one of my biggest regrets. Behind marrying an abusive asshole, of course."

Mom's eyes grew wide. "I . . . thank you. I mean, obviously I moved on."

I raised an eyebrow at her. "Did you?"

She crossed her arms. "Of course I did! I barely think about this town!"

"Ah, well. I'm happy for you." Jackie smiled. "I'll let you check out and get back on your way."

Her voice was soft, and I wondered if she was disappointed by Mom's stubbornness. I would have been.

Jackie grabbed the basket and weighed it before handing it back. We all lapsed into silence, broken only by the sound of small feet hitting the earth.

"I'm calling you Grandma now!" Eric's voice yelled.

"I said to wait until you were away from customers!" Cain called as he jogged behind them. "Sorry!"

"These are my parents!" I called back.

Cain paused and his back straightened. I thought he might run, but instead he walked over. "Then I'm doubly sorry about that. I'm Cain."

"Jim," Dad said, shaking his hand. "Wow, that's one powerful shake. You're dating my daughter, right?"

"I am."

"I hope you treat her right, but judging by what happened to the last one . . . she would let you know if you don't."

"She would," Cain said. "And this is my son, Eric."

"*Your* son?" Mom asked. "But he said he was calling Jackie Grandma."

"Ah, yes. I took Cain in as a foster mom when he was a teen. I'm kinda like a mom."

"You *are* a mom," Cain corrected.

She laughed, but there was a dusting of red on her cheeks. "He helped me see how awful Donny was. And your daughter helped me learn to admit it. So I suppose I have you to thank too."

Mom looked between Cain, me, and Jackie. "I . . . have so many questions. When did you take him in? How did he help you see it?"

"You wanna know?" Jackie asked, raising an eyebrow. "I thought you were done with this place."

She considered it. "I suppose since my daughter's living here, I could . . . hear some of the things that have happened. As long as the town doesn't turn on me, that is."

"I can whip them into shape," I said.

Jackie laughed. "Just like she did a few weeks ago. We're all on the right path now thanks to her."

"Is Center Point still open?" Mom asked.

"It is. They'll be doing dinner now. Tammy runs it."

"Please tell me she doesn't do the cooking."

"Nope. That would be her husband."

"Well then . . . honey," she turned to Dad. "Do you mind if we stay for dinner?"

"Are you sure this is what you want?" he asked.

"Yeah . . . I think I am."

"Then we'll stay. I wanna see the farmhouse Mollie loves so badly. She was hunting for a house forever. This one had better be good."

"It is," I said. "You're welcome to come in."

"I can show you my marble run!" Eric offered.

"Is it in the hallway again?" Cain asked. "Because if it is and our guests fall—"

Eric tore off in the direction of the farmhouse.

"That answers *that* question," I replied.

We closed up the farm while Jackie and Mom talked. Eventually, they rode in Jackie's car to the town square while I showed Dad the house and the barn. They stayed late into the night, and instead of driving back, I offered to let them sleep at the house.

"It's not too bad out here," Dad eventually said as I handed him towels. "And who knew you were good with kids?"

"Just the right one," I replied.

"Can you believe the entire town has a grant to make rent cheaper?" Mom asked as she took the extra toothbrush I offered. "I didn't think those kinds of things existed!"

"It's almost like magic," I replied.

"Goes with the town slogan." She brought me into a hug. "I'm *so* happy for you, honey. You were right about this place."

"Thank you for coming to see it."

"I suppose we'll be here more often. I can't let you do all the driving. Especially with a child."

"Technically, he's Cain's."

"Sure. Is that why you have a book in your hand to read to him?"

"He likes my voice better."

She smiled before she pulled Dad into the guest room, wishing me a good night. I took a breath, absorbing the fact that I'd done it. The farm had done well. Mom and Dad had seen it *and* were proud of me.

And I had the perfect boyfriend waiting for me to read to his adorable kid.

I'd thought I needed to make everything exactly as it had been before. Instead, I'd created something new, and it was perfect as it was.

I couldn't be happier.

CAIN

Strawberry Springs Neighborhood Watch
Mollie Wilson
Guys. I'm begging you to watch Renovating with Love. It's so good, and my best friend is on it.

Comments:
Kerry Winsor: I've been watching it! Does she work in the back?
Mollie Wilson: No, she's the main lead.
Kerry Winsor: YOU'RE FRIENDS WITH WREN?

"The romance was an unnecessary plot point."

Mollie gasped dramatically and threw popcorn at me. "How *dare* you! It was perfect! It had me on the edge of my seat!"

"But they *kissed*." Eric stuck his tongue out. "Ew."

"I got to see my best friend fall in love with her dream man, and both of you are ruining it." She rolled her eyes. "Seriously, he's gonna be invited to holidays after this."

"I was trying not to say it, but it felt . . . forced," I said.

"Forced? How could it have been forced?"

"A lot of things in show business are forced."

Mollie shrugged. "I could ask her. When she's done with filming."

"Shouldn't she be? The show's over."

"Maybe she's planning the next thing," Mollie replied. "But you're right. There should have been some sort of break or something. I haven't heard from her in a while." She frowned as she looked at her phone.

"Is that not like her?"

"No, not at all. Before the show, we talked constantly. But I must have gotten used to not doing it as much. I should message her and check in." She typed on her phone. "I'm worried."

"It's probably nothing," I replied. "She could be busy planning, like you said."

"I just miss her," she replied. "When I told her I moved here, she was so excited to see the place. Why would she up and vanish?"

I hated seeing Mollie sad, and I hoped this friend of hers wasn't abandoning her just because she'd moved out of the city. I'd only ever heard good things about Wren, and from what I'd seen on TV, she was the most real part of that show.

The only time Mollie was inside was when we were watching it. As strawberry season wound down, she'd taken to planting new bushes and planning out the farm for next year, which would provide a lot more income on top of what the animals produced.

I reached out to her, planning on bringing her into a tight hug as she thought things through, but there was a knock at the door.

"That might be Kerry. She said she was gonna bring a pie over that she made. I'll get it."

Mollie nodded, a small smile on her face. "Thank you," she replied.

I got up and walked to the door, but right before I opened it, I noticed a truck in the driveway, one that I'd never seen before.

This had better not be like the last time I opened the door to a stranger. If another one of Eric's family members came out of the woodwork, I would be telling them to kick rocks. The adoption was well underway, and I would be damned if anything stopped it.

I opened the door to a woman with strawberry-blonde hair tied into a ponytail. Freckles dotted her cheeks, and she looked just like the woman I'd seen on TV, but dressed down.

"Uh, hi. You must be Wren."

She raised an eyebrow. "You know me?"

"Mollie makes me watch your TV show."

She slowly nodded, but I saw the way her shoulders slumped downward. "Right . . . It's nice to meet you, by the way. Hopefully you're treating her right."

"I'm trying to."

I didn't know her, but I did know she looked more downtrodden than I would have expected. I had a feeling she didn't want to be talking to me.

"Hey, Mollie!" I called. "Come here a sec."

"Is it pie-tasting time?" she asked as she walked around the corner.

But when Mollie saw Wren, her eyes went wide. "Oh my *God*! You're here." She pulled her into a hug, a wide smile on her face. "I was worried about you!"

"No need to be worried," she said. "Just needed some time to get affairs in order."

She sounded flat even to me, and Mollie pulled away, her eyes narrowed. "You're sad."

"No, I'm not."

"Come on. I know you. What happened?"

"Nothing."

"Wren . . ."

"I'm done with filming," Wren said. "And that's what's important. I wanted to see the town you moved to and . . . get away for a bit."

"Get away from what?"

"Everything." Her voice was dark, and Mollie raised an eyebrow. Wren didn't answer.

"Okay," Mollie said slowly. "You're welcome to stay with us. Right, Cain?"

"Yep. I can get the guest room ready."

Mollie nodded and gave me a look that said we would definitely be talking about this later. I barely knew the woman, but something *was* off. I could only hope that Strawberry Springs could work its magic on Mollie's best friend.

Because it had definitely worked for us.

THANK YOU

I can't thank you enough for coming to Strawberry Springs with me. A lot of my teenage years were spent in a small town, and it was incredibly healing for me to journey to one of my own and stay there for a while. I wasn't sure if I would be able to capture the feeling of it since I've spent so long in cities, but through writing this, I found a new home. One that's all my own.

To my personal cheerleaders, Lizzie, Josh, and Cass, thank you for helping me through all of the self-doubt I struggle with. It still follows me around, but the support system I've found is incredible, and I can't say enough how much talking about my stories help.

To my editing team, Mae and Kasey, thank you for helping me develop and write this book. I struggled so hard in the beginning stages, but once the ball started rolling, I blinked and had an entire novel in my hands.

Last but certainly not least, I have to thank the developer of the game that loosely inspired this series. In 2020, I started playing a game called Stardew Valley to pass the time, and it changed my life. It reminded me that I do, in fact, love small towns, and that while they may not be perfect, they can be home. So, ConcernedApe, thank you for making an incredible game. If any of my readers haven't played it, I can't recommend it enough.

WANT MORE?

Get a bonus chapter about life a few years in the future here!

ARE YOU READY FOR WREN'S STORY?

Pre-order here!

INTERESTED IN AMY AND LEVI'S STORY?

Read *Ill Will* here!

OTHER BOOKS BY ELLE

The Failure to Thrive Series

Failure to Thrive

Under Any Conditions

The Aisle and Error Series

Contractual Obligations

Ill Will

Summers in Christmas

Snow Stuck

The Family Business Series

Forces of Nature

Man of Action

Movers and Shakers

Strawberry Springs Series

As It Was

As They Are (Coming Fall 2025)

Standalones

To Make Matters Worse

Fakecation

ABOUT THE AUTHOR

Elle Rivers writes fun romance books filled with real-world problems wrapped in beautiful, heartwarming happy endings. When not writing, she can be found speed-reading other authors' amazing romance novels, curling up next to any warm object she can find, or singing obnoxiously loud to Taylor Swift.

Elle was born and raised in Nashville, Tennessee, and she considers herself one of the few native Nashvillians who does not like country music. She has eight cats who fight for the spot on her lap and eight chickens who couldn't care less about her unless she is bringing them food. She lives with her romance hero of a husband who endlessly supports her writing endeavors, and her son, who is the biggest, but most adorable, distraction.

www.ingramcontent.com/pod-product-compliance
Lightning Source LLC
Chambersburg PA
CBHW030329120726
47901CB00007B/1731